AFWAt

AUTHOR	CLASS
Roberts C	F

TITLE	No.
So immortal a flower.	07503226

So Immortal a Flower

On the Island of Crete in wartime, Sylvia Day from peaceful Marlow-on-Thames discovers the excitement and the rewards of fighting for her country and caring for those who are wounded and in need of help. And against a battle-filled background of violence and bitterness she discovers too the friendship and love that overcome the boundaries of race and belief.

By the Same Author

Novels

Scissors
Sails of Sunset
The Love Rack
Little Mrs. Manington
Sagusto
David and Diana
Indiana Jane
Pamela's Spring Song
Havana Bound
Bargain Basement
Spears Against Us
Pilgrim Cottage
The Guests Arrive
Volcano
Victoria Four-Thirty
They Wanted to Live
One Small Candle
So Immortal a Flower
Eight for Eternity
A Terrace in the Sun
The Remarkable Young Man
Love Is Like That
Wide is the Horizon
A Flight of Birds
The Pilgrim Cottage Omnibus

Miscellaneous

Gone Rustic
Gone Rambling
Gone Afield
Gone Sunwards
And So To Bath
And So To America
And So To Rome
Half Way
Portal to Paradise
One Year of Life
The Grand Cruise
Selected Poems (1910-1960)
A Tale of Young Lovers (Poetic Drama)
The Diary of Russell Beresford
Alfred Fripp: a biography
A Man Arose

Autobiography

The Growing Boy—Book 1
Years of Promise—Book 2
The Bright Twenties—Book 3
Sunshine and Shadow—Book 4
The Pleasant Years—Book 5

So Immortal a Flower

Cecil Roberts

HODDER AND STOUGHTON
LONDON   SYDNEY   AUCKLAND   TORONTO

CONTENTS

BOOK I
PROLOGUE

CHAPTER | | PAGE
I. EXCURSION IN TUNIS — 7
II. SICILIAN SPRING — 39
III. SCHLOSS GARSTEIN — 49
IV. THE TORCH PASSES — 58

BOOK II
CRETE

I. SYLVIA DAY — 68
II. SUNSHINE IN CANDIA — 92
III. ENTER HERMES — 108
IV. VILLA VOUNI — 125
V. FAREWELL, DEAR MOUNTAIN — 140

BOOK III
SO IMMORTAL A FLOWER

I. THESEUS MEETING ARIADNE — 151
II. WINGED ICARUS — 188
III. AIR AND WATER — 202
IV. RETREAT TO SFAKIA — 216
V. THE BRAVE BUT ONCE — 241
VI. CALL OF THE BLOOD — 260
VII. WINDS OF AUTUMN — 276
VIII. WHO IS SYLVIA? . . . — 292
IX. GREATER LOVE HATH . . . — 306

Ὃν οἱ θεοὶ φιλοῦσιν ἀποθνήσκει νέος.

TO THE MEMORY OF

L. B. R.

Lieutenant, R.A., Killed, North Africa,
May 2, 1943. Aged 22.

It may be again that Life will mould a young face
To break a heart with, in some new day unseen,
But never again, for one, can return the grace
That was yours, dear Lucien—beyond Fate's malice, serene.

BOOK I

PROLOGUE

CHAPTER I

EXCURSION IN TUNIS

AT five o'clock life seemed extinct up at the Villa Byrsa. Although it was still April the African sun was hot. Not a breeze ruffled the Mediterranean or the lagoon, with La Goulette at its sea entrance. White Tunis rose beyond the quay at the end of the shipping channel traversing the shallow blue water. The great sky was cloudless. In the distance the faintly grey mass of Jebul-bou-Korneïn broke the sky-line. Towards evening it would turn mauve, when the pink-billed flamingoes went winging across the crimson lagoon, and the great sun, a ball of fire, was eaten up by the dark western mountains.

The awnings of the Villa Byrsa were blue and white. They shrouded a dozen windows of the flat-topped house on the road side, visible through the palm trees bordering the long drive behind the iron ornamental gates. On the sea side, a wide terrace with a marble balustrade of Moroccan design was covered for half its length by an orange awning, and the windows of the two stories above had awnings of the same colour. The green latticed windows of the house were shut. But all the inhabitants of Sidi-bou-Saïd knew its owner was in residence, for the tricolour flag hung from the pole at the eastern end of the terrace. When Count Pierre de Beaumarchais-Fontaine went off on one of his desert expeditions with his English house-mate the flag was absent.

The garden of the villa was small and exotic. Its five acres were excessively manicured, to use the slightly derisive phrase of Russell Beresford, the count's friend and fellow

archæologist. Two gardeners, one a Scot, Sanderson, one
an Arab, Ali, and a native Berber boy, Selim, somehow
found all-round employment trimming the parterres, pruning
the orange trees, and preserving, despite the summer heat,
a verdant half-acre of grass. The garden was on three
terraces, each faced with a white marble balustrade. At the
end of each of these terraces a fountain threw a silver jet of
water that splashed into a faïence-tiled bowl. From the
lowest terrace the cliff fell sharply to the sea, with a path
cut in the rock that went down to a bathing pool, so con-
trived that water from the incoming tide could be trapped
in it.

A little before six o'clock the shutters of a window on the
terrace opened, and Randell Dunning stepped forth from
his bedroom, where he had taken a siesta after an alfresco
lunch in the arabesque loggia beyond the fountain, where
meals were served in spring and summer. Looking up, he
discovered that neither Pierre nor Russell was stirring yet.
The only sound besides the pleasant splashing of the fountains came from the kitchen quarters, hidden behind an ilex
hedge, where François, the old family chef, sang as he
prepared the evening meal, served at nine o'clock, under the
lanterns hanging from the mosaic ceiling of the loggia.

Randell Dunning surveyed the pleasant prospect before
him : ancient Cap Carthage, the white-and-blue walls of
Sidi-bou-Saïd clustered on the headland, the lighthouse
that watched the ships passing La Goulette, the blue vista
seaward, the minaret of a mosque below, a belt of olive
trees beyond Pierre's property, some dark cypresses silhou-
etted against the great gulf, and, in the distance, a pleasant
pattern of white and grey, the houses and minarets of Tunis.
Like himself, the city was now waking to life. This was
the cool and pleasant hour when a French civilisation grafted
on to an Arab one, enticed the lounger with its alluring
variety. He decided to run down to the city and sit at his
favourite café on the tree-lined Avenue Jules Ferry. He
had been there yesterday, and a vain hope lodged in his
mind that he might again see the woman with the white
lace gloves.

§ 2

Le Chat Noir never closed its doors. Less celebrated than Florian's in the great piazza at Venice, it served a similar purpose. It was a social centre of Tunisian life. In the spring, summer, and autumn the tables beneath the gay tricolour awning were filled with the better-class French, Italian and Arab population of the city, and with a large proportion of tourists in the season. On the raised terrace, behind the tables spread out as far as the trees lining the avenue, a string orchestra played in the early evening and until one in the morning. Its dais was advanced in summer to the front of the restaurant, enclosed by large glass windows, now removed.

The cuisine maintained the reputation of the French and of M. Charles in particular, once of the Hotel Crillon, Paris, and now, since his discharge from the army with the Croix de Guerre for services in the Great War, the pride and mainstay of Le Chat Noir. Those services had not been culinary. A general of France had hinted in vain that M. Charles was not using his gifts to the best advantage. "*Mon Général*," replied M. Charles proudly, "as a captain of artillery I am as skilful with shells from my battery as ever I was with shells over my frying-pan. I make an omelet the enemy respects!" No further hint menaced the patriotic zeal of M. Charles.

Gassed on the Aisne and demobilised in February, 1919, the damp air of Paris drove him south, first to the Riviera, and finally to the coast of North Africa. Here he had prospered, married a pretty Italian beauty specialist, and produced Etienne, his son and heir. A Breton *bonne* carried Etienne past Le Chat Noir at 6 p.m. exactly each evening. M. Charles advanced to the back of the orchestra and blew Etienne a kiss over the bass fiddle. At the same moment a lustrous-eyed young woman waved her hand from a balcony across the avenue. The sign beneath the window proclaimed *Mlle. Lenoir. Salon de Beauté.* Actually its proprietress, leaning out of the window, was Madame Charles. Her gesture embraced both father and son. If affairs continued as at present, M. Charles might achieve his high ambition and be the father of a son in the Corps

Diplomatique.   Already he had bespoken a nomination
from M. Cambon, one of his oldest patrons.   At forty, with
an industrious wife of twenty-eight, a son four months old,
and twenty thousand francs in the bank, M. Charles considered himself a fortunate fellow, despite two damaged
lungs.

Most of the regular patrons of Le Chat Noir sent their
compliments to M. Charles.   Once every evening, towards
ten o'clock, he made a grand tour of the tables, a *corbeille*
of fruit in one hand, a *corbeille* of flowers in the other.
With these he saluted the ladies at each table.

Randell Dunning had been introduced to M. Charles by
his hosts, Pierre and Russell, on his first evening in Tunis.
They had dined there, extremely well, and Pierre had been
at great pains to introduce Randell as " one of the foremost
writers of England."   " That would do nothing for you at
home," said Pierre.   " When you name one of your battleships *Shakespeare* or *Milton* you may have some standing
among your own people—but even then it will not produce
a superlative omelet such as Charles now feels inspired to
create.   For us an *écrivain* is an *artiste* ; for your nation a
writer is only a vagrant !   Why you have bothered to produce one of the great literatures of the world I have never
understood ! "

Pierre always enjoyed talking in this fashion.   " As one
of the few Anglophiles of France, I claim the right of a
devastating candour," he would say.

" A dinner like this makes any insult of yours digestible,"
retorted Randell, raising a glass of Château Yquem.

In his two weeks' sojourn in Tunis they had dined at
Le Chat Noir several times.   M. Charles had never failed
them.

The food was superlatively good, but the restaurant had
other attractions.   The fashion of Tunis filled its tables at
the cocktail hour.   When Randall arrived at the café, having
reached Tunis in a few minutes in the workaday Citroen
that Pierre had placed at his disposal, there was scarcely
an empty table.   The orchestra was playing gaily, but the
overture to *Thais* was drowned by the babel of voices.
Curious eyes watched Randall as he threaded his way
through the tables.   He was vain enough to enjoy the

attractive figure he cut with his tall, spare body, his sensitive face, and black, short-cropped curls. He dressed well and had a flair for colour that annoyed his conventional friends. This evening he wore a thin mauve suit of tropical worsted, made for him in Cairo, with a cream silk shirt from Jermyn Street and a light grey Homburg from Lock's. Three months in the Sahara had tanned his face to a rich brown that enhanced the brightness of his dark eyes. Early success had given him an air at twenty-eight. Four years of war, from which he had emerged as a captain with a Distinguished Flying Cross, and two years of travelling about the world had made him self-possessed in manner, deceptively so, for he had a more volatile spirit than his manner suggested. The tonic quality of conceit had provided a cover for a certain diffidence derived from beginning life as the fourth son of a poor country clergyman.

Pierre had exaggerated, of course, in introducing him to Charles as one of the foremost writers of England. But it was a prophetic exaggeration, and Randell had not felt embarrassed by this intelligent anticipation. He had already written two successful novels. Neither of them had sold very well, one of them scarcely at all, but they had enjoyed a *succès d' estime*, and people who found them boring were intimidated by their style, and the respect of the critics showed for what they called his " nervous prose." Oddly enough, his books were full of repressed violence, and Randell had felt aggrieved with a famous critic who had called him " a volcano ever on the verge of eruption." It sounded a little like sarcasm. " But his characters are all encompassed by the lava of incandescent passion," redeemed the volcanic note. That sentence had run through the American reviews, caught from the blurb on the cover.

His last book had been given the Blackstone Memorial Prize, awarded " to the most distinguished book of interpretative realism of the year." Randell did not know quite what the phrase meant or why the prize was awarded, but it had pleased his American publishers. What had pleased him most was that it had moved a snippet magazine of immense circulation to print a précis of his story at a price that was twenty times the sum derived from the book itself. On that sum he had travelled for a year and thereby found himself now in Tunis, after a thrilling trek from Uganda and up through the Great Sahara Desert via Lake Chad.

He found a seat at last and ordered a vermouth cassis. American voices reminded him that a liner on a world cruise had anchored off La Goulette yesterday evening, where she had ridden luminously on the indigo sea. At the next table three Arabs, with snowy-white burnouses and red fezzes, displayed, as they talked in French, thin brown hands, well-manicured and lavishly jewelled. The eldest, with the white beard, wore a diamond ring that glittered with every movement. He was probably a wealthy merchant with a shop in the Souks.

A boy in a dirty *jerba*, that day-nightgown of the poor natives, hawked the evening paper, an Italian one, *Il Gazzettino*. Randell bought one and read it as he sipped his vermouth. It contained news of a strike that was convulsing Italy. Communists had seized the docks at Genoa ; there was a train derailed at Forli ; the country was paralysed, and the King had issued a proclamation. In Bologna an ex-Socialist journalist, who had formed a society of blackshirts, called Fascists, had made a violent speech threatening the government. This rabble rouser, one Benito Mussolini, had joined forces with the melodramatic Gabriele D'Annunzio. Ugly battles had broken out between blackshirts and the strikers. Thirty-five people had been killed.

The *Gazzettino* had a good sale among the café's customers. Half the population of Tunis was Italian. For generations poverty-stricken Italians from Sicily and southern Italy, peasant stock mostly, had been spreading themselves across Tunisia. The Moslems regarded them with contempt. Europeans, these immigrants were as poor and worked at jobs as menial as themselves. The well-to-do Italians were mostly Jews from Leghorn, who ran many of the commercial agencies that the French had let slip into their hands. The road-makers, the field labourers in the olive, orange, and lemon groves were mostly Sicilians. The Arabs watched them toiling without envy. Since one could exist without work, why this foolish industry ? In turn, the Italians ignored the Moslems and scarcely hid their resentment of the French, for Tunisia should be Italian, part of their empire. They should have obtained it at the Peace Treaty, together with Trieste, Fiume and Dalmatia. They had been cheated. Mussolini and D'Annunzio had said so. Well, one day it would all be theirs—Tunis, Malta, Corsica, Spalato, Fiume.

Pierre, who had lived in Tunis for three years, said the Tunisian Moslems were the best politicians of all. They made little noise ; they kept their people in subjection and possessed rural properties, which the French greatly improved with their irrigation and other government projects. They had lost their independence. The Bey of Tunis was a puppet, but better a puppet pulled by the French, who kept a firm hand, softly gloved, than a rapacious and wayward Bey, as of old.

A fierce argument broke out between some Italians at a near table. They were hotly divided over the Italian government and Signor Mussolini. The names of Wilson, Clemenceau, and Lloyd George were interjected into the argument, always with invectives, and by the pro-Mussolini faction. The whole argument, which had become very intense, collapsed on the appearance of an Italian lady of ample charms, whose hand all the perspiring debaters kissed in turn.

The motley crowd on the boulevard was now at its densest. French, Italians, Arabs, Americans, and English strolled by. There was not a vacant table at Le Chat Noir. The orchestra was now playing selections from *Madame Butterfly*, and, as if out of the wings, an almond-eyed Annamite nursemaid, clad in saffron, with heavy black hair, led her two daintily-dressed charges past the café. Randell's eyes, following this oriental note, were suddenly arrested by the occupant of a table near the newspaper kiosk. He saw her, with a pleasant surprise ; she was the lady who had commanded his attention the previous evening. The hat was changed, and the costume, but nothing could alter the high distinction of that fine profile, that delicate feminine grace. He was seeing her, of course, at a time when he was particularly susceptible. Three months in the desert, with lice-infested Arabs and hide-strong camels, had pressed heavily upon his sensitive nature, and a forced continence had severely tried the flesh through the heat of sub-tropical days and a provocative imagination stirred by the lovely starlit nights. A thirst had been stored pending the return to human contacts, and his turbulent blood worked in him for the fulfilment of manhood.

Alert, intense, the movement of human beings about him again evoked his pleasure in society. He loved most a cosmopolitan scene such as this. It touched his imagination and inspired a succession of situations upon which his mind played with the author's gift of creation. This unknown young woman of yesterday evening, for instance. He had first observed her because she was outstanding, in dress and manner, among all the other women at the tables. She was French, of course, for she had the Frenchwoman's flair for chic, achieving ostentation without offence. She might be thirty. Her figure was slight, her face unlined, with a perfect throat. The full mouth, well-defined with its scarlet lipstick, gave her an air of maturity that was wholly refuted by the lovely dark eyes under the broad, pale brow. But the extremely sensuous quality of her face resided most in the delicate perfection of her nose. It was flawless in shape, with beautifully turned nostrils. He had had, of course, no opportunity to observe her closely or at length. She indicated more of an atmosphere than a presence. She had, he would say for want of a better definition, an " aura " to which he found himself instinctively drawn.

A love of women was fundamental to his nature. With them he breathed deeper, lived more acutely, and felt an adventurous joy in the possession of youth and health. He liked the flattery their pleasure in his company revealed, as much as the vanity they evoked in him by his ability to attract them. Cynical, he resigned himself to finding them superficial and wayward. A witty woman delighted him, but a really clever woman—he had met only a few of them —created a diminishing ratio of attraction. Her femininity was less potent in the mental atmosphere she created. Clever young women seldom had charm ; clever elder women had discarded frailty. He did not know it, or perhaps he did not choose to know it, but he liked a woman who was subservient to his mind, while provocative to his body. He liked to find in the object of his attention the mirror of his egotism. Brilliant, good-looking, adventurous, an excellent companion always, with much to give in exchange for what he sought, he had the determination of all men who, having trafficked successfully with Death, have no fear of the future, but are determined to extract the maximum pleasure out of the remainder of life, in the mood of profligacy that characterises the gambler with his profits.

She had changed her position slightly. The brim of her crimson hat, trimmed with gardenias, hid her face from him. An elbow rested on the table. French lace gloves gave a cool delicacy to her hands, a feature he had observed the previous evening. He followed the line of her, slim and chic, to her diminutive scarlet shoes, again expressive of her utter femininity. She was smoking with a long ivory cigarette-holder.

The lovely evening spread its calm splendour over the city. The minarets caught a tone of rose from the west. The upper sky was a fathomless void of lapsing light. The serene dusk had an illimitable beauty. Randell ordered another vermouth and tapped a cigarette on his gold case. He had been made tense by that woman in the crimson hat, and he had an absolute certainty of their awareness of each other. Yet to his knowledge she had never looked his way or seen him.

The orchestra was now playing a selection from Tchaikovsky's *Nutcracker Suite*. He decided that she was not a tourist from the cruising liner at La Goulette. Tourists, certainly women, never went about alone, and never had her repose. They carried the impetus of their transit with them everywhere, and the excitement of the next port of call broke the serenity of every scene they invaded. No, she was not a tourist. She expressed unconscious repose.

How ridiculous ! He had not seen her at all clearly yet, neither moving, nor speaking. Her loneliness suggested that she might be a resident of Tunis, the wife, perhaps, of some French *fonctionnaire*. For that matter he had no reason for assuming she was married.

The Italians at the next table reached a new height of discord. The youngest jumped up, shook a mane of black hair, and. spluttered, staccato-like, firing adjectives into the bodies of his opponents. " *Mache !* " he exclaimed finally, inarticulate with anger. With a wide flourish of his expressive hands he rushed from the table and fled along the boulevard.

" *E pazzo!* " observed the bearded Italian. " That Mussolini makes them all like that. I have to live here, to work here, to send my children to school here. Why make trouble ? We live here comfortably. The French do not bother us. We prosper. *Non è vero ?* "

His companions gravely agreed. They lapsed into a brooding silence. Suddenly the old Italian picked up his copy of *Il Gazzettino*, and tore it demonstratively into halves. Something in it must have offended him.

" It will make trouble for us," he cried, tearing it again into quarters. " I want to live in peace. We have gone through one war and won it. *Che buono ?* "

He spat out his cheroot and mopped his brow with a dusky diamonded hand. His companions seemed awed.

A movement across at the fair one's table drew Randell's attention from the political scene. She had summoned the waiter and was paying the bill. The depth of the bow suggested an unusually generous tip. The *garçon* obsequiously made a way for her through the tables towards the boulevard. Perhaps he, too, felt a sudden resurgence of romance through his dilapidated frame, for even old waiters might be decayed Romeos.

Randell pulled out a note and placed it under his saucer. Surprised at himself, he rose and made his way out of the café. For the moment he had lost her, but knew her direction. He glanced at his wrist-watch. It was a quarter to seven. Dinner at the villa was at nine. He would pander to curiosity awhile. It would be interesting to see where she went, where she lived, perhaps.

The gardenia-trimmed hat was a little ahead of him. She could have no idea he was following. The pavement was crowded with strollers under the plane trees. It was the hour of the promenade. European tourists, fezzed Arabs in their voluminous robes, French officers, prosperous *locataires* and their wives, sauntered along the wide avenue, quizzing one another.

Intermittently he had a full view of her. Her movement was all that he had surmised in one so graceful. She had a swan's serene air of effortless motion. Medium in height, he appraised her straight legs, the high-arched feet, un-splayed and vital The tailored beige skirt, box-pleated from the slender hips, expressed the sensuous contiguity of her figure beneath the thin cloth.

He lost her for the moment in the enfolding throng and then caught the crimson hat again, threading the human pattern beneath the trees. Suddenly she halted and drew toward the curb. She raised a pointed, gloved hand, sum-moning a perambulating carriage with a yellow tasselled canopy. The driver on the box seat drew up and saluted her. She got in. Randell saw the crimson hat recede, visible beneath the swaying canopy.

He looked around and found what he sought, another Jehu with a vacant carriage. He summoned it and got in.

" M'sieur ? "

" Do you see ahead of you that carriage with a crimson hat in it ? Follow it discreetly," said Randell.

" *Mais oui, m'sieur*," replied the old man, jerking the reins.

They ambled onwards. In this direction they were going towards the old town. Perhaps she was visiting the Souks to make a purchase. In a quarter of an hour the leading carriage turned to the right, towards the coastal road. The Souks were not her destination. It was probable now that she was going home, to one of the villas, towards Sidï-bou-Said.

He lit a cigarette, enjoying his adventure. The delightful creature in front had no idea she was being followed. She was not aware of and not interested in him. No, that might not be correct. It might be vanity on his part, but he could not dismiss a suspicion that she had seen him the previous evening and that again she had seen him this evening as he looked for a table. Something in the aversion of her face under that obscuring hat told him she was aware of his presence. But she knew nothing of his pursuit of her carriage. She had not turned once to look.

The carriage did not turn in at any of the gates on the lower road. It went off on the upper road and began to mount the hill. So she lived in one of the larger villas set in their ornate grounds with a view towards the gulf ! Ten minutes later there could be no doubt about her destination.

The carriage was mounting the winding road that led towards the Restaurant de France, from whose terrace there was a renowned view of Tunis and the gulf. She might be driving there or merely going to view the sunset, which promised to be unusually splendid. He faced a dilemma. It was somewhat obvious if he followed now. Theirs were the only carriages on the road. Well, the belvedere of the restaurant was a public place. He had equal reason and right to view the sunset.

They had arrived now. She dismounted from her carriage, which she did not dismiss. It seemed unlikely she had come here to dine. Dinner was usually later. He watched her cross to the belvedere and stand there, resting her hands on the balustrade as she surveyed the view. Halting his carriage when it reached the far end of the terrace, he told the driver to wait and strolled leisurely along, pausing from time to time to gaze at the superb panorama before him. He drew level with her at last, her back turned towards him. It was impossible that she had not heard someone approach. What now?

With a pounding heart he halted and rested a hand on the balustrade a few yards distant from her. She turned her head towards the stranger and observed him with a steady, unembarrassed gaze. For the first time he saw her fully, clearly, and a shock of pleasure struck him. She was so much more beautiful than his former glimpses had revealed. Her expression, reposeful and sympathetic, was lit with intelligence. Her eyes were large and filled with a light that made them an eloquent index of her nature which, he felt instantly, was dignified but flexible. He could not be mistaken in believing she expected him to speak to her. Her whole attitude was one of expectancy, though expressed with an air of calm dignity. It caught him unguarded, so that, their eyes meeting, he flushed. Then, to mask confusion, he raised his hat and addressed her boldly.

" *Bonsoir, mademoiselle. C'est magnifique, n'est-ce pas ?* " he observed, indicating the view before them.

" *Oui, c'est revissant*—but need we speak French to each other ? " she asked, a smile lighting her eyes.

" Ah, I hear you speak English perfectly ! " he replied, laughing in surprise.

" Not perfectly—but sufficiently well, I hope. I should
be able to—I'm English ! "

" Oh ! "

" Do I look very foreign ? " she asked.

" You are so very chic—I assumed you were French."

" That is flattering, and you are almost right. My clothes
are French."

A brief silence fell between them. There was no sound
in this upper air until one of the horses shook its harness.
The evening was scented with honeysuckle.

" I thought perhaps you lived here," began Randell,
breaking the pause.

" Why ? " she said quickly, looking at him with candour.

He knew at once that her question was provocative, that
she had trapped him.

" Because I frequent Le Chat Noir ? " she continued, not
waiting for him to attempt any evasion of the implied
accusation that he had been watching her. " But all tourists
go there—it is the centre of everything ! "

" Yes—the music is good," he agreed lamely.

" It seems so. I've been there twice—yesterday and to-
day. I've been here only three days. Oh, how lovely this
is ! " she exclaimed, gazing out across the gulf.

The sunset had advanced to its crowning magnificence.
In the distance, on the headland, a white blade of light
flashed from the Phare, a light which, of old, Hanno may
have watched for, home-coming after his journey with a
fleet of sixty sail through the Pillars of Hercules. Dido's
city had gone, as also Hamilcar's, Hannibal's, Saint Augus-
tine's, but the setting remained. Behind them rose the
Byrsa, the ancient Punic acropolis, now disfigured by the
hideous cathedral, Christianity's retort to the dethroned
worship of Baal. As seen from that acropolis, little of the
landscape had changed—the ports of vanished Carthage
gleamed in the evening light, the round naval harbour with
its island, the commercial harbour where Scipio had built
his mole.

The falling sun had crimsoned the great lagoon before
them, stretching from La Goulette up to the water front of
modern Tunis. A flight of flamingoes, with pink-tipped
wings, crossed the evening sky. It was a double flight,

mirrored in the turquoise lagoon below. These birds were
the descendants of those who had witnessed the triumph
and ruin of nation after nation coveting these waters and
the great African continent behind them.

Far off, across the still lagoon, in a veil of indigo and rose,
twin-peaked Djebel-bou-Korneïn faded through the dusk,
and the last light of evening lingered in the folds of the
distant mountain-sarcophagus of the Zaghouan range,
whence the Romans had brought water in an aqueduct
whose massive arches still spaced the plain between
mountain and city.

The silence of the upper sky was broken as they watched.
A distant vibration drew their eyes seaward. Like a bat
skimming the twilight, an aeroplane came in. It banked
and turned over the ruined castle-fort of Chikli, in the
lagoon, an old stronghold of the Corsairs. Then it flew
across the isthmus dividing the lagoon from the salt shallows
of Sebkha-er-Riana. It followed the line along which had
run the triple fortifications of ancient Carthage, before Rome
had erased them, and dipped towards the aerodrome at
L'Acuina. Behind that aerodrome lay the salt lake which
was once the Gulf of Utica, the famous Phœnician emporium,
now twelve miles inland, blocked in by the alluvial deposits
of the Medjerdah River.

"That plane probably came from Sicily," observed
Randell, after having described the geography of the scene
before them.

"You must have lived here a long time to know so
much," said his companion. "How interesting you make
it!"

"No—I'm a fraud," he replied, laughing.

Her voice was as lovely in its tones as it should be,
belonging to one of such physical distinction. He began to
think now she might be thirty-five. She had a certain
maturity, and her manner was assured.

"Actually, I have been here for only three weeks," he
explained. "I happen to be staying with a friend of mine
who is in the Service des Antiquités and has a lot to do
with the excavations here."

"You are not an antiquarian or an historian? You've
made it most interesting for me, Mr. —— ?"

She paused and gave him an encouraging smile with her eloquent eyes.

"Randell Dunning's my name. I'm a novelist, English, of course. And you—you are visiting for the first time?" he asked, leaning his elbows on the balustrade and scrutinising her face frankly.

Her delicate white lace gloves fluttered in the air. He thought of mating butterflies as she raised them, gesticulating, and laughed musically.

"Yes—for the first time. My name is Kleber. Madame Carlotta Kleber. Carlotta I owe to my mother. She had an Italian friend of that name and named me after her."

"I think it's a beautiful name," he said.

She made no reply and looked out over the lagoon. He wished he had not made that remark. It sounded trite. The glory was fading from the upper sky. A mauve light came with the tranquil tide of evening. Then it turned to jade, with a sickle moon of silver, bright in the east. Lights began to twinkle coolly in the villas around. The shaft from the lighthouse scythed the deepening dusk. A dog barked, staccato in the stillness.

The sound of horses and wheels over gravel came to them. Others were visiting the belvedere. Presently an open carriage discharged a family of five, a man and his wife, two little girls, and a lanky boy, in tight white shorts, for whom trousers seemed long overdue. The little girls, with bunches of almost Negroid black hair tied up with blue ribbons, ran across to the balustrade and peered over. Their shrill, excited voices sounded like quarrelsome sparrows. The parents, ignoring the view, walked across to the restaurant after dismissing the carriage.

"*Venez! Venez!*" cried the boy impatiently, easing his tight shorts before following his parents. "*Dépêchez-vous!*" he called in a half-broken voice. The sisters detached themselves from the balustrade on which they clambered and ran after him.

"Have you any children?" asked Randell as they went.

"No—and you?"

"I? Oh, I'm a bachelor—so far!" He laughed. "I like wandering. I find material for my books that way."

"Have you been away long this time—you live in

London?" she asked, pushing back a glove to glance at
a gold wrist-watch.

"Yes, in London. I've been away six months now. I've
just made a trip through the Sahara, from Lake Chad, by
camel."

He felt a little peeved that she took no interest in what he
had written. Generally, when he disclosed his calling,
there was a sudden quickening of interest and a desire to
know the titles of his books. He was still young enough to
be proud of his creations. Like a young mother, he was
ready to parade his offspring. But this strange, lovely
woman gave him no encouragement. She seemed indifferent to his calling, though not, he felt, indifferent to
himself. She was disconcertingly self-possessed and yet
combined with it an air of sensitive reticence. He found her
increasingly hypnotic, with a beauty that baffled analysis.
Her features were good, her brown hair glossy and beautifully coiffured as far as he could discern under that sweeping
hat. She was *soignée* to a degree that had justified his
error in believing her to be French, though she had a little
of the harder brilliance that became the pattern of rich
American women long resident in France. She was
strangely un-English in every sense, lacking the casual and
careful independence of her countrywomen.

Kleber was not an English name. He wondered about
her husband. Of course he might be an American living in
France. She referred to herself as Madame. Or he might
be a French-Alsatian with a Teutonic name. There might
not be a husband at all. She might be a widow! He had
a lot of questions he wanted to ask. It would be pre-
sumptuous to do so on such slight acquaintance. Moreover, he felt she did not encourage inquisitiveness. Her
glance at the wrist-watch had not escaped him. He had no
feeling that she wanted to be rid of him, but, possibly, she
had an appointment. Her carriage was still waiting, as his.

Over at the restaurant the French family had awakened
the place to sudden activity. Two waiters in Arab burnouses, with black-tasselled fezzes, were hovering behind
the head waiter. A prolonged conference ensued between
M'sieur and the head waiter as they discussed the menu
almost passionately. Madame took no part in this serious

preliminary. M'sieur seemed to know her tastes exactly.
The scene gave Randell an idea. It was a bold move that
might lead to a rebuff, but he took the risk.

" It's so charming here—the afterglow will last for some
time—that I'm tempted to ask if you won't give me the
pleasure of dining here. The food is good, I believe. The
pleasure of your company would make it delightful. But
you may have an engagement or feel that, as our acquaintance is so brief——"

She interrupted him with a gay little laugh.

" The situation is one that, as a novelist, I am sure you
could use, and you have phrased it charmingly ! Thank
you. I should love it ! To be frank, I was going to ask
you, as my guest."

" Splendid ! I'll dismiss the drivers," he said, and went
over to them. He paid them off so handsomely that they
had no growls left in them.

" I think an *apéritif*, while we discuss the menu ? They
make an excellent daiquiri here with local limes—but
perhaps you——"

" I should love one," she replied, as they crossed to the
restaurant.

They chose a table that had an uninterrupted view. New
colours had invaded the higher reaches of the sky. A large
cloud was edged with an incandescent glow, the sun's ex-
piring effort. He ordered *vichyssoise*, trout with a Château
Lafite, 1912, quails in aspic with a 1908 Pommard, and
crêpes Susette to follow.

She removed her lace gloves, to reveal exquisite hands.
The fingers were slim and long. She wore two rings, one
plain and one with a cluster of small diamonds about a large
ruby. Obviously she was a woman of some wealth, according to her appointments. Her cigarette case, gold, with a
lizard inset with emeralds, was beautiful and unique.

" Fabergé ? " he guessed as she offered him a cigarette.

" Yes—how nice of you to know ! I treasure it," she
said. " It was given me in Warsaw—after one of my
concerts."

" Ah—you are a singer, an opera star ! " he exclaimed.
It explained so much, her travelling alone, her poise.

" No, nothing so romantic. When I was a very young

woman I studied the piano—in Paris. Later I gave a few concerts in various capitals. But it was no use."

" No use ? "

" Many are called, but few are gifted enough," she explained.

" I would like to hear you and know just what we have lost."

She laughed, this time with a lightness she had not hitherto shown. What distinction she had ! He wondered about her background and how she came to be alone in Tunis. Perhaps she was not alone. He alluded to her remark about giving up music.

" Didn't your husband want you to continue playing ? " he asked.

" No. I don't think he cared much. Really, I have no talent."

" Is he here with you in Tunis ? "

" No."

At that moment the waiter returned with the daiquiris.

" I first met these in the Ritz bar at Paris. I like them, don't you ? " she asked.

" Yes. I believe they originated in Havana—but who knows where a cocktail has birth ? It is one of the great illegitimates ! "

She had steered him away from her husband. He would not try again. How foolish of him, anyway. This was immensely enjoyable. She was so completely stimulating to eye and ear, as well as to mind. It was an almost impossible combination.

Their eyes met over raised glasses. The French family at the corner table watched them covertly. The fact edified rather than worried Randell. They were a good pair for a Frenchman to observe.

" Your friends at the villa—will they be worried about you ? " asked his companion.

" Oh, no, I have thoughtfully established a reputation for eccentricity. Dinner is at nine, and we never wait for each other."

She made a few polite inquiries about them.

" I like Beresford ; I was up at Oxford with him. Poor fellow," he said.

" Poor fellow—why ?   He is unhappy ? " asked his companion.

" Oh, no, not that.   He's the brightest of fellows, and very gallant.   No—he's consumptive and makes a wonderful fight for it.   He goes through life with a collapsed lung and has never really recovered from an attack of rheumatic fever following the Gallipoli campaign.   Pierre, poor chap, who's devoted to him, came out of the war minus one kidney and with a burst eardrum.   You'd never know anything's the matter with either of them.   They're crazy about their work and are, outwardly, the most robust and active pair imaginable.   I hope you will come and see us—the villa is really charming, with a magnificent view."

She thanked him.   " But I am leaving in a few days," she explained.

" So soon ?   Oh, but I had hoped——"

" These brief contacts are part of the pleasure of travel— if one is sufficiently unconventional to seize the opportunity," she said, smiling at him.

He found he could not dive deep enough into the unfathomable loveliness of her eyes when she smiled like that.   An exquisite aura enveloped her, and the ache of frustration pervaded him.   Many adventures, in which he had enjoyed his prowess, told him that here was a woman beyond his experience.   He felt commanded rather than commanding.   His egotism was challenged and yet not hurt.   He noticed again a luminous quality in her skin, pearly, rose-tinted, with a singular coolness.   Her mouth expressed every nuance of her swift mind, perfectly matched to the changing light of her dark eyes.   He would have to keep a clear head.   One false move would defeat him, he knew.

" Are you often at the Chat Noir ? " he asked, forgetful of her early remarks.   " I wonder how long I have been missing you."

" I've been twice—so you've never missed me," she answered frankly, with a challenge in her eyes.   " We saw each other the first time I was there."

He gave a start of surprise, which she saw.

" I didn't know you had seen me at all, either time," he replied.

" Yes—I'll be quite honest. Yesterday, at about six o'clock, you wore a Wykehamist tie. To-day——"

" Good Lord ! " he exclaimed, looking hastily down at his tie.

" No, to-day," she continued, laughing, and looking at his bright yellow tie, " you are somewhat un-English, somewhat Latin Quartier ! "

" Oh, really ! Actually I bought it at Sovrani's in Venice last summer."

" Very pretty—and a perfect match with your coat."

" Thank you. And if I were to remark on your appearance——"

" Please do ! "

" Even if I were a master of English I should fail miserably. So you recognised the old school tie yesterday ? Do you know Winchester ? "

" My brother was there."

Again he started and at once became inquisitive.

" Oh—when—what was his name ? "

" He must have been there before your time. I was a little girl then. He was killed on the Marne."

" My elder brother might——" began Randell.

" Can I have a little dry toast ? This quail is delicious," she said.

He called the waiter. She had headed him off again. One thing was plain. She wished to keep her anonymity. Madame Kleber, perhaps of Paris, with a husband somewhere—that was to be the extent of his knowledge.

The lights on the tables had been switched on. The sunset had gone. The restaurant had filled up in the last hour. A small orchestra had made its appearance. There was a central space for dancing. The musicians, obviously French, were dressed in embroidered Moroccan jackets, with red-frogged fronts. They wore fezzes with coloured tassels. The night was deliciously warm. Occasionally a stirring wind brought the scent of honeysuckle. The service at the tables was slow, but the food was good. Randell Dunning, having eaten well and drunk well, felt stimulated. It was a stroke of unbelievable good fortune to be sitting here with this very lovely woman. He had only one desire unfulfilled. He would like Pierre and Russell to see him and envy him.

" Will you dance ? " he asked.

She rose and he followed her on to the floor. Again he marvelled at his good fortune. She danced perfectly. Their rhythm was flawlessly matched. She came into his arms completely relaxed. The perfume of her hair, the cool smoothness of her hand, the lightness of her in movement, it was all a blend of enchantment. She did not talk ; a serious and perfect dancer. The two-step ended. A tango began. They went into it, each finding the other adept. When it had ended and they made their way back to the table, his utter enjoyment made him exclaim, " You were wonderful ! " But the moment the words escaped him he knew he had erred. She made no response, but her eyes lingered on him for a second, and he felt like a schoolboy reproved for his exuberance. It was curious how she never lost her poise even in their most genial moments. It was something more than good breeding. What it was he could not find words for. She kept him watchful and a trifle anxious.

At half-past ten, after two more dances, she expressed a wish to go.

" Shall we take a drive ? " he asked.

" Thank you, no. It has been such a lovely evening, but I'm rather tired," she replied.

When the carriage arrived he escorted her out.

" I may see you home ? " he asked.

" Thank you. The Palace Hotel," she answered.

The horse jogged along, down the curving road, past the white villas with their dark, guardian palms. The clear night was full of stars. The moon had gone down. The air was noisy with tree frogs. Presently they came to the town, with lamps embowered in foliage. Odd voices from open doorways, strains of music, noisy *boulevardiers* strolling in the leaf-shadowed night revealed the city as still full of life.

He ventured to suggest lunch for the morrow, but she was engaged.

" Will you be at Le Chat Noir ? " he asked.

" Yes—I think so."

" Let me suggest a change. Do you know the Café Marabout ? "

" No."

" I think you will find it interesting. Let me call for you
to-morrow and take you there. It's an old café in the Souk
of the Fabric Sellers."

" That sounds perilous," she replied, laughing. " I can
never get through the bazaars without spending money.
They are such wheedlers ! "

They came to the Palace Hotel, and he escorted her to
the entrance. She held out a gloved hand.

" Thank you so very much. It's been a most delightful
evening. Then to-morrow at six I'll be ready. Good
night, Mr. Dunning."

" Good night."

She gave him a radiant smile, withdrew her hand, and
left him.

He paid off the driver and, walking along the avenue, his
head full of speculation on this astonishing evening, began
to look for a taxi to take him back to Sidi-bou-Saïd. Suddenly he remembered that his car was still parked opposite
Le Chat Noir. He walked briskly in that direction.
A woman like Madame Kleber would make one forget
anything.

§ 3

Randell Dunning saw Madame Kleber on three consecutive days following their dinner at the belvedere. He
met her and took her to the Café Marabout in the native
quarter, as arranged. It was an old building full of
columns pillaged from Carthage after the fall of the Roman
Empire. It took its name from being built over the tomb
of a Marabout, a holy man of Islam, or, as Randell explained
it, a human monument to dirt and superstition, " Anyone
can set himself up as a Marabout if he will dedicate himself
to complete inertia and complete filth," he observed.

The café delighted Madame Kleber, with its Kairouan
carpets, its Arabs squatting on the floor, drinking coffee and
smoking hookahs, and its native orchestra that made a
plangent dissonance on a number of strange string instru-
ments and drums. The vocal accompaniment seemed like

the distressed love call of a tomcat to Dunning's ears, though Pierre always claimed a fine discernment of tonal values.

When they left the café they wandered through the Souks, resisting the persistent touting of Tunisian merchants who, in the doorways of their bazaars, sprayed scents, rustled silks, rattled beaten copperware with silver inlay work, and displayed oriental rugs and cloths. It seemed to Randell that his companion was singularly unfeminine in her firm indifference to these alluring objects, but when she learned that some of the most beautiful rugs were a product of Kairouan, the ancient Holy City south of Tunis, she expressed a wish to visit the place. Randell at once suggested the excursion in his car. It was about four hours' drive and an extremely pleasant outing over the Zaghouan range and across the plain, with its olive and palm groves.

Accordingly, he called for her the following morning at nine o'clock. The occupants of the Villa Byrsa were now filled with active curiosity. When would he bring the alluring one to the villa ? asked Pierre.

" It's odd, but I can't awaken in her the slightest interest about you," answered Randell.

" Oh, nonsense ! " retorted Russell. " I'll bet you've made us out to be a pair of bearded ancients—your twin octogenarian uncles who don't like company."

" I've built you up in every possible way and turned the villa into a dazzling palace. I've offered lunch, cocktails, dinner, all to no effect. She doesn't want to meet anyone, very obviously."

" Very obviously you're not risking any competition," said Pierre as they sat at breakfast.

" It may be, of course, that the literary touch has led Randell into difficulties—these writing fellows have perfervid imaginations," remarked Russell, feeding crackers to Pierre's great saluki hound.

" What do you mean by that ? " asked Randell, looking out across the terrace. It was going to be a perfect day.

" The lady may have warts, whiskers, or a waddle. Or she may not exist at all, in the manner of the importance of being mysterious. The whole story is very fishy, my dear boy. I've never hooked pretty widows in public cafés," said Russell.

" And never in Le Chat Noir with Italians and French-
men biting—very fishy indeed, Randell. You produce her,
or we'll regard her as one of your greater works of fiction,"
bantered Pierre. " Now why can't we motor you down to
the rendezvous this morning? My God! You look
frightened at the idea ! "

" When Madame Kleber wants to come, she'll come.
I've invited her often enough," said Randell.

" Is she quite alone ? " asked Pierre.

" Quite—so far as I know."

" It's odd, isn't it ?   No friends, no husband—travelling
quite alone ? " queried Russell.

" Women do travel alone these days. She's not a young girl."

" No—but if she's half what you say, she's a siren, and
sirens without sailors seeking shipwreck are phenomenal.
I think our curiosity is quite legitimate," exclaimed Pierre.
" I shall spy on you to-morrow at Le Chat Noir, so be sure
to fix the date. You needn't acknowledge me."

Randell escaped from them after breakfast. He had
informed them of the excursion to Kairouan, and Pierre, in
his way, could not resist a final quip as he left them.
" There's a good hotel at Kairouan, the Splendide. The
beds are comfortable and no curiosity is shown. So if we
shouldn't see you at breakfast——"

" How very French you are ! " retorted Randell, getting
into the car.

As he motored into Tunis he thought how his friends
had underlined his own speculation on this exhilarating but
odd encounter with Carlotta Kleber. Easy to talk to,
always bright and full of interest, she maintained a reserve
he had not penetrated thus far. It was tactful not to show
too much curiosity at first. After all, why should she give
him her life's history after so brief an acquaintance ? Her
marriage may not have been a happy one. Women as
beautiful as she had a habit of making unhappy marriages.
He had seen it so often. Perhaps, with their beauty, they
were the prey of uninhibited males ; possibly some of them
had only their beauty for a magnet. Carlotta Kleber was
not in this class. Half an hour with her showed her to be
a woman of character. She talked well and she listened
well, an even greater gift.

An absurd idea visited his mind. Perhaps she had just left her husband and was travelling to mitigate the shock. It would explain her cultivated solitude, her reticence about her past. There was one other possibility. She might even be a widow. He could recall no occasion when she had spoken, the few times she had spoken, of her husband as a living person. He would like to clear up that point. Then he laughed to himself. What did it matter whether she was married or widowed? He had a conviction this encounter would not proceed to an adventure. For the first twenty-four hours he had nourished that hope. Every unknown woman evoked a sense of adventure in him; it was his touchstone of interest, being young, ardent, and uninhibited.

Madame Kleber was waiting for him in the vestibule of the hotel, cool, lovely, vivacious. Again, she was exquisitely dressed, in a tailor-made cream jacket and skirt, piped in red, with facings and cuffs of striped blue and white silk. A slender rope of pearls looped her brown throat, firm and unwrinkled. He noticed, as before, the slight exaggeration, provokingly feminine, in her mascaraed eyelashes and carmined mouth. The perfume she used was sparing and indefinable. He had never met it before. Her footwear was impeccable. This morning she wore dainty cream calf shoes with red heels to match her costume. She carried a deep reticule with a red-white-and-blue-tasselled fringe and pink jade handles. One of her singularities was punctuality. She had never kept him waiting, and also, he had observed, she never fumbled. She knew exactly where her purse was in her reticule, or her compact, or sun glasses. This morning she was not wearing the small diamond-set wrist-watch; instead, a small watch hung from the lapel of her jacket, set in a crystal cube. He remarked on its singular beauty as she sat beside him in the car.

" Fabergé ? " he asked, admiring it.

" No, not this time ! " She laughed, turning it for him to see. The tiny hands in the form of arrows radiated from a gold heart at the centre.

" It's really unique and exquisite," he said, examining it.

" It's from Cartier. I love it. My husband gave it me on the tenth anniversary of our wedding," she said simply.

That was his chance. He took it.

" I hope he'll mark the next decade with something equally lovely ! "

" I hope he will ! " she laughed.

So he knew that much. She was not widowed. And she had been married at least ten years. His thirty to thirty-five estimate seemed correct.

They were outside Tunis now. The early sun was warm. The sky clear. Pierre had lent him his new drop-head Delage coupé. It moved almost soundlessly.

The road towards Zaghouan was a good one. It ran parallel with the great Roman aqueduct which had carried water from the nymphæum on Djebel Zaghouan, across the plain to Carthage. It was an impressive chain of arches, some sixty feet high. It covered the desolate country for about forty miles, a monument of blood and tears, built in the slave era. The plain was being cultivated in places, but the general expanse was barren and sad with forgotten history. They came to the poverty-stricken village of Mohamedia, built by one of the beys, with its vast ruin of a former palace and barracks. Bedouins were camping among the ruins now.

They descended from this bleak spot, crossed the stony bed of a river, and left the spur of the Saharan Atlas range. They began to climb again, through more cultivated country, past terraces of olive, orange, and cypress trees. They came to the town of Zaghouan, hanging picturesquely on the precipitous extremity of the mountain, whose head was still obscured in mist. Below them stretched a panorama of gardens and cultivated plains of fruit and olive trees set in geometrical patterns. An old arch cut the sky, witness to past triumphs of Roman power. The semi-circular nymphæum up in the mountain, and a ruined temple, marked the honour shown the goddess of the source, for this mammal mountain had nourished Carthage of old and nourished Tunis to-day.

Enfidaville, orderly, modern, French, greeted them as they gained the plains, with the wide salt marshes of Sebkha Djiriba glistening on their left. They stopped for a drink at a little café set out on the main street of the town. It might have been anywhere in Provence, so perfectly had these settlers reproduced the atmosphere of the home-land.

"If the *garçon* wears a short black sateen jacket and a white apron round his middle, I shall cry," said Madame Kleber as they selected a table under the orange awning.

He did, and, true to the Place Pigalle, had not shaved that morning.

"There's France, the quintessence of it, look!" cried Randell, pointing across the road. Two small boys, bare-legged *gosses*, with berets, and carrying school satchels, went by. Their black linen *tabliers* were belted at their little waists. They gazed at the observant lady with large dark eyes, long-lashed, in their coffee-coloured faces.

> "*A la Saint Jean,*
> *Tout oiseau perd son chant,*"

quoted Madame Kleber. "That was the first thing I learned in my French reading book. We had a governess called M'mselle Meuniére. She was always in tears, poor girl, for she had never been away before. My father called her the Sole Meuniére, but he was so kind to her that she fell in love with him, and it became terribly embarrassing. She went home when her father had arranged a marriage for her with the local attorney, a man twenty years her senior. She wrote at first. She had a son—I wonder what happened to her. Her boy may have been killed in the war ; it would just catch him. How those children bring it all back!"

She surprised Randell by beckoning to the two small boys. They came towards her diffidently, wondering what she wanted. She asked them their names. Etienne and Paul. She gave them each a chocolate bar, wrapped in silver paper, from the *pâtisserie* the waiter had brought. They were coming home from school. Yes, it was very hot here in summer, but they went to the beach. With little bows they went off, all smiles, shrilling, "*Merci, madame!*"

The *garçon* brought them a newspaper. They glanced at it. That man Mussolini was in the headlines again with a provocative speech. He had ranted about "Mare Nostrum" and mentioned Corsica, Malta, and Tunis. Clemenceau had made a forceful retort.

B

" We're all going to have trouble with that fellow,"
observed Randell.

" Oh, no ! The Italians are such charming children."

" Charming children can get swollen heads if they go
unspanked."

She laughed. " How severe you sound ? One might
think you enjoyed spanking children ! "

He paid the bill and they resumed their journey through
the olive groves and across the flat land. Presently Kairouan
loomed out of the distance, dazzling white in the brown
plain, with barren hills rising in the western background.
It was wholly oriental in character as they came to it,
walled, with a massive gate, and dominated by the great
minaret. A camel cavalcade blocked the road as they
entered the city. The narrow streets were filled with
shouting Arabs and mules laden with merchandise, through
which an impatient motorist tried to blast his way. It was
a little like a scene from the *Arabian Nights*, declared
Madame Kleber. Two French officers of the Zouaves
sauntered by in their vivid uniforms. They ogled Randell's
companion with Gallic effrontery. They were to be excused.
Pretty women were scarce in this lost place.

The French had been here for forty years, but the character
of the city had not altered much. It contrasted vividly with
Enfidaville. The city, founded in A.D. 671 by Okba Ben
Nafti, the Mussulman conqueror of Africa, and the parent
city of Cairo, had retained it oriental ways ever since three
French generals had stood before its walls in 1881, and a
young officer, riding up to the studded gate of the Casbah,
had commanded it to open. It opened. Fear reigned
within. All the women and children had been hidden. But
the place went unsacked, the women unraped. The Cross
did not wage war like the Crescent. As the gate opened
a white flag fluttered from the minaret of the Grand Mosque.

" We can be grateful for one thing," explained Randell.
" The mosque was unwittingly desecrated by some French
soldiers who accompanied their Algerian allies when they
went in to worship at the shrine of Sidi Okba. So we can
go in to-day. I was here last week. It's worth a visit."

A small boy with diseased eyes and an unwashed *jerba*
jumped on the running-board. " *Je suis le guide official,*

m'sieur!" he shouted. "*Viesitez le Grande Mosquée!*
Eenglish? *Américain?* I speak both, mister!"

In vain Randell ordered him off.

"Poor child—he looks famished. Let him take us,"
said Madame Kleber.

"We'll have no choice—anyhow, he'll knock off the
others."

And at that moment the boy placed his foot full in the
stomach of another urchin who attempted to board the car.

They removed their shoes at the entrance to the mosque
and shuffled around the vast courtyard in the slippers provided. They performed the tourist's set piece, squeezing
between two columns by which they qualified for entrance
into Paradise. The great hall of the mosque was a maze
of columns, of Roman origin obviously. Their young guide
tried to move them to ecstasy over the mihrab, the carved
eighth-century prayer niche. Finally they ascended the
tower above the white-roofed city. In an unwary moment
Randell dropped a few centimes to the clamouring urchins
below. Immediately the place became vocal with countless
shrill voices that rose in a supplicating chant.

"No good cheeldren, m'sieur!" asserted their guide,
envious of the largess. He spat down on them in a gesture
of contempt.

They paid off young Ali, but with the persistency of glue
he clung to the car until they had reached the Hotel Splendide
and went in for lunch. He insisted on guarding the car;
it might be stolen, despite the hotel attendant—"Sleepy,
bad man," asserted Ali.

The lunch was better than they had hoped. Leaving by
a side door, they evaded Ali, who had adopted them, and
made their way to the bazaars. In the Souk des Tapis
tremendous haggling was going on between the bazaar-
keepers and a party of American tourists from the liner at
Tunis, who had preceded them here. Sharp black eyes
flashed; hands were spread out in despair at the appalling
reductions they were prepared to make to give the customers
satisfaction. From this noisy scene they went to a quiet
one, an Arab carpet manufactory. Here they watched the
incredible patience of the hand weavers knotting cords in
the intricate design.

At five o'clock, exhausted, they began the return journey. It had been a delightful day. Madame Kleber grew in attraction and mystery. Randell wondered if he dare make love to her. He found a tortured pleasure in her company, but not once did she afford him an opening. Two things happened on this journey which showed some kind of advance in her interest. She suggested he should call her Carlotta, and she questioned him for the first time about his work, the books he had written, the books he proposed to write.

" I would have taken you for an athlete rather than a man of letters. You arrested my attention at once when you came to the Chat Noir. There is a slight arrogance in your figure ! " she commented.

" Do you find me arrogant ? " he asked.

" On the contrary, I find you very pleasant to talk to and most considerate ! "

" Thank you."

" And me ? " she queried with a mischievous glint in her eyes.

" If I were to say what I thought, like my friends Pierre and Russell, you would accuse me of an imaginative flight," he answered boldly.

She laughed this time as he had never heard her laugh and gave him one of those disturbing glances of her lovely eyes. Then she began to ask him about the caravan routes as they halted by a line of over-burdened camels slowly lurching forward.

They dined together that evening at her hotel, and when again he invited her to visit them at the Villa Byrsa she declined. " I am so bad at going out among strangers, so please excuse me."

He was certain that no woman of his acquaintance could be so self-possessed among strangers, but since this was her wish he made no further comment. She declined a suggestion for lunch or more sightseeing. She was behind with her letters.

" Let's meet at the Chat Noir to-morrow at six," she said.

" And dinner somewhere ? I'd like you to see the ruins at Dougga, in moonlight—there's a lovely Temple of the Triad."

" May I leave it till to-morrow ?   Let's go into the palm court ; I find these voices very unpleasant," she said, rising.

A large party of Germans had suddenly appeared in the hotel.   They guzzled sonorously and were unlovely to behold.   Evidently a German cruise ship had put in.

At eleven o'clock Carlotta retired, thanking him again for a delightful day.   He drove back to Sidi-bou-Saïd that slept on its hill, dream-like in the clear moonlight.

How far had he progressed with Carlotta ?   She had seemed much nearer to him to-day.   Now he was less certain that she shunned all romance.   How could a woman of such beauty resist the advances she provoked ?   She was married.   He had never found husbands insuperable obstacles.   He divided them into three categories, the possessive, the trustful, and the casual.   He had a feeling that M. Kleber belonged to the third category.   Well, whatever ensued, she had made his sojourn in Tunis a high note of enjoyment.

§ 4

They were not destined to meet again at the Chat Noir. The following morning, as Randell came up from the bathing pool, the butler met him with a note which had just been delivered by hand.   Randell saw at a glance it came from the Palace Hotel, marked " Urgent " in one corner. This was the first time he had seen her handwriting.   It was full of character, firm and easily legible.

He opened the envelope with suppressed excitement, fearing a disappointment ; was she putting him off ?   Pierre and Russell politely walked on into the house.   He unfolded the single sheet of paper and read :

Dear Randell,
   This will surprise you.   When you get this I shall have left Tunis.   I am going to the Grand Hotel Villa Igeia, at Palermo.   Will you come as my guest for a week ?   If not possible, good-bye and a thousand thanks,
                                   Yours sincerely,
                                          Carlotta.

Standing still, he read the note three times, stunned by the abruptness of her departure, by the invitation she gave him. What did it mean exactly? There was no reason why she should not have a guest, no reason at all. But their friendship had been very short, three days in all. Impulsiveness was the last quality he ascribed to her.

Why had she asked him? Evidently she liked his company. He had no false modesty about his attractiveness, physical and mental. Women had always been drawn to him, but not women like this. And why, oh, why, had she flown so precipitately? Baffling, magnetic creature! How little he still knew her.

He made his decision instantly. He would go. He would have to face a barrage of banter from Russell and Pierre, for it would be quite useless to deny that she had caused his sudden departure. The best he could do was to make it appear that her invitation had not wholly surprised him, that he had suggested continuing his rôle of cicerone in Sicily, which he knew well. Anyhow, let them make what they would of it.

In the study he telephoned a cable, saying he would leave to-morrow afternoon by boat for Palermo. Then he went out on to the loggia to break the news to Pierre and Russell, who looked wise, but exhibited the most tactful restraint.

CHAPTER II

SICILIAN SPRING

RANDELL DUNNING rose early on board the *Santa Lucia*, awakened by the noise of scurrying feet overhead. They had put in at a port. It could not be Palermo, for it was only six o'clock, and they were not due until nine. He looked out of the porthole of his state-room. The sun had risen, breaking in splendour through the morning mists which still shrouded the headlands of the mainland before him. Putting on a dressing-gown, he went up on deck. The port was Trapani, on the west coast of Sicily. Beside the harbour there were large lagoons where the sea water was evaporated, leaving the salt, which was a government monopoly. It was stacked up in white pyramids that glistened in the morning light.

He found himself talking with an amiable Italian who had come aboard. He proved to be a professor of literature at Palermo University. In a short time, delighted to display his knowledge, he had given Randell the history and topography of the place.

" There, look ! Do you see that headland coming out of the mist ? That's ancient Eryx, on the top of Monte San Giuliano. There used to be a temple to Ashtoreth, the Phœnician Venus. The Greeks believed it was founded by Heracles and was the abode of Venus Erycina. King Minos of Crete, who was murdered, is said to be buried there. Of course, this sea is just liquid history," went on the professor. " It was here, you know, off Trapani, which was the ancient Drepana, that the Carthaginian fleet was destroyed by the Romans in 241 B.C. at the end of the First Punic War, thus wiping out a previous defeat. Phœnicians, Greeks, Romans, Moors, Normans, Spaniards—they were always fighting one another. You English were here ; you held Sicily under Lord Bentinck, when your Nelson was waiting for Napoleon. And then, in 1841, Garibaldi came and kicked out the

Bourbons. That's nearly a hundred years ago—quite a long time for anyone to be at peace! I wonder how long it'll last this time. They're still squabbling over the peace terms. The war to end war! Why do men talk such nonsense?"

The professor pulled out a cigarette-case and offered Randell a cigarette.

"You don't believe we've entered the era of reason?" asked Randell, aroused by the voluble little man.

"Signore! Reason—who, that's ever read a line of history intelligently, can believe in reason? The race of man is incurably stupid! For centuries and centuries he's been fighting and dying heroically—for what? These Carthaginians, Romans, Saracens, Normans, who were at one another's throats and died choking in this very sea, does anyone care why and for what they died? My dear signore, as a historian I have the greatest difficulty in finding out for what they died! Their freedom, their faith, their honour, they would have told you, doubtless. But they never had any freedom; they were driven to fight either by tyrants or demagogues. What folly! A man's expectancy of life is about sixty-five years. For the first twenty years he's growing up, being educated; for the last ten he's getting old and full of pains and worries. That leaves him a space of thirty-five years in which to enjoy this wonderful world, with all its treasures of art, literature, music, to say nothing of the variety of the scene. A mere thirty-five years out of Eternity for enjoyment! And what does he do? He starts a war, shouts a few catchwords manufactured by politicians, and is snuffed out. For what, I ask you? Two thousand years ago that bright Roman lad, Julius Cassius, the pride of his father, came here in a trireme, had a pike stuck in him by a Carthaginian lad, fell overboard, and floated like a dead fish. In Rome his mourning parents erected a memorial. *Dulce et decorum est pro patria mori*—to quote Horace—you know how it runs. He died that freedom might live, that his nation should flourish. Now, I ask you, signore, does anyone care a damn for what poor Julius was snuffed out, aged twenty, two thousand years ago, or Giovanni, carrying a rifle for the Bourbons, eighty years ago? Does anyone care what the squabble was about, and did it really matter to them or to us, looked at historically ? Poor lads, with only sixty-five years at the best, and lopped off at twenty, dying for racial or religious superstitions, for plots of land, for parrot cries, for kings or parliaments, for autocracies or democracies, all the same folly dressed up in different costumes ! No, signore, man never gets wiser. He always finds a more ingenious plan for behaving better *next* time—like Mr. Wilson's League of Nations that they've emasculated—but he never carries it out. One day this sea and these beaches will be stained again with young blood, with Juliuses and Giovannis dying for the same illusions."

" Do you teach this in your history lessons ? " asked Randell when the little man paused in his tirade.

" Signore ! " he exclaimed, spreading wide his arms in a gesture of futility. " I am the father of two splendid boys, eight and ten. I have a wife I love and a comfortable home. Do you think that I, Professor Campanelli, could change the folly of the universe ? Any bugle can silence me, and drum drown me out. They prefer the feathers in a Field Marshal's hat to all the books of history I might write. Man is not interested in the truth ; he is only interested in the confirmation of his own misconception of it. For myself, having escaped one catastrophe—I was a soldier on the Piave, signore—I can only hope that I may enjoy a space of time before we are overwhelmed by another. I may be fortunate. But, knowing history and the nature of man, when I look at my two little boys I am filled with despair. Forgive me, signore, I do not wish to depress you on so lovely a morning."

" You don't depress me. All that you say sounds very logical, except for one thing," said Randell, smiling. " Man is an imperfect animal, I agree, but he is something more than an animal ; he has the divine spark. Animals fight for defence, or sex, or food, sometimes for the sheer love of killing, but never for an ideal."

" For an ideal ! What kind of a divine spark, as you call it, what kind of an ideal is this which makes men for ever butchering one another, destroying in a few hours of frenzy all that they have achieved through years of laborious peace ? "

Randell slowly drew at his cigarette and let his eyes rest on the increasing splendour of the dawn. They were leading mules over the side of the ship, belabouring the poor beasts mercilessly as they drove them down the ramp.

" We've embarked on an interminable argument, my dear Professor—the ways of God to man," replied Randell slowly. " I will say only this. Does it really matter much when and for what a man dies ? What really matters is how he reacts. He can fight and die in a bad cause nobly if he feels he is fulfilling his sense of duty."

" But it is a fallacious sense ! " interrupted the professor.

" Maybe—but having sacrificed himself to an ideal, to a sense of duty, or only to a sense of comradeship in that he will not desert his friends or his country, he has kept his self-respect. I don't think it matters what the verdict of the historian is. As for the better part of life that your Julius or your Giovanni sacrifices, I look at it in another way. Would they be any happier or nobler by having preserved themselves ignominiously ? A dead man in the lap of Eternity has no sense of time. If he has an imperishable soul, what are twenty or forty or a hundred years of life to him ? And if he has no soul, if he is a mere foolish animal, if all he can ever get is confined to his life here, then I have no answer to your problem, and neither have you, for man then becomes such a sorry joke of a callous creative force that he could not hope to live by pure reason, even if he possessed it. He has then as little chance of an orderly progress as a ball in a roulette wheel. But I'm hungry ; do you think we can get anything to eat ? "

" Yes, I'm sure ; let's go down—if I may have the pleasure of your company ? We do not agree, but we are good friends, *non è vero* ? " replied the smiling little professor, leading the way to the saloon. " There is at least one certainty in which you and I can rejoice—the unfailing friendship between your country and mine."

At ten o'clock they drew into the port of Palermo, with its noble bay, its rich plain of the Conca d'Oro and the great amphitheatre of the mountains as its setting. For a moment Randell wondered whether Carlotta would be there to meet him and dismissed the hope. The uniformed porter from the Grand Hotel Villa Igeia met the boat and led him to the hotel omnibus. Randell bade Professor Campanelli good-bye, having been introduced to his slim young wife and two dark-eyed little boys, neatly dressed in dazzling white suits. He accepted an invitation to dine with them during the week.

The hotel omnibus set off for the Villa Igeia, a mile and a half distant, facing the bay at the foot of the towering Monte Pellegrino. He had stayed there briefly last autumn. It was one of the most agreeable hotels in one of the loveliest scenes in Europe. All the shining richness of the Mediterranean seemed gathered in this noble palm-girt valley.

He was the only person from the boat. A few guests were still eating a late breakfast on the terrace when he arrived. The reception clerk expected him ; he was taken straight up to a suite that had been reserved. It was on the first floor, a bedroom and a sitting-room, with a balcony. The servant threw up the shutters, flooding the room with light. He stepped out into the radiant morning. The sea sparkled before him. The mountains were partly shrouded in a morning haze. The rich plain, with the city sprawling over it, was a green vista broken by old towers and buildings. The garden of the hotel was vivid with exotic blooms.

He found a note awaiting him in his room, along with two new English novels and a recent copy of *The Times*. They were from Carlotta. She would see him at noon, and they would lunch together. She had ordered a car for the afternoon, and they could make an excursion. Randell unpacked and took a bath. He had a feeling of adventure. After four years of war and two of travel, thank heaven he was still young enough for that.

At noon he went downstairs and found Madame Kleber awaiting him in the palm court. She looked as cool and lovely as ever.

" You must think me quixotic to go suddenly like that ? " she said, taking his hand.

" Yes—but what kindness, to let me know where you went, to have me here ! " he responded.

" Shall we lunch on the terrace ? I'm really hungry. I've just had a sitting with the hairdresser."

They found a table well in the shade. The noon blazed

around them. The head waiter remembered Randell and
broke into smiles. A lad with a perfect Greek profile and
black cropped curls waited on them. His name was appro-
priately Apollo, attached to an unpronounceable surname.
This was indeed the perfect setting of a perfect idyll. If
only Time would fold his wings and pause a little in rich
content.

§ 2

Five days fled. Five perfect days in a flawless setting of
quiet and warmth and springtime beauty. The mornings
were fresh ; the afternoons, charged with the scent of
flowers, were languorous. The warm, still evenings passed
from the crimson and gold of sunset to the purple dusk and
the starlit beauty of the sub-tropical night. They made
delightful excursions, to Montreale and its Norman cathedral
with the superb mosaics, to Soluntum, for its view of the
valley and coast, and to Piana dei Greci, the Albanian
settlement up in the mountains, where for some five hundred
years these people had preserved their costumes and customs. There was a day of such heavenly beauty, when they
lunched between the massive columns of the ruined temple
at Segesta, that, in the silence of the golden air, looking
over the great valley, they seemed to feel the presence of
those who had once laboured to voice their faith five hundred years before Christ. The Arthenians had besieged
their city ; the Carthaginians had looted their treasured
Diana ; the tyrant Agathocles in his fury had massacred
them ; the Romans had avenged them. Now only the
lizards and the field mice scurried over the deserted threshold
and the weed-grown floor of the roofless temple, immense
and eloquent against the blue sky.

Randell lived in a state of serene happiness. He was not
in love ; there was no quality of restless fever in this tranquil association with a woman of beauty and character.
Her poise had never left her, and he was aware now of her
clear determination to possess him as a lover. His suite,
he discovered that first evening, adjoined hers. Her wish
was instinctively realised by him. The fulfilment was
mutual and unvoiced. He lived these days and nights in
a trance of happiness, like some character in a romantic

French novel. The very setting conspired to give an unreal, almost theatrical background to the idyll. The Carlotta he had found so alluring at the Chat Noir had grown in attraction at the Villa Igeia. She still baffled him. There were reticences of mind and soul he could not invade. A hundred years with her would not elucidate the enigma that she presented. He never flattered himself he knew her inner thoughts, or that he possessed her wholly, even in her complete surrender to their moments of passion. Like Cupid, he visited his Psyche in a kind of darkness, only it was she who forbade the lamp and any investigation of this palace of love. Wisely he accepted the conditions. Who was ever given so much, with so little effort?

There was one occasion when he felt he had almost touched the spring of her inner being. They had made an excursion to Santa Maria di Gesú. A fat old monk had escorted them round the monastery and through the beautiful gardens. He left them on a terrace, with a stone fountain and a basin into which the water fell musically in the hot afternoon. Below them lay the valley of Palermo, a garden by the sea, backed by Monte Pellegrino and the amphitheatre of the mountains. The olive groves shone silvery in the wind. Peach, lemon, pomegranate, pepper, cherry, and orange trees filled the kaleidoscope before them. In the distance, under the azure sky, lay Palermo, russet gold, and white, with domes and *campanili* rising from the still valley. Then human voices came faintly on the air, voicing chanting in the chapel below them.

Randell saw her face quiver with the beauty of that moment, and his hand went over hers on the warm stone balustrade.

" I shall never forget this," she said, breaking silence. " What absolute peace and beauty ! "

" Must we ever leave it ? " he asked, smiling at her. " You are completely happy ? "

She looked at him and did not answer, her eyes looking into his so that he saw their candour.

" Completely happy ? I don't think that is ever possible, for me, Randell," she said.

They said nothing for a space, looking out over the plain, listening to the chanting voices.

" Carlotta—forgive me, but your marriage—it isn't a
happy one ? " he asked quietly, with averted eyes.

" Randell, you mustn't assume anything," she said, with
a smile of delicate reproof. " I should find it difficult to
explain—and why is it necessary ? We are here. This is
enough."

She withdrew her hand from the balustrade.

" Shall we go ? " she asked, linking her arm in his.

" My dear, I'm sorry," he exclaimed, seeing tears in her
eyes.

" It's nothing, Randell. We mustn't be foolish."

They went down the steps and picked up their old horse
carriage at the gates. The light was reddening and the
whole city glowed as they drew near to it under the falling sun.

On the morning of the sixth day he alluded to the ter-
mination of his visit. His period as her guest was ending.
He proposed, if agreeable to her, to stay on.

" Why can't you be my guest in turn, Carlotta ? "

They were breakfasting on the terrace. She did not
answer him at once and poured out another cup of coffee.
Then she looked at him and spoke calmly.

" I am leaving for Marseilles to-morrow afternoon,
Randell. There is no boat again for three days. I must
go to-morrow."

He was about to protest. There was a note of finality in
her voice, and he knew it was useless. His pride, too, was
hurt.

" I'm sorry if it must end so soon," he said, limply.

" It's been a wonderful week. I shall always remember
it. You have been so kind and thoughtful."

" I ? Carlotta, this is a shock," he exclaimed, folding his
napkin. " Very well—I'll leave on the evening boat, to-
morrow, for Naples. I shall go on to Venice," he said
affecting indifference.

" Randell, you sound hurt. But it couldn't go on, my
dear—I've never misled you on that."

" No, that's true, Carlotta," he admitted.

She glanced round. They were unobserved. Her hand
took his on the table momentarily, and she gave him one of
her irresistible smiles. Then she rose and he followed.

§ 3

He went with her to the boat soon after lunch the next day. The baggage went in the hotel omnibus, but for this last ride they took their old driver and his two trotting ponies. Randell covertly examined the labels on her baggage. It was consigned to the Bristol Hotel, Marseilles. She gave him no clue whatever.

" Are we never to see each other again ? " he complained, a little exasperated, when he asked if she would give him an address, and she had refused.

" It would be too difficult, Randell."

" Well, if you think so—there's nothing to be done," he said, masking the hurt to his pride. He was being dropped firmly. Dropped was the only word. He, Randell Dunning ! It had never happened before. He found it inconceivable now.

He stood waving until the boat left the quay, sad, angry, playing his part in pride. His last sight of her was one of utter loneliness, of the serene distinction which had never left her since that first evening of their contact at the belvedere. Lovely, maddening woman, lovelier for the aura of sadness he sometimes felt about her ! In their most intimate moments she had a childlike wistfulness, in contrast to her power of decision.

The carriage was taking him back to the Villa Igeia, when, compelled by a sudden idea, he halted the driver and told him to drive to the Banca d'Italia in the Corso Vittorio Emanuele. It was a horribly mean thing to do, to track her down like this, but his curiosity would not be restrained. She had gone there with him to cash her letter of credit one day. They might have no information, or they might decline to give it.

He found them affable and obliging at the Banca d'Italia, after a light lie about desiring to cable some money to her account in a bank whose name he had forgotten. They turned up the record. Frau von Kleber's letter of credit had been issued by the Wiener Bank-Verein, Vienna.

He thanked them and went out to the waiting carriage. Frau von Kleber ! Frau—not Madame !—*von* Kleber, of Vienna—not Paris ! She had never mentioned Vienna.

Now he came to think of it, she had never mentioned living in Paris, but somehow he had always assumed she lived there for a dozen indefinable reasons.

There were four hours before he sailed. The hotel seemed deserted without her. He filled in the time by writing letters. He recollected he had never seen her write a letter or receive one. She must have registered in the hotel, producing her passport. But he could not ask them at the desk. It would seem too odd, and he felt ashamed of himself already.

What an adventure, what an incredible adventure ! One day he might be able to use it in a novel, if only he could make it plausible.

He left that evening. As his boat beat its way slowly out of port the day died in a crimson conflagration that seemed like the end of the world. A lighthouse on a mountainside blinked coldly. He thought of another boat beating northward in the falling darkness.

CHAPTER III

SCHLOSS GARSTEIN

CARLOTTA VON KLEBER stayed one night in Marseilles and
two nights in Paris. Then, having completed her shopping
she took the train to Innsbruck, telegraphing her husband
the time of her arrival. Franz had already gone to their
summer home at Garstein, twenty miles out of Innsbruck.
The great gloomy Schloss was the property of Franz's
uncle, the General Graf Rudolph von Kleber, whose heir
he was. Perched on the spur of the great Karwandel
range, it had splendid views, but was isolated and grim, and
too large. It was always raining, too, or if not raining,
enveloped in swirling mist. The few fine days did not
compensate for the wet summer months. Schloss Garstein
was renowned for its shooting. For generations the family
had impoverished itself with the annual visit of the Emperor
for the *grande battue*.

The Graf Rudolph was a sick man now. The old
Emperor was dead ; the new Emperor was in exile. Austria
had been dismembered, and no one seemed to care about
its fate. The Socialists were in the saddle, completing the
ruin a lost war had wrought. The Graf's two sons had
died in battle. Only one of them had married, leaving two
daughters, by a woman he detested. He had made his
nephew Franz his heir because no other male of the line
existed. Franz was a gay, handsome, worthless spend-
thrift, like his father, who had died in Franz's infancy,
leaving a mountain of debts. The Graf, now sixty-five
and confined to his room by chronic arthritis, had only two
pleasures left in life, his collection of Holbein prints, and
his nephew's wife, Carlotta. The prints and the Von
Kleber wealth, such of it as survived, had come from his
Swiss grandmother, the only daughter of a Basle banker of
the eighteenth century.

Graf Rudolph had warmly greeted the English bride his

nephew had brought back to Austria after his two years as military attachê at the Austrian Embassy in London. When Franz had first broken the news to him of his sudden marriage to a young Englishwoman he had been angry and perturbed. The sight of her, young, lovely, vivacious, had dispelled all his fears. That was in 1912, when Franz was twenty-eight and his bride twenty-four. They seemed a devoted pair. The Graf hoped all would be well and that Franz, who had been rescued from several wild affairs, would now settle down. He had been responsible for him since the death of the boy's father, and the responsibility had not been a light one.

The young couple took an apartment in Vienna when Franz was recalled from London. Then came the war, in which the general lost his two sons, and Franz rose to be a major, decorated for gallantry in the Galician campaign.

In the horrors that followed defeat, the general, his sons dead, turned more and more to Franz, who, after appalling experiences, including a Russian prisoners' camp from which he escaped, had lost none of his charm and dash. Discharged from the army, his diplomatic career obliterated with Austria's disappearance from the Great Powers, Franz became, in turn, a ski-ing coach, a bank clerk, and the Continental agent for an American engineering business.

Carlotta von Kleber, through all these trying years, managed to keep herself attractive in appearance and cheerful in disposition. Cheerfulness cost her more effort, due less to economic reasons than to Franz's successive infidelities. He was fortified in his infidelity by the knowledge that his wife, despite the difficult scenes between them, was deeply in love with him. He had one excuse when some glaring irregularity provoked his wife's protest. " If we only had a family it would be different. Give me a son, my dear, and I'll be a reformed character."

Twice they had come to the breaking point. On both occasions it was Uncle Rudolph, now a chronic invalid, who healed the breach. " If you leave the scamp, Carlotta, I shall have no one to keep me going. Let me talk to him."

When the Graf talked his nephew listened, aware of an inheritance that could not be too far distant. The Graf and Carlotta drew nearer to each other in every crisis. She came to love the splenetic old man in the wheel chair. While Franz travelled about Europe on his agency business, which always coincided with the gayest seasons in the Continent's reviving capitals, Carlotta come to spend more and more time at Schloss Garstein.

Franz von Kleber would have been indignant had he been charged with not loving Carlotta. He loved her as much as on that day when, at a Leicestershire hunting-box, she had swept him off his feet, the fresh young daughter of a local squire. With his entrancing accent, his graceful body and quick mind, he had speedily cast his spell. Prince Charming stormed the castle and carried off his princess. Only her love for him gave her courage for the frightening adventure in a wholly new world.

It was difficult at first. She had to placate two prim, old-fashioned sisters, openly hostile to Franz's mad adventure. The general, correct but aloof, wished to show his disapproval of Franz's independence in marrying without consulting him, his guardian and benefactor. Within a year Carlotta had no truer friends than Mitzi and Maria Kleber, no firmer admirer than the Graf. Franz was received back into grace, which he so repeatedly fell from. " *Liebchen*, you can do anything with the old boy," he would say to Carlotta, and then urge her to extract some favour that she would not attempt. The Graf's sons, two grave young men, became her devoted cavaliers. They were mere boys, children of a late marriage, with a mother who had died in their infancy. Carlotta, only a few years their senior, emphasised a motherly rôle towards them, to defeat their amorous affection. Soldiers, like all the Klebers, they were the first to fall. By Christmas, 1914, General von Kleber was childless. Franz became the torchbearer of the line.

The years went by. After five years of marriage the general tried to hide his disappointment at Franz's failure to provide the new generation. Carlotta's hopes waned. Franz became reproachful. There had always been boys in the Kleber line. The inference was clear. He found in it an excuse for his wandering fancy. Then, as if ashamed of himself, he would show a new warmth to Carlotta and again be the lover who had won her. Gay, gallant, and

gifted in the light arts of entertainment, even his incon-
stancy could not lessen her devotion. And with this knowledge he began to grow cruel. Carlotta hid her suffering.
" Carlotta, if only you could have a child, it would make
a difference. Franz would be more considerate," said
Maria one day, when another of her brother's indiscretions
had created a scene between the general and his nephew.

Carlotta made no reply and set her mouth. Even his
sisters imputed to her the barren bed. As for the old
Graf, no words that could be twisted into a reproach ever
left his lips, but she knew his long-deferred hope was
changing to a sad acceptance of her failure. He had
weathered the vicissitudes of fortune through all these dis-
astrous years and kept the inheritance intact, to no purpose,
it seemed to him.

Carlotta, as the train drew into Innsbruck, was thinking
of the Graf now, a prisoner these days in his invalid chair,
dressed, fed, and moved by old Otto, his army servant for
forty years. Grim, splenetic, a rebellious cripple, twisted
and tortured, he was an impressive hulk of a man, with the
will to live still strong in him. Once, in one of those recurrent scenes with his nephew, when extravagance had
aroused him, Carlotta heard him bellow, " You're lucky
I'm paralysed, or, by God, I'd get me another family at
sixty-five, which you can't do at thirty-five."

The blood burned in Carlotta's cheeks as she hurried
down the corridor to her room. In that moment she hated
all men. Then she remembered, as she stared out of the
window down into the courtyard, that Franz had refrained
from making any defence against his uncle's charge, and her
anger vanished. She loved Franz and knew in his fallible
way he loved her.

The train drew into Innsbruck. The tourist season was
beginning. The platform was filled with dismounting
passengers and friends who had come to meet them.
Carlotta stood for a few moments amid the cheerful confusion by the door of the *wagon-lit* and surveyed the long
platform. There was no sign of Franz, who always came
to meet her. She had been away five whole weeks. She
wanted Franz now particularly.

A voice addressed her. She turned to find a smiling,

chubby-faced youth in a green jacket, bare-kneed, in leather shorts and white stockings, respectfully raising his feathered hat. It was young Hans, the house-boy, grinning from ear to ear.

" Welcome, *gnädige Frau!* Herr Franz is in Budapest. He comes home to-morrow. You have had a pleasant journey ? "

" Very, thank you, Hans."

" How many pieces, *gnädige Frau ?* " he asked, surveying the luggage.

" Seven. How's the Herr Graf ? "

" Just the same, *gnädige Frau*. He is expecting you eagerly. The Graf and Gräfin von Hatzfeld are visiting him."

Hans obtained a porter. They divided the baggage, the stocky youth taking the heavier. Carlotta followed them out to the limousine. Hans carefully wrapped the rug over her knees. It was a chilly day. They had a long drive.

For the next hour she leaned back, with closed eyes, a sense of fatigue enveloping her. She had braced herself for the meeting with Franz, and now it was postponed. The adventure was over. Back again, exhausted nerves swept her into utter lassitude. She was dismayed to hear there were guests, although they would take from her some of the strain of attending the Graf, who always wanted her within call.

She opened her eyes. The air was sharper. They had climbed steadily. The scene was wild and splendid, mountains capped with snow, the meadows in their spring colours, the larch woods in their feathery green. How different from Palermo, with its languorous heat, its exotic vegetation !

Randell Dunning would be in Venice now, unless he had lingered in Rome or Florence. How unreal and far-off he seemed already. He had not succeeded in hiding the hurt to his pride, which her departure had given. She had been as gentle as possible, but a man of his vanity could never conceive himself as the object of a woman's design. How confident of himself he was ! She had diagnosed him correctly from that first moment in the Chat Noir. He had strolled in among the tables with the air of a grand seigneur, dressed for notice, although flawless in taste. Even without his careful attire he would be a man to command attention anywhere, tall, with an athlete's spare frame, and the air of a well-bred young Englishman. He had more than this. His handsome face was lit with intelligence, marked in the quick, dark eyes, as well as in the broad brow, with its widow's peak of black shining hair. They were eyes alert to any woman's presence and inviting to a pretty one.

She had seen all this at a glance and had turned her head before he had noticed her. That she would soon be observed by him she was assured by her instinct. The use of the mirror in her compact confirmed the fact.

It was at the belvedere that an idea she had once considered, and dismissed as impossible to fulfil, returned to her. With a swiftness and certainty she had not believed herself capable of she made her tremendous decision. Frustrated in her own deep desire, she was losing her hold on the man she loved and disappointing those who loved her. She was certain it was no fault of her own. The best doctors had reassured her on that. Here was a man who would serve her purpose, put her faith to the test.

So she had gone through with it and had never wavered, but her mood of cool determination towards the chosen instrument had changed to one of affection. He had been so considerate, so ardent and sensitive a lover, despite, or perhaps because of, his conceit in his rôle of Romeo. His perfect body had been at her command. She had to confess to moments of ecstasy that made her forgetful of the purpose of her design. Almost fiercely, because she was afraid of herself, she had repulsed his suggested extension of their holiday at the Villa Igeia. Moreover, every day increased the chance of some accidental discovery of their liaison. The sudden descent of a horde of German tourists on the Palace Hotel had warned her that Tunis was no place for her adventure. Certain he would follow, she had fled to Palermo. There she had succeeded in stifling, if not in eradicating, his growing curiosity about her. He had become reconciled to her desire to divulge no details. She was a little astonished at herself and at the resolution and ease with which she had gone about her purpose. It was all over now, safely. It remained only for her to wait, hoping.

Schloss Garstein came into view. For once it was in bright sunshine, with the Alps glistening behind. They swept through the little mountain village, clean and sunny in the spring morning. The moment they entered the courtyard the hall door opened, and two borzoi hounds came bounding out. Emil, the butler, stood smiling on the steps. It was a cheerful home-coming. She had a feeling that things were going to be well with her. A telegram awaited her. It was from Franz, in Budapest —

Welcome home. Missed you terribly. Back Friday evening Love.

She smiled at the exaggeration. Franz never really missed anybody. He had a genius for evading loneliness and for making the person at that moment in his presence seem the only one that mattered. His photograph smiled at her now from her dressing-table. He was still a young man in appearance, handsome, vital, with ample blond hair and serene blue eyes. His strong hands were folded over the chair he straddled. He was her lover still, intermittently, in gusts of passion. He was stirred by an intense sensuality, utterly unlike Randell Dunning's lyrical but controlled passion.

Just before the lunch-bell sounded, she went to Uncle Rudolph's room. There he sat, in his chair, looking down the valley and over the village, with the onion-shaped steeple of the church and the calvary on the foothill of the mountain behind it. The Graf's valet was reading to him from the newspaper. He looked up on her entrance.

" Carlotta ! " cried the Graf, raising two twisted hands in greeting. " How good to have you back ! I've missed you, my dear."

She took his poor hands and kissed his cheek.

" Now sit down and tell me about your trip. You wrote only once. You didn't say a word about what sort of a place your brother was in. I never went to Algiers— burnt-up place, and dirty, like all French towns, eh ? "

She laughed at him. Outside Austria, the world to him was a rubbish heap.

" Not at all, Uncle Rudolph. Except the native quarters, which are kept picturesquely dirty, the town's clean and well laid out. My brother lives outside Algiers on a farm. He's on a mountain slope, with a heavenly view of the Mediterranean."

She answered his questions, giving him a picture of Algerian life, of her excursions. Franz had sent him her letter from Tunis. What made her go there?

" I wanted to see it. It's easy to get to. It's more Italian."

" So we've always heard. How did you come back? " asked the Graf.

" Oh, by Marseilles and Paris, where I had some shopping to do."

" I'm glad you didn't come through Italy; they're having a lot of trouble there, railway strikes and street fighting. An ex-anarchist called Mussolini's stirring them up, assisted by that mountebank D'Annunzio. Why don't they shoot them or lock them up? "

The luncheon bell rang. He motioned to the valet standing near, who turned the wheeled chair towards the door.

" I hope you're hungry? " asked the Graf, who always sat at the head of the table, though he had to be fed in his own room.

" Ravenous! It was cold driving from Innsbruck," said Carlotta, walking beside the chair.

" We've the Hatzfields here. I was glad to see them. They came last Monday. That husband of yours hasn't been near since you left. Business in Budapest. I've never heard of any business being done in Budapest. They wouldn't know how to do it," growled the Graf.

They came to the large, heavy dining-room. Graf and Gräfin von Hatzfield were there, awaiting them. They greeted Carlotta very formally. They were a dowdy old pair, whose presence would account for Franz's absence. He had suffered from these visits for so many years. The Graf von Hatzfield told hunting stories about the Emperor, who always admired his English gun. The repertoire had not altered in twenty years. The Gräfin had such thick legs that Franz felt sick when he saw them. He also hated the brown mole with the white whisker on the left corner of her mouth. His cousins and he had always dared each other to pluck it when she fell asleep on the *chaise-longue* after lunch, but they could never find sufficient courage.

The slow meal proceeded, with the Graf watching in his chair and talking, while the antelopes looked down on them with glassy eyes. Nothing had been changed in the long, dark room for fifty years. The heavy German Gothic furnishings were hideous. Carlotta thought of her own cheerful little apartment in Vienna overlooking the gardens. In July she and Franz would be back there. In July she would know.

CHAPTER IV

THE TORCH PASSES

THE old General heard, above the humdrum voice of his
valet reading to him, the gale mounting in violence outside
the Schloss. The wind howled and buffeted the old castle.
The gutters rattled and the piercing wind of a January
night started all kinds of ghostly noises along corridors,
around chimneys and roofs. The Graf listened while his
valet read the *Wiener Tagblatt*. He lay in bed, his eyes
fixed on the ceiling. The days of the wheeled chair almost
over. His illness had progressed these last nine months.
He grew more and more a prisoner of his paralysed body.
He could only lie still now. He had to be washed and fed,
and Death, whom he would have welcomed, mocked him
and made him a living corpse. For his mind was vividly
alive, and it was as if with each curtailment of his physical
body the brain received new energy. He wore out those
around him with his fretful insistence on detail, his ceaseless
curiosity regarding all the affairs around him. A little
push-bell was pinned on the lapel of his jacket, and his
twisted hand could just reach it. One ring summoned
Otto, the valet; two rings, Steiner, the male nurse; three
rings, Emil, the butler. The bell was always ringing in
the servants' hall.

Graf von Kleber, lying in his bed, was not listening to
Otto this wild night. He had ordered the shutters to be
thrown back that he might look on the snow-laden mountains and the moon riding the scudding clouds. Otto was
reading an account in the *Wiener Tagblatt* of the alarm felt
over Italy's growing tyranny in the Tyrolean provinces that
had been filched from Austria by the peace treaty. The
German names of villages and railway stations were Italian-
ised. Bozen had become Bolzano; Italian was made com-
pulsory in the schools; all the state officials had been
dismissed; even the names on some of the tombstones had

58

been changed by fanatical Fascists, growing in power every day. General von Kleber was not a little bewildered by the rise of this thick-necked new leader, Mussolini. The fellow had been chased out of Switzerland for his socialistic activities, then he had turned into a patriotic soldier and fought for his country. The general had applauded the manner in which he dealt with strikers and Socialists. If they had poured castor oil down the throats of that Socialist rabble now in power in Vienna it would have been better for poor, plundered Austria, dismembered by her enemies abroad, and tyrannised by a Bolshevik rabble at home. But this man Mussolini, who had shown so much sense, was now becoming swollen-headed. The poor Tyrol groaned under these self-appointed Fascists. Not forty miles over the border, good Tyrolese, men born free, with a long tradition of sturdy independence, were being bullied and dispossessed and imprisoned by popinjay Italians. It was time someone reminded them of Caporetto—the monkeys.

Otto heard no grunts of approval as he read the *Wiener Tagblatt's* vigorous protest, and, pausing, he looked at the old man on the bed. The storm reached a new height of fury, and the gale beat upon the windowpanes. The dense fir forests on the mountain slopes grew black each time the moon raced out of a cloud. In the hall below the massive Nuremberg clock struck ten.

" Otto, I can't keep my mind on anything. Go and see if Dr. Boehm has arrived. And bring me some news of Frau Carlotta," said the old Graf.

Otto put down the paper and left the room. Poor Carlotta, the Graf hoped she was not suffering too much. He felt anxious about the doctor. The storm had broken down the telegraph wires, and Franz had driven out into the night to fetch him. For Carlotta's hour had come. Schloss Garstein was to have an heir after all. The line of Von Kleber was not going to fade out. His lovely Carlotta was giving him an heir. The young couple had done their duty by him.

Not for a moment did the old general accept the possibility that the child might be a girl. When the nurse had reported that the labour pains were severe he felt reassured. He had always heard that midwives believed that the labour pains with boys were greater than those with girls. It might be only an old wives' tale, but the general was prepared to believe it, and he heard of Carlotta's heavy labour with increased satisfaction.

" Well ? " cried the Graf as he heard the door open.

" Dr. Boehm's just arrived—he's with the nurse," said Otto.

" Tell him I want to see him," commanded the general.

" Very good, Herr Graf."

A few minutes later Dr. Boehm came into the room and greeted the general. He was the family retainer, an old friend, and was wholly trusted. Unwearying, thorough, and kind, his name touched all hearts like a benediction. He should have retired long ago, but there were too many poor in Garstein, and he was the heart's historian in every village home and lonely chalet. The general bullied him, but Dr. Boehm always replied gently. He had never been intimidated by his old friend, whose selfishness he had measured but whose nature he knew was honourable, fearless, and just.

" Well, what do you think ? How is she ? " demanded the Graf.

" I've not seen Frau Carlotta yet, but it can't be long."

" *Lieber Gott !* Why haven't you ? "

" You demand priority. I'm on my way, dear General," answered Dr. Boehm, smiling down at the old man.

" I want no damn nonsense about a girl ; you know that ? " said the General.

" Do you think I'd be sitting here in Garstein if I had the knack of turning unwanted girls into lucky lads ? It's a good thing for you someone welcomed Carlotta on her birthday. And if it's a girl you'll get over it and be just as silly as all grandfathers," said Dr. Boehm.

" I'll throw it out of the window ! It's to be a boy. Carlotta knows that ! " growled the Graf. " You'd better be getting on with your job. You're staying the night, in case ? "

" There are other expectant mothers who might want me," said Dr. Boehm teasingly. " My profession knows no discrimination."

" Rubbish ! Those village women are tough old mares.

Foaling's nothing to them. You're to stay on the job. I find it a terrible strain."

" You ? You monstrous fellow ! " laughed Dr. Boehm.

The General turned his head with a great effort and looked at his friend.

" It's going to be all right, Heinrich ? " he asked quietly.

Dr. Boehm put his hand on the shoulder of the prone figure.

" Of course. Carlotta's a very healthy woman. I'm going to see her now. Get some sleep. We might wake you with some good news."

§ 2

Carlotta lay in her dimly-lit bedroom, listening to the storm. It seemed to be mounting with her own spasmodic pain. This was her hour, and now it had come. In the marshalling of her courage she knew now what all other women had told her of childbirth. Between the recurrent pain she had moments of clarity in which she reviewed episodes of her life. She had wished to face this event in a nursing home in Vienna, but the almost pathetic protest of Uncle Rudolph could not be ignored. Tradition insisted that a Kleber who was ultimately to inherit Schloss Garstein and the estates should be born here. Franz laughed at tradition and was prepared to ignore his uncle's great desire, but Carlotta felt impelled to humour the old man, always her ardent admirer and never more so than since that hour when his despondent spirit had leaped at her news. So to Schloss Garstein she had come in this final month to await the event now imminent.

Franz had come with her, laying aside his work. He had become again her devoted companion in these last few months, and the Franz of her first years of marriage had returned. Volatile and handsome as ever, he was a little chastened now with fear. But most of all, he was transported with pride, and she realised how deeply hurt he had been with the inward suspicion of his own failure. Hitherto with a lack of gallantry that had wounded her, he had never shown any doubt that she had failed in the chief duty of a wife, in this case the perpetuation of the proud line of the Klebers. The change in him, his renewed devotion, and a badly disguised penitence of his own faithlessness that did not delude her, in no way altered her judgment of his character. He was unreliable and vain. Like all men of weak natures whose character did not match their physical and mental attraction, he responded to flattery wherever it might be found, and a man of Franz's charm would never lack flattery.

But how useless all her insight was in face of the fact that she loved him, that he had never lost for her that shining fascination of her early youth when, so slim, so alert and good-humoured, he had wooed her passionately and conquered her swiftly. She had overruled all the objections urged on her. He was a foreigner ; they had known each other for so short a time ; she would be transformed to an alien world, to customs and traditions that would be strange, and perhaps antagonistic. She listened to all this and found it as nothing to set against her love for Franz von Kleber.

At this moment, after ten years, with many and bitter experiences, she did not regret her act of faith and love. In the last three years she had been losing him. Loneliness began to be her lot ; the gnawing pain of jealousy grew as she saw what other women were gaining. There had been a time when she felt a bitter hostility to Uncle Rudolph. Franz's reproaches, his undisciplined despair when there was no promise of a child, were clearly intensified by his uncle's constant chiding. But as Franz lapsed in his conduct and his infidelities became more blatant, she found a sympathetic ally in the blustering old tyrant. Whatever his disappointment, he had a code of conduct, an inflexible chivalry. He castigated Franz, called him a barren blackguard, an indolent libertine, and threatened him with disinheritance, things all ignored by Franz, who knew he would not be hurt, because Carlotta could not be hurt. In Uncle Rudolph's eyes Carlotta could do no wrong. It was not her fault that their marriage was barren.

The great clock in the stone hall had boomed ten, and then the half-hour. She was afraid now and called out. The clamour of the storm on this wild January night seemed to threaten her. The grim old castle had always repelled her, so large, so cold, so isolated amid these snowbound mountains, roaring with avalanches and torrents and swept by winds. To die here was a frightening thought.

The pain swept over her and, as if in exultation, the wild elements smote the castle again. Out in the night there was the sound of a crashing tree. The electric light by her bed wavered, went low, and burned on again. She summoned her courage. She would not die and be cheated of everything for which she had taken so great a risk.

Calm came again. She closed her eyes. She heard the nurse moving at the end of the room.

" The doctor's come. So we're all right now," said the woman's kind, confident voice. " What a terrible storm ! Herr Kleber was lucky to get him."

Carlotta heard her, but did not answer. Her mind was far away. The unconscious partner of this approaching birth, Randell Dunning, where was he now ? How faint he had become ; how little he mattered, his purpose having been served. She had read his novels these last few months and had found some of his own traits portrayed in his characters. Somehow this made him less real, less distinct. He faded into his own fiction. Perhaps, to him, she had been no more than an episode, hovering in the writer's world of mingled fact and fable. It was better so. Like an intangible dream seemed now that week in Palermo, with the moon on the sparkling sea, with the grey wall of the mountains and the black silhouette of palm trees below their balcony in the still and aromatic night.

Her son had been conceived in beauty. How much of his nature would be moulded thereby ? A son ; she had never doubted that. She could not have made so tremendous a sacrifice, in the very name of love, to be cruelly cheated.

The pain surged through her again.

" Franz ! Franz ! " she breathed with clenched hands.

She heard the door open, voices, the nurse's and the doctor's. A cry escaped her again ; her brow was damp. She opened her eyes. Dr. Boehm stood there. Then her hand felt his, steady, reassuring. The fear in her large eyes died, to meet his with a faint, brave smile.

§ 3

The Graf fell into a heavy sleep about midnight, worried with anxiety over the forthcoming event in the room above him. Dr. Boehm had been in thrice to answer his impatient queries. Satisfied by having extracted a promise that the doctor would not leave the Schloss until the child was born, the old general slept.

Shortly before two he was awakened. The storm was still raging, but it was not this that aroused him from his sleep. Otto was gently shaking him. For a few moments the old man stared absently at the ceiling.

" It's come, Herr Graf, it's come ! " cried the valet excitedly.

The Graf was fully awake now. He turned his head.

" What's come—what's come ? " he demanded.

" The baby, Herr Graf ! "

" I know that, you fool—but what is it ? Boy or girl ? "

" Oh—a boy, of course," answered Otto.

" *Gott sei Dank*," murmured the old man.

He lay silent for a few moments. The wind howled. A driving snowstorm beat against the windows. The room was cold, the fire in the porcelain stove having burned itself out. Otto put in some more logs and relit the fire.

" Otto, how is she—Carlotta ? " asked the voice from the bed.

" Very well—she's sleeping now, Dr. Boehm says. Herr Franz is sitting in her room with the nurse."

" Where is Dr. Boehm ? I want to see him," cried the General.

" He came a little while ago and didn't want to wake you. He's in the pantry having something to eat. Emil is up ; we're all up, Herr Graf," said Otto excitedly.

" Fetch Dr. Boehm—and raise me."

The valet raised him and then went out.

A few minutes later Dr. Boehm came in.

" Well, she's a proud mother. It's a fine boy ! " cried Dr. Boehm jovially as he advanced from the door.

" Carlotta's all right ? " asked the General.

" She's come through it splendidly, and it wasn't a quick delivery. She's sleeping now." He pulled out his watch.

It's past two. I'll be going now, and I'll come back about
noon."

"Don't be a fool! Emil'll give you a bed. You can't
go into this storm, and you want a rest," said the Graf.

"I'll take a rest at home. I may be wanted any moment.
Lotte Schmidt's expecting."

"What, again! Why, that's her eighth, and the man's
a half-wit!"

"Her ninth. It's her annual event. Nature doesn't
apply intelligence tests to creative powers."

"More's the pity," growled the General. "The state
should stop people like Schmidt."

"Ah, come now," remonstrated Dr. Boehm, smiling.
"You mustn't deny the poor their pleasures! Can't you
go to sleep again?"

"No; however do you imagine a man can go to sleep on
a night like this, with a raging storm and a baby just born?
When am I going to see it? I'm its great-uncle, aren't I?"

"The claim isn't very strong," laughed Dr. Boehm. "But
we'll humour you. We'll bring young Herr Whatever-
you're-calling-him down to you at once."

"His name'll be Rudolph, after me, of course!"

The doctor was about to question this assumption, but
thought better of it. That was the parents' battle, not his.
Bidding the General good night, he quietly left the room.

By ten o'clock the Graf had been washed and had break-
fasted. Otto had put the earphones on his head so that he
could hear the morning news broadcast from Vienna. The
storm had ended suddenly. The day had cleared and the
sun streamed into the room. Across the valley the mountains shone dazzlingly. There was a patch of blue sky. It
was a transformation that made the night seem evanescent
as a nightmare. The Graf had had the gardener bring a
bouquet of gardenias from the conservatory. With enormous difficulty he had scrawled a message to Carlotta on a
card and sent it, tied on to the flowers, to her room.

He was listening now to the news. Those infernal
Fascists had perpetrated further outrages in the Tyrol.
There had been street fighting in Trento. Suddenly the
door opened, and Franz came into the room, white-faced,
tears running down his cheeks.

C

" Carlotta ! Carlotta's dying ! " he cried hoarsely.

The old Graf painfully turned his head. He had not heard because of the earphones. Otto, who had heard, came running out of the bathroom and removed the head-piece.

" What's the matter ? What is it ! " asked the Graf, his eyes fixed on his nephew.

" Carlotta ! She's worse, she's dying ! Carlotta's dying ! " stammered the young man, his eyes streaming.

The Graf made no reply for a few moments. Then he spoke.

" Franz, don't lose your head ! Send for Dr. Boehm," he said calmly.

" Hans has gone for him. Oh, my poor Carlotta ! " cried Franz distractedly, and hurried out of the room.

The Graf and Otto looked at each other.

" Go and ask the nurse. Get the truth. And don't let Franz make a scene," said the general calmly.

" Very good, Herr Graf."

Dr. Boehm arrived within half an hour and went straight to Carlotta's room. One glance had told him the truth, but he had in vain exercised all the professional skill at his command. Carlotta was conscious, her eyes abnormally dark and large in her blanched face. Pneumonia had set in. Dr. Boehm had to order the sobbing Franz away from the bed. Carlotta tried to speak, and, although inaudible, Dr. Boehm knew what she wanted.

" The baby," he said, turning to the nurse.

She brought the child, and Dr. Boehm placed it in the mother's arms. Carlotta lay still, closing her eyes. Dr. Boehm sat quietly by the bed, watching. Presently she opened her eyes again and her lips moved, and she looked up from the child. " Franz," she said, so faintly that Dr. Boehm only just heard it.

He was not sure whether she meant the child or her husband. He turned and beckoned him, but before the distraught young man reached the bed Carlotta had closed her eyes again. Dr. Boehm leaned over her, spoke to her. She was unconscious.

He lifted the baby gently from her arms. Franz, holding

one hand of his wife's in choking grief knelt by the bed.
For half an hour he stayed there. Then Dr. Boehm touched
the young husband on the shoulder and led him away.
Carlotta had slipped from them, as gently as a stream
joining the great river.

BOOK II

CRETE

CHAPTER I

SYLVIA DAY

UNDER the date April 5, 1939, Sylvia Day wrote in her diary : " Marlow-on-Thames. Twenty-five to-day. Slipping into middle age. Where is romance ? Feel very old. Will do the shopping, go to the cinema, go to bed, and then march onward to my twenty-sixth birthday. Feel nothing ever will happen to me."

She looked at her diary as it lay on the small bureau in her bedroom and reflected that she had omitted one thing in her day's programme. This afternoon in Reading, after lunching with her uncle, she was to take her Army Nurses' Examination. She had hoped it would be London, for that would have given her an excuse for a trip. She could have seen her friend, Muriel Stanway, who had just been appointed secretary to a general. Muriel had been lucky. She said the general always had roses on her desk and vowed she made the best cup of tea of anyone in the War Office. Over two hundred cups of tea were made in the War Office at half-past four each day, so that Muriel triumphed over keen competition. The general, alas, was fifty-eight and married. He also had a habit of slipping off his shoes under his desk because his corns hurt him.

When Sylvia got downstairs she found half a dozen packages on the dining-room table, set for breakfast. Her grandmother never came down until noon and indulged in an orgy of telephoning from her bed. Old Mrs. Day waged war over her telephone with the grocer, the butcher, the greengrocer, the garage, with Harrods' Store in London, with Heelas' store in Reading, with the local hairdresser, and most of all with the local telephone exchange. The day they changed to automatic dialing she would lose her most enjoyable battle. She was eighty, sharp-tongued, combative. But she was a local institution. " What do you think old Mrs. Day said this morning ? " someone would ask, and then relate her latest *bon mot*.

Sylvia loved her though she was often exasperated by her. It was impossible not to admire the old lady's grip on life, her unfailing common sense, her immense courage and generosity. Against all these there were her ruthless will, her complete self-centredness, her contemptuous use of everybody to fulfil her plan of life. This tyranny bore heavily on Sylvia, since she was the only one to carry it. An orphan since nine years old, together with Richard, her brother, aged fourteen, she owed everything to Grandma Day, except the income she had inherited on her aunt's death. Gratitude and custom kept her a prisoner in the empty Georgian house. Richard had escaped long ago, immediately after Sandhurst. And as if to make his escape doubly sure, he lived out of England.

Sylvia thought of him now, for among the letters on the table there was one with the Crete postmark and the Greek postage stamp that she always saved for the gardener's boy. Sylvia looked at the envelope and was disappointed to see that Richard's letter was addressed to her grandmother. This was rather unusual. He wrote witty and cynical letters. Mrs. Day called him " godless." " How can he be anything else, spending all his time with the pagans ! " commented Mrs. Day. For Richard was with an archæological mission in Crete and had no interest for anything else except the Minoan Era, 3000 B.C. Privately, in his letters to Sylvia, he always alluded to their grandmother as H. D., which stood, not for Henrietta Day, as the old lady imagined, but for Holy Day.

Mrs. Day not only deplored Richard's interest in the pagans ; she deplored the world's interest in the Pope. In her eyes he was the fountain of all wickedness. He was behind the Irish who were placing bombs in London cloakrooms, behind Mussolini, who had so cruelly misused the poor little Emperor of Abyssinia, behind the Duke of Windsor's abdication. Inconsistently enough, and Mrs. Day was a past mistress of inconsistency, she loved the local Catholic priest, Father Duffy, and had him in for dinner once a week. He was her favourite bridge partner. and everything she won she gave to his church fund. She was the donor of the new heating installation in his church. She observed grimly, " I wouldn't wish chilblains on the Pope."

Sylvia put aside four letters for Mrs. Day and glanced at three for herself, but she turned hastily to the parcels, all addressed to her. Obviously these were birthday presents, One was stockings from Muriel ; she always sent stockings. One was from her aunt at Reading, and it was always the same sensible thing, a cheque for five pounds. A very small registered packet raised her greatest hopes. Its contents, as its sender, were unknown. It bore a London jeweller's label. She swiftly opened it. Her heart gave a leap. It was an exquisite gold wrist-watch set in small diamonds. A card enclosed said it was sent on instructions of Mr. Richard Day.

Sylvia put it on, showed it to old Mary, the maid, who exclaimed over it, and, hastily finishing her breakfast, picked up Mrs. Day's letters and went to her room.

The old lady was sitting up in bed, clad in her pink bed jacket. The breakfast tray had been removed. The telephone was on her bed. She was talking on it, a gleam in her eye.

" They were tough, I repeat ! Did you eat them ? . . . Then how do you know they were tender ? The lamb that produced those chops was the one that followed Mary. It was exercised to death ! I want half a pound of liver, one pound of steak, undercut. . . . Thank you, Mr. Reece. . . . And before eleven ! "

She put down the receiver and turned to Sylvia.

" Good morning, my dear, many happy returns." She put out her arms and kissed Sylvia. " My present is on the dressing-table, on the end there. I know nothing about it. It looks frightening to me, but I heard you say you wished you had one."

She glanced at her letters while Sylvia opened the box. A cry of delight came from her. It was a Leica camera. Sylvia rushed to her grandmother and kissed her. Then she showed her Richard's present. " Richard is always munificent ! " commented the old lady.

Mrs. Day picked up the telephone and gave a number. The letters lay unopened before her. They might lie there an hour yet, while she telephoned the world. Sylvia never could understand how anyone could leave letters unopened for a second.

Sylvia left the room and prepared for the morning's shopping. She had to motor into Reading for lunch. Just as she was getting into the car, garaged in the old stable, Helen, the second parlourmaid, came running across the courtyard.

" The mistress wants you, Miss Sylvia," she called.

Sylvia smiled and patiently got out of the car. She seldom set out without a call back. She went indoors and went up to the old lady's room. The telephone receiver was on the stand. One letter only had been opened, Richard's. Something in it must have been quite unusual. Mrs. Day had a sad expression.

" Read that," she said, curtly, passing the letter.

She read the letter through. Her brother had been dangerously ill with rheumatic fever. It had affected his heart. He would have to be nursed for some time. He would, as soon as he could, be moved to his villa up in the hills near Vori. He wondered if it would be possible for Sylvia to come out and nurse him and be with him for about six months. It would not be a holiday, though he had always hoped to show her Crete one day.

Sylvia looked at her grandmother, when she had finished reading, with exciting eyes and pounding heart. It would be wonderful, but she knew how impossible it was.

" You see, he doesn't think of me for a moment," said Mrs. Day.

" Oh, Grandma, I'm sure——" she began, but was interrupted by the old lady, who went on :

" You want to go, of course, and it would be selfish of me to stand in your way, though what I shall do, I don't know."

" But I'm not going," cried Sylvia. " I simply couldn't leave you ! I'm sure Richard wouldn't wish you to be left."

" Fiddlesticks ! I know exactly what the boy is thinking. This illness of his is a chance for you to get away. He knows you can get nurses from England, even if there aren't local ones."

" Need we talk about it any more, Grandma ? " asked Sylvia. She was very near to tears. Disappointment, anger, revolt, and a sense of duty all battled within her.

" Yes, of course we must ! Richard may be as ill as he says, or he may not. You're going, whatever it is," said Mrs. Day, firmly.

Sylvia, stared at her, unable to believe what she had heard.

" Old women like me, flattered to death because we're cheating Time and thinking ourselves very clever about it, are a menace to the young. If I wasn't here you'd have been to all sorts of places by now. Mary can look after me. If her forgetfulness finishes me, and it probably will, what does it matter ? All my friends are on the other side. I can't see any more of them even in the obituary columns now. I expect Richard wants you at once."

Mrs. Day vigorously dialled the telephone.

" Operator, I want a London call. Cook's Tourist Agency. . . . Where ? I've no idea ! They do exist. . . . No, I don't mind which office as long as it's intelligent. And the shipping department, please. . . . Thank you ! "

She put down the receiver firmly.

" They'll call me as soon as they've got them. You'll have to think what things you will want, Sylvia. Perhaps you can get them when you're in Reading to-day."

" Grandma, I can't believe it ! " exclaimed Sylvia.

" Neither can I, but we shall get used to it. I am very glad I bought you that camera. You'll see some things worth taking," observed Mrs. Day.

" I shall never pass my examination to-day—I'm much too excited," said Sylvia. " My head's in a whirl ! "

" That's it ! " declared Mrs. Day, emphatically. " That explains it ! When Richard heard you were taking up nursing again he saw your usefulness at once. That boy always had a genius for looking after himself ! " Mrs. Day opened *The Times* and scanned the shipping page. " I see nothing about Crete."

" Richard always went on an Italian boat, from Brindisi," said Sylvia. " That the quickest way—unless you fly to Athens."

" That would cost far too much."

" Oh, I don't want to fly. I'd like the voyage."

The telephone rang. Mrs. Day picked up the receiver. It was Cook's, of London. She told them what she required. A long conversation followed. Sylvia waited breathlessly. There were boats from Marseilles and Brindisi. The boat sailed every Friday. It took sixty hours to reach Brindisi by train ; that would mean leaving London next Tuesday. The Brindisi boat went to Athens via Patras. At Athens one took a Greek boat for Crete.

" Very good. Send me all the particulars and I'll send you a cheque. The name is Day. Miss Sylvia Day, *Glenarvon*, Marlow-on-Thames. . . . Passport ? Gracious, no, she hasn't got one. . . . No, she's not a minor ; she's a level-headed young woman. . . . You can ? . . . . Very well, we'll return the forms at once. . . . Yes, the number is 4422. . . . Mr. Green ? . . . Thank you very much."

Mrs. Day put down the receiver and smiled at Sylvia, now a little white and tense with excitement.

" A very nice man," said Mrs. Day. " Mr. Green, if we want him. He's sending the passport forms and says he can rush them through. When I went abroad we never had nonsense like that. You only heard about passports in Russian novels, when Nihilists were trying to escape from the Czar's police. They're relics of barbarism. Now, my dear, don't look so frightened. It's better to get it all settled in case I changed my mind."

§ 2

Just one week later Sylvia stood on the deck of the *Dante* as it steamed out of the harbour of Brindisi. Only two hours earlier she had driven through an Italian town for the first time in her life, conscious of the blaze of light, the vivid azure sky, the heat of the sun on her skin. She had taken an open carriage from the railway station, down the Corso Garibaldi, to the quay. The strange names, the buildings, the colours, and the people on the street, after the long train journey, seemed like a scene out of the theatre. Her head reeled with the novelty of these last three days : the Channel crossing, the *wagon-lit* train through France, across the Swiss Alps, down into the Italian plain, then Milan, Bologna—magical names. She regretted having to pull the blind and go to bed. In Brindisi, carefully piloted by Cook's agent, she had had time to breakfast on the open terrace of the Grand Hotel before embarking. She wondered who the other passengers were, where they were going, whence they had come. This was one of the gateways to the Near East.

The *Dante* was a trim little ship with about twenty first-class passengers. The aft deck was filled with a motley crowd of men, women and children who seemed to be camping on it. She found later they were mostly Greeks, returning to Corfu, Patras, and Athens. There were two Greek priests among them, with comical black hats and magnificent long beards. They wore heavy chains with silver crucifixes suspended.

Sylvia, having arranged things in her cabin after she had seen the port fade away, went up on deck and took possession of a chair. She tried to read, but she could not concentrate. She watched the gulls circling over the ship. The brilliant sky had not a cloud. Italy lay far off, a flat line on the horizon. According to her Baedeker, they were in the Strait of Otranto and leaving the Adriatic Sea. The island of Corfu was the next port of call.

A steward passed, carrying a tray. The sight of the tray, immediately evoked Mary taking breakfast to Mrs. Day. She would be doing it just about this time at *Glenarvon*. How far away it all seemed in time and place, and yet it was only three days. The old lady's gallant bearing in these last moments of farewell filled her with contrition. It was shameful ever to have been so rebellious and to have had such hard thoughts about her. At twenty-five one's life was not ruined. There was time yet, though not too much. She had never had a lover. Somehow she had never seemed attractive to young men. They found her too serious, and she found them too flippant. Until Richard had gone to Crete, four years ago, he had been almost her only masculine contact. They had always been very close to each other ever since they had been left orphans and had been sent to their grandmother. Their grandfather, Dr. Day, was alive then. They adored him ; he was so full of fun. Grandmother Day had always frightened them a little with her dominating manner and her precision.

" You are English, please ? " said a voice, cutting suddenly into her reverie.

Sylvia started and turned to the occupant of the deck chair next to hers. He was a young man, Italian, according to a Fascist pin in his lapel. His teeth were brilliantly white as he smiled, offset by his golden-brown skin. Despite the sun he wore no hat, and his thick hair, glossy and raven black, was in character with his dark, nervous face. In her few hours in Italy, Sylvia had noticed how handsome were the very young men, and that there was a touch of the dandy in the better classes. This was the first time a young Italian had spoken to her in English.

" Yes, how do you know ? Oh, my book, of course," replied Sylvia.

" May I ? " he asked, extending a hand towards it.

She passed the book to him and noticed how beautiful his hand was, the nails light and firmly shaped, with slender fingers. His linen was flawlessly clean. He wore a bright blue suit that would have been loud in England, but here it was in keeping with the vivid day.

" *The Hall of the Battle-Axes : Excavations in Crete*," he read, and turned the pages, glancing at the illustrations. " Oh, archæology ! You are very learned, I see. You are a professor ? "

Sylvia laughed, and the young man looked more closely into her eyes. He had not been wrong. She had very beautiful blue eyes. He had been studying her covertly ever since he had seen her coming up the gangway at Brindisi. You had to notice her. A lovely figure, perfect legs, a fine free air in her movements, and a face that was beautiful at a glance. And now the first pleasure she gave was confirmed. He noticed how lovely her profile was and the cream colour of her skin. These English girls so often looked as if they lived in a wind that kissed them into such artless beauty. She had blonde hair with a gold glint over her small ears. He loved them blonde. Blonde hair and blue eyes and a pink-and-white skin ; he tingled with excitement.

" Oh, surely, I don't look like a professor ! " protested
Sylvia.

" Of course not. You are too young and beautiful ! But
I once met a pretty American girl, very young. She was
a professor of domestic science at an American university.
I did not know it was a profession, but I could have learned
anything from her," he said smiling.

" And did you ? " asked Sylvia.

" The American girl can be very hard," he replied,
quietly, giving her back her book.

" There are times when it is necessary, I'm sure," commented Sylvia, a little surprised at her boldness.

He looked surprised, too, and then his dark eloquent eyes
smiled at her.

" My name is Cesare Manetti," he said.

" Mine is Sylvia Day."

" How d'you do ? What a lovely name ! It is a poem.
' Shall I compare thee to a summer's day, thou art more
lovely and more temporate.' Shakespeare wrote that ! "

" I know, and he would be shocked at your pun, like
me," said Sylvia. This young man needed no encouragement.

" Please excuse me. It is always such pleasure to talk
English," he said, chastened.

" You talk it very well," observed Sylvia, now apolo-
getic.

" Thank you. I lived in London two years ago. I loved
London, but I was too young. I was only twenty."

" That can't be so very long ago. Why were you too
young ? "

" Ah," exclaimed Manetti, spreading his hands. " One
is either too frightened or too bold. But that is another
story, as you say."

Sylvia did not ask what the other story was. A silence
fell between them. Bold mountains filled the distant
horizon as the ship steamed south-east.

" That's the Albanian coastline. Those are the Acro-
ceraunian Mountains," said her companion, breaking the
silence.

" Oh, how wonderful ! I never thought I should see
those. Shelley's mountains," she exclaimed, and, seeing

his incomprehension, she recited the lines she had liked
since a girl :

> " *Arethusa arose*
> *From her couch of the snows*
> *In the Acroceraunian Mountains,—*

And now I am looking at those famous Greek mountains ! "

" Not Greek—that's Albania. They're ours now," said
Manetti, smiling.

" Yours ? "

" Italy's. Albania's ours now. We'll reach Corfu this
evening. That will be Italian one day also."

" You mean, you'll take it, like Abyssinia ? "

He winced at the name and then smiled tolerantly.

" It was always ours, signorina. The Mediterranean is
a Roman sea—Mare Nostrum. We are at last recovering
what has been stolen from us. But we must not talk
politics," he said catching a glint in the English girl's eyes.
" Let us enjoy ourselves."

" I enjoy talking politics. All over Italy, as I came
through, I saw how you've covered your buildings with
Viva Il Duce, and with his face. Why does he glower ?
Doesn't he smile ever ? "

" Yes, but he is a serious man. Look what he has done
for Italy ! We were torn with internal politics ; we were
trampled on by the other nations ; my poor country was
despised. Now——"

" Now," interrupted Sylvia, " it's getting itself into
trouble everywhere. Fiume, Albania, Abyssinia. My
brother tells me you are trying to stir up trouble in Crete.
You claim Malta, don't you, and Corsica and Tunis ? "

He spread his hands and smiled. He had not expected
this. She looked so docile and pretty.

" We must not quarrel. You English have everything.
Why cannot poor Italy, overcrowded, expand her terri-
tory ? " he asked, a little irritably.

" It's the way you go about it. It was dreadful what you
did in Abyssinia, attacking those poor natives and that
harmless little King. I'm afraid we shan't agree, so we'd
better not talk about it," said Sylvia, seeing he was hurt.
She picked up her book.

But he had been stirred by her remarks, and ignored her intention.

" Have you spent much time in Italy, signorina ? " he asked.

" No. In fact, I've not really seen it at all, only what I saw coming through in the train to Brindisi. It looks very beautiful. We English have always loved Italy and its people. Our poets have made it a second home—Byron, Keats, Shelley, the Brownings——"

" Walter Savage Landor, Leigh Hunt, John Ruskin. Oh, yes, you have written charming things about us. But always as if we were children living in a museum or in a cheap asylum for impoverished spinsters. That Italy is quite dead. We are a disciplined people, awake to our destiny," he exclaimed, with a gleam in his dark eyes.

" What is your destiny ? "

" To take our proper rank among the Great Powers. To be respected. To rid ourselves of dead faiths——"

" Does that include religion, the Pope and the Catholic faith ? " asked Sylvia, interrupting.

" Of course not. I am a good Catholic. I speak poli- tically. The Church is a necessary part of the State. I meant all the cant about democracy, the rule of an ignorant, Press-ridden public, operated by slick politicians. We had that in Italy. It brought us to ruin. Look at us now. We have recovered our dignity ; we are respected because the Duce had made us powerful. There are no strikes, no beggars in the streets. We are a different people."

" You are indeed ! You invaded Abyssinia and interfered in Spain, and bombarded helpless Corfu, and locked up your critics at home, or drove them into exile, and strangled your Press. Why do you have armed Fascists patrolling your trains ? What are you afraid of ? " asked Sylvia, spiritedly.

" We are afraid of no one, but the Fascist regime has many enemies. They are not there to menace tourists. We have desperate enemies at home, signorina."

" Who made them desperate ? The decadent democracies don't seem to have that trouble. You can't find any armed guards on trains in America and England and France. We respect the law and we are free to say what we think."

" So are we, signorina, within proper limits."

" Who determines what is proper—Mussolini ? Who's filled Pantelleria with political prisoners ? Who's poured castor oil down the throats of helpless men and women ? Who murdered Matteotti, because he dared to stand up and say what he thought in your puppet Parliament ? Why does Mussolini have to bellow from a balcony and talk about eight million bayonets, and living like a lion ? "

" Signorina, I beg you," cried Signor Manetti, looking around nervously. Half a dozen heads were turned towards them. " You are on an Italian boat. It's not wise to talk like this. Anyone might——"

" So that's how free you are ! " said Sylvia, throwing caution to the winds. " We can't even have a harmless discussion in the middle of the sea—your sea, as you declare. I know you think England's decadent. We often think it ourselves. Democracies are stupid. We do muddle along with Baldwins and Chamberlains——"

" I never mentioned them, signorina," protested Manetti. " Please, please, let us not talk about it."

" Who began talking to me ? No, I apologise for that, Signor Manetti," said Sylvia. " I'm very glad you did talk to me—but you wear a Fascist pin in your coat, and you've got a Fascist pin in your brain, and I suspect you go around pinpricking everybody who believes in old-fashioned ballot boxes and freely-elected parliaments, and that somehow, despite some very discordant notes, the voice of the people is the voice of God and won't be silenced by a Duce and his millions of bayonets."

" *Scusi, scusi, signorina*," murmured Manetti, rising and bowing. Then he hurried away.

Sylvia sat on in her chair, fixed by her determination not to show fear. Faces had glared at her from neighbouring chairs. She had been warned before she left England not to talk politics in a country where Mussolini had to be called Mr. Smith, if one wished to be safe. But her wisdom had been overcome by a number of barbs that had got under her skin before the handsome Signor Manetti began the theme of Italian greatness. In the hotel she had seen a pictorial paper, with headlines gloating over Hitler's rape of Czechoslovakia last month, and even in the lavatory there

was a card over the mirror adjuring Italians never to forgive
Sanctions and " *il buffone Eden.*"   She had no illusions
about Mr. Eden at Geneva, who might have known a little
more a little earlier about Mr. Baldwin at home, but a buffoon
he certainly was not.   That hotel was frequented by British
tourists coming and going from India and the Near East, so
the insult was well calculated.

§ 3

Dinner had been served, and darkness had descended
when they drew in to Corfu.   Sylvia went up on the deck
to look at her first Greek town.   They had anchored in the
bay.   There was a tremendous commotion among boatmen
who were taking the passengers off.   They were unloading
cargo under the glare of arc lights.   There was little to be
seen save the twinkling lights of the town and two dark
masses which she learned were the old and the new fortresses.
Sylvia was leaning over the taffrail when Cesare Manetti
came up to her.   She had not seen him since lunch-time,
when he had sat far across the saloon, perhaps to avoid her.
She felt she had been a little too rough with him and was
prepared to be more gracious when he again approached
her.   But he carefully kept away all the afternoon, and he
was still invisible when she went down to dinner.
There were two other English people on board, judging
from their conversation.   They sat at a nearby table in the
dining-saloon.   One of them was a very thin, elderly man,
who was somewhat deaf, and his companion was a middle-
aged woman with a high-pitched voice and a patrician
manner.   She talked incessantly through dinner, complained of the food, and was very peremptory with the
perspiring steward.   Sylvia disliked her intensely.   The
old man had only two words.   " Oh, yes ? " he would say,
punctuating the incessant flow of his companion.   The
woman certainly talked about extraordinary things, among
them the father of one of her friends.   He was rich and
eccentric and, it appeared, he was obsessed with the idea
that he was a bird, so much so that he had a favourite perch
up in a large tree on his lawn !   He could only be induced

to come down by the butler bringing out a large wicker cage on a wheeled platform. He deliberately left the door of the cage open and disappeared. The old man would then come down and get into the cage, whereupon the butler would emerge, shut the door, and wheel his master into the house.

The woman told this preposterous story with the greatest solemnity, and at the conclusion her companion said, " Oh, yes ? " Sylvia was convulsed with laughter and suddenly caught the eye of the young Italian, who had also heard the story and was in a similar state.

Now, as she leaned over the taffrail, Manetti alluded to the couple in the dining-saloon.

" Do you think it was true ? " he asked.

" I shouldn't be surprised. They were both very serious about it," answered Sylvia.

" We've an hour here before sailing. Would you like to see the town with me ? I know it well," he asked.

" I would love it ! "

" I'll get a boat, and we can have a short drive and a drink."

They were rowed across the velvety dark water to the quay. Here Manetti hired a carriage, and they drove up into the town. They saw the Royal Palace and the old Fortress. He showed her the statue of Sir Frederick Adam, who was Governor of Corfu from 1822-32.

" The Corinthians were here seven hundred years before Christ. We had it for over four centuries, then you had it for fifty years, and now the Greeks have it," he explained.

" And soon you'll have it again ? " asked Sylvia provocatively.

He looked at her, alert and lovely, as she sat hatless in the carriage beside him.

" If you think we're going to quarrel again, you are mistaken," he said, smiling, and flicking off the ash of his cigarette. . . .

She noticed a large diamond flashed in a ring he wore, and thought how very un-English it was. He had also a diamond tiepin. Otherwise he was well and unostentatiously dressed in his light blue suit.

They drew up at a café on the Esplanade. He led her to

a table on the pavement, keeping the carriage. They had half an hour yet. Sylvia was nervous about losing the boat.

" Don't worry, it won't sail without me," he said quietly.

" Are you a diplomat ? " asked Sylvia. It seemed to her only kings and diplomats could keep ships waiting.

" Oh, no," laughed Manetti. " I play cards with the captain ! He doubles his salary on me."

" Do you make this journey often ? "

Manetti raised his glass. Sylvia raised hers.

" To you, Signorina Day," he said, clinking the glasses. " I make the trip once a month, but never in such pleasant company."

" On business ? "

" Yes ; we have branches in Athens, Alexandria, and Tunis. I come from Rome. My father is a diamond merchant."

" How thrilling ! But I know nothing about them. I couldn't tell a real once from a paste," confessed Sylvia.

" You've no diamonds ? " he asked, watching her eager face.

" No."

" There must be lots of people who want to give you diamonds," he said quietly, his eyes very soft and liquid.

Colour flushed her cheeks, and their eyes met for an embarrassed moment. Then she laughed and, to recover herself, drank again.

" Look," he said, drawing his chair nearer and pulling off his ring, " I'll show you how to know a real diamond from a fake."

He pulled out a small magnifying glass and placed it over the stone which shot fire.

" Look at those facets. That was cut in Amsterdam ; all the best cutters are there. I've learned cutting there myself, and in London, in your Hatton Garden. Do you know how many facets that's got ? Forty-eight ! You can't get paste to look like that."

The ring burned under her fascinated eyes. He produced another out of his pocket. Fifty-four facets. It had fire that seemed wicked, lying there in his thin brown hand. Then he pulled out his tiepin, a ruby encrusted with small diamonds, the cutting minute but many-faceted. He twisted the pin in his fingers to make it sparkle. Then he replaced it in his tie, with a laugh. Again she noticed his fine hands, so alive, so sensitive.

It was time to go. They got into the carriage. The wine must have been strong ; already she was heady, a dizziness increased perhaps by these sparkling stones. Half-way along to the quay they entered a shadowed section. His arm had gone around her, and suddenly he had drawn her to him and kissed her deliberately, with a warm passion that flowed through her.

She drew away from him, surprised at her own calmness, her lack of anger. The intoxication of it, as she sat closely by him in the dark night, seemed to belong not to her, but to some character in fiction. He held her hand, pressing it, his passion communicated through his smooth fingers. He was still holding it when they came to the quay.

On the way out to the ship the cold air revived her. She would not let him take her hand. He smiled at her quizzically.

As soon as they reached the ship she said good night and thanked him, going to her cabin. She was tired after a lovely day. She had not slept too well on the train, being excited, and had been up early on arrival at Brindisi. Now, early again in the morning, the ship would reach Patras, on the Corinth Canal, where she was taking the train for Athens.

Sylvia had no idea how long she had slept, when she was awakened by a noise she could not at first define. Then she heard it again. There was a gentle scratching at her door. She switched on the light and sat up. The noise came again. Her heart thudded within her. She listened. It was repeated, very gently.

" Who's there ? " she called, startled by her own voice.

The scratching became a slight tapping.

" A moment ! " called Sylvia, now wide awake. She got out of her bunk and put on a dressing-gown, swiftly tidying her hair. Glancing at her wrist-watch on the table, she saw it was twelve-thirty. What could be the matter at this time of night ?

She unfastened the cabin door and opened it a few inches. Cesare Manetti stood there in a blue dressing-gown over yellow silk pyjamas. He smiled as she glared at him.

" Yes—what do you want ?   Is something wrong ? "

For the moment she thought perhaps the ship was sinking.

" Oh, no, nothing is wrong, signorina.   But it is such a warm night, I thought perhaps you, too, could not sleep and would like to talk."

He smiled, showing his beautiful teeth, his throat strong and brown in the open pyjamas.   His bright eyes rested on her hair and shoulders, on the pink and white beauty of her flesh under its fair halo.

" Talk !   I was fast asleep ; you woke me up.   I don't want to talk at this time of night ! " protested Sylvia, scarcely hiding her annoyance with this quixotic Italian.

" Please, may I come in and talk to you ? " he pleaded, and simultaneously stepped forward towards the cabin, pushing open the door.   " Signorina, you are so beautiful. Why shouldn't we talk awhile ? "

His eyes shone ; his voice had a low, vibrant tone.   It flashed upon her suddenly what his insolent overture meant. She drew back a step, momentarily afraid.   He came forward again and was now in the cabin and, taking the door from her hand, was closing it with a confident smile.

" No one has seen me," he said, coming towards her. " *Cara mia*, how lovely you are ! "

She found words at last and recovered from the paralysis his deliberate action had imposed on her.

" Get out of the cabin at once, or I shall ring for the steward !   How dare you ? " cried Sylvia.

" Oh, signorina, please !   I only stay a little, *Io voglio fare l'amore con te*," he pleaded, attempting to kiss her hand.

She scarcely listened to what he said.   There was no doubt of his intention.   He had the insistent assurance of a successful Lothario.   His face, handsome, flushed, was so near to her she could smell the scented pomade he used on his hair.   It made her faintly sick, with its odour of violets. As she stepped back from his advance, snatching her hand away, she felt something hard on the dressing-table.   It was her silver hand mirror.   Instantly she seized it and crashed it with all the force of desperation against his brow. The mirror broke.   The blood flowed from a cut on his forehead.   He started back with a cry of pain and surprise.

His hand went to his brow, and he felt the blood on it.
Shouting at her fiercely in Italian, he opened the cabin door,
looked at her for a moment with a curious expression of
anger and hurt vanity, and then withdrew, closing the door
with a bang.

Sylvia slipped the catch at once and stood still, her heart
thudding, her mind still unable to believe the reality and
nature of this man's intrusion. How could he think his
insolence would succeed?

The ship's engines pounded in the still night. Through
the open porthole she could see they were riding a calm
sea on which the dim moonlight placed a leaden glaze.
She had made one mistake, forgetful of all she heard about
the young Latins. She should not have allowed him to kiss
her in the carriage or have made the half response when his
arm went around her. Yet it had been so pleasant. The
warm night, the scene, the propinquity in that carriage as
it went under the dark archway—for her it had been of the
very nature of romance. To him, of course, it had been
the promise of further opportunity.

She was a little frightened now by her savage attack, to
which witness was born by the smashed mirror now lying
on the dressing-table. He would appear with a badly cut
forehead to-morrow. She might have blinded him in her
panic.

Shivering now, Sylvia got back into bed, leaving on the
light. For some time she lay reviewing the incidents of
the day, and then she must have fallen asleep again, for she
was awakened by the stewardess tapping on her door. It
was six o'clock. Outside, a newly-risen sun had burnished
the blue-grey water, and through the haze the barren slopes
of mountains faintly gleamed. The light still on in her
cabin recalled the scene of the night. But all was well.
In an hour they would be at Patras, where she took the
train for Athens. The day, breaking with such beauty and
excitement ahead, dispelled her nightmare.

§ 4

In two swift days of utter enchantment Sylvia saw the chief sights of Athens. She made the excursion to lovely Daphni, with its Byzantine church set amid the olive trees, and then along the Sacred Way by the Bay of Salamis to famed Eleusis. But of all her crowded memories, it was that first breathless sight of the Acropolis that stood out unfading, for her whole life, she was certain. She saw it, ever present, from all parts of the sprawling city, and then ascending that historic hill, where the famous names of the greatest age of Greece had sounded on men's lips in that ambient air, she came to the towering solemnity of the shattered Propylæa, where marble bled and every shadow had a voice.

Then through that rocky gateway, high above the murmuring metropolis, she saw how much grander than all imagination, more sacred, was the roofless Parthenon. Here in the stillness, set high above the city and the guardian mountains, Sylvia listened, her body pressed against a golden column, feeling the pulse of a vanished race beating immortally through her transient flesh.

And now, as Crete drew up the southern sea, faint, with the snow-crowned White Mountains rising into the peerless blue, Sylvia began the last stage of her wonderful journey. She stood now in the prow of the little Greek steamer, fanned by the soft, cool air of early morning. The mountains fell away ; the headlands grew bolder, and dimly on the coast a fringe of white houses told her they drew near Canea, their first port of call.

When the ship anchored in the roadstead a boat drew out of the little harbour, to take off the passengers to Canea, and to bring out those making the coastwise trip to Retimo and Herakleion, Sylvia's own destination. The harbour looked very small, with its breakwater and the finely carved Venetian lion. A Greek on board, who had lived in Chicago, and eagerly seized an opportunity to talk English, told her that in stormy weather the steamers sought anchorage in Suda Bay, the other side of the headland. Sylvia, through borrowed glasses, could see minarets and domes amid the pink and white houses, which gave the place an Eastern air.

The ship was away again in half an hour. It had filled
with peasants going along the coast. The men wore baggy
blue Turkish trousers and leather top boots, showing a few
inches of bare leg between the trousers gathered in below
the knee and the top of the boot. Sylvia marvelled at the
waste of material in these trousers, with clumsy folds hanging down between their legs like the udder of a cow. The
men's embroidered jackets were made of light blue worsted,
and seemed hot for such a climate. The evidence of the
long Turkish era in Crete was plain to see.

A dominating peak, snow-crowned, gleamed inland, and
they approached Retimo.

" Mount Ida ! " exclaimed the old Greek. " The birthplace of Zeus."

Retimo, off which they anchored in the heat haze of
midday, also had its slender minarets and a strong wall and
a lighthouse. There was another exchange of peasants and
merchandise, borne by a medley of rowing boats. The
deep ravines of the mountains took on a purple tone. Most
of them seemed barren of trees.

Sylvia chatted with the old Greek who knew the island
well. He had been in exile there once, a follower of Venizelos, the patriarchal politician who had been so clever at
the Peace Conference at Versailles.

" He got us Smyrna, but that fool, King Constantine, lost
it for us by trampling too much on the Turkish toes," said
the old man bitterly, spitting into the sea.

In the late afternoon they approached Herakleion, still
called Candia in Sylvia's guide book. It was to be her home
for the next few months. For three years she had been
receiving letters from this little town. She felt she knew
it intimately through her brother's chatty letters.

They were in the bay now, and she could see the quay
and lighthouse and the villas dotting the hills that swept
down to the shore. Again they anchored some distance
out and there was a tremendous commotion of small boats
taking off passengers and cargo. The blue sea was smooth
as glass. The hot sun beat down upon the launch that
chugged its way to the harbour, filled with small sailing-
boats and tramp steamers. Sylvia's heart beat quicker as
she drew near the quay. A week ago at this time she was

sitting down to tea at *Glenarvon*, with Grandma Day in her
arm-chair, so placed that, between the weeping willows on
the lawn, she could get a glimpse of the Thames, of the
weir, the bridge, and the Cookham woods rising from the
lush meadows, now golden with buttercups. It had seemed
to Sylvia as if through all the years of her life she was
destined to run errands, to fetch the evening paper from
the letterbox and new books from the library. Romance
had been confined to the covers of a book or the dark
interior of the local cinema.

And here she was disembarking on Crete, the island of
Theseus and the Minotaur, to live in the mountains with
her adored brother, after a journey across Europe—including
attempted rape by an infatuated, young, and very handsome
Italian! She had now adopted the word "rape." The
alarming violence of the word gave her a strange pleasure
and enhanced the peril in which perhaps she had never
been. Already she regretted her attack with the hand
mirror. She had caught a glimpse in the station at Athens
of a young man with a bandaged head, hurrying away to
the ticket gate. Here, to Sylvia's surprise, a young woman
had thrown her arms around Manetti, embracing him passionately. His wife, or his fiancée, or—— Then in the
scramble of hotel porters she lost them.

There was no scramble of porters here when the launch
touched the quay. For a moment she experienced a sudden
panic. Suppose no one came to meet her! She had sent
a cable from Athens announcing her arrival. Richard, when
he had last written, was still in the hospital at Herakleion.
She had only his address, care of the Bank. Then all at
once her fears were dispelled. She saw a young woman in
nurse's uniform waving to her. When Sylvia ascended the
steps she came forward.

"Miss Day?" she asked. "I have been sent to meet you
by Mr. Day. I hope you have had a comfortable journey?"

The young nurse spoke with an accent. She was Greek,
obviously, with large black eyes and jet-black hair drawn
severely back from her olive face.

"Your baggage?" she asked.

"Those two pieces," answered Sylvia, pointing to two
bags which the porter had passed up on to the quay.

" How very little ! Then we can go at once. I have a car. My name is Helen Paulos. I am with your brother at the Villa Crane."

" He is out of the hospital ? "

" Yes ; a few days ago. He has gone to the villa of a friend. Of course he will have to take care for a long time. I am with him now, but I cannot stay. We are very short of nurses at the hospital. . . . Ah, here we are ! Sit in, please. I'll get your baggage.

Sylvia got into the open car. Helen Paulos found a man, who brought the bags. Then she seated herself at the wheel.

" It is only a short drive ; we are up here," she said, and pointed to some villas scattered over the spur of a mountain behind the town.

They were in a wide street now. It seemed an odd jumble of the old and the new : an old fortress, a minaret with the top lopped off, which had been made a museum, and some cafés, one called Haï Laïf, spread over across the pavements, the chairs mostly empty now under their yellow awnings. They came to a stone fountain with four guardian lions ; very obviously the sign of former Venetian occupation. They turned into a labyrinth of back streets and began to ascend from the town. The mountains looked very barren, of dove-coloured limestone, except for patches of cultivation, olive and lemon groves among the foothills. The arid mountains looked sun-baked and inhospitable.

They turned off into a dusty white side road, and then stopped before an iron door between heavy stone piers.

" Here we are," said the nurse, getting out and swinging open the iron door in the high walls.

There was a garden behind the walls, a green oasis, with a long vine pergola leading up to the villa, a two-storey house of white limestone, with green awnings and shutters. There was a wide, raised veranda, shady and covered with a purple wistaria in full flower. On a chaise-longue lay Richard Day, his eager face smiling at his sister.

Sylvia went up to him and kissed him. It was three years since she had last seen him in London. It was obvious from the shape of their faces that they were brother and sister, both having the same light brown hair, the same

blue eyes, and the rather wide Day mouth, dimpled at
each corner.

" Well, I've got you here at last, out of the clutches of
the Kind Dragon," cried Richard, holding both her hands
as she looked down at him.

" Oh, don't say that, Dick.   Grandma was so very sweet
about it.   She didn't hesitate for a moment, and it's a
terrible wrench for her," said Sylvia, smiling at him.   She
was shocked by his appearance.   He seemed so very thin,
and lined in the face.   The bright air of youth, which had
always clung about him, had vanished.   This was a grown
man she saw, with tired eyes and a voice that had lost its
old ring.   He must have been very ill.

" I thought she would be, bless the H.D.'" he answered.
" I laid it on pretty thick in the letter.   I hope the poor
old dear didn't think I was a goner !   But I had to scare
her to get you."

He turned to his nurse, who stood waiting, after a youth
had brought in the bags.

" Will you take my sister in and show her her room and
introduce her to Anastasia ? " he said.   Then, addressing
his sister, " You'll have to do a lot of pantomime with old
Anastasia.   She's seventy and has no teeth.   Don't be
scared ; she's so sinister and dark she looks as if she came
straight out of hell.   But she's my treasure.   Oh, I ought
to tell you—this is Jack Crane's house—he works with me
out at Knossos.   At present he's honeymooning in Athens.
He's lent me the place until we move."

" Where—and when ? " asked Sylvia.

" Up to Villa Vouni, near Vori, in a week, I hope."

Sylvia went into the house with the nurse.

" He looks very ill," said Sylvia.

" He is very ill," answered Miss Paulos.   " He can't
think of moving up to Vori in this condition.   Have you
seen the villa ? "

" No—I've never been here before."

" Oh, of course not !   Well, Vori is about as remote a
spot as you'll find in all Crete.   And Crete is the most
forgotten place in the civilised world."

" Don't you like it ? " asked Sylvia, surprised.

" I hate it.   I'm getting back to Athens as soon as

possible," answered Miss Paulos, leading the way up the stairs. " You know, it is the island of the Greek legend— where the Minotaur devoured the tribute of youths and maidens from Athens, until Theseus killed the brute. Well, you get devoured here still. Yes, I'll be glad to see Athens again. I was born there," said Miss Paulos, opening a door. " This is your room. Don't forget to shake your shoes before you put them on."

" Why ? "

" Scorpions like to hide in them. It's a cool room. The bathroom is next door, but it's only a name," she said, and added, " There's always a water famine here— you'll have to be content with a jug. Now I'll leave you to unpack. We'll face Anastasia later. By the way, Mr. Day calls her ' Nasty ' for short, but it's only a nickname. She's a good old tyrant, really, and a grandmother with countless grand-children. She'd have had a hundred, they say, if they'd all lived."

CHAPTER II

SUNSHINE IN CANDIA

WITHIN a week the spell of Crete had fallen upon Sylvia Day. Spring is lovely all the world over, but never before had she imagined such enchantment as was around her on these scented, golden days. The sun did not yet burn, as she was to find later. It rose early and clear, drawing up the veil of mist over the mountains and sea. The sky was a vast canopy of fathomless blue into which a luminous fleecy cloud strayed as if to emphasise its finite nature in the azure mirror of Eternity. As the day grew, the shadows in the mountain ravines deepened, mauve in the afternoon, purple towards evening, when a crimson light touched the whitewashed houses. The snows still lay on the mountain tops, dazzling and virgin in that wild hinterland where remote villages, ancient as Time, lived their isolated lives. It was now the time of the white crocus, and the asphodel flowering in the meadows. The vines were in fresh leaf ; the butterflies haunted the flower beds ; the evening littered with the first fireflies, and the monotonous chant of the tree frogs filled the warm, starry night.

Her brother Richard rested most of the day on the veranda of the Villa Crane. From it he could see across the valley to the mountains opposite, and, below, sprawling with its squat buildings, lay the town of Candia, or Herakleion, as it was now called in its free Greek era, with its fortress and old Venetian walls and the mole of the little harbour in the blue bay.

At the end of the week Helen Paulos left, and Sylvia took charge, but her duties as a nurse were not onerous.

" I'm a fraud, really, and as soon as I get rid of this infernal weakness we'll leave for the Villa Vouni," said Richard. " I want to see what's going on at Phaistos."

Phaistos was the scene of further excavations among Minoan ruins. Richard's villa at Vori was near ancient Phaistos, a city of the Minoan kings whose neighbouring

mountains looked southward across the Mediterranean to
Libya.

" You've been warned to take it easy for the next three
months," said Sylvia, as she sat with her brother on the
veranda after breakfast.

" If I take any notice of Dr. Phokias I shall never leave
this chair. He's developed a violent passion, not for the
patient but for the nurse ! I warn you, he's a desperate
widower of sixty, with three marriages behind him. Is he
coming to dinner to-night ? "

" Yes, with Mr. and Mrs. James, the Consul, and Madame
Kaledemas."

" I'm afraid you're going to find it dull here, Sylvia."

" Dull ! I love every minute of it ! " protested Sylvia.

" In a month you'll know every face, everything the silly
face is going to say, all the gossip, and all the best and
worst hands at bridge. Socially, this place is the world's
worst dump."

" I didn't know archæologists cared anything about
modern society. You've never shown any interest in anything that doesn't go back to two thousand years B.C."

" Oh, my dear, what a libel ! Knossos and Phaistos are
over two thousand. We are not so frivolously modern as
that ! As you'll see, when you visit Knossos with the
extremely charming guide I've procured. You'll know then
why I can't get excited about ranting dictators. If only
they would read history ! "

" But Hitler and Mussolini are going to upset our lives
unless we do something," said Sylvia. " Look how Hitler's
just gobbled up Czechoslovakia ! A young Italian on the
boat coming here told me Italy was going to have the whole
Mediterranean—he called it Mare Nostrum."

" Perhaps she is," commented Richard, and then, seeing
the shock of surprise on his sister's face, he put his hand on
her arm reassuringly. " As an Englishman, I should fight
them to the death over it. As an archæologist, I contem-
plate the possibility calmly. The folly of the human race
is persistent through the ages. There is always a crusade
in which men will slaughter one another with titanic fury
—and always for an excellent reason. It used to be racial,
then it was religious ; now it's ideological—dictatorship

versus democracy.   In our particular case it's demodictator-
ship *versus* thalassocracy."

" That's quite beyond me—what's thalassocracy ? "

" Britain is now what Crete was four thousand years ago,
a thalassocracy—a sea power.   Having built our greatness
by control of the seas, we can only keep it either alone, or,
failing that, by getting allies.   Crete was a contented kingdom, enlightened, with a long culture, and powerful.   But
she was not a warrior nation ; she built no defences on the
island ; she raised no large armies.   For over a thousand
years she was safe.   She traded with the known world ;
she had a writing script, even before the Phœnicians.   She
sent her wares and pottery to Egypt—they found it in the
palace of King Akhenaton at Tell el-Amarna, in the fourteenth century B.C.—she seemed eternal.   She was the
birthplace of Zeus, the father of the Olympian gods.
According to legend, Zeus was suckled in a grotto on Mount
Ida, there, and nursed by the nymphs.   They will show you
his tomb on Mount Jukta.   Crete's great King Minos was
the son of Zeus, according to tradition.   He ruled a kingdom
that seemed as if it would last for ever, a constantly
recurring fallacy, for it was a kingdom built on sea power.
So long as her navy ruled the seas she was impregnable.
But a day came when someone conquered that navy.   She
was wiped out, her palaces and cities devastated.   We dig
up a few stones, find a few vases, and conjecture how
powerful she was four thousand years ago.   This island is
a good example of man's slippery hold on empire, his utter
inability to inhabit the earth peaceably.   After the Cretans
came the Dorians ; after the Greeks the Romans, for some
four hundred years ; after the Romans the Byzantines, then
the Saracens in A.D. 823, and again the Byzantines, in 960
until 1204, when Crete fell and it was sold to the Venetians.
Later, there came three hundred years of incessant strife
between Christians and Moslems, until 1913, and, after
that, Venizelos, Pangalos, Metaxa, the everlasting politicians
working on the everlasting mob.   Your young Italian thinks it's
his turn now ; the German's sure it's his—and we do everything we can to encourage them by thinking a sweet logic
can halt an implacable determination.   By the way, as my
nurse, you should stop this tirade.   It's bad for a weak heart."

He lit a cigarette and laughed when he saw his sister's face wearing such a serious expression.

" What is demo-dictatorship ? " she asked, quietly.

" That's something of my own to describe a new form of folly. It's government of the people by intoxication of the people, by a man deriving his power from some of the people, through forcible regimentation of all the people. It promises the triumph of a self-chosen people over all the other goddamn people. Mussolini invented it on a balcony, and Hitler propagates it on a microphone. It's just as wicked, and no more wicked, than all the other crusades through history by which men have sought to cut one another's throat. And since man is fundamentally heroic, as well as fundamentally stupid, he will go on fighting and dying for his own conception of his rights."

" You are very depressing, Dick."

" As a student of history I am always depressed."

" Would you let the Italians take the Mediterranean—as the Fascists demand ? "

" Certainly not ! " answered Richard. " As a nation we are lost if we lose control of the Mediterranean."

" And you'd die fighting, if necessary, to keep it ? "

" Certainly ! "

" But in view of what you have just said, and what you know as a student of history, isn't that illogical ? " asked Sylvia.

" My sweet, of course it is. But have I ever asserted that man is a logical animal ? In the view of Time I am foolish to fight for anything. In the view of my own life-time I am wise to fight for the kind of life I find most pleasant. I should not find it pleasant if Hitler ruled the British and Mussolini forbade me to enter his Mediter-ranean. Dear me, how did I get on to this dreary subject ? "

" I don't find it at all dreary—I find it very vital," said Sylvia. " Do you think there's going to be a war with Germany and Italy ? "

" With Germany, yes. Hitler can't go on shouting for ever, with all those soldiers behind him, and we are so flabby whenever he spits in our face. As for Italy, I really don't know. They've got everything ready, and yet I can't believe they'll risk anything that isn't a certainty. But you'd better ask Morosini, who's coming to lunch to-morrow."

" Morosini ? " queried Sylvia.

" He's the lad who'll show you Knossos to-morrow, I hope. Cesare is our prize Italian.

" Cesare ! "

The tone of her voice made Richard look sharply at her. He saw her cheeks flush as their eyes met.

" You haven't met him ? " asked Richard, wondering what had caused her sudden confusion.

" No—who is he ? "

" Cesare Morosini is really part of the history of Crete. His family is a Venetian one that gave doges to Venice. One of his ancestors was Francesco Morosini. That public fountain down in the town is a memorial to him. Can you bear a little more history ? "

" I love it ! Go on. You're talking to one of the world's most ignorant women," asserted Sylvia, tucking one leg under the other as she sat on the large stool by his chair.

" To admit that would give me a family pain, sweet sister. Well—when the Greeks and the Romans and the Saracens had all taken Crete, the Emperor Constantine of Byzantium took it back for a time, in 906. After the fall of Constantinople, in 1204, a gentleman called Boniface, Mar-quis of Montferrat, an ex-Crusader, got hold of it, and he sold it to the Venetians."

" Then Crete was Italian once ? " interrupted Sylvia, recalling the young man of the *Dante*.

" Venetian actually, as the Morosini fountain and loggia show, as well as the fortifications, and those old arches down by the harbour, built to house their galleys. The Venetians hung on to this place for four centuries, while they fought for control of the Mediterranean with the Genoese and then with the Turks. It all ended in a terrible tussle with the Turks—it gave a phrase to the Italian language, a ' *vera guerra di Candia* '—a real Candian war ; that is, to go on bitterly to the very end.

" That's what Francesco Morosini did here against those Turks. In 1645 they captured Canea, and Retimo the next year. Candia braced herself for a siege which began in earnest in 1648, with fifty thousand armed Turks on land

and the whole Turkish fleet off the shore. Morosini put up a terrific fight, while all Christendom watched. It was the longest siege on record. It lasted over twenty years, but at last the Turks took it in 1669. The people had been reduced to skeletons, but they won so much respect from the Turks that Morosini and his garrison got an honourable peace and sailed out of her unsubdued. Even then they clung to Grabusa, Spinalonga, and Suda—you can still see the old Venetian fortress in the bay there—until 1718, when the Turks finally got them. Morosini was an old war dog who never let go. He was at the Turks again in 1684, when he fought in the League against them. I find it hard to forgive him one thing, though it was equally the Turks' fault. He captured Athens, and it was one of his shells which struck the Parthenon that the Turks had made into a powder magazine. It had survived for two thousand years almost intact, but that Venetian shell finished it. It was a German gunner who fired the shell—in keeping with the Teutonic passion for violence. People at war don't bother about historical treasures ; their politicians or soldiers can always make necessity appear the better reason. It always has been so ; it always will be so. In the frenzy of battle men have no time for the fine points of æsthetic arguments—even if they are capable of appreciating them. You'll see. When the next big row comes, it won't be a Venetian shell blowing up the Parthenon ; it'll be bombs blowing up all our cities, and the accumulated loveliness of the centuries."

" Oh, Dick, you can't think that we'll be such fools ! " cried Sylvia.

" Yes, such fools. You'll never change human nature. But I'm off on politics again. To come back to Cesare Morosini. He's naturally very proud of his descent from the great Francesco, and it gives him a sort of family hold on this place."

" What does he do here ? "

" He's been attached to the Italian Archæological Mission at Phaistos, and he's worked at Knossos—we all co-operate. And—well, perhaps I shouldn't prejudice you," said Richard, breaking off and lighting another cigarette.

At that moment the garden door opened, and an old man, in baggy Turkish trousers, top boots, and a worsted jacket,

came up the path to the villa. " Ah, here's Pericles with
the mail. I wonder if there's anything from home," commented Richard.

" *Kalemera sas kameis !* " he called.

The old man approached with a bundle of letters. " *Kala
eucharisto, Kyrie,*" he responded, and began a long story,
punctuated with many gestures and laughter.

Sylvia could not understand a word of their amiable
chatter. When he had gone they examined their mail.
There were two magazines, four letters, a *Times*. One
letter was from Grandma Day. The old lady was well and
happy. Uncle Charles came in to see her regularly. There
had been a plague of caterpillars in the garden. Miss
Whissitt, from Henley, had made a stirring speech at the
Women's Guild, on behalf of the Red Cross. She had
been appointed organiser for the district. " As she knows
everybody and everything and has a greater capacity for
suffering fools and cajoling jackasses than any other woman
living, she'll make a great success of it. She has also got
the job of distributing gas masks, and, to encourage the
idea, motors round in hers. Unkind people say they don't
notice any difference. We seem to have been leisurely
organising for war ever since Mr. Chamberlain came back
from Munich, quoting Shakespeare and promising ' peace
in our time.' I made the electricity company refund six-
and-fourpence. Their man misread the meter. You see
how wise it is to learn to read one's own meter. I am
having the dining-room repapered a bright green. Scott
says wallpapers will become very scarce if there's a war, and
if there's to be a war, then we must be as cheerful as possible.
Personally, I don't believe a word of all this war talk.
Hitler and Mussolini are windbags. I hope you are taking
precautions against bad drinking water. Miss Whissitt says
the water in Crete is very bad. She has not been there,
though she gave me a long lecture on the ruins of Knossos,
particularly about some room with battle-axes, of which she
said Richard had sent her pictures. I hope they were
decent ones. I once saw some frescoes at Pompeii which
should never have been dug out. Miss Whissitt says she
had a fearful illness after drinking some water on Lake
Como, and Greek water is probably more dangerous than

Italian water. I have taken four seats for the Enclosure at
Henley Regatta. I shall miss you very much arranging our
lunches that week."

When Sylvia had finished reading her letters she found
Richard engrossed in *The Times*.

" Can I interrupt you ? " she asked.

" Um ? " murmured Richard, still reading.

" Not more war rumours ? "

" No—Woolworth's have risen sixpence. I think I'll
buy some more," he said.

Sylvia burst into laughter. Her brother looked up from
his paper.

" Why do you laugh ? " he queried.

" You're such a funny mixture, Dick. You say you're
only interested in ruins three thousand years B.C., and here
you are, really excited by a rise of sixpence in Woolworth's ! "

" There's nothing funny in it at all. I've no doubt that
goatherds at the Court of King Minos were vitally interested in the Goat Exchange, or whatever they called it. We are
finite creatures first, and feast our immortal souls afterwards."

" Miss Whissitt has been to see Grandma Day and gave
her a lecture on the ruins of Knossos."

" Good lord ! That must have subdued even Grandma."

" Does she know anything about Knossos ? "

" The first time I ever heard of the place was when she
kept me quiet as a kid by giving me some pictures of naked
girls doing gymnastics over the horns of bulls, and told me
all about King Minos, and Theseus and the Minotaur.
I'll bet if she were here she'd tell us one or two things we
don't know about our own excavations. That old girl's
uncanny. What else did she tell Grandma ? "

" Oh, nothing. But she told her to warn me against
drinking the water here."

" Well, she's right on that, of course."

" Dick, I want to learn modern Greek. I must be able
to talk to these people. I didn't understand a word you
said to Pericles."

" Do you really mean that ? It's a tough job," asked
Richard. " I haven't the time, old girl."

" Oh, I don't mean that. There must be someone here
who can teach me."

" I expect so.   I'll ask Çesare.   He's a fluent linguist in six languages."

" Tell me more about Cesare Morosini—you've kept something back," asked Sylvia.   " What is it ? "

Richard gave his sister a quick look.   He regretted his indiscretion, which she had so quickly detected.

" Did I ? " he parried.   " Well, I don't think I'll say— I've really no justification."

" You're making him frightfully interesting."

" He is frightfully interesting.   Cesare has all the gifts. He's the most preposterously handsome boy I've ever seen, and the most attractive.   They say he finds women in his bed every night ; they crawl in up the drainpipe or get in with the laundry."

" He sounds very conceited.   I don't like him a bit," said Sylvia.

" You're wrong.   Cesare hasn't an atom of conceit.   He's one of the nicest dispositions I've ever encountered.   With a tenth of his looks and charm, women would have made me a bounder."

" Has he brains ? "

" Yes—lots."

" Good health ? "

" Radiant ! " answered Richard.

" Good-tempered ? "

" An angel."

" Lazy ? " asked Sylvia.

" No, very industrious—and he's plenty of money."

" How old ? "

" Twenty-five.   Though, like all Italians, he looks more mature."

" Just what does he look like ? " persisted Sylvia.

" Well, of course, I may spoil him for you."

" I believe you're pulling my leg ! "

" He's got a blue chin, hairy paws, and toothbrush eyebrows."

Richard laughed aloud, and put an arm across his sister's shoulders as she made a grimace.

" So that's what you don't like.   Well, Cesare's lucky. He's a smooth, tawny skin and an Italian's hands."

" How tall ? "

" Nearly six feet. Slim, broad-shouldered, with dark brown hair, bleached gold on top. Dark eyes, with a smiling light in them, a good speaking voice, and the best possible manners. He dresses perfectly. Apollo Belvedere, born in Venice, educated in Paris, tailored in London, and polished in Rome."

" And too good to be true in Crete. I don't think I shall like him. I find Apollos too dazzling."

" How many have you known ? " asked Richard.

" None," confessed Sylvia.

" Ah ! Just wait and see," said Richard, smiling at her.

She loved him when he smiled like that. Every line of his neat head was dear to her, and to be with him, to know that he needed her, filled her cup of happiness. She had missed him dreadfully in these last six years of separation, three in India and three in Crete. He was old enough and dominant enough to take the lead in everything, and yet they had never ceased to be the closest of companions. In their childhood in India, when the death of their mother had left a void that was never filled, he had been like mother and father to her, though he was only fourteen and she was nine. They had been sent home to Grandma Day's, and a new life had opened for them in what seemed a strange land, for they had been born in India, where Colonel Day had his command. She had seen less of Richard in England than in India, for he was sent off to Wellington College before entering Sandhurst, destined to soldiering, as all the Days. But there were long holidays, and although Richard brought back his own friends he never neglected her, and, determined to keep up with him, she could ride, shoot, and swim as well as any boy friend he brought home. When it came to handling boats—rowing, sailing, or punting—she made them look amateurs. " You'll put nothing over that kid," Richard would say proudly, surveying her from the lordly height of seventeen. She was twelve then, and they had been three years out of India, and her father was getting dim. Perhaps, realising this, Colonel Day flew home on leave to see little Sylvia and, above all, to talk to young Richard, who was showing the strangest streak and was kicking against Sandhurst and an army career.

Colonel Day never saw his children. His plane crashed

taking off from Cairo on a bright June morning. Thus
there was no stern talk to Richard, but, constrained by his
father's wish, he dropped his opposition to the army. He
did well at Sandhurst, was commissioned in a cavalry
regiment, and, so far as they all knew, seemed quite happy.

Then one day Sylvia heard the dreadful news. Her
beloved Richard's regiment was ordered to India. She was
a happy undergraduate at Oxford, and it seemed as if her
world had crashed. Richard came down to see her. It was
Eights Week, her last term before she went to Guy's Hospital. They attended bump races, college lunches, and
dances that went on until dawn. She had found how much
her own youthful looks meant to the young men around her,
and yet it was Richard, tall, whimsical, neat, who filled the
whole scene. One day, she knew, she would not be the
first in his life. Some unknown girl would walk in and
possess his love, but until that time Richard had her complete devotion. And now he was taken out of her life just
when she was most aware of him, most needing him in the
bright, wonderful world unfolding before her.

She had never forgotten that week, the music, the flowers,
the doom that hung over her, making every moment of
their companionship more intense. And she fretted for him.
He was unhappy, too. He had no wish to go; he hated
the Army, though he never completely confessed it to her.

So he went, and two years passed, and she lived for the
third year when he returned on leave. She had graduated
then and had begun her medical course, when, without
warning, the whole future changed. Aunt Ella, the devoted,
patient burden carrier of all affairs at *Glenarvon*, suddenly
died. Grandma Day could not be left alone in the large
house. Sylvia saw her career vanish. Her disappointment was lessened by one piece of fortune which led to
another. Aunt Ella had left both her niece and nephew a
comfortable legacy. They were each independent financially.

Richard came home, having resigned his commission.
He was tired of the heat, playing polo, and having to listen
deferentially at mess to a gallant colonel with a primary
mentality. Sylvia was once more united to her beloved
Richard. She took over the duties so admirably performed
by Aunt Ella, always under the firm supervision of Grandma

Day, whose autocracy increased with age, and heroically defied infirmities.

Richard now had leisure to pursue his natural tastes, antiquarian and archæological studies. Then three months after his return home the bombshell fell. He met and married within a month a former secretary to the director of the British School at Athens. Barbara Haskitt was an interesting example of the new woman. After a brilliant career at Oxford, Paris, and Munich, where she absorbed degrees like a hydrangea absorbs water, she had worked in Rome and Athens. Thin, dark, direct in manner, her black hair drawn tightly back from an ascetic brow, she frightened Sylvia, although there was no flaw in her behaviour towards her sister-in-law. Sylvia wondered how Richard could have been swept off his feet by this hard young woman of thirty.

One thing became immediately clear. Barbara was not going to share Richard with anyone. Grandma Day and the new Mrs. Day crossed swords at once. Richard's wife, not being a woman who spent her energy unnecessarily, made a clever move. Her contacts and interests were the same as Richard's. It was not long before they announced their decision to go to Knossos, to work with Sir Arthur Evans' mission there.

Grandma Day took her defeat philosophically. Richard was lost to a wife and archæology. He had always been difficult and had delivered a hard blow to the family tradition. Grandma Day's line of action was clear. She altered her Will concerning Richard, without announcing it, and sent for her son Charles, a not-too-prosperous solicitor in Reading, on whose wife she had always made war. Now she healed the breach by a generous gesture. She offered to provide for Gerald, their eldest son, if he would give up his boyish ambition to take holy orders and go to Sandhurst to become a soldier. The offer was so generous that the conversion was complete. Grandma Day dialed her telephone more firmly than ever. Days had fought at Malplaquet, Torres Vedras, Waterloo, Balaclava, Khartoum, Majuba Hill, on the Marne, and in the Khyber Pass. She had now maintained the tradition so callously broken by Richard, in the grip of " that chryselephantine creature," as Grandma Day termed young Mrs. Day, in allusion to her white skin, black clothes and necklace, and bangles of yellow amber.

Sylvia had suffered intensely, but hid her pain. It deprived her not only of Richard's companionship, but also of his letters, of which she had been the sole recipient. They had been such warm, vivid letters, touched with the lambent flame of his humour. She was also more of a prisoner at *Glenarvon* than before. Young life rarely came to the house and, when it came, quailed before " the grand tortoise," as Miss Whissitt once called her, in one of her unguarded moments of enlightened candour. The old lady seemed quite oblivious of Sylvia's need of young companionship and of the possible effect on her future. She pressed her grand-daughter, perhaps unconsciously, into that army of complaisant virgins indentured to spinsterdom and immolated on the altar of selfish old age.

Grandma Day had her revenge, though at the cost of Richard's happiness. Without any warning, news came that he and Barbara had separated. The news as it came to *Glenarvon* was bald and brutal. The tragedy was announced in a few sentences. He would continue in Crete. The reconstruction of part of a ruined monastery near Vori, planned as a summer home in the mountains, would go on, and he would continue his work at Knossos. Barbara had been appointed professor of archæology at a Californian university.

The marriage had lasted fourteen months. Richard's letters to Sylvia were renewed. They had lost nothing of their humour and vivacity. There was never a reference to his domestic tragedy. At home the mystery remained unsolved. Richard seemed engrossed in his work up at Phaistos, to which he had gone after Knossos.

Sylvia wondered what she would find at the old monastery at Vori, now called the Villa Vouni. She had seen photographs of the amazing ruin hidden away on a mountainside and accessible only by a mule track. It had been founded by monks in the fourteenth century. In 1866 some four hundred Cretans, men and women, had taken refuge there. The Turks stormed it and killed them. Then they had pillaged it, and it had been left in ruins.

Richard's reference to Morosini's work at Phaistos made Sylvia wonder if he visited the villa and knew Barbara.

" I suppose Signore Morosini comes to the villa a lot ? "
asked Sylvia, getting up from the stool, conscious of house-
hold duties awaiting her.

" He comes over when he's working at Phaistos. Visitors
are rare. It's two hours' journey by mule after you leave
the highway."

" How long have you known him ? " asked Sylvia.

" Oh, ever since I came here—though he often goes to
Rome for three or four months. He's in the Fascist hier-
archy."

" That's something I don't like about him," exclaimed
Sylvia. " If he believes all that Mussolini says, he's a fool,
and if he doesn't, he's a hypocrite."

" My dear girl, it's not as simple as all that," replied
Richard, smiling at her. " Most of the young Italians are
ardent Fascists—it gives them a progressive spirit as well as
a uniform. Some of them know Mussolini's a braggart, but
he has made people take notice of Italy, cleaned up the
place and made them work, poor devils. He's gone a long
way on wind and castor oil. He knows the trick with
homo sapiens. Put a tassel on a timid man's hat, give him
top boots with which to stamp on the corns of other timid
men, and he'll make his weight felt. I don't fear Musso
nearly as much as Hitler. He's poorer material to work
with, and bullfrogs can't keep inflated for ever. But we
mustn't ignore the Fascists. They're sitting here in the
middle of the Mediterranean, holding the door open for
Hitler. They've got their hands on the Dodecanese, on
Rhodes, Leros, Libya, Pantelleria, Sardinia, Albania, and
Abyssinia. They've sharpened their knives on the throats
of the Spaniards in Spain, Arabs in Libya, Yugoslavs in
Fiume, Greeks in Corfu, Austrians in the Tyrol, Albanians
in Durazzo, and Abyssinians in Abyssinia. They've
torpedoed our boats in the Mediterranean—and we've pre-
tended we don't know who did it, to such straits are we
reduced by our politicos—and clapped their hands over the
mouths of that hypocritical Non-Intervention Committee.
My God ! Only last January Chamberlain was taking the
salute in Rome from the eight million bayonets Musso's
threatened to stick in us, and went home assured that ' a
Gentleman's Agreement,' signed between a soft statesman

and a brazen thug, will help ' peace in our time.' Do
you wonder these young Italians sitting on the doorstep of
Africa, Egypt, Palestine, and the Balkans, believe one push
will give them possession ?   It's going to take a lot of lives
and bloodshed to disillusion the young Morosinis. We
cheep like canaries in a pretty cage while the Italians sharpen
their claws.   We've done everything we can, from Corfu in
1923, to Prague in 1938, to encourage these Fascists to
believe in Mare Nostrum. Perhaps they're right. Perhaps
we're not fit to hold on to what we have. I get very sick,
these days, seeing how we are kicked around Europe. I've
stopped work at Vori. We may be flung out of here one
day."

" You can't mean that ? " asked Sylvia, astonished by the
bitterness in his voice.

" Indeed I do.   And I know Cesare Morosini believes it,
too.   There's not a detail he doesn't know on this island."

" You mean he's a spy ?

" I don't think we can use that word. He's every right
to be here, and to look around and to make notes. I offered
to do the same thing and got snubbed by our people. We
still believe the Italians are inalienably attached to us
because we once helped Garibaldi. A whole army of
English *rentiers* live there because it's beautiful, warm, and
cheap. They bleat endlessly of the devotion of their *cara
Marias*, their *caro Giovannis*, who cheat them of the house-
hold bills and wear their old clothes."

" Then you don't trust Signor Morosini ? " asked Sylvia.
Richard was coughing now, hoarse with too much talking.
She was scandalously abusing her duty as a nurse, but
curiosity and an excitement charged with apprehension led
her on.

" I don't trust any politician. ' Our country, right or
wrong.' An American, Stephen Decatur, said that, and it's
still a universal belief. But I admire Morosini ; he's intelligent, industrious, well bred, brave, and proud. He
believes in the gamble."

" And you ?   This is really my last question."
Richard did not answer for a few moments and watched
a pair of blue butterflies hovering over the scarlet geraniums.

" I would like to believe in pure reason, but mankind can

always find an honourable reason for a dishonourable act. It can be incredibly brave in fighting for something over which a coward shows more sense. All men in uniform are brave and noble, in theory, though at home, out of uniform, they are often cowardly and ignoble in fact. An idea elevates them ; a mass instinct moves them ; a cause excites them. But the fact remains, philosophically regarded, that William James' words are true—' Man, biologically considered . . . is the most formidable of all the beasts of prey, and indeed the only one that preys systematically on his own species.' Young Nazis and young Fascists will die heroically for the dictators they believe in. We, when we can't back down any longer, will die equally heroically. I have no quarrel with the Guidos and the Karls. I respect them, and I must respect all men who hold their own lives in contempt and will die for their own way of life, however duped. Between us we shall trample the earth into a bloody bog, this time with a thoroughness unknown in history. As an individualist I am sunk in pessimism, but the philosopher in me knows the irrepressible buoyancy of life. The greatest tragedy of war is that the young die and the old linger on. But let us remember that, dying young, they bequeath no legacy of folly to the world, and they leave us in the height of their physical faculties, knowing ecstasies they could not prolong, full of honour unstained, faith uncompromised, and hopes that can no more be deferred. The weight of suffering is upon those who remain. If they have learned nothing they are doubly damned. It is not unjust that they must live on to expiate their sins. Hitlers and Mussolinis are not born ; they are made—made by the conditions that arise from human greed, or political casuistry, or, more simply, by mental and moral laziness. There, Miss Day, you see what I've dug out of four thousand years of ruins. Since history's taught us so little we might try a course of archæology."

"Thank you. I've forgotten the first thing in nursing—that the patient must not be fatigued. I'm off to the kitchen to struggle with Nasty," said Sylvia. "And I think *The Times* should be stopped ; it agitates you too much."

"That's a cruelty I could not survive !" called Richard, as she went into the house.

CHAPTER III

ENTER HERMES

SYLVIA had sufficient experience of her brother's whimsical mind not to accept his statements without caution. When Morosini arrived for lunch and she went into the library where he sat talking to Richard, she was prepared to see a fat, swarthy little fellow of fifty. Richard had played tricks like that on her before. She was surprised, therefore, despite her brother's account, when she saw the young man who stood up on her entrance. While Richard introduced him she suppressed a flurry of excitement and pleasure. He had not exaggerated. For the first few minutes she avoided any careful examination of their guest, knowing only that a handsome young man was talking in a very pleasant voice with hardly any accent.

He was long in the legs, and it seemed at a casual glance that his head was a little too small for his body. He wore no socks, and open sandals. His brown feet were perfectly formed, and, for once, the ugliest part of human anatomy evoked no distaste in her. She covertly watched his hands. They were strong but fine, and he used them without the excessive expression of the Latin when animated. She noticed the long fingers, the nails pale against the brown flesh. He was dressed in a suit of spotless white, uncreased and well cut. A yellow tie hung loosely on his white silk shirt. His teeth were flawless, his eyes full of animation. Sun-bleached hair, well brushed back, showed a smooth, neat head. Sylvia thought of the god Hermes rather than Apollo. It was impossible that a young man endowed with such good looks could not be conceited, and she watched him with a slightly defensive hostility. He was not going to charm her in his infallible manner. She had suffered already from one young Italian of charm.

They went into lunch, and Richard, sensitive to everything, was aware of Sylvia's cool but perfectly mannered reticence. In turn, though perhaps not aware of her defensive air, young Cesare Morosini chatted on, his remarks addressed generally to them both.

He certainly talked well, and Sylvia listened to his easy, correct English and envied him. If only she could talk any language with that easy perfection ! She had fair French and halting German. Nasty, on her first entrance with one of the dishes, had been greeted by him in modern Greek. There was a rapid and fluent interchange between him and the old woman, whose lined face suddenly shone with animation.

" How long did it take you to learn Greek like that ? " asked Sylvia.

" Oh, I don't know, Miss Day, I took in demotic Greek with my garlic," he replied, laughing.

His eyes lingered on her. She had the delicate English colouring, and if he had his way he would not let her go out into the sun. He had no liking for this modern craze on the part of women to look as if they had Aztec blood. Her lovely creamy whiteness, the soft tinge of pink, made her incomparably more beautiful than any of the roasted beauties of the beach.

" You see, my people are bankers, and that was my planned destiny. I am the family disappointment. But since money circulates so widely and flows through so many channels, I was carefully prepared for a nomadic life. My first governess was French, my second Scotch. I spent my summer holidays with Greek cousins in Athens, my Christmas holidays with banking connections in Stuttgart. I was two years at Oxford—oh, what lovely years——"

" When ? " interrupted Sylvia. His eyes, she thought, at that moment, as they gleamed with reminiscent pleasure, had an indescribable vitality.

" Nineteen thirty-two and three," he answered.

" But I was there then ! "

" Ah—you must have been one of those Dianas on bicycles that I could never surprise at their baths. Did you know a girl called Jojo ? " he asked, a smile lighting his eager face.

" Jojo ? No ! What an odd name ! Jojo what ? "

" Ah, I don't know ! I never did know, and perhaps it

wasn't Jojo. But it sounded like that. She was dressed as a page to the Duke of Illyria in a performance they gave of *A Midsummer Night's Dream* in Worcester College garden one warm June night. When I saw her my heart went right down, then right up, and turned over—you know——"

" I don't think I do, but still—" commented Richard.

"And someone behind me called " There's Jojo ! ' Somehow the name was just right ; she seemed Jojo. I hunted her down in the programme. There was a frightful jumble of names among the supporting cast, and it must have been one of fourteen. It took me a month to track down nine of them. I never got round to the other five, for term ended, and I went back to Rome, and Oxford was over for me. But I did see her once again. Where do you think ? I went to Naples to see some friends off to America. We had champagne, and then the gong rang, and we had to go ashore. We stood waving as they warped the ship out, and there, leaning over the taffrail of the promenade deck, with a great Sicilian straw hat on her head, was Jojo. ' Jojo ' I screamed. ' Jojo ! ' Everybody was screaming too, of course. You know those boats going out full of Americans ! She looked down and saw me, a little surprised. I waved madly, and then she thought perhaps she should know me somehow, and she waved back. And that was the last I saw of her ! I wonder what happened to her ? Perhaps she's the wife now of some director of the Guaranty Trust, or the General Electric, and lives in a large wooden house on Long Island, or in a concrete box on Park Avenue. Jojo ! Ah——"

He spread his hands and raised his eyes.

I have seen the angel Gabriel, thought Sylvia. I am slipping. This is not to be, and then in a voice that did not sound like her own, she said to him :

" So much for learning English. And the French language ? "

He thought she was mocking him, and the sunlight faded out of his eyes.

" I am sorry. It is very silly to talk like this. French I found very easy. It's so near to Italian. But German —ah, what a language to expect anyone to learn ! And for an Italian—we have nothing in common," exclaimed the young man.

" Come now, Cesare. You've got an Axis in common," said Richard.

" Oh, that ! It was only to frighten you into being good about Abyssinia. I am so happy. Don't let us talk about politics. It is like a cloud. Do you like it here, Miss Day ?" he asked, turning to her.

" Immensely."

" Sylvia hasn't seen Knossos yet. I can't think of a better guide, if——" began Richard.

" Or a happier," cried Morosini quickly, and turned to Sylvia. " When may I take you there ? To-morrow morning ? It is better early, before it gets hot."

They agreed for the morrow. Morosini departed after a visit of two hours. It had seemed like ten minutes.

§ 2

At nine o'clock the next morning, just before Morosini was due to fetch her for the tour of the excavations at Knossos, Sylvia sat in front of her dressing-table mirror, having come up from breakfast, and put on a large, shady straw hat.

It did not suit her. It made her look dowdy, so she discarded it for a very small hat made of netted white silk. It gave her the air of a young page, but after a few moments' contemplation she took it off.

" He'll think I'm trying to look like Jojo," she said to herself. " Sylvia, you are not going to make a fool of yourself over Hermes. He's got wings on his feet, and you'll be left standing."

She put on the large straw hat. It was practical and would keep the sun out of her eyes.

He was prompt, arriving in his large red Fiat automobile. For a few minutes he talked with Richard on the veranda, and then they set off. Unlike yesterday, he seemed quite solemn and a little pedantic. He inquired how much she knew about the history of Knossos and the vast palace of the Minoan kings. She told him she had read accounts of the excavations, and of course Richard's letters had been full of information.

"You know the legend of King Minos and Theseus and the Minotaur?"

"I don't know it too well. I once read it as a child in a book of Greek fables."

"Not fables—there's a solid substratum of truth in the story of the Minotaur and the labyrinth," observed Morosini.

"Perhaps you had better tell it to me," said Sylvia, very conscious of his brown hands on the steering wheel.

"You are back in the nursery, and I am the Scotch governess," he said, with a sudden smile. "We will start with Zeus. Once upon a time, in fact, in the very beginning of time . . ."

She listened as they drove through the bright morning land. It was as if Hermes were carrying her to the abode of the gods.

'. . . . the great Zeus saw fair Europa in a meadow of Phoinikia. It was spring, and she stood naked and knee-deep in flowers. He was smitten at sight of her with the flame of desire. Wishing to draw near her without causing alarm, he changed himself into a bull and browsed quietly as he drew nearer and nearer to the lovely Europa. Seeing him so strong and so gentle, she and her maidens came near to stroke him, and presently Europa sought to ride upon his back. Then suddenly despite her cries of fright, the gentle bull ran across the meadow and leaped into the sea. Thus, finding herself transported by the great Zeus, disguised as a bull, she was brought to Crete, where he wedded her and begat many sons and daughters, among them Minos, Rhadamanthus, and Sarpedon. Here they grew to manhood. One day they fiercely quarrelled over the beautiful youth, Miletus. Minos triumphed, and the brothers fled, leaving him the supreme lord of Crete, for Zeus had passed to his Olympian state, ruling over the gods.

"Now every ninth year King Minos visited Mount Ida, yonder"—Morosini pointed to the vast mountain crowned with snow, and draped in morning mist, that towered upon the south-western horizon. "There he conferred with the mighty Zeus. King Minos had married the lovely but fickle Pasiphae, and that lady conceived a guilty passion for a bull—you see how the tauric symbol runs through this legend—and she brought forth a dreadful monster, with the body of a man and a bull's head. She was assisted in this intrigue by a very skilled craftsman named Dædalus, who had built for King Minos a palace and a labyrinth. The King shut up the monster, which they called the Minotaur, in the labyrinth, and proceeded to throw Dædalus and his son Icarus into prison.

" Dædalus was a wily and ingenious man. He made wings for himself and his son, warning the youth not to fly too low, since his wings would get wet, nor too high, since the sun would melt the wax with which they were fastened. But the poor youth forgot the warning. He flew too high, and the sun melting the wax, he fell headlong into the sea, which ever afterward was called the Icarian Sea.

" Now King Minos had made successful war upon King Ægius, King of Athens, and had placed upon him every ninth year a tribute of five noble youths and five maidens. And he made of these a sacrifice to the devouring Minotaur.

" It chanced that to the court of the King of Athens came a noble youth, Theseus, already renowned for his deeds of strength. He was an illegitimate son of the King, who welcomed him in his troubled and enfeebled old age. Theseus, confident he could overcome the Minotaur, offered to go as part of the tribute. The ship, because of its sad mission, was furnished with a black sail, and King Ægius gave to his son a white sail that he might hoist it should he return triumphant. Theseus departed with the youths and maidens to Crete. But before they were locked in the labyrinth, to be devoured by the monster, beautiful Ariadne, a daughter of King Minos, had seen young Theseus, and her heart took flame from his beauty, whereupon she devised a means for his rescue. She gave him a sword and with it a skein of wool, that he might trail it in his wanderings in the vast labyrinth and, if successful in his contest with the Minotaur, retrieve his steps by it.

" Theseus met the Minotaur and slew it, and led his companions out of the labyrinth. In making his escape from Crete he took the enamoured Ariadne with him, and, setting sail for Naxos, married her. Alas, later he deserted

her and returned to Athens. The old King, acquainted of
the return of the ship, rushed to the cliffs. But Theseus
had forgotten the white sail the King had given him as a
symbol of success, and seeing the black-sailed ship approach,
the King threw himself from the cliffs in despair and was
drowned. From that day they called it the Ægean Sea."

They were approaching Herakleion when Morosini
finished his story. He drove at a great pace, the white dust
swirling behind them. Yes, thought Sylvia, the god Hermes,
messenger of Zeus, at the wheel of an automobile, telling a
story of the ancient gods.

" Have I told it well ? " he asked with a boyish laugh.
" Those old gods were so prolific that I often forget important members of their families."

" Very well. I think I shall now behave intelligently,"
answered Sylvia.

" Have you read Sir Arthur Evans' four monumental
volumes, *The Palace of Minos* ? Certainly you should read
them if you get the chance."

" I have read them," said Sylvia.

Morosini gave her a sharp look and saw she was laughing
at him.

" *Dio mio !* I suppose you're going to check up on me this
morning. Have you been to the museum here and seen all
the exhibits ? "

" Yes. They're magnificent," she said, and saw a swift
look of dismay and suspicion flit over his face.

" Are you pulling my leg ? " he asked. " Haven't you
seen the palace ? "

" No, I wouldn't go until Richard or someone equally
intelligent could take me."

" Thank you. That revives me a little. We shall be
there in a quarter of an hour," he said, as they took the road
by the old Venetian wall and started up the valley.

On their right lay the great massif of Mount Ida. Beyond
rose Mount Jukta, the reputed burial place of Zeus. Nothing
in the contours of these mountains could have been changed
in four thousand years. The warriors of King Minos,
perhaps Theseus himself, had traversed this valley of
hundred-citied Crete, as Homer called it.

They passed several old Turkish estates, the site of a

Roman villa, and the remains of an amphitheatre, and then,
where two small valleys joined, at the foot of the mountain,
she saw the Palace of Minos, for so long only a name to her,
a fabulous wonder, filling the letters from Richard, and now
a reality.   It lay before her, still and ruinous, covering the
valley floor, under the blinding sun of this Cretan day.
A holy quiet pervaded the air when Morosini stopped the
car and they got out.   Yet it was a quiet full of bodiless life,
as if the dead generations dwelt in the roofless chambers
and looked at the snow-girt mountains under the azure sky.

She followed her guide over the threshold and, familiar
with it all in theory and booklore, learned from his scholarly
store, which he brought to vivid life in his young enthusiasm.   They followed the site of the first palace built
twenty centuries before Christ and destroyed two centuries
later, after a brilliant era.   Here at the gate of Asia and
Europe the kings of the island empire had founded their
courts.   The ruins through which they now stepped, so
patiently disinterred from the debris of the centuries were
those of the new palace, built in the eighteenth century
before Christ, which had endured in its vast splendour
through four hundred years, until some force unknown had
swept down and with fire and with terror had destroyed for
ever the proud Cretan supremacy.   What force had it been
and whence had it come ?   History could only vaguely
surmise.   Only the evidence of that overwhelming catastrophe remained, in broken walls, fallen columns, fragmented
pavements, and the haunted stillness where a footstep sent
the lizards scurrying into the crannies of the crumbled rock.

They passed the ruined theatre of the palace, where the
court had held its displays of boxing and dancing.   A long
corridor, whose walls had carried a processional fresco,
brought them into a large interior court, rectangular and
open to the sky.   They traversed a maze of rooms, a great
hall of three columns, vestibules, a throne room, the treasury,
the long galleries, the storage vaults, and saw great vases,
a man's height, wherein the oil, wine, wheat and provisions
had been kept.   They came to the Queen's chambers, the
baths, the cabinets, the sanctuaries, with their lustral basins,
sacred to the mystic cult.   And then, in each centre of two
small rooms, they saw the columns bearing the sign of the

double axe, the emblem of Zeus. Here was the very heart
of the mystery about which this vanished race, so gifted, so
powerful, half lost in legend, had built its sacred cult.

" We once thought that the labyrinth of King Minos was
at Gortyn, in the vast quarries there," said Morosini.
" We're now almost certain the labyrinth was this maze of
rooms opening out of each other. It is significant that the
name of the double axe is *labrys*, and here, we surmise, is
the source of the legendary labyrinth of Theseus' contest
with the Minotaur. Who knows? The mists of time
drift here, now hiding, now revealing, the life of this
vanished race, of King Minos, Theseus and Ariadne,
Dædalus and Icarus."

They sat on a sun-warmed rock. Half a dozen tourists
with a guide disappeared down a corridor. Their footsteps
died. Through the stillness came the shrill whirring of the
cicadas. The scent of wild thyme was in the air. Sylvia
thought of those long-dead female toreadors of the Cretan
bull ring, incredible athletes who vaulted over the bulls'
horns ; of those small-waisted slim Cretan youths, with
their gold and silver belts and loin-cloths, cup-bearers and
pages to King Minos. Four thousand years ago these pavements had been thronged with lovely women, grave warriors,
statesmen, craftsmen, courtiers, pressed with daily problems, sustained by ambitions and hopes. The tides of time
had ebbed and flowed through the centuries. Race upon
race and war upon war had come and gone, would come
and go. But the mountains, the sea, the air, these remained,
unchanging, under the endless procession of dawn and
sunset.

" Please don't look so sad ! " cried Morosini's voice,
breaking upon her reverie.

" Doesn't this place—do something to you ? " asked
Sylvia, unable to find the words she searched for.

" Yes, but it doesn't make me sad. They died, but they
lived as we must live. They ate and drank and made love
and had children and said little prayers to whatever gods
they believed in. They sailed the seas and conquered, or
died young in battle in strange places, or were massacred by
the strong foe that breached their walls. That's the unchanging history of men. It all matters so little. A minute

dead is the same as ten thousand years. Time is an illusion,
life a conscious moment."

He smiled at her and, seeing a doubt in her eyes :

" Oh, yes, the moment is very real and important ; we
must live exploiting every sense. *La vita comincia domane*
—life begins to-morrow, says the poet. How wrong, how
stupid ! It begins now, here ! "

" I believe you are a pagan," said Sylvia, feeling the
intense vitality of his physical ecstasy as he sat there, every
line of his body quick and graceful in the bright air. Had
the flutes of Pan sounded across the glade and he had
bounded away, shaggy-thighed and horned, the apparition
would not have startled her. They were so near to that
mythical world of unruly gods, ravished nymphs, and fleeing
fauns. Hermes might suddenly catch her up and bear her
away through the incandescent air to some cool grotto
where, in sweet resistance, his ardour would prevail.

Sylvia started. Hermes had lit a cigarette, and the age
of the gods vanished with the snap of his automatic lighter.
He looked at her inquisitively while the blood mantled her
cheeks. A zephyr played with a stray curl over her ear.
The miracle of the flesh touched him like an æolian harp.
Perhaps she saw his deeper inbreathing, the wordless ecstasy
briefly revealed in his gaze, for she rose abruptly, saying,
" Shall we go ? "

He made no answer, and together they crossed the court.
At a rough passage, over the stones, he gave her his hand.
It was so surprisingly cool and firm. They came to the car.
The growing heat of noon filled the valley. The mist had
rolled off the mountains, and their arid slopes boldly took
the sun. The silvery olives dotted the foothills. Against
a ruined tower in the thick shade of a cypress tree a boy
tended a flock of kids and waved to them, happy to break
his loneliness. The wild rhododendrons blazed in the
vivid noon. The vines and early tobacco stood in green
patches of cultivation, but no one was in the fields, for the
peasants had gone to their siesta.

They did not talk much on the return journey. The
visit to Knossos had cast its spell upon her. Those dead
generations had not left the voiceless palace. And more
disturbing, because more vague, the living had intensified

her consciousness. A voice, the touch of a hand should not have challenged so strongly the influence of the shadowy dead. She simply must not lose her head because of a singularly handsome and pleasant young Italian.

§ 3

A whole month had passed, and the end of May had brought the growing heat of summer to the Mediterranean island. The spring cruises had ceased, and there were fewer visitors to Candia, as they called it always, in preference to the Greek name of Herakleion. The afternoons were so hot that the siesta reigned from noonday to early evening, when the workers went forth to the tobacco fields, the goatherds shifted their flocks, and the donkeys renewed their patient circuit at the water wheels, drawing water for the parched land. Two-wheel mule carts came noisily rumbling down the dusty roads into Herakleion, laden with early produce. There were other carts laden with pigskins bursting with wine. Sailcloth windmills on the lowlands by the coast pumped water incessantly, as they had done through the centuries for Saracen, Venetian, and Greek. Up in the mountains, where the winds swept through the passes, similar mills were used for grinding corn.

Richard gained strength each day, and there was such a change in his appearance that Sylvia no longer watched him with anxiety. He rode out in the evenings, making visits to the small society that the town afforded, though he by no means confined himself to the few English and Americans, or to those connected with the various archæological missions. In this way Sylvia came to know many delightful Greek families and also the Italian circle in which Cesare Morosini moved. But she soon discovered that this small island, so halcyon in its setting, was a hotbed of political intrigue and unrest. Political exiles from Greece had been banished here from time to time, leaving behind them feuds of astonishing fierceness between the restless political parties in the Greek capital. The native place of Venizelos, here, everyone seemed to be a fierce politician. Politics, said

Richard, had ruined ancient Greece and were the plague of
modern Greece.

To remote Crete came other rumours of a larger unrest
spreading over Europe. The world had scarcely recovered
from the shock of Hitler's rape of Czechoslovakia when the
quarrel over Danzig mounted in intensity, and the relations
between Berlin and Warsaw grew more and more strained.
Mussolini in Rome and Franco in Madrid made hectoring
speeches, directed against the confused democracies, who
were still clinging to the hope that what they were quite
unprepared for was not likely to happen. Somehow it
would all be settled by compromise, by conferences and
peripatetic politicians. The world could not be so mad as
to plunge into a second war. The growth of air power
would bring unimaginable horrors on mankind. The United
States at a safe distance, gave notice that it would not again
be drawn into the quarrel—Europe was a congenital epileptic
beyond all cure. France, locked in incessant political turmoil, proved that progressive division led to a sum total of
ineptitude. England affirmed its faith in the evanescent by
a Peace Ballot, and then, in a sudden fury of apprehension,
distributed gas masks and dug waterlogged ruts in its public
parks and gardens.

A Cassandra-like instinct worried Richard. He never
made a plan but what he prefaced it with the remark : " If
the war doesn't stop us." Some of his colleagues scoffed ;
others were simply annoyed by the reminder of something
they wished to dismiss. Cesare Morosini, whenever the
subject came up, was a buoyant balloon. There would be
no war ; there could be no war. Hitler and Mussolini were
too strong. France was a broken reed. England would
exercise her genius for compromise. Why worry ? They
were planning a World Exhibition at Rome, which showed
how little the Duce believed that war was inevitable.

Richard was now well enough for the journey to his
home at Vori. Happily they would not be deprived of
Morosini's company. The excavations at Phaistos, the
royal palace second in importance and size only to the one
at Knossos, where he worked with the Italian Archæological
Mission, were only an hour away. At one time he and
Richard had shared a small peasant's house, before the old

monastery had been acquired.   Morosini was now his guest there.   For a whole month Sylvia had been taking lessons in modern Greek, and Morosini, who spoke it fluently, had offered to continue them at Vori.

Early one June morning Richard and Sylvia said good-bye to the Villa Crane.   Sylvia was a little sad at leaving a place where she had been so happy.   There had been long mornings on the veranda in the cool shade, with distant Mount Ida, often crowned with clouds, as a background. The vine pergola was crowded with grapes ;   the garden was bright with scarlet cannas, tall yuccas, the large saucer-like flowers of the purple cyclamen, roses, pink oleanders, and the green fig and lemon trees that provided a grateful shade.

Anastasia and Nikephoro, the boy of all work, had been sent ahead to the Villa Vouni, to prepare for their coming. To avoid the heat they started early, soon after six o'clock, in Richard's car.   They followed the old southern route southward through the ravines and over the mountain passes that for centuries had connected the two palaces of Knossos and Phaistos.   It had been the only highway, a mere mule path between the north shore and the south.   For some miles they threaded the valley and the foothills above the stony bed of a withered river.   They had now entered the province of Malvoisie, a land of vineyards, home of the once-renowned Malvoisy wine.   The ravine grew narrow ; they entered a fastness of mountains and ascended by a series of bends towards lonely Prinias, a tiny village crouching in the shadow of the massif of Mount Ida.   They were still climbing, in a desolate wild country of glaring limestone crags and sparse vegetation, when they came to Hagia-Varvara, a small village from which they began the ascent of the pass, two thousand feet high.   Below them now opened a lovely vista, the rich valley of Messara, with its lush meadows, orchards, and plantations.   Deep in the pocket of the mountains stretched the garden of Crete, from the great chain of the Lassithi in the east, to the blue bay of Messara.

They began to descend now, and Richard made a side excursion to show Sylvia the site of ancient Gortyn, set in the plain crossed by the River Lèthe, famous in classical lore. Gortyn had been the Roman capital of the province of Crete and Cyrene. Here had been a sanctuary of the Egyptian gods and, near by, a temple of Apollo.

The dim centuries and the lost generations had left their successive signs : a temple built six or seven centuries B.C., showing the Minoan influence, a Doric terrace of six half-columns, and, witness of the imperial era, another temple, divided in three sections by a colonnade. Before the temple there still remained the basin for the sacrifices and the Roman altar. Near by the temple lay the ruins of the Governor's residence, built for some homesick Roman, in the first century A.D., rebuilt in the fourth, and inhabited until the Byzantine era. How many Romans had sat and dreamed beside the little nymphæum ? wondered Sylvia. It was all so desolate, so sweetly sad. These temples crumbled, forgotten by time, washed by the rains, burned by the suns, and visited by the soft beauty of the moon.

A little more distant, a Christian basilica of the sixth century stood close by a theatre of the second, and, close by the latter, as if to chide the cults of these upstarts, a wall carried the text of the Law of Gortyn, the fundamental source of all Greek law, pronounced six centuries before Christ. A little distant lay the fragmentary ruins of the market-place and the acropolis of the dead town.

They made one more detour, to the subterranean quarry from which ancient Gortyn had been built. The innumerable bewildering recesses of this quarry, which they did not dare to penetrate, had for long created the belief that this was the original labyrinth of the Minotaur. Whatever its true nature, it had seen dire events in the human calendar. It was here, in the War of Independence of 1824, that the hunted Christians had sought refuge from massacre by the Turks. It had been explored once by an English engineer from Retimo, who, taking a hint from the skein supplied by Ariadne to Theseus, had entered the fearful labyrinth by means of a bag of chaff with which he laid a trail as he went.

" Do the natives go into it ? " asked Sylvia as they stood by the entrance of the excavation, plainly a work of deliberate art.

" They're frightened to death of it," replied Richard.

" I could find only one man in the surrounding villages who would make the attempt with me.   I followed the method of Theseus and went into it with a reel of twine.   It was an eerie experience, walking along those silent corridors, and wondering how many centuries had elapsed since men had first been lost in it.   In the twenty-third corridor we came across human bones.   They wore Roman manacles, and we surmised they were runaway slaves who hid there and never got out again.   If you like, one day we'll go into it, with the proper precautions.   Cesare and I found a secret exit.   I've got a plan of it."

" A secret exit ? "

" It would seem like it.   A track mounts up through an interior cavern and comes out in a chimney of rocks.   From there a passage leads to the stables of our old monastery. It's possible, of course, that the monks may have made the secret entrance for a refuge when the Turks began to invade the island.   The labyrinth could hold a thousand people without crowding, and the cave, from which the passage runs to our stables, could hold five thousand.   What it was all made for remains a complete mystery."

" Do you think the Cretans put their prisoners in it and left them ?   Or was it a prison used by the Romans of Gortyn ? "

Richard shook his head.   " We've thought of everything like that.   The Cretans were not a cruel race, judged by contemporary standards.   Also, they wouldn't waste prisoners.   Like the Romans, they always put them to work in the mines or the galleys.   One day we may solve the mystery.   I've been charting the labyrinth for a couple of years and have almost finished, but so far we are no nearer a solution."   He glanced at his watch.   " We must go. It's two hours to the villa from here, and climbing all the way."

A mile farther along the road they left their car at a peasant's house and found five mules, with a man and a boy awaiting them.   Their baggage was loaded on two of the mules, and they mounted.   Their mules followed a stony mountain track, with perilous turns above rocky precipices overhanging the barren ravines.   They were now turning towards the west and from time to time had glimpses of the distant sea in the Bay of Messara. The old muleteer and his boy prodded the animals. The plain was misty below them. The air was fresher ; the scrub gave place to the arid slopes of the sun-baked mountains. They descended, traversed a gorge and mounted again, and then turned a sharp corner of the cliff's face. Sylvia gave a cry of delight, staring incredulously at the scene spread before her. From a wide terrace high on the mountainside they looked over the successive ranges that shut in the wide valley below, to the blue sea stretching south to the hazy horizon.

" Over there lies Libya. In a direct line of about two hundred miles you'd strike Tobruk, and south-east you'd hit Egypt and Alexandria. Well, what do you think of it ? " asked Richard.

Sylvia was wordless for a few moments of wonder, gazing at the vast blue dome of heaven, the mauve mountain ranges, the olive-green plain of Messara, the amethyst sea fading mistily on a horizon beyond which lay the vast African continent, with Libya and Egypt but a day's sail southwards. It was a scene wherein the world of fabled history stood suddenly revealed.

The old man with the mules began to name the squat villages in the long valley, little white settlements of houses set amid orchards and groves of lemon trees. The sun burned fiercely in this thinner air wherein utter silence reigned, save for the rattle of stones beneath the hoofs of the restless mules. At last Sylvia found some poor, inadequate words for the ecstasy of the moment.

" Oh, Dick, it's like waking in Paradise ! I could live for ever with this view. I know now how the ancient gods felt on Parnassus, hearing the planets sing ! "

" I'm afraid they heard a lot more ! " laughed Richard, pleased with the delight he had given her. " Well, this is the view you'll live with for some months. We're home."

" Home ! But I don't see anything ! " exclaimed Sylvia.

Richard made no answer and signalled the muleteer to move on. In a hundred yards they made another turn around the face of the cliff. Even then Sylvia found no answer to her question until a gateway, hewn from huge limestone blocks, gave access to a long, level terrace.

Beyond it, and of the colour of the rock against which it crouched, so closely that it was almost indistinguishable, stretched a ruined monastery. The whole sunlit world lay at their feet, valley and mountains and sea.

Their mules halted at the far end of the terrace. In a restored section of the ruin a door opened and an old woman appeared, accompanied by two other smiling women, all chattering. It was Anastasia and the servants of the Villa Vouni.

CHAPTER IV

VILLA VOUNI

THERE are halcyon periods in the lives of the fortunate when to be aware of them is to be fearful. The perfect hours must inevitably breed the storms that threaten the tranquil scene. The days passed, days of smiling skies, of sunshine and clear mountain air, of vistas of light and of luminous clouds, of morning's fresh glory on a world that seemed untouched from the birth of Time. The evenings brought sunsets of rose and purple. The gorgeous pageant of summer unfolded itself through days filled with the aromatic scents of the mountain wilderness and the happy day-long shrilling of cicadas in the bushes. Sylvia touched the peak of human felicity. Sometimes a shadow came, now faint, now strong, but it could not endure in the utter peace of this mountain eyrie. Even the reminder of the dead generations, of the monks who had lived here until the Turks shattered their domain, could not diminish the loveliness of these days, with the fair promise of each crimson evening, each silver dawn.

June passed. The lemons on the trees ripened, hanging in arched arbours like golden globes. Heavy clusters of purple grapes weighted the cool pergolas. Huge jars of blazing oleanders, zinnias, dwarf quinces, and pomegranate bushes spaced the long terrace. Aromatic thyme, mingled with the scent of roses, drifted in the zephyrs of the noon. Loveliest of all was the soft and tranquil night, the star-spangled dome over the dim shapes of mountains sleeping in the silver flood of moonlight.

Richard had begun work again. Cesare Morosini had joined him. Together they spent their mornings over at Phaistos, where they were now excavating behind the ancient theatre, among ruins that belonged to the First Minoan Period, some three thousand years before Christ.

Sylvia, under the guidance of Cesare, had made several

excursions across the plain of Messara that lay below them, to the three mountain terraces on which the old palace had been built. It possessed a splendid staircase, eighty feet wide, from which there was a magnificent view. Perhaps the most enthralling sight for Sylvia was a series of beehive tombs, the necropolis at Kalyvia. These tombs consisted of domed rotundas, some fifty feet in height, with a diameter of about sixty feet. From each tomb one passed into a small rectangular room, the sepulchre chamber. Here the Minoans had placed the dead, without coffins or embalming. The entrance to the tomb had then been sealed by filling in the earth of the descending approach. Buried as in bottles, they were hidden from sight and the passing centuries. Solid, dry, and long ago despoiled of all their contents, the tombs now stood empty, as if awaiting new interments.

Richard and Cesare were employing about a dozen natives on the present excavations. It was slow work, for the exciting discoveries had passed with the main work, now completed, on the vast palace, which had never received the publicity that had been accorded the palace at Knossos.

Morosini returned to the Villa Vouni each day with Richard. He had a room at the eastern end of the terrace which had once been the library of the monastery. Every day, since there were no interruptions in their isolated lives, Sylvia had a lesson in modern Greek from Morosini, who proved an excellent teacher. She had also begun to practice with him in the Italian tongue. He congratulated her on proving an apt pupil. In the long, cool evenings they dined on the terrace in the shadow of the mountain that rose precipitously behind them. The food was simple and wholly of native origin. It was imported by mules from the nearest village of Hagi Deka.

" This must be the most secret place in all the world," said Sylvia one afternoon as they sat under the pergola, having finished lunch. " How did anyone find it ? "

" Those old Greek monks had a passion for the inaccessible. They wanted no contact with the visible world. You should see all those monasteries in Greece, clinging to their mountain eyries," said Richard.

" But how did they exist financially ? " queried Sylvia.

" Look at the size of this place ! It probably housed three or four hundred monks."

" Ah, they didn't neglect to collect their rents down there," said Richard, indicating the misty valley below. " They owned farms and orchards. They even owned a line of boats at Matala, in the bay there, that took produce to Greece and Egypt."

" They sometimes owned something much more profitable, too, the old scallywags ! Some of these monasteries had interests in Siberian mines. The Russian Revolution hit them hard," Morosini added.

" The complete history of this place," said Richard, " if one could obtain it, would cover several centuries of astonishing facts. When we cleared out one of the rooms here we found an old parchment, from the Grand Master of the Knights of Rhodes, saying that a new consignment of wounded was on the way, if the ship got through. They were wounded Crusaders from Acre, if you please. The hospital at Rhodes was full."

" When was that ? "

" It was the Third Crusade, in 1189, a grand flop, except for all the profiteers in Venice and Alexandria. Oh, and I mustn't forget a very successful one at Cappadocia—possibly our friend Saint George, who had more to do with army contracts than with dragons," said Richard.

" Dick's an iconoclast—you know that, Sylvia ? " exclaimed Morosini.

" My authority is Gibbon's *Decline and Fall of the Roman Empire*," retorted Richard.

" I can't believe that this was once a war hospital ! " said Sylvia. " Why was it left to fall into ruins ? "

" Oh, that's very simple. The monks scurried out when the Turks came in, in 1669. Then they came back and stayed until the massacre of 1866, by the Turks, who had a short way with Christians. When they got tired of killing them they'd go to sleep for a while. But every decade or so they'd massacre a few, to keep their hand in. You might take Sylvia to the Melidoni Grotto one day," said Richard, turning to Morosini.

" Well, it's rather horrible still," he answered.

" What is it ? " asked Sylvia.

" There's a grotto on the road from Retimo. It was dedicated in antiquity to Hermes," began Morosini.

" You should feel at home there," said Sylvia quickly, and then regretted her folly.

Morosini looked at her with his serious brown eyes.

" Why ? " he asked, watching her.

" Oh, nothing ! " she returned, blushing. Not for the world would she let him know that when talking to her brother she referred to him as Hermes.

Morosini's quick eyes saw the blush and the swift glance of comprehension that passed between brother and sister. Sitting there in the mottled light of the pergola, framed against a background of hanging grapes, with his golden hair, his white teeth and brown skin, he might have come straight from Olympus. His sandalled feet lacked only wings. Perhaps he had laid these aside with his caduceus and towards evening would retrieve them and fly over the darkening Ægean on some mission of the gods.

" The grotto's enormous," continued Morosini. " You go in under a low arch and then descend into the yawning blackness, with your lamp emphasising the darkness. After a time you come to a cavern, eighty feet in height, propped up in the centre by a tremendous stalactite pillar. All around you hang stalactites, rows of them in weird masses and folds. It looks like the shrine of the Titans. Then you crawl down a passage into a second cavern, over a hundred feet high, the whole surface covered with stalactites of all shapes—flutes, columns, and uprising bases of stalagmite that almost touch the descending giant icicles. It's all very terrifying even if you don't know what's happened there." He paused and, seeing Sylvia engrossed by his description, continued : " In 1822 there was one of those periodic insurrections of the Cretans against the Turks. A Turk, Hussein Bey, marched against Melidoni to wipe it out. The people, about a hundred of them, took refuge in the grotto, with several weeks' provisions. The Turks couldn't get in, and when the Cretans refused to come out Hussein Bey ordered sulphur, resin, and straw to be burned in the entrance. The smoke rolled into the grotto, and the trapped victims retired to the second cavern, but ultimately this was filled with smoke, and they were all suffocated.

The Turks waited for some days. Then, hearing no signs of life, they went in and plundered the bodies. Then they departed. A week after they had gone three of the villagers went to see what had happened to their relatives and friends. What they saw was so terrible that two of them died of shock within a few days. Some years after, the Archbishop of Crete blessed the grotto, and the bones of the victims were gathered together in the outer cavern. There's still a sickening odour of corpses in the place, and you feel stifled and choked with horror. No, I don't think it's a place to visit."

They were silent for a few moments, then, breaking the silence with a sacrilegious levity, came the raucous music of a band playing jazz music. It was Anastasia's radio, tuned in to Athens and the Harlem Sextet at the Hotel Grande Bretagne.

" O God ! Can you explain why an old Greek crone of seventy conceives a passion for twentieth-century Negro jazz ? " protested Richard. " Shades of the old monks addicted to Gregorian chants ! "

" They probably love it, for a change," said Morosini.

" Just imagine—here, a thousand miles from anywhere, to find yourself bombarded by ukuleles and trombones blown by corybantic niggers in Athens ! Tell Nasty we want our siesta, and she'll have to postpone her dose of Harlem blues," cried Richard as Sylvia went along the terrace to the kitchen quarters.

The blare died away ; the two men lay back in their long chairs. A profound silence reigned. When Sylvia returned an hour later, Morosini had drowsily opened his eyes. He made a sign and, stealthily rising so as not to wake the sleeping Richard, he tiptoed along the pergola until he had reached Sylvia. It was the hour for her Greek lesson, which they usually took in a corner of the terrace built over the ruin of the former refectory. From this corner they had a superb panorama of the mountains, the fertile valley with its summer-shrunken river, and, in the clear light of afternoon, the blue-green sea stretching to the horizon.

They seated themselves on a swing couch beneath a yellow awning. Sylvia had now progressed as far as reading

E

the Athens newspapers, and from articles in this they made conversations. Little by little, arising from out of these discussions, she had gleaned more and more of Morosini's life, his views, his ambitions. He had an unshakable belief in the resurrection of the ancient Roman Empire, in the indisputable hereditary right of Italy to govern the Mediterranean, and in the quasi divinity of the man who symbolised this new era of Italian greatness. Often they fell into dispute, but with his knowledge of political history, his nimble mind and burning faith, Sylvia rarely succeeded in gaining her own viewpoint. She began to wonder, a little uneasily, whether, after all, a faith so passionately held by this new generation of the Fascists might not succeed in achieving its goal by pertinacity, if not by active aggression. The rape of Abyssinia had stirred England from her lethargy into a temporary indignation. But the mood had passed. The pathetic and dignified little Emperor, in the topee and cloak, had pleaded the cause of Abyssinia before a morally bankrupt assembly of the League of Nations, which had been too cowardly to apply its Sanctions. Now, in sleepy old Bath, he nursed a grievance that had become, for most, a bore. Hitler, profiting by this diversion, had marched into the demilitarised Rhineland, his success assured by a corrupt France and a peace-indoctrinated England. *Sanzioni!* hissed Italy, with the leer of a gunman holding up a saloonful of craven politicians. And then Italy had attacked Albania, choosing Holy Friday for her brigandage. " *Christos aneste!* (Christ is risen !) " said the Greek peasants, greeting Richard Day. " *Alethos aneste!* (Truly He is arisen !) " he replied, and saw in their faces the apprehension that Eastertide had brought. They remembered the murderous attack on Corfu in 1923, in those early years of the Fascist dictator. When would he strike again, menacing the Greek homeland ?

The veil had now been torn from the designs of the two dictators. The Greek newspaper which Morosini had opened before them, intended for the reading lesson, was full of the menacing Albanian situation. Greece was alarmed. France and England, no longer able to evade the issue, tactfully deplored Italy's provocative step.

Sylvia began to read the paper aloud, with Morosini's

help. They had carefully worked through two columns of political comment when Sylvia felt she could restrain herself no longer.

"Can't we read something else?" she asked, putting down the paper.

"Yes, but don't you find it interesting?"

"How do you think I find it, Cesare? You must know what all this means!"

"If you think war, you are wrong; there will not be a war. I am certain of it. Strong men prevent wars; the weak permit them."

"You think England is so weak that she will let Italy and Germany hold a revolver at our head?"

"Oh, my dear, isn't that a little melodramatic? There will be no need of such a thing. Your country will recognise our right to an honourable place in the world."

"And if we shouldn't—if we don't happen to think that what you are doing is honourable, Corfu, the Tyrol, the Dodecanese, Abyssinia, Albania, the Italians in Spain, the backing of Hitler—what then?" demanded Sylvia spiritedly.

"Why, then we might have to deliver an ultimatum. There are millions of our people and millions in Germany who will no longer be denied their rights," said Morosini.

"You believe in Mussolini and Hitler? You would support them even to declaring war on us?" asked Sylvia.

"I think you are taking an extreme view. There are sensible men on both sides," said Morosini, smiling. "But need we discuss it, Sylvia?"

"Yes, it's no use our going on and not being honest with each other. You believe in your Duce to the point of fighting for him?"

"All of Italy would do its duty. Mussolini is the voice of all of us."

"Out of jail, or in internment camps, and driven into exile? Sforza, Salvemini, Toscanini, Ferrero?"

"My dear, I can't see where this discussion will land us. And you're not learning your Greek," he said smoothly, picking up a book. "Shall we try the *Fables*?"

Sylvia suppressed an angry retort about Italian fables being more important just now than Greek ones. He could not know that something more than dislike of the whole

totalitarian creed lay behind her protest. It hurt her to
hear Morosini propagating the Fascist doctrine. A man of
intelligence, of honour and fair play, how could he condone
these bludgeonings, the blackshirt tyranny with its castor-
oil discipline, its screaming sycophantic press, led by the
vitriolic Gayda ; how could he support the prancing of the
playboy Ciano with the simian Goebbels, Bruno Mussolini's bombs unfolding " like beautiful flowers " on the
helpless Abyssinian peasants, the trussing of Libyan *kaids*
like hens, and dropping them as high-altitude bombs on
their own too-independent villages ? How could he, so
charming and cultured, with such a proud history behind
him, heir of one of the great civilisations of the earth, pros-
titute his soul and intellect to support the balcony bellowings
of a sawdust Cæsar ?

She could understand the young German filling his mind
with the Nietszchean nonsense of a perverted house-painter.
The bovine stupidity of the German people was unaccount-
able. They had missed the civilising influences of ancient
Rome, the sensibility born of the Latin spirit. But these
Italians, the race of Dante and Petrarch, Da Vinci and
Michelangelo, Bellini and Raphael, Palestrina and Verdi,
heirs of the golden Renaissance, the fetter-breaking *risorg-
mento*, sons of Rienzi and Garibaldi, how could they descend
to a creed of brute force ?

Cesare Morosini, with the grace of his youth and the
vivid play of his alert mind, combined in his personality
qualities so attractive that he seemed the natural heir to the
Medicean splendour. He had appeared to her in this
bright light of the Ægean day like some young knight
stepping from the canvas of Giorgione. Love, if that was
a name for the exaltation of spirit she had known through
these three months of happiness, had pierced her with
shafts. The lean brown hand, the gold of his sun-bleached
hair, that sudden light of his inquiring eyes, physical attri-
butes all, superimposed themselves upon her consciousness
of his voice, his swift mind, his pleasure in her slightest
interest. She loved him, despite the warning voices that
would guard her from folly. He was a foreigner ; he had
a philosophy to which she was fundamentally opposed. His
life would be passed in scenes that were strange to her,

among people who could never receive her as one of themselves. The children of such a union—she let her thoughts go as far as that—would have to straddle two worlds, or grow indifferent or even antagonistic to the racial inheritance of one of the parents. There was also the difference of religion. To all these difficulties must be added another, the threat of a break between two nations, more bitter because of the long accord it would shatter.

No, said the voice of caution within her; and yet how strong was the attraction of his presence, setting all warnings at nought! His body, his mind, they combined to hypnotise her senses so that she found herself helpless in the bondage of his charm.

Sylvia looked at him now as he sought the page in the *Fables*. He was so kind, so patient; his presence was so invigorating, that she lived in the fullness of her faculties only when he was near. And all her feeling might be founded on a false assumption. He had given no clear sign, shown no awareness of anything but casual pleasure in her company. He was always gay and supplemented every whim of hers with his own eager interest.

Sometimes she led him to talk of his own home, his parents and brothers and sisters. She began to know the life in the vast old palace in Rome, or in the rambling villa in Tuscany, a community life of grandfather and grandmother, of parents, of single and married brothers and sisters, with bewildering titles and names : the *principessa*, the *duchessa*, the *marchese*, the *conte*, and a brood of *fanciulli* and *bambini*, mixed up with English and French governesses and family retainers. It seemed to be a dignified communal life bound by the patriarchal spirit. They were poor, as the old families of Italy were poor, sacrificing all independence to fruitless dignity.

One sister, Cesare's favourite, had broken with tradition. She had defiantly married a French artist of peasant stock, an irreligious, impecunious fellow twenty years her senior. They lived in an unbelievable state of cheerful disorder in a Provençal village. Emilia's worst offence, after five years of this mis-alliance, was that she was happy and defiant. She had married a bad artist, but a good fellow, who made fun of the Church, the aristocracy, and, what was the greatest affront, the august traditions of the Morosinis. Sylvia hoped to meet the adventurous Emilia one day. She must have much of Cesare's zest for life.

" I think we got as far as here," said Cesare, finding the page.

She did not seem to hear, and he looked up from the book. She lay back on the cushions, staring skyward, her eyes and mind far away. He made no comment for a few moments and took his pleasure in the lovely line of her throat and profile, the crown of her soft brown hair. Then, aware of his watchful waiting, she smiled.

" They must be very pleasant thoughts; you are so lovely like that," he said, paying her one of the few compliments he had made in words.

She did not move for a few moments or betray by any sign that he had said anything unusual. Then, leaving her train of thought and half turning her head, she smiled at him.

" Cesare, do you think it's any use my learning Greek ? " she asked.

" Of course ! You're doing very well. I heard you talking to Nike after lunch. The boy understood you quite well," he answered.

" Oh, I don't mean that. Is it going to be any use ? Where do you think we shall all be a year from now ? "

" I should be very unhappy if I thought I shouldn't be here then," he said, looking down at her.

" Cesare, I think sometimes you are a little like your— whatever his name was—that politician who trusted nobody."

" Dear me ! " laughed Morosini. " You don't mean Machiavelli ? If so, I'm not flattered ! "

" Yes, I'm sorry, Cesare, but you're not a fool, and I'm not a fool. Everything's going wrong, very wrong. The Rome-Berlin Axis—it means something. It must lead to war. What'll be the use then of having learned modern Greek ? We shan't be here ; that is, we English. You might, since you claim it's your sea."

Her earnest face searched his, but if she had hoped to find him disconcerted or provoked to candour, she was disappointed. His eyes looked into hers with a playful mocking smile in them as he spoke.

" Very well, perhaps I am Michiavellian, and the Duce also. If that is so, why worry ?   The Axis is a piece of bluff to make your elegant Mr. Eden and your truculent Mr. Churchill take serious notice of our serious grievance."

" We might call your bluff ! "

" If you did, nothing would happen.   There is too much good will, even after Sanctions, between us—the traditions are too strong," he answered.

" But you say you resent all that tradition means—a grateful Italy, subservient to the rich tourists who want Italy to be an impoverished nation of hotel-keepers and waiters."

" My dear Sylvia, I believe this is just a skilful distraction to get away from our Greek.   I'm not going to argue with you any more.   The clouds will blow away and the sky will be as serene as this."

He waved towards the deep blue heaven above them. " Now, here we are—the tenth fable of Æsop.   Read ! "

He passed the book, giving her one of his conquering smiles, while he corrected her from time to time.   They worked hard ; the sun began to fall down the sky.

" Very good !   You're a brainy girl," he said when she came to the end of the fable.   " And now——"

" You want your drink !   I'll wake Richard.   Will you make the cocktails ? "

Morosini went into the house.   Every evening, before they dined under the pergola, they drank their cocktails at this end of the terrace, watching the light turn from gold to purple on the deepening folds of the mountains.

Richard was not asleep.   He was reading the latest London *Times* when Sylvia approached.   He folded it up and walked to the terrace with her.   He was angry at a speech he had just read, made by the Prime Minister in the House of Commons.

" Either he's the biggest humbug that ever lived, or he's a silly old man.   He's ' deeply shocked ' by Mussolini's latest move.   Shocked !   My God !   Churchill's been telling 'em for the last five years ! "

" Don't say anything, Dick," said Sylvia, and seeing her brother's questioning look, added, " I've been arguing with Cesare again.   He'll think we're crazy on the subject."

" I agree.   It's useless to discuss it with Cesare.   Don't do it. The Fascists know what they're after. They haven't put guns on Leros, Sardinia, and Pantelleria to shoot ducks with. If we don't——"

He broke off. Morosini approached with the tray and set it on the stone table.

" What a glorious evening ! " he exclaimed, surveying the scene as he vigorously rattled the shaker. He had begun to fill the glasses when Richard lifted his hand and checked Sylvia, who was talking to him.

" Listen ! " he said.

There was silence except that a faint throbbing filled the upper air.

" Planes," said Morosini. " They're coming this way." The rhythmic throbbing slowly increased in volume.

" There must be a number of them," observed Richard, scanning the sky.

" Look ! There they are ! " exclaimed Morosini, pointing.

They followed his hand. Far off, like small birds, the blue-grey shapes moved steadily across the upper sky. They slowly drew nearer over the immense dome of space.

" They're flying in formation. They must be military planes. Do you think they're landing here ? " asked Richard.

They were nearer and larger now, proceeding in a V formation, strictly held. The reverberation of their engines filled the sky.

" Why, they're bombers ! " cried Richard. " They must be Italian."

Morosini made no answer for a while. He watched them intently. They had come down to a thousand feet and were bearing directly for the island.

" Yes, Savoias, our finest. Fifteen of them," said Morosini, his gaze fixed on them.

They watched and waited. Nearer and nearer they came in beautiful, steady formation.

" They make you feel quite powerless—they're so sinister," said Sylvia. The drone of their powerful engines almost buried her last words.

" Where have they come from ? " asked Richard of Morosini.

" Possibly Rhodes, or Leros. I think they must be going

to Tobruk or Benghazi in Tripoli. We have aerodromes there. What a beautiful sight ! " exclaimed Morosini.

" Yes, beautiful, until you think what they can do," commented Richard, lifting his glass. " Well, here's to your night-mary-nostrum," he added, drinking.

" Dick, what an awful pun ! " protested Sylvia, raising her glass. In the act of doing so she detected a shadow of hurt pride in Morosini's eyes, but it passed instantly, and he smiled back at her.

" We've admired your navy so often, sailing our seas, that you mustn't begrudge us a little display in the air," he said amiably.

" And you still say there won't be a war ? " asked Sylvia.

" My dear Sylvia ! I'm pinning my faith on the common sense of two far-seeing men who will seek to pre-serve peace in Europe," he answered.

Richard laughed and held out his glass for Morosini to replenish.

" Meaning Hit and Muss, I suppose ? " he asked. " To preserve us from what ? "

" Communism and anarchy," replied Morosini.

Richard was about to make a retort when he saw the appeal in Sylvia's eyes.

" What a perfect evening, now the bumblebees have gone," he said calmly.

They dined as the light waned and the streamers of crim-son and orange dissolved in the pale emerald sky. Their eyrie was the last outpost of the dying day. Before they had finished the meal, Leander, their soft-slippered waiter, brought out the candles, whose flames burned upright in the still air.

Morosini was an excellent talker, never forcing his views or monopolising the conversation. Laughter was never far distant from his talk. Art, music, literature, and human folly, all contributed to his delight in life. But those who would have ascribed to his easy talk the character of a dilettante would have erred. In his master passion, arch-æology, he had the equipment of the scholar, allied with the spirit of the pioneer. Only once did their animated conversation turn a dangerous corner. The subject of aerial

surveying for archæological purposes, and some of Morosini's experiences, came up.

" You don't fly yourself ? " asked Sylvia, surprised.

" Oh, yes, I love flying ! "

" Do you do much of it ? "

" Yes, I've taken the regular courses," he replied, and,
seeing she had not quite understood, he added : " I am a
reserve officer in our air force. I know those Savoias that
came over quite well."

Richard's next remark carried them away from a confession that seemed like a challenge to Sylvia.

" What about that guitar of yours, Cesare ? " he said.
" I feel like a little music."

" Certainly, I'll get it," he answered.

When he had gone into the house, Richard spoke.

" Sylvia, my dear, let me give you a little advice. You're
upset by Cesare's blind faith in the Duce and all it means.
Don't worry over it, and, above all, don't make a contest of it
with Cesare. You'll only hurt one another, and you can't
change him. Avoid the subject. Patriotism isn't a matter
of logic or justice. I hate these Fascist and Nazi creeds.
They'll bring the whole world to bloodshed, because they
can't be lived with, but I can understand young Italians
and Germans, reared in the faith of self-sacrifice for the
Fatherland. It's a chance for the bullies and blackguards,
but there are also thousands of starry-eyed young men who
feel they are white knights in a sacred cause. You can't
persuade them otherwise. Cesare's one of them. You
must accept the fact. The stars in their courses will show
which of us is right."

He smiled at her, putting his hand over hers and
pressing it.

" Did you know he was an aviator in their air force ? "
asked Sylvia.

" Yes ; he's been away from time to time for training.
I know what might happen some day, but it doesn't alter
my affection for Cesare. He's honourable and fearless and
well bred. And, for all his brave talk, he had heart-
searching moments of apprehension, like all of us. Well, if
you'll——" He broke off at the sound of footsteps.

Cesare sat down and strummed the guitar, tuning it.

It shone in the faint candlelight.   It was now dark; the
stars were brilliant.   As he bent over it, his hair tumbling
from his brow, Sylvia had a sudden vision of a young squire
at the court of some cinquecento prince.

Cesare shifted his guitar and raised his head.   " What
shall I play ? " he asked.

" You might sing us a ballad," said Richard.

Cesare paused for a moment.   The air was very still and
warm.   Crickets chirruped in the garden.   Over the shoulder
of a grey mountain the moon had risen and threw a veil of
silver on the dim valley.   Perhaps the sight of the moon
suggested his song, for, softly strumming the guitar, Cesare
began to sing.   He had a light baritone voice, and his singing
was easy and spontaneous.

" *Quando la bella luna . . .*"

he began.   Sylvia had heard him before, and his voice
always aroused in her an almost unbearable melancholy.
And as she listened the thought ran in her : This is so
beautiful because it will be all gone so soon—the warm
night on the mountainside, the moonlight, the black
shadows of the branches, the voice of a young man playing
his guitar, my brother, myself, young in a word that is so
transcient.   Hold it for this moment ; let nothing of it
escape.   In other days to come you will wish to recall it,
to remember then how beautiful it was.

So thinking, she listened and watched the singer in the
moonlight, knowing happiness and love and fear.

CHAPTER V

FAREWELL, DEAR MOUNTAIN

JUNE, July fled ; August came with greater heat, it seemed to Sylvia. The maize and the tobacco had been cropped, the vintage completed. There had been festivals in the villages of the Messara valley, the women dancing in their vivid native costumes, the men in their brightly embroidered and tasselled coats and loose blue Turkish trousers. The long-bearded priests of the Greek Church, grave old patriarchs living in near poverty, gave thanks in their churches for the abundant harvest.

Richard, now completely restored to health, had insisted on making excursions, chiefly on mules, to show Sylvia the countryside. They had been down to the sea several times by the tortuous path that went through deep ravines and stony gullies until it struck the floor of the rich valley and followed the banks of the shrunken Ierapotamos.

In a short time Sylvia knew every secret path, the tracks used only by the mountain goatherds going from village to village. She knew the trail from the high plateau, across the barren face of the mountains, or through the stunted olive groves and cypresses of the lower belt, down to the dense vegetation of the steaming valley.

Most thrilling of all was the excursion they made from the stables of the villa, by the secret route down to the great caves and the labyrinth near Gortyn. It had been an unforgettable, awesome experience. She knew the people now. Morosini's able teaching bore fruit in friendly contacts with the proud and austere peasants of these mountain ways. " *Kalos orizete !* (Welcome !)," or " *Kaliméra sas !* (Good day to you !)," they called to her. It was a wholly new world and one whose life passed in eventless days, encompassed by the solitude of their remote and hidden dwelling.

The days were passing, and for Sylvia the end of this summer dream came like a lengthening shadow. The six

months of her visit had almost gone. Grandma Day's
letters began to sound with a more urgent note. The inter-
national scene grew daily more disquieting. That monstrous little man in Berlin, Herr Hitler, had raised his voice
to a higher pitch of hysteria in denunciation of the Polish
Corridor and " enslaved Danzig." Yet it was difficult in
the bright and peaceful air of Crete to believe this menace
of darkening clouds far to the north. Those disturbing
agents, newspapers, arrived late, and always there was a new
conference that might achieve something. No one had
warned the English in Crete to go home. Morosini was
still sure that the democracies would back down before the
aggressive resolution of the two dictators. They were too
strong for the soft and procrastinating democracies.

One voice, more than that of newspapers or of persons,
brought to them in their mountain retreat the growing
unrest of the world. It was the radio. Every day now, on
the short wave, they toured Europe. Athens, Rome,
Vienna, Berlin, Warsaw, Paris, London contributed their
contradictory versions. Politicians and diplomats seemed
to be in continuous transit from one capital to another.
Special correspondents said the situation was grave or less
grave, that a crisis had arrived or that there was no crisis.
The air was filled with bewildering versions, but the sum
total seemed to them, here in the Villa Vouni, that the
Germans grew more adamant, more threatening. By the
first week in August even Morosini seemed a little shaken
in his optimism. Russia's defection had alarmed the
English and had warned the Poles. But the Poles were
defiant, conscious of their good case, and the English cham-
pioned them. Nations began a semi-mobilisation. The
skies darkened.

Sylvia had arranged to return to England in September,
when Richard moved down from the villa to Herakleion for
the winter. She had never seen Rome, and Morosini
planned for her to return via the capital. He would go with
her and show it to her. He had to return there by the
second week for a training course. He held a pilot's commission in the air force reserve.

In the second week of August the situation looked better.
Chamberlain was exerting every effort as a mediator between

Germany and Poland. There would be no war, asserted
a leading British newspaper. But the tourist traffic began
to flow back from the Continent to England. A British
boat on a holiday cruise, scheduled to call at Herakleion—
obstinately advertised as Candia—curtailed its itinerary,
cut out Crete, and sailed for home.

"It's getting very serious," said Richard, after shutting
off the radio. "I'm wondering if you ought not to leave
earlier."

"And you? Will you stay?" asked Sylvia.

"Until it's quite definite war will break out, yes. Even
now I can't believe it's possible."

"What would you do if it did?" asked Morosini, across
the dinner table.

"I? Oh, I don't know. Offer my services in the army,
I suppose. It'll seem very odd, going back to that nonsense again. I always hated it," answered Richard. "It
would be odd if you and I ended up as deadly enemies,
Cesare."

"It is not possible. There will be no war. At the last
moment the Duce will step in and settle it."

"I haven't your faith in the Duce, my dear Cesare. Oh,
God, here we are on the old subject again. Let's have
some music on that guitar of yours."

Morosini fetched his guitar and strummed and sang. It
was a hot night; the air was heavy, the sky moonless.
To-night the music somehow failed to dispel their fears.
At eleven o'clock Richard again toured Europe on the short
wave. Germany came bellowing in; Rome was vigorous.
Nothing seemed to come out of London. Berne quoted
New York. The President of the United States had sent
a message to Herr Hitler. The British Ambassador in
Berlin had visited London for a consultation with the Prime
Minister and was now returning to Berlin with fresh
instructions. Prices on the London Stock Exchange had
rallied a little.

"Well, let's go to bed and see what to-morrow brings,"
said Richard, turning off the radio.

Another week passed, of rumours and counter rumours.
They began to tire of the incessant turmoil coming over the

air. At Phaistos Richard and Cesare had struck a promising vein, and a call had gone out for more labourers. Even the news that Germany, Poland and Russia, were mobilising somehow failed to stir them. But when they returned one early afternoon Sylvia rushed to meet them, as their mules came into the yard.

" Germany and Poland are at war ! Hitler's invaded Poland this morning at dawn ! Warsaw's already in flames," cried Sylvia. " I got it on the air after you'd gone this morning."

" And England ? " asked Richard, after a silence.

" There's nothing, nothing yet. The Cabinet's meeting."

" France ? What's France doing ? " asked Morosini.

" She's ordered full mobilisation, but nothing beyond that yet," answered Sylvia.

They walked into the house in silence and sat down. The first to speak was Richard.

" Well, here it is. A madman has set the world alight. It's a fire that won't be put out for many years," he said, quietly. " Sylvia, I'd like a drink— whisky and soda."

" You ? " asked Sylvia, of Morosini, going to the cabinet.

" Oh, thanks," he said, getting up and joining her.

She noticed his hand trembled as he held the siphon.

They drank in silence. Then Richard turned on the radio, and the world in agony leaped in on them. The German station was the first to come through. The army invading Poland was smashing all opposition. The *Luftwaffe* had driven the Polish planes out of the air. Warsaw, Cracow, Lwow were in flames.

The staccato German voice continued its catalogue of triumphs. Richard turned to Paris. Ministers were conferring with the President. He tried London next. The Cabinet was in continuous session. Richard switched off.

" But aren't we going to declare war ? " asked Sylvia.

" Inevitably, but England has to consult the Dominions," replied Richard. " Well, Cesare, what are you going to do now ? It's the hour of Mare Nostrum."

To Sylvia's surprise he looked at them with tears in his eyes. All his assurance had vanished.

" We shall stay out—we shall stay out ! " he repeated, as if to convince himself.

" Well, to-morrow we must get down to Herakleion and see about getting home, somehow," said Richard. " I hope Italy does stay out. We might then get back through France, instead of going by the sea the whole way." He stood up, emptying his glass. " I'm going to change. I hope it's a good dinner, my girl. Good dinners are going to be very rare soon," he said, and left the room.

§ 2

It was Saturday before they got away on the return journey to Herakleion. Richard was now irritable and worried by the news from England. Two days had gone and she had not declared war. Neither had France. Germany was sweeping through Poland, raining death from the air.

They reached Herakleion late on Saturday afternoon, going again to the Cranes', who had returned to their villa but gladly took them in. Young Crane had all the particulars about the journey to England. He was going with his wife to Athens and Brindisi, and then through Italy and France. The British Embassy in Athens thought it was possible. Italy was not coming in, and the frontier at Chiasso was open. This news revived Morosini's spirits, and he began to recover from the black depression that had settled upon him. He would go to Brindisi with them, and on to Rome.

On Sunday morning, towards noon, all Richard's angry impatience vanished. Over the air came the harsh, tired voice of the British Prime Minister explaining that all of England's efforts for peace had failed. Hitler had drawn the sword. The challenge had been accepted. England was now in a state of war with Germany.

" And France ? Where's France ? " asked Sylvia.

They agreed it was strange there was no word of France. Then in the evening came word that France, too, had declared war. Morosini's prophecy seemed to be true. Rome was calm. There was no word from Mussolini.

The next two days passed in frantic preparations, including a visit by Richard to Canea to see the American consular agent, to whom he entrusted his interests. The agent was buried in an avalanche of interests being thrust into his hands.

" Have you thought of one thing, Day ? I might have to unload all these interests on someone else. Everybody knows Greece will be in it. What about us ? We might come in. By God, we ought to ! " he exclaimed, turning the cigar in his mouth.

Richard looked at him for a moment or two without speaking. Then slowly he said :

" I'm glad to hear you say that. I hope America thinks what you think. If she doesn't, we're sunk. We've got nothing except our navy. Look at the *Luftwaffe* in Poland. We'll hold out perhaps for a few months, but we've practically no planes, no pilots, no guns. Our folks just wouldn't believe it could happen and France's the same."

" I guess we're the same, too. We're all caught with our pants down. Say, what's the matter with the democracies ? We can't say that Hitler fellow didn't give us plenty of notice. Holy Moses ! And there's Mussolini, too. He plans mischief around here. This island's lousy with Italians. You'd better look out for Cyprus and Malta. Say, this ain't very neutral, is it ? " he asked, grinning. " I'll be getting fired. If I do—and I wouldn't holler—let me tell you, I'll hand over everything to the Swiss Minister in Athens. Extraordinary people, the Swiss. They always hold the stakes and don't seem to make much out of it."

Richard said good-bye to the cheery fellow and spent a hectic hour with the shipping agent. It was absolutely impossible for him to guarantee the rail journey from Brindisi to Chiasso. And there were no cabins on the *Tasso* to Athens. They would have to sleep on the deck unless someone cancelled. The boat left at six on Tuesday evening.

Richard bought three tickets. They were travelling light, with only their clothes in handbags. All the furniture and other things up at the Villa Vouni had to be left. He had arranged for a man at Vori to go over and look after the place But it was an act of empty faith. The villa would certainly be pillaged. The peasants were not dishonest. They could not understand that anything left unguarded was not there

for anyone who wanted it.   That philosophy had reigned
for four thousand years.   Greeks had pillaged Minoans,
the Romans the Greeks, the Byzantines the Romans, the
Venetians the Byzantines, the Turks the Venetians.   It was
foolish to expect these Cretans to ignore the tradition.

A few English and French inhabitants of the island were
remaining and taking a chance.   They were mostly people
who had properties and had been settled for many years.
They were too bewildered to move.   It was unlikely Greece
would be involved.

And so the last day dawned, and the hour came when the
three of them, Richard, Sylvia, and Cesare, stood on the
little steamer's crowded deck and watched the island recede
from sight.   First they said farewell to Herakleion, its harbour and town, its villas and foothills, with regal Mount Ida
beyond.   The great range of the mountains shone clearly in
the morning sun.   Then followed the coastwise run to
Retimo, through the green-blue water, dazzling white where
it thrashed the rocks, and on to Canea in the dusk, with the
White Mountains holding the last light of evening, and all
the folds of the hills fading under the purple veil of night.
A lighthouse on the Akrotiri Peninsula blinked across the
dark water, and Crete was gone.

The silence that had held them as they watched a phase
of their lives float away on the widening sea was broken by
Morosini.

" *Dio   mio !* " he exclaimed.   " I left my guitar at the
villa ! "

§ 3

They had to wait two whole days at Brindisi before they
could secure places on the Brindisi-Milan express.   They
could not book beyond Milan.   A report came that, following France's declaration of war, the frontiers at Chiasso and
Domodossola had been closed to all trains coming from
France and Switzerland.   At Milan they could find out the
best route open to France.

Cesare Morosini became more hopeful as each day went
by with Italy not ordering full mobilisation.   He still hoped

and believed Italy would stay out of the war. Everything could be adjusted. Richard was sceptical and caustic. Everywhere in Brindisi there was enthusiasm for Germany's smashing success in Poland. Mussolini was backing the right horse. The war would be over soon. The Allies would have to make peace. Then Italy would realise her proper status in the Mediterranean. The Italian press was ecstatically pro-German, exhorted by the frenetic Signor Gayda. But a few Italians in the hotel who talked with Richard very covertly deplored the pro-German mania. " We have gone mad," said a little Italian to Richard.

" But you are wearing the Fascist pin ! " retorted Richard.

" Signore, we all wear Fascist pins—we are all good Fascists simply because life would be intolerable if we were not ! " the little man replied.

" Don't you see what that is leading you to ? If some of you haven't the courage to make a stand, you'll all be rushed over the precipice. Liberty has to be earned and fought for."

" Ah, you have no idea how we are spied on. *E terribile !* Signore, someone is looking ! Good-day, and *buon' viaggio* when you get away."

They made a few excursions, but the heavy shadow was upon them. Cesare had lost all his buoyancy, and yet his faith in Italy's destiny was never impaired. But he realised that a clash between Italy and England might occur at any moment. The newspapers were full of rumours. The French had been pushed into the war by England and had not wanted to fight. They had offered to concede Corsica to Italy if she would stay out. London had been bombed and was in flames. Three British battleships had been sunk by German submarines. England had no hope of survival.

" Dick, are we going to lose the war ? " asked Sylvia, on the last day as they went up to their bedrooms.

He did not reply at once, then :

" Do you want my honest opinion, or do you just want to be reassured ? "

" Your opinion."

" I know no more than most people, but being out of England these three years, here in the middle of the Mediter-ranean, has given me objectivity, I think. If England is not knocked out by air attack in the next six months, the decision will be reached here. If the Mediterranean goes, the British Empire goes. The Germans know that. That is the sole value of Italy to them."

" Can we hold the Mediterranean ? "

" I'm not sure. In our blindness we've given the Italians a long start. France is rotten ; Spain is antagonistic ; Turkey will remain neutral. We shall be on our own here —with the whole Atlantic and the Pacific to guard. I don't see how we can do it, even if Goering doesn't bomb us to bits. We have only one hope—America. It's a faint hope. She's disgusted with Europe ; she doesn't want trouble, and she imagines she's safe. At the moment she's so self-righteous she's passed laws to stop anyone buying munitions, hiring ships, or raising loans from her. Germany knows that, too. It plays her game admirably. Can you tell me how we, England and France, eighty millions, a hundred millions if you take in the colonies, all miserably unprepared and in a day-dream, can stand up to Germany's eighty, Japan's forty, and Russia's one hundred millions, to which you may add forty millions of the Italians ready to jump when we're going down—nearly three hundred millions, all fanatical, all armed to the teeth ? "

" Then you've no hope ? " asked Sylvia.

" I said America. I can't believe she's so blind that she doesn't know what happens to her if we go under, with the Atlantic and the Pacific hostile, and the Fascists and Nazis organised south of Panama."

" And she's our stock. We're cousins."

" I wouldn't count on that. The British stock's pretty well swamped, and I've never noticed that relations find blood's thicker than money. The real thing that may put us together is that we believe in the same things, the right of a nation to say what it wants, to live as it wants, and to kick out its government when it doesn't like it. If we go under, and all that goes with it, America would find that it's her turn next, for she'd be too obstreperous to the victors. America is vital to us and we to her, but will she know it in time ? "

They had reached their bedrooms. Sylvia stood a little dismayed. Richard smiled at her.

" Don't let me depress you, old girl. We're going home, whatever happens. And whatever happens, we wouldn't want to be anywhere else. Good night ! "

" Good night, Dick."

He kissed her and watched her until she had entered her room.

§ 4

The train for Milan was crammed. It seemed full of English, from India, from Egypt, from Palestine, from odd little islands all over the Mediterranean. There were old ladies and retired officers and officials uprooted from their villages and pensions. They took their seats with a defiant dignity, but even in their common distress they found it difficult to talk to strangers. There was only one sleeping-car, monopolised by government bigwigs from Cairo and Athens. They would have to sit up two nights and then might not get a rest at Milan. The previous train, they heard, had been fourteen hours late, delayed by troop move-ments. This one was heavily guarded by Fascists with revolver belts. The carriages were full half an hour before the train left.

In those last minutes, their places secured, Richard, Sylvia, and Cesare walked up and down the platform. They had said everything they had to say, and the minutes dragged. But at last the call to entrain was heard.

" Good-bye, Richard. Good fortune to you," said Cesare, gripping his friend's hand.

" Good-bye, Cesare, old boy—all the best," responded Richard. Then, going to the carriage, he left Cesare and his sister together. The poor boy was on the verge of tears, he saw !

" Cesare ! " said Sylvia.

" Sylvia ! " he cried in a strangled voice, taking both her hands. Suddenly his arms went around her, and he kissed her passionately. The tears welled in his eyes. " Cara mia ! I love you ! " he said, distractedly, his boy's face pressed to hers.

They clung together in utter despair. The train began to move. Richard, by the steps of the saloon, turned anxiously. Cesare stood back, and Sylvia hurried towards Richard, mounting with his assistance.

"Good-bye!" called Richard as the train quickened. "*A rivederci!*"

"*A rivederci!*" echoed Cesare.

He stood there, hatless, so young, so handsome, the tears now streaming down his face as he watched the train recede.

When they reached their seats Sylvia buried her face in her handkerchief, blinded with tears. She felt Richard take her hand and hold it. The train gathered speed. Presently she wiped her face and desperately smiled at her brother. An elderly Englishwoman opposite said very gently, " I've a new copy of the *Tatler*; would you like to see it ? "

Sylvia took the magazine and thanked her. She opened it and looked at the photographs of shooting parties on the Scottish moors, of country houses and seaside groups, a smiling England, now in deep shadow.

Sylvia turned the pages, scarcely seeing them. Cesare had always wanted to say he loved her ; he had wanted for a long time, but he knew the difficulties ; the impassable barrier the Moloch of war had placed between them.

BOOK III

SO IMMORTAL A FLOWER

To have fought, to have lost, to have fallen
to have won from the losing such glory ;
Under a rain of death so immortal a flower
to have planted ;
In the hush of even that falls
when the strife of the day is a story,
In the breaking of waves will their voices
sound o'er a sea enchanted ;
Here shall we know how their valour
gained them a raiment immortal,
Listen, and grieve, and be proud
where, deathless, they passed the Portal.

CHAPTER I

THESEUS MEETING ARIADNE

It was early dawn when she woke. In the grey light of the
April day she could dimly make out the figures sleeping in
the cabin which the destroyers' officers had put at their
disposal. Through the porthole the leaden face of the
Ægean Sea shone dully, touched with the breaking light of
the April day. Sylvia Day lay back in the bunk for a few
moments. The ship's engines pounded ; overhead there
was the sound of restless feet. They were at sea after the
nightmare of those last days during the retreat from Larissa
to Volos ; the Greek expedition had ended, ended in utter
disaster for the Greeks, the British, the Australians, and the
New Zealanders. All that courage, all those lives had been
expended in vain. Before the onrush of the Germans,
triumphant in the air, overwhelmingly supplied with everything, mere courage had not been enough. The gallant

151

Greeks, triumphant so long before the Italians, had been broken. Epirus and Macedonia had surrendered ; the King had fled to Crete. Athens, they had heard, was being mercilessly bombed, with terrible destruction among the transports at the Piræus. It could only be a matter of hours before the Nazi flag flew over the Acropolis.

Sylvia tried to remember the date in this year of 1941, this month of April. But all dates were jumbled in her mind. Fatigue, desperation, the stench of wounds, the sight of men dying, the ravaged countryside, the roads crammed with refugees, soldiers, broken-down transport, all under the same terror of those deadly Stuka bombers harassing their retreat, the crowded events of these past days had become a blur in her mind. She remembered one date. She had arrived in Larissa, her hospital base, on April 5, her birthday. Who could have foreseen the astonishing pattern of her life in those two years since she had written in her diary, on her twenty-fifth birthday, that nothing would ever happen to her ! There had been that dream-like holiday in Crete with Richard, ended by the outbreak of war ; then life in England, a stupefied, half-awakened England for those first six months, it seemed to her, when none of the dreadful things everyone had expected had happened to them. But the stunning collapse of France, the terrible retreat from Dunkirk, the nearly mortal blows of the *Luftwaffe* over London in the October raids, had shown them that all that had been imagined, and worse, was their lot.

That life in England seemed very dim now. She had been nursing at Aldershot for the first few months. She was near enough to run over to Marlow at odd times and see Grandma Day. The old lady was magnificent. Six rooms of *Glenarvon* were filled with East End refugees, noisy children and disgruntled women pining for their battered homes and the excitement of London. Grandma Day had subdued them as she subdued everybody. The children were fed, clothed and disciplined ; the mothers were sternly reprimanded for their ingratitude and lack of patriotism. Slowly they came under the reassuring influence of the firm old lady. She solved all their domestic problems, including a couple of wayward husbands whose affections had wandered with the more glamorous appeal of uniforms. Never before had Sylvia had such admiration for the old lady, and a deeper love had grown in the place of her former dutiful affection. Not for one moment had Grandma Day hesitated when Sylvia suggested her line of service. " Of course you must go, my dear. You have every qualification. I shall be quite all right," she said at once.

Richard, too, had been in her life during that time in England. She had odd week-ends with him in London during his training for an air pilot's commission. Then he had been sent to the North. There was a final rendezvous at *Glenarvon* during his forty-eight hours' final leave. Then she heard he was in Libya. His last letter had found her in Alexandria, of all places, to which her unit had been drafted. It had been written from Greece.

The next day her unit received orders. Then they heard their destination. British, Australian, and New Zealand troops were being rushed to Greece. The Germans in a downward sweep through the Balkans were at the Greek frontier. The Greek army, whose stand had surprised the world and smashed back the Italian invaders, was breaking before the tremendous force of the Germans. At the end of March, after a northern journey by rail and lorry through the mountains, Sylvia had seen snow-covered Mount Olympus and, later found herself installed with her nursing unit in a school on the outskirts of Larissa, the capital of Thessaly, in the wide plain commanding the roads from Macedonia. Behind them lay Thermopylæ and its proud memory of Leonidas, the Spartan King; to the south-east, on the Bay of Lamia, was Volos, their port of supplies.

At Larissa, Sylvia knew, for the first time, the horrors of war. Shattered bodies poured into the base hospital. To the north the Allies were making a desperate stand in the attempt to hold the Germans on their easterly route down through Greece. The line was thinly held. The equipment, in artillery and transport, was desperately impaired. Their few planes were being shot out of the sky. For three desperate weeks the port had been held, but the pressure grew hourly. The Germans had broken through in the

vardar Valley and at Salonika. The Allied position was
untenable. The Germans in the west were racing towards
Athens, the Morea was in their hands. On April 13 came
the order to withdraw. Only the highest courage, the will
not to be bombed from the face of the earth, made possible
the dreadful march through the terrible biting coldness of
snow-locked mountains and wind-swept passes.

Those days in the hospital had been a nightmare, yet it
was strange how you got used to anything, how your mind
and body performed their functions mechanically. No one
had failed in those frightful last days.

The ship heeled over, making a sudden turn. Sylvia
braced herself against the bunk. Closing her eyes, she
could still see the shrapnel-pitted white walls of the hospital.
A bomb had smashed the north end, killing five men and
two nurses. Hour after hour there were raid alarms, but
they just went on.

The smells were worse than the raids. Dead bodies no
longer had any terror for her. She could never forget those
living wounded, nor gaping stomachs, smashed arms and
legs, and limbs going black ; nor, when all was over, the
yellow faces of the newly dead. How hideous those men's
beautiful bodies could become ! A Greek Adonis with half
a jaw, an Australian Hercules with strips of bloody flesh for
a leg, a Scotch Perseus with golden curly hair and blue
eyes, but a terrible raw mess that had once been a mouth—
the wards had filled and filled with such as these, until
horror died and one went on, from bed to bed, amid basins
and scissors and blood-clotted bandages, amid men who
cursed, and men who whimpered, and, worst of all, men
who lay quite still, staring up at the ceiling in a resignation
that accepted death.

It was not the dying she could see most clearly now, but,
just before the end, when they were drawing out of Larissa
and going to Volos on the day, where the transports were
waiting, that tired medley of men piling into trucks. They
were New Zealanders mostly, with some dark-skinned
Maoris and stubby, tough little Greeks. For them there
was no embarkation at Volos. They were going south to
Thermoplylæ. Across more than a century, Byron's prayer

was to be answered. There in the Pass, making a last desperate stand to hold up the German hordes, with the shade of Leonidas to marvel at them, these men would make a new Thermopylæ. She saw them now, grinning and waving good-bye, unconscious of the new glory they were to add to the scene of an ancient one.

The destroyer heeled over again, rapidly changing course. Through the porthole, in the growing light, Sylvia could now see other ships, a medley of merchantmen, all and every kind that had been collected for the evacuation. They were all crammed and weighted down above their Plimsoll line with their human freight. Two watchful destroyers herded them, a sitting target for enemy aircraft.

Sylvia sat up. The sun had risen ; the sea caught the light and took on a purple sheen. The little cabin, sacrificed by three officers was crammed. Three nurses lay in the bunks ; three were on the floor. They were all in their uniforms, two of them in the grey of the Australian units. They had worn their clothes for three nights and days.

One of the girls on the floor sat up. It was Janet Farr, who had been with Sylvia ever since they had left the Athens base. She was a shock-headed sturdy girl from Yorkshire. Thirty years of age, out of a Leeds hospital, she was an experienced campaigner. The men did not like her. She was hard and brusque and used her authority. But Sylvia knew at once her sterling quality. Nothing would ever break her. As a nurse she was rough, with a coarseness in her manner, but she was a rock, unyielding constant. She had never flinched. Once, when a bomb had blown out the side of a room in which she was doing dressings she had gone on with her work, making one brief comment—" Bloody awful ! " From then on she was known to patients and staff as " Bloody Awful." It fitted perfectly the men's grudging admiration of this rough martinet.

" Have you slept ? " asked Janet, pushing back her untidy tow-coloured hair. " Eh, I could do with a drink ! "

" Like a log—look at them ! " answered Sylvia, pointing to two nurses on the floor. One had her mouth wide open and was snoring ; the other had unbuttoned her skirt and tunic, and lay in disorder.

"Who talked about sleeping beauty!" commented Janet. This was their second night on board. They were still sunk in fatigue.

Sylvia swung her legs over the bunk's side. There was the problem of washing again. Janet Farr began to straighten her dress, examining some photographs over a locker.

"That's mine," she said, pointing to the photograph of a young officer, handsome, smiling. "One of the lieut.'s brothers, I expect. I wonder where those lads are sleeping. They must bless us."

"I don't suppose they've slept at all. They all look worn out," replied Sylvia, remembering the tired face of one of the lieutenants who had come down to his cabin to ask for something.

Janet stepped over the two prone bodies. "Let's get out; it's a grand morning. I wonder where we are," she said.

Sylvia followed her along the gangway. They had not gone a couple of yards when the quiet morning burst into uproar. The Bofors began to hammer. A raid was on. They had been expecting it all yesterday. It had come now.

Sylvia and Janet clambered up on deck to be met with a stern cry all around them. "Lie flat! Lie flat there!" A young officer came along. "Take cover, Nurse, take cover!"

Janet laughed insolently at him, for the whole deck was alive with soldiers still hunched up in sleep. They had remained where they had dropped on the deck. Had they tried to move, there was not an inch of space below.

"That's all right, my lad, but where?" demanded Janet.

The lieutentant laughed. "It's an order, Nurse!" he said. "I have to give it!"

The guns answered. The ships all around them filled the sky with their raking fire.

"Where are they?" asked Sylvia.

"There!" pointed the lieutenant. "Three Savoias."

White puffs filled the sky. The bombers were at an immense height. They were right over now. A few moments later the dull roar of explosions spread through

the air. Great fountains of water rose around them, white,
glistening, beautiful in the morning sunshine. Near her an
Australian sergeant was hopefully firing heavenward with
a Bren gun. Three more Savoias came out of a cloud.
They wheeled and came in towards the convoy.

" Six of 'em ! This is it ! We've been lucky," said the
lieutenant. " Here—get in here. Move up, you fellows ! "
He pushed her in the lee of the bridge.

" Where did you sleep last night—or did you ? " asked
Sylvia, recognising him as one of the owners of the cabin.

" Oh—I dossed in the wardroom for a couple of hours.
I hope you were comfortable ? "

" Shamefully," said Sylvia, smiling.

A fresh burst of gunfire drowned conversation. More
bombs came down, one so perilously near that the destroyer
lifted in her course. Sylvia waited, with that tight feeling
inside her. One was so helpless under raids.

" They've got one—a Greek boat, the poor bastard ! "
said a voice near her.

Sylvia scanned the smooth water as the sound of the
explosions struck her. She saw a towering sheet of water
subside again into the sea. Then, with a flame springing
from midship, she found the victim, a two-thousand-ton
steamer. She had a tremendous list and was sinking by
the head. She went down quickly, so smoothly that it was
like a scene in the cinema. Suddenly she was not there
any more. The water swirled over her. But around her
were black dots of men swimming desperately amid the
litter and debris of the missing ship. Sylvia watched in
voiceless horror. It was her first sinking.

" Too 'ot for 'em. They're off," said a voice.

The six Savoias were dropping southward down the sky.
Everyone on the ship was awake now. The destroyer was
racing over the morning sea. Sylvia went forward with
Janet to find some breakfast. In an hour they would sight
Crete, an officer said.

§ 2

Just before eight o'clock land came up over the horizon,
a greyish line at first, indistinct in the morning haze. Then

it grew in length, and a range of mountains lifted their snow-crowned heads, lovely as they caught the sunlight above the belt of mist.

They watched the island draw nearer. The convoy had spread out now. A cruiser raced past them, flinging the spray up nobly from her bow as she cut the blue water. Then voices filled the air. The ships were giving her a cheer. They knew her mission ; she was bound for Greece again, to rescue more troops. She passed, a beautiful vision of courage and hope.

" What's Crete like ? " asked Janet as the island drew nearer.

" Mountainous, wild, beautiful. But I don't know Canea. I was only in the harbour a short time, when the boat called there on my way to Candia," said Sylvia.

More men had come from below, men in all kinds of uniforms : British Tommies, New Zealanders, Australians, stocky, unshaved Greeks. They all looked dirty and tired, and most of them stood around or squatted on the deck, not talking much. They had come out of hell, with a sense of defeat upon them. The odds had been too great. They had lacked guns and transport, and, above all, air cover. A few of them talked and showed some curiosity about the island to which they were drawing near. There was a lad with a mouth-organ, playing music-hall ditties that his pals chanted around him.

" Did you like living there ? " asked Janet, staring out across the sea. Crete was nearly in view now. The White Mountains rose majestically under the vivid blue sky. The rocky headlands caught the sun. They were nearing the Akrotiri Peninsula. Suda Bay, their port for Canea, lay on the eastern side of it.

" I loved every hour of it—it was Paradise. We had a place up in the mountains. It's funny to be coming back like this, just two years after. I wonder where everybody is," said Sylvia.

A little while back, when she had heard someone say " Savoias " on the approach of the bombers, a name came at once into her mind. Whenever those Savoias went over them in Greece she thought of Cesare Morosini and remembered how, one August afternoon on the terrace at the Villa

Vouni, he had identified the Savoias flying over. He flew one, he had said then. She wondered where he was and if he was flying one now, if, by the strange trick of fate, he had been in one of those planes scattering death over Larissa. How far off those days of the Villa Vouni were, their talks, his fierce defence of Fascism, her Greek lessons, his guitar playing in the tranquil evenings. She had never foreseen to what use her knowledge of Greek would be put. In the hospital, when the Greek cases came in, emergency ones dealt with before they could be sent on to their own bases, she had always been called for. She had interpreted for the doctors, assisted the operations, written down messages for dying men, and tried to hearten them in their own language. She had spoken to Italian prisoners also, emaciated, frost-bitten lads, with all the spirit beaten out of them. Her Italian was more halting than her Greek, but somehow she established relations with them. Once, when a youth said he came from Rome, she asked him if he knew anyone called Cesare Morosini, a young flying officer. The youth shook his head. It was a foolish question, but she had to ask it. There were the oddest coincidences sometimes. There was an occasion when, dressing the leg of an Australian flight sergeant, he had asked her name. "Day?" he repeated. "You haven't a brother in the R.A.F. in Libya, have you—Dickie Day?"

"Why, yes! That must be my brother! When did you see him last?" cried Sylvia.

"Oh, about three months ago—before I got in this Greek show. He was in Derna then. He's a great lad. I can see you're his sister now. Same eyes and mouth."

The men were assembling on deck. A nervous air communicated itself through the ship. As they drew nearer to the island the danger of air attack increased. Every gun was manned. The convoy had begun to close in. They were close to the headland now and could see the light-houses, the white villages on the mountainsides, the olive groves covering the lower slopes, the steep, rocky shores that seemed to offer no opening for a ship.

Sylvia went below to collect her kit. The cabin was empty; her companions of the night had gone. She was about to leave when the door opened and a young man burst in.

" Oh—I'm awfully sorry—I didn't know you were here, Nurse ! " he exclaimed.

" Don't apologise—it's your cabin, I expect ? " replied Sylvia. He was the young lieutenant who had spoken to her on deck. He was slim, with nice grey eyes and a good mouth. That must be his brother in the photograph Janet Farr had commented on. " You'll be glad to see us out, I'm sure—and many thanks," added Sylvia, picking up her kit.

He stepped forward and took hold of it.

" Here, let me take that, please."

" Oh, no, thanks. We let no one help us. You've all plenty to do," replied Sylvia, holding firmly to her bag.

" Yes, we are glad to see you out, but not for your reason," he said laughing. " We're glad to get you landed safely—as I hope we shall."

" Is this the first trip ? "

" No—the second. And we're turning round immediately."

" For Greece ? "

" Yes—a new cargo ! "

" You are magnificent ! " said Sylvia simply.

" Thanks—but what about you ? You girls are marvellous. God, what you must have gone through ! "

There was a moment of embarrassment. They looked at each other and smiled.

" What's Canea like ? " asked Sylvia, to break the silence.

" Lousy—it's half in ruins now. I expect it'll get well plastered soon. I'm cheering you up, aren't I ? You're going to the hospital at Maleme ? "

" I expect so."

" Well, if ever I get there I'll ask for you."

" I hope you won't—not for the usual reason."

" Then the unusual reason. That doesn't sound right either ! " he exclaimed with a ringing laugh. " How do I find you, in case ? My name's Derek Whatley."

" Mine's Day—Sylvia Day."

" Thanks. That's a lovely name. Well—you won't let me ? " he asked, pointing to her kit.

" No, thanks."

He took a box out of a locker drawer and then turned to her before leaving the cabin.

"Well, good-bye—and good luck, Nurse!" he said, saluting.

"Good-bye, Lieutenant," she answered.

He went out, and she wondered, as she always wondered these days, if ever she would see him again. Then, hugging her kit, she went up on to the deck packed with soldiers. They had rounded the peninsula and were drawing into Suda Bay, a U-shaped anchorage locked in by the mountains. Woods came down to the shore. The white houses lined it, and she saw they had been battered. They passed an old Venetian island fortress. There was a cement works at the head of the bay. The low pass, breaking the mountain line, must be the road to Canea, on the other side of the peninsula. This was a good anchorage, the best in Crete and the enemy knew it also.

It was a medley of shipping gathered here. It had been called from the distant parts of the Mediterranean and pressed into the desperate task of equipping Crete for the coming ordeal. There were ships from Alexandria and Athens, ships from Salonika, Bristol, Liverpool, and Haifa, British naval vessels, Greek naval vessels, tugs, lighters, tramps, merchantmen, scarred, dirty, weather-worn, waiting their turn at the little stone quay. They bristled with anti-aircraft guns. The 8-inch cruiser *York*, torpedoed by an intrepid Italian, had foundered, but was still formidable above the water-line.

Shortly after noon Sylvia and her companions were put ashore. They trod the red soil of Crete and were marshalled and allotted their transportation. They left Suda Bay and its crowded shipping in a lumbering army lorry, going along the battered waterfront and the cement docks, and up the dusty rise across the neck of the Akrotiri Peninsula, and down again towards Canea, white and sprawling along its bay. They went on through the town, hot and dusty in the noon, and thronged with troops and transport. They skirted the coast, and a valley of olive groves opening up to the foothills of the White Mountains. Here, at the edge of the luxuriant plain of Maleme, between the orchards and the sea, they found their new home, a series of tents, a few low buildings that were the Army Hospital and a Field Ambulance Dressing Station.

F

" But it's lovely ! " exclaimed Janet, as she got down from the lorry and looked around at the sea, the olive groves, and the snow-covered mountains.

" Lovely ! You must wait, miss ! " exclaimed a corporal with a grin, throwing out their kits.

§ 3

Sylvia's unit slowly gathered itself together in the next two days. Twenty-eight of them had come safely through from Volos, with four doctors, including a Greek surgeon. Two of the nurses, Australians, were missing. They had been on the ship bombed in their convoy, and had been either killed outright or drowned.

The living quarters were some distance away from the hospital, up among the olive groves on the slope of the mountain. A refugee camp had been made here for the British women and children evacuated from Greece or sent in from the Cretan towns that were being increasingly bombed. Later, when transport permitted, they would be sent to Alexandria.

This respite from war restored them. The April sun was not yet too hot. The mountains, still heavily covered with snow, were a beautiful sight, especially at evening when the snow fields caught the rosy light of the setting sun. The tents where they slept were scattered for safety, through the dense olive groves planted on the rich red soil, and they commanded a superb view of the blue bay and the rich plain rising from the shore to the great wall of the White Mountains. Broad and fair was the valley before them, relieved by the vivid colours of the spring and backed by those shining masses of untrodden snow that filled the whole of the blazing southern heaven. Over the silvery groves of the olive trees shone the deep blue of the Ægean Sea, and afar, higher than all her sister peaks, Sylvia recognised with a thrill the great snow-crowned dome of mighty Mount Ida, nursery and throne of immortal Zeus. Beyond that gleaming peak lay the mountainous road that led from Candia to Gortyn, and Villa Vouni on its precipitous rock looking southward across the Libyan sea. Would she ever see it again ? wondered Sylvia.

After a few days at Canea she began to inquire about the journey along the coast to Candia, or Herakleion, as everyone now seemed to call it. It was only eighty-five miles distant, but the road was jammed with transport. At intervals it was bombed by enemy planes. Even had she been able to obtain leave, the trip would have been almost impossible, and the journey to the Villa Vouni quite out of the question. Later, when things were more settled, she might make the attempt.

Gradually she became aware that things were not going to get better but worse. After those terrible days of bombardment, of wounded streaming in, of continuous retreat and threatened encirclement at Larissa, and after the nerve-racking scenes of the hurried embarkation at Volos and the suspense of the voyage down the Ægean, Canea had seemed like Paradise. The quietness of the nights, the loveliness of the sunny days in a sub-tropical panorama of vineyards, olive groves, wheat fields, and tobacco plantations, the wooded foothills dotted with little white villages, the palms, the scented air, the cicadas shrilling on the hot mountainside, all created an illusion of Arcadian peace. There were reminders of another world ; raiders flying over induced a scurrying to shelters. The dull roar of an exploding bomb sometimes shook the air. There was a continuous procession of wounded from Suda Bay ; and the last forces evacuated from Athens, where the Nazi flag now floated over the Acropolis, had brought a final phase of the Greek disaster. But slowly the successive tides of humanity spread themselves out, subsiding in the dusty, walled city, along the coast, and in the tented communities hidden through the shady olive groves. An army was licking its wounds, reflecting bitterly on the errors and the reckless gambling of someone, as it seemed, who had thrown them, ill equipped, inadequate in all things except plain physical courage, to hold back an arrogant and triumphant enemy. The Greek army, broken and defeated, was being rounded up. Athens, after those heady months of triumph, was suffering bitter humiliation.

What next ? Crete was feverishly preparing for the day of wrath. Wavell had come and held a council in a cottage somewhere along the road to Retimo. It seemed a little late for a council of war. Where were the guns? Where were the prepared defences, the aerodromes, the planes? Could a war-worn army, rushed from the sandy wastes of the Libyan Desert to the snow-smitten, windswept fortresses of Greece, stand again and fight after those nightmare weeks when they had battled so desperately against the tide of defeat? It seemed they had to stand. If Crete went the Middle East was imperilled—Libya, Egypt, Palestine, Syria, Iraq, and Iran, and with them would go the eastern Mediterranean Sea, the Suez Canal, and eventually the Indian Ocean. The dream of Mare Nostrum might become a reality. Cesare Morosini had not been just a wild young man, one of the millions intoxicated by the Duce's oratory. All around them these days the threat grew.

Sylvia dreaded the hour when the radio broadcasted its summary of news. That voice in the far-off homeland was so desperately reassuring amid a growing menace. In the first weeks of May, here in this beautiful Mediterranean island, a sense of doom began to pervade the air, though to each other they showed a resolute front. The British army was retreating in Libya, and the great prize of Tripoli had slipped from their hands. It had slipped because of an army weakened for the desperate Greek adventure, desperate and inevitable if one more gallant diminutive ally was not to feel itself deserted and betrayed. London had been heavily bombed; the old Guildhall lay in ruins; great areas of the city were consumed by fire, reduced to rubble. Syria was in revolt; an insurrection had broken out in Iraq. Poland, Norway, Belgium, Holland, France, Czechoslovakia, Yugoslavia, and now Greece had disappeared. There was near panic in Cairo, someone brought news. The elegant officers with the fly whisks, the occupying army of the terrace at Shepheard's Hotel, were wondering where next they would go in this uncomfortable war. The Russians were winded; the French were out; the Americans were not in. Here in sunny Crete, in these few days of respite, it was like the hushed prelude to a thunderstorm.

" We're going to get a packet, my girl," said Janet Farr, snapping the cotton thread with her teeth as she sat sewing one afternoon in the olive grove. " We can't go anywhere from here. General Wavell's said so. So here we stay. Have you made your will, Sylvia ? "

" Long ago," answered Sylvia. " And you ? "

" Me ! Oh, Lord—you should see what I'll leave ! Two Marks & Spencer camisoles, a piano with twenty instalments to go, and some glass beads and bangles."

" Did you have a very hard time, Janet ? "

" Well, depends on what you call hard. I suppose you'd call it hard. I left school at fourteen and went into a mill for seven bob a week—on your feet from eight to twelve, one to five, half-day Saturday. It wasn't much of a life, come to think of it. Up the street and down the street, milk on the step at seven, insurance dues, a piano lesson once a week, the cinema twice, p'raps a dance at Fairyland if you collared a boy, and once a year a week at Blackpool, if you'd not blewed in your savings in the meantime. We lived in a grey brick street, cheerful as a piece of wet tripe, three overgrown brothers always polishing themselves up in the bathroom, and my sister Fanny and Mom and Dad. Sundays we went to chapel and got excited at a revival meeting or screeched madly in an oratorio. And then I got ambitious. A doctor was kind to me and he got me into the Infirmary Hospital—a scullery maid at first. Well, to cut a long story short, I became a nurse at last—it nearly killed me, but I did it. Yes, I suppose it was a hard life, and, good lord, wasn't it dreary ! If it wasn't for the killing of all these lads I'd say thank God for this war, the longer the better ! "

Janet Farr put down her sewing and looked across the valley, through the branches of the olive trees, to the sparkling sea. Then, after a pause, she said :

" I never knew there was anything as beautiful as this— the sun like a kiss all over your body. Even at Larissa I was happy. It's wonderful to feel you're wanted. I don't envy you, but I've missed a lot. I'd have missed everything if it hadn't been for the war. It's the same with all these boys ; they'd have been factory hands and clerks and counter-jumpers all their lives, and now they're all over the world, seeing places. They're hating it at times, but not really, deep down. When they look back they'll think it was the time of their lives. My dad was always croaking about that last war. To hear him, you'd have thought it was one long picnic, except when he put a bit in to show you what a hero he'd been ! "

Janet laughed and stretched her arms above her head, gazing into the blue sky.

" Tell me more about yourself. I love hearing about lucky people. You'd a lovely house in a nice little town on the Thames, two maids and a cook, a car of your own, a good-looking brother who gave you a grand holiday here I've heard all that. Oh, yes—and an expensive camera and a grandmother and the right kind of voice."

" The right kind of voice ? " asked Sylvia.

" You know what I mean, the ' don't-you-forget-I'm-a-lady ' voice."

" Oh, what nonsense, Janet ! "

" Nonsense, is it ? The office boy'ld always show you in to the boss. Look how the men melt—' Yes, miss.' And the officers are on to you at once. Don't think I'm resentful. What's there's there ! "

" Janet, you'll perhaps be surprised if I say you're a bit class-conscious ? "

" Of course I am ! Do you remember that captain in B Ward—him with the tricycle name ? "

Sylvia laughed aloud. " Oh, you mean Captain Tyrwhitt-Menzies-Marjoribanks."

" Yes. How was I to know he called it Mennies-Marshbanks—what an idea ! ' How did you become a nurse ? ' he asked, with a mouth full of adenoids, as I was washing him."

" He was merely curious."

" Yes, with the emphasis on the ' you '."

" And what about Lord Brierwood ? "

" Oh, he was nice—he was a gent, poor lamb," said Janet quietly, and, after a pause : " He's the only boy who died I've cried about. To have all that, looks, and money and title and lose it at twenty ! Sylvia, you never say anything about your boys ! "

" Boys ? "

" Yes—you must have lots, with your looks."

" And expensive camera and voice ! Janet, you're an *enfant terrible*."

" That's something for what ? "

" French for ' an irrepressible child.'   I might ask about you ? "

" Me !   What !   With my face and legs ! "

Janet spread out her legs and lifted her skirt, to feel the sun on them.

" I don't suppose this is very ladylike, is it ?—but my, it's good ! " she exclaimed with a twinkle in her eye.   " Sylvia, it's funny about me and you, mud and porcelain, and yet we got on so well together."

" Janet, you mustn't say such hard things about yourself. Of course we get on together.   You're clever, and very brave, and full of good humour.   I'm very lucky to know you."

Janet did not answer.   She watched Sylvia sewing for a few moments, and then said very quietly :

" With a face like mine, it doesn't matter what you have. Men'll run after nitwits if they've a pretty face.   Funny how six square inches'll put out all the rest."

There was a note of such sadness in her husky voice that Sylvia looked at her keenly.   Their eyes met in complete candour.

" Oh, my dear, someone will want you," she said, earnestly.

" No, Sylvia, I'm thirty and I've missed it.   I hope I I don't get too hard."

So that was it.   It was a defensive façade against life hurting her too much.   How unfair it all was.   She had such splendid qualities of heart and mind, and all anyone could see was her poor ugly little body and face.

" You haven't told me what I want to know.   Have you a boy ? " asked Janet, sitting up and renewing her sewing. " Don't tell me if it hurts."

" No, I haven't a boy—not really."

" Now what do you mean by that ? " asked Janet.

" Oh, it was all rather complicated.   I think every-thing went to my head a little.   It was really quite impossible."

" Oh, then there was someone—' was ' or ' is ' ? " queried Janet.

" ' Was,' " replied Sylvia, firmly.

" Come on, I want details. Tell me," urged Janet.
" You don't mean he's been killed ? "

" Oh, no. At least I don't think so—I hope not. You
remember I told you about our life up at the Villa Vouni
here ? We had a guest there. He was a young Italian
excavating nearby. Cesare Morosini. I only knew him
for four or five months. He was a friend of Richard's, very
clever, a wonderful linguist, and highly educated. He came
of a very distinguished family."

" Describe him. Young, of course ? " asked Janet.

" Twenty-five. Fairly tall, with an athletic figure,
bronzed with the sun. He had beautiful hands and very
eloquent eyes. Hair dark, but bleached with the sun. His
voice——"

" Oh, my dear, I can't bear it. Weren't you mad about
him ? "

" Not exactly. I didn't know, really ; it was so con-
fusing, so wonderful, that I——"

" But you must have known ! " interrupted Janet eagerly.
" You can't help but know if you're really in love. Didn't
he say anything—didn't he hold you and kiss you ? "

Sylvia made no reply and looked down at her sewing,
embarrassed by her companion's searching questions.

" Oh, Sylvia, I'm sorry," exclaimed Janet. " I'm a bit
cracked on the subject. That's what happens when you're
frustrated."

A dull roar filled the air, punctuated by heavy explosions.
They looked up. The sky was clear.

" They're bombing Suda Bay again," said Sylvia.

" We'd fourteen come in this morning—stevedores.
Three amputations. They knocked out a Greek caïque and
caught a destroyer. I wonder what's happening at Herakleion."

The noise died down, then a heavy vibration and a rattle
of anti-aircraft fire leaped up from the valley and the hills
around them. Sylvia and Janet looked up. There were
four faint shapes fleeing down the sky. Over at Maleme
aerodrome half a dozen planes tore up the sky to intercept
them. A pattern of spirals filled the bright air, and they
watched the climbing acrobatics of the gnat-like machines.

" Savoias—and a 109F," said Janet as the chase went down

the sky, out seaward. The town grew quiet again. It was
now an everyday occurrence. The night bombings were
more worrying.

"Cesare Morosini—the young Italian I spoke of—is a
pilot. He flies a Savoia," said Sylvia.

"Oh! That might be him. How odd it all is," commented Janet. "A red-hot Fascist, I suppose? What
makes them so red-hot? That young Nazi in 5A spewed
out his venom. He wanted to die for his Fuehrer—and
there we were, patching him up! He'll probably get home
and breed some more of the *Herrenvolk*."

"It's a religion; they get converted and see the light.
Cesare was like that. We had fierce arguments."

"And that spoiled it? He was in love with you?"

"I didn't know—not until the war broke out and he came
to Brindisi with us on our way home. Then just as the
train drew out he told me," answered Sylvia.

"And you?"

"I suppose I was—he was young and handsome, and
I lived in another world then—it was so new, so wonderful.
I had never met anyone quite like that before. He talked
well, knew things; there was a quickness and beauty about
him. We called him Hermes—the messenger of the gods."
Sylvia broke off and laughed softly. "You see how badly
I had it. And we both knew it was hopeless. He saw this
coming. There was nothing to be done."

"But when it's over?"

"No—I don't think so then. Our worlds are so different,
really. Foreign marriages are always difficult. One of the
two must surrender so much. And somehow it's all
different and could never be the same again. I think we
were just children then, carried away with the excitement
of life. We both know so much more now—and we'd find
ourselves wide apart. I see now it was a physical ecstasy,
and that's not enough. One's grown up tremendously these
two years."

"I don't know how you kept your head. A handsome
young Italian sitting at your feet—offering himself. It
sounds like a novel, except for the ending," said Janet.
"But I'd have liked him a little wicked, and dark, and a
real count."

"He was certainly not wicked, but he happened to be dark, and a count."

"Oh, Sylvia, you should have snatched him!"

"Janet, you're a little snob!"

"Of course I am! I love a title! Who doesn't? Fancy the Countess—what would it have been?"

"Morosini, I suppose. You know, Janet, you're a funny mixture. The men all think you're so hard, and some of the girls, too, and you really ooze romance."

"A young man crazy about you—a handsome young man, a foreign handsome young man, a foreign handsome young man with a title. Sylvia, it's sheer Hollywood, and you kept your head!"

"I nearly lost it. A moving train and a war saved me," said Sylvia, shaking out the dress she was repairing.

Janet suddenly pulled down her skirts and sat up. Someone was coming towards them through the olive grove. It was a man dressed in white shorts and stockings.

"Who's this?" cried Janet. "It's not an orderly."

They were in the women's compound and strangers were not allowed by the guards at the wired fence to come into this part of the grove.

Sylvia looked up. In the patchwork of shadow and sunlight playing over the approaching figure it was difficult to see clearly. He was obviously coming straight towards them. A few moments later she saw he wore the peaked cap of a British naval officer. There was something familiar in the young man's face. He was nearer now, and recognisable. It was the young lieutenant from the destroyer, but she had forgotten his name. Sylvia stood up as he approached them.

"I was told I should find you here," he said, saluting as he smiled at her. "I hope you don't mind my looking you up—I had to come to the hospital."

"But how nice of you!" exclaimed Sylvia, genuinely pleased to see him again.

They shook hands. There was a momentary pause. Janet had risen, with the slightly truculent air she always affected towards men.

"Oh—I don't think you know my friend—Nurse Farr?

Janet, this is——" She paused awkwardly, searching
vainly for his name.

" Derek Whatley," he said, smiling.

" Of course ! Janet, it was Lieutenant Whatley's cabin
we slept in."

" How d'you do ? " said Janet severely, in a voice that
was quite foreign to her.

" How did you find us ? " asked Sylvia pleasantly.

She examined him more leisurely than had been possible
before. He had removed his hat, and she observed the
slight waviness of his brown hair rising from a broad, smooth
brow. The Mediterranean sun and weather had not driven
a boyish pinkness from his cheeks. She recognised again
the merry glint in his grey eyes.

" I got hold of the matron and asked for you."

" How clever of you to remember my name," laughed
Sylvia, " and I hope we're not so recognisable now we're
washed and cleaned up."

He laughed with her. He had good teeth, even and white.
Janet looked him over very thoroughly, and he must have
been aware of her scrutiny, for he said :

" I hope you don't mind my ferreting you out ? "

" We feel it's a compliment. Where have you been—to
Greece again ? "

" Twice since we landed you. This last trip we caught a
packet coming in early one morning. A couple of Stukas
dive-bombed us. A near miss—with six of our men
wounded. Operation job, I'm told. We've just brought
them in. So I looked for you."

" We can't offer you a chair—— " began Sylvia, when her
companion interrupted her.

" Oh, have mine. I must go," said Janet abruptly.
" Good-bye—see you later, Sylvia."

She gave a curt nod and hurried off down the grove.
There was an embarrassed silence for a few moments.

" I say, I hope I haven't butted in—— " began Whatley.

" Of course not. I'm very glad to see you. My friend's
a little nervous," explained Sylvia. " Don't take any notice
of her manner. She's a grand person really."

Sylvia forced herself to say this. She was feeling angry
with Janet for her gauche manners.

" I couldn't resist asking after you—and as you were here "——said the lieutenant, nervously.

" It was very nice of you. The Navy's a refreshing change. Won't you sit down ? " asked Sylvia, pointing to the camp chair vacated by Janet.

" Thanks. It's rather a lovely spot. Are you comfortable here ? "

" Well, as much as one can expect. There're four of us in a tent. Thank heaven it's not midsummer ! Can you give me any news—or shouldn't I ask ? How've we come out of Greece ? "

" Well—pretty badly. There's a lot of the poor devils left. They were wonderful—they've fight still in 'em. We were shot out of the skies. We made a last run to Argos just before Jerry plastered it. God, it was awful ! Those poor Greeks—I never saw anything so tragic. They knew they were doomed. We picked up a fellow who'd been shot down at sea. He said the sky had been black with Stukas and Heinkels and Messerschmitts. We got in on a lull, luckily, and had to wait off while the troops came out in small boats. Those fellows were marvellous. They'd fought ; they'd marched ; no food, no sleep from bombing, Argos in flames when they reached it, and there they waited patiently on the beaches. We put into the Piræus—it was almost bombed to pieces. The faces of those poor Greeks ! They know they're for it now. I never saw such despair—and after such high hopes."

He pulled at the grass savagely. She looked at him, his sensitive face, the glistening hair on his brown legs, the smooth hand with the seal ring. Twenty-four or five, she thought, more of the artist breed than the man of action, nervously taut, and with charm.

" You've told me nothing of yourself—what the navy's done. Pretty desperate, I gather ? " she asked. " We've some of your ratings."

" Oh, well—it's no picnic for anyone. You've seen it. Jove—it's like a dream here ! " he exclaimed, looking down the grove with its vista of blue sea. " What a beautiful world it could be ! "

He glanced covertly at his wrist-watch.

" I'm supposed to be on a mission. Are you off duty ? " he asked.

" Yes—until seven."

" Could you get away ? I've got a car. The S.N.O.'s asked me to drop a signal at a place called Mournies."

" S.N.O.—that's a new one in the war alphabet."

" Oh, no—quite an old one to sailors—Senior Naval Officer. He's in charge of the port at Suda. I say, could you come ? I'd love it ! We'd be back in plenty of time."

His voice was so appealing she could not have refused him, and she had no desire to.

" I think it would be very nice," answered Sylvia.

" Would your friend like to come ? It's a five-seater."

" I think we'll leave her—and I'll let her know what she's missed," replied Sylvia with a laugh, getting up. Janet had behaved badly.

They walked down through the tents, past the hospital. She asked him to wait while she got a hat. The guard at the gate saluted. They reached the car, a shabby old Ford.

" It's not elegant, but it goes," he said as they went down the dirt-track, past another guard, on to the road. They ran towards Galatas and Canea. Through the battered town they took a road beyond the walls and mounted up the valley. The countryside began to spread out below them as they came to the foothills. The lyric beauty of spring was in the fields and groves around them. It was impossible to believe that azure sky could rain death, and the still afternoon break into a staccato uproar of guns, exploding shells and bombs. At a turn of the road they could see the bay, a blue-green, velvety semicircle of water, translucent, with the fire of a sapphire. The air above it had almost a purple bloom under the cloudless heaven. The young leafiness of elder trees marked their way, spaced with tall Grecian poplars now broken into a green mist of spring leaves. Almond blossoms lifted their vivid pink petals over old garden walls, and by a stream the willows drooped their emerald tresses Below them a light breeze rippled the young wheat in waves of colour. The vines had put forth their new leaves, unretarded by the savage pruning of the old shoots. They stood in orderly rows, while even now, in sturdy faith, the peasants raked the mounded earth about the roots. In wilder places Nature ran riot with splashes of scarlet anemones amid the young grass, with clumps of asphodel springing into fresh leaf. As the car ran on they talked and laughed. For a while their hearts were young and gay in this scene of Nature's indifference to man's folly.

They came to Mournies, a small white village, asleep in the afternoon sun. Whatley stopped an old man and asked for direction to a certain villa, but he was not understood, and Sylvia proffered her help. The man's face was wreathed in smiles when she spoke Greek to him, and he gave her a voluble and minute direction. As Whatley restarted the car he looked at her in open admiration.

" Wherever did you learn Greek ? " he asked.

" Here. I once lived in Crete before the war."

He stared at her, his grey eyes surveying her wonderingly.

" I really know nothing about you, do I ? " he said.

" Nor I about you," retorted Sylvia.

" But I'm a very ordinary person. A stockbroker's son, born in Guildford, somewhat educated at Dartmouth—that's all. But you—I always felt you were an unusual person."

" How frightening, or perhaps frightful ! " she exclaimed.

He looked at her with such undisguised admiration that an embarrassed silence followed. A few moments later they came to the gates of the villa. It stood superbly at the foot of the White Mountains, with a large garden. There were three cars in the road. To Sylvia's surprise two New Zealand soldiers stood on guard before the house, fixed bayonets gleaming in the sun. They clicked to attention when Whatley got out of the car and approached the gate. After a brief interrogation they let him pass through. In a few minutes her companion returned and got back into his seat.

" Is that a general's place ? " asked Sylvia as he started the car.

" No. King George of Greece is living there with his cousin, Prince Peter, and the Greek Prime Minister. The whole government of Greece is in that villa ! "

Outside the village, at a fork in the road, he halted the car.

" Shall we make a little excursion ? It's only four o'clock," he asked.

" Oh, let's ! " answered Sylvia vivaciously.

" God only knows how long we'll be able to do this."

" Are you pessimistic about our chances ? "

" Professionally, I'm never pessimistic. But we are in a tough spot. The *Luftwaffe's* not half an hour away. They're laying down aerodromes like mad. We've no planes to speak of and three aerodromes—Candia, Retimo, and Maleme. Maleme's the only really good one. Then there's only one possible anchorage, Suda Bay. Unfortunately that's on the north. There are no harbours on the south, which we could reach easily from Egypt. Still, the men who should know believe we can hold it, or we shouldn't be here. If Crete goes we may lose all the eastern Mediterranean. Alexandria and the Suez Canal are only a short hop. We're being pushed back now in Libya. Tobruk's only two hundred miles, Mersa Matruh's two-eighty. We'd be in a hole if this went. And the Germans'll go all out for it. I've got it in my bones. But it's only a sailor talking, and I really know nothing."

The road suddenly disintegrated into a mule-track. The vegetation was thicker here. Three or four villas stood on the rising ground, commanding views of the rich plain and the distant sea.

" Oh, let's walk ! " exclaimed Sylvia. " It's entrancing ! "

They took the rough track between two garden walls. When they had gone about a hundred yards a door in one of the walls opened and five men came out and began to come down the lane. Four of them wore uniforms. One of them, leading the way, had a walking-stick. As they came abreast, and Whatley saw them more clearly, he stood aside and saluted sharply. The man with the stick raised it in acknowledgment, and then, seeing Sylvia, said very pleasantly as he passed, " Good afternoon ! "

" Why, that was King George ! " exclaimed Sylvia when they had gone.

" Yes, with Prince Peter. But did you see the big gun behind him ? "

" Yes."

" That's tiny Freyberg."

" Who ? "

" General Freyberg. He's running the whole show."

Sylvia stopped walking and looked down the track again.

She saw the back of a man, hat in hand, and strove to recall what she had seen : a small bullet-head with the hair lying flat upon it, a pair of gimlet eyes that had glanced at her, and thin lips compressed in a straight line above the clean-shaven jaw. She had seen a legend. And it was not of the man, oiled and painted black, who swam for over an hour through the dark night to light flares on a Dardanelles beach that she thought. Nor of the man who won the V.C. in France and became a brigade commander at twenty-seven ; all that was dim, in a great war now engulfed by a greater. The man she really knew, whose face she had seen at last, was one she had been so near to when he made that incredible retreat with his men from Olympus. The brave wonder of it had surrounded her in the field hospital. She heard of him on a hundred lips of those rugged Anzacs, smashed in body but unbroken in spirit.

" I'm glad I've seen him at last. He's a lion of a man," said Sylvia simply, resuming her walk.

" They've produced the toughest man they've got. That's something to be hopeful about," observed Whatley.

The path rose steeply now. They came to a wood of carob trees. Some catalpas were just bursting into flower and threw up a fountain of creamy saucer blossoms. They sat down on a bank scented with thyme and removed their hats. The air was loud with the shrilling of cicadas exulting in the glorious day. The prospect before them transcended any words which they could find. They were conscious, for this hour at least, of a complete happiness, with all apprehension dismissed, with no vision of the past and the future. It was transitory, and, in the changing circumstances of these days, an interlude that had no more permanence than a dream ; but to be alive and to be young on this day and hour was supremely good.

They talked of a dozen patternless things : of England, of their homes, of the possible shape that life might assume if they and their homeland emerged from this ordeal. The garrulous politicians would have been surprised and dismayed by the utter simplicity of their needs. Utopia was not their goal. They merely wanted personal freedom, a pattern of life not moulded or warped by tiresome idealists. A chair by the fire, a quiet day in a garden, the easy company of friends, and enough money to fend off adversity in old age : that was all. " I sometimes think the highest achievement of our civilisation would be the ability to read a book in bed, with safety," said Derek Whatley, puffing at the briar pipe he had lit.

He asked her about her home, and then about her brother, and particularly of her life here in Crete before the storm broke. She wore a ring, set with a little Cretan seal, three thousand years old, a precious thing, given her one day by Richard out of his collection. Whatley examined it closely, holding her hand. When he had finished looking at it he still held her hand, and, conscious of a slight caressing of it, she smiled at him.

" Do you mind ? " he asked, and then, a little shyly, " You can't think what it means to touch a woman's hand, to sit with you and talk. One gets so sick of men."

They laughed then. He had leaned back on the bank where he sat. Her hand, in his, rested against his smooth thigh. She felt one arm creep behind her and turned, smiling at him. Their eyes met, and all speech hung suspended between them. Swept by the impulse of their youth, they drew nearer each other, and their lips met hungrily. His arms held her to him, and they lay there breathless, intoxicated with the heady moment, the loud shrilling of the cicadas filling the bright air.

Sylvia sat up and pushed back her hair in an embarrassed silence. He picked up his pipe and pressed down the tobacco in the bowl. From the bank where he still lay he watched her, happy, admiring.

" Sylvia—you're wonderful," he said, his hand seeking hers again. She let him take it and laughed down at him.

" Thank you ! " she answered brightly.

" Don't laugh at me ! "

" Am I laughing at you ? We've both been silly."

" Silly ? I don't feel it's at all silly, my dear."

" Sentimental, then. We're being very young ! "

" We are young. What's wrong with that ? I am so happy. Bless you ! "

They looked at each other, a little seriously this time. She pushed a fallen lock of hair back from his brow. Somewhere a bird began a sustained level trill. They listened.

" I wonder what that is ? " he asked, and then, " I suppose
we should be going. Sylvia, you've made me very happy—
to see you, to hear you, to touch you. One gets very,
very——"

He sought for the word and, failing, he sat up, put his
arm about her, and kissed her deliberately. Then he
helped her to her feet. They went down the track towards
the car. It was nearly six o'clock. The lovely purple
light began to grow in the folds of the mountains. The sea,
afar, lay tranquil and burnished. They came to the car and
set off for Canea. When they reached the hospital he said
good-bye at the gate.

" I'll be over to see our men to-morrow—about six. Will
I be able to see you ? " he asked.

" I'm on until eight."

His face fell. They looked at each other, frustrated.

" After eight—would you be free ? We could find a
place to eat somewhere. There's a cabaret show and
dancing at the hotel—of a kind. I'll probably be gone
Friday," he said, giving urgency to his plea.

" That would be lovely."

" I may not be able to fetch you. This is the S.N.O.'s
car."

" Don't worry, Derek—I'll get a lift. I'd like to ask
Janet," she said, " or would you rather—— ? "

" Of course, bring her along. I'll be at the Palace at
eight. Bye-bye ! "

" Good-bye ! "

He watched her pass the guard and go up the path through
the olive trees. He was unbelievably happy. At the top
of the rise she turned and waved to him. They were
bombing Suda again. The anti-aircraft guns were popping
away, but he did not hear them. Olivious of everything
except the singing of his heart, he set off for Suda Bay.

The next day there was a great increase in the tempo of
the bombing. The Germans were stepping up their raids
on the Maleme aerodrome. It was their chief target. The
machines lined up there were gravely menaced. All around,
in the groves and hills, the army was feverishly digging slit
trenches. There was an appalling lack of equipment :

Bofors, field guns, small arms, even shovels and barbed wire
for the creation of defences, were totally inadequate. Steel
helmets were used to scoop out slit trenches. There were
only eighteen anti-aircraft guns, four howitzers, six heavy
and sixteen light tanks on the island. Transport was almost
nil. Worst of all was the lack of fighter aircraft. It hardly
existed after the losses in Greece. It was worn by five
months of incessant fighting against a numerically superior
foe in the Middle East, in Libya, in Greece. Only a merest
remnant had reached Crete, a scratch lot of Hurricanes,
Blenheims converted to fighters, Brewster Buffaloes, and
some obsolete Gladiators. The three aerodromes, at
Meleme, Retimo, Herakleion, were hastily improvised. For
some reason, or by a fatal lack of reason, other aerodromes,
more strategically placed, had not been begun or completed.
A site had been surveyed in the Messara Plain ; levelling
had begun, but it was too late, and other possible sites up
in the mountains, more protected from the enemy than
Maleme and Herakleion, had not been utilised. And if
they had been, where were the planes to come from ?

Freyberg was painfully reducing the chaos to order. The
dumped refugees were sorted out. There were sixteen
thousand Italian prisoners on the island, a grave menace.
Six hundred of their officers were sent away. There was no
transport for the rest. The original inadequate three battalions held for the defence of the island had now grown
into an army of forty thousand men. To the original force
made up of the 2nd Black Watch, 2nd York and Lancaster
Regiment, 1st Welsh Regiment and Royal Marines, had
been added the survivors of the 4th and 5th New Zealand
Infantry Brigades, and the 6th Australian Division. In
addition were men of the 2nd Leicesters, 2nd Argyl and
Sutherland Highlanders, and the 3rd Hussars. It was a
mixed bag composed of some fourteen thousand British,
seven thousand New Zealanders, six thousand Australians,
and about twelve thousand Greeks.

Equipment, lost in the Greek evacuation, was desperately
scratched together. The Greeks had five patterns of rifles—
Greek, British, American, Canadian, and Italian—with
corresponding problems of ammunition. Specialised units,
their equipment lost, had to be absorbed into various corps.

All day and night there was an influx of Greek caïques and odd boats filled with stragglers who had somehow made the perilous trip from Greece to Crete. Supplies arrived from Egypt, ill spared by the desperately pressed army in Africa, and many were sunk on the hazardous journey from Alexandria. Lacking southern ports, ships had to make the menacing trip round the east end of Crete, to Herakleion and Canea, the prey of German and Italian aircraft and submarines.

Reconnaissance reports emphasised the growing menace in Greece. The enemy aerodromes were choked with fighters, bombers, troop transports, and gliders. In the harbours, fleets of small boats for the invasion were being assembled. Men and equipment poured down all the roads of Greece to the southern shore. But the first week had passed and the blow was not struck. Each day the tensity grew. There was a full moon on the twelfth, a bomber's moon. The news from Libya was bad : the British Army was retreating ; an insurrection was sweeping vital Iraq ; London had been terribly blitzed ; the Suez Canal had been bombed. Mysteriously, but with an element of comedy, Hitler's confidant, Herr Hess, had descended by parachute on a Scottish moor.

Since the battle for Crete would resolve itself into a battle for landing-grounds for enemy aircraft, the defending forces were most heavily deployed at the three vital points along the northern shore : Maleme, Retimo, and Herakleion, the sites of aerodromes. But in these early days it was Suda Bay, with its transports, that drew most of the fire. Enemy aircraft had devised an effective and economical mode of bombing. They came in low, too low for anti-aircraft fire, delivered, and skimmed away just over the neck of the Akrotiri Peninsula. Daylight unloading of the ships became impossible. Crews of stevedores were drawn from the Australians and New Zealanders. They worked under cover of total darkness, with improvised tackle. They were the jugular vein of Crete in these days of feverish preparation. But the cost was high. A steady stream of undaunted stevedores poured into hospital, and Sylvia heard the heroic chronicle of a phase of war that went unheralded.

Through all these days the navy kept its constant vigil, since the main invasion would come by sea. There were transports and merchantment to be convoyed ; there was a sea to be kept clear between Greece and Crete ; there was a constant vigilance over that water upon which all manner of desperate craft bore its human cargo towards Crete. And ever from the sky above, the land-based enemy darted in for the attack and sped away again. Every route to Crete was guarded despite the high-level and dive bombers who came in again and again. With luck, the elusive Italian fleet might be caught making a bold bid for the mastery of Mare Nostrum.

The hospital, situated on the coast between Canea and Maleme, was a barometer of the increasing tension upon the island. The houses, the tents, the staff, and equipment were under extreme pressure all the time. The doctors, nurses, and first-aid staff who had been evacuated from Greece were all suffering from the strain of those weeks when, hurried from camp to camp, bombarded and raided from the air, they had toiled night and day to deal with the swelling ranks of the wounded.

Sylvia's unit from Larissa had been gathered together again. They would never forget those last days in that battered town, a deserted shell from which the inhabitants had fled. It had been once upon a time a pleasant country town composed mostly of little white buildings built of native stone, with uneven cobbled streets, a pretentious highway, and a square with a " modern " hotel and restaurant. The civil life of the little town was dead. The noises in the streets had been of army trucks lumbering through to and from the front, of the clattering feet of soldiers, the rumble of artillery in the hills around, and, at intervals, the sudden uproar of raiding planes, anti-aircraft guns, falling bombs, and the staccato bursts overhead of machine-gun fire.

Through all this, through the harassed evacuation, the perilous sea transit, Sylvia's unit had gone. Here in Crete, the strain, after a short period of relaxation, had been renewed. They were tired, with ragged nerves, and faces set for the ordeal that was surely coming, despite these halcyon days of spring. Death, the courage of man, the smells, the crushed bodies and torn limbs, had become part of the unending procession that passed through the operating theatre and wards. Fortunately hard work and immense fatigue numbed the mind. Some of the nurses grew hard, a few callous, most of them fatalistic. It never occurred to them they were heroic. Doctors, nurses, and staff were composite parts of a machine that functioned steadily. It was odd how everything came to be accepted in time ; the stench of putrefying wounds, amputations, intestines spilled out, men blinded, the filth of old bandages, black clotted blood, smashed jaws, emasculated manhood. All this and a mixture of faith and blasphemy were combined with cool science pursuing its course and discipline holding all in its rigid mould.

There were moments when Sylvia thought she could not hold on, but they were singularly few, and most surprising of all was that they came when there was least cause, in those intervals when the pressure lessened. The former Sylvia, the young woman of *Glenarvon*, of the Villa Vouni, and of England in that first year of war, had vanished. Another Sylvia, a woman sure of herself, poised, a realist ready to challenge nonsense and prepared to be aggressive towards personal or general injustice, had been moulded in Greece and hardened in the furnace of war. She had had so much more to learn than Janet Farr, long toughened in the battle for survival. The hard little Yorkshire woman had only changed the field of operations. Sylvia had been thrust into a new world, horrible, but vital. A singular bond had grown between them, created by the utter difference in the preparation for life they had received. Sylvia envied Janet's ruthlessness, her hard sense, her disdain of subtlety, her thoroughness in achieving her goal. She made a characteristic remark when Sylvia told her of Lieutenant Whatley's invitation for the evening in Canea.

" I'll bet I give him a pain. You asked him to ask me, didn't you ? " queried Janet bluntly.

" Oh, Janet—we want you to come."

" He doesn't want me hanging around ; neither do you."

" I shan't go without you," said Sylvia.

" We may neither of us have the chance—we may have to work all night, as things are shaping. They brought in sixteen men, ground crews from Maleme, an hour ago. The Jerries don't give that aerodrome an hour's peace. They shot up six Brewster Buffaloes this morning, sitting on the ground, and Suda had a noisy night."

But a little after eight o'clock they were free for ten hours. Sylvia was so tired that she hesitated about going into Canea, and oddly enough it was Janet who insisted on their going.

" I ache in every limb, and I stink of ether, but if I don't see some men that aren't half pulped I shall go dotty! Come on, my girl ! "

They found a truck that took them into Canea, where they arrived half an hour late. Derek Whatley was waiting for them on the hotel steps when they arrived. A lurid sunset still lingered in the sky. There would be an hour before black-out. Whatley's face lit up when he saw them. Hope had been running low. He had failed to get over to the hospital that morning, and their lateness began to dim his hopes.

He led them through to the back of the café into a room opening on to a courtyard. For the present, until the black-out, all the windows and doors were opened. The place was packed. A babel of voices rose above the tumult of a band playing jazz. The variety of the uniforms was bewildering : Greek, British, Australian, and New Zealand. There were a lot of civilians also, in the oddest of scratch clothing, refugees from Greece and the Balkans. The surprising thing was the number of women, speaking Greek, French, Polish, Italian, German, English, and some indeterminable languages. The jazz band of six, sweating profusely, consisted of Austrian Jews who had fled southward from Europe, their last refuge having been the Hotel d'Angleterre at Athens.

The food was bad, the service desperate, the noise frightful, but no one seemed to mind. When the black-out came the heat in the long room became intense. The band played louder ; the people at the bar screamed at everybody ; the crowd dancing was so great that a mass of congealed bodies rotated on the board floor. The boys began to whoop it up, the hair falling over their brows. The girls they had picked up clung to them, or were pushed around, or half collapsed, with dazed eyes and mouths smeared stickily

with rouge. Then a clearing was made for the floor show.
A howl went up, and whistling rent the air, when girls
dressed as houris took the floor. They were a troupe of
Circassians who had fled from Salonika to Athens, and
Athens to Crete. There had been nine of them originally,
but the caïque in which they had crossed the Ægean Sea had
been machine-gunned by a German plane and set on fire.
Half of the passengers had been killed or drowned. None
of the girls looked older than twenty.

They were an acrobatic troupe and they went through
some astonishing contortions which the audience greeted
with increasing frenzy. Some of the boys rushed the stage
as the troupe went off, but the girls were hurried out into a
room behind the band. Whistling and catcalls rent the air.
It was their last show. They were being transported to
Alexandria on the morrow. The band struck up ; a mob
invaded the floor. Sylvia and her partner found themselves
jostled.

" Would you rather we got out of this ? " asked Whatley.

" Oh, no. I'm enjoying it immensely ! "

" It's getting a bit rough."

" I like to see them enjoying themselves," shouted Sylvia
above the din. She wondered how many of them would be
alive a month hence. The jetsam of Europe was floating
in this motley sea. So many of them had nightmares to
dispel, horrors to drown. Their gaiety was semi-delirious.

They fought their way back to their table after a dance.
It was past midnight.

" We must really go—we've duty at six o'clock," said
Sylvia. She looked around for Janet. She had last seen
her dancing with a Greek officer. For an hour she had
been in the crush around the bar, but now she could not
be found.

" What shall I do ? " asked Sylvia, perplexed. " Where
is she ? "

" Oh, she'll get back somehow ; don't worry," said
Whatley.

They fought their way outside. In the still street a few
stragglers stood around in the moonlight.

" I'll have to find a lorry," said Sylvia. " I hope I'm
lucky."

" Don't worry, we'll pick up something. Let's walk until we do," said Whatley, linking his arm in Sylvia's.

At that moment she saw Janet in the deep shadow of a house. She was talking to an Australian, who towered over her.

" Janet ! We've been looking for you ! We're going home," cried Sylvia, pausing in front of them. " Are you coming ? "

She looked at the man who was with Janet and saw now that he was a sergeant, a heavy-jawed fellow of about thirty.

" Come on, baby ! " he said, taking Janet by the arm and pulling her towards him. In that moment, as Sylvia looked from one to the other she was conscious of some kind of understanding between them.

" You go along," said Janet abruptly. " I'll find my own way back."

She gave Sylvia a truculent stare as she spoke to her, and pressed herself closer to the enormous Australian.

" Janet—do come ! It's very late," urged Sylvia, a sense of alarm sweeping through her.

" It's all right, miss. She's with me. We've fixed it," he said, with a warm, confident smile. " Haven't we, kid ? " he asked confidently, bending over Janet.

" Yes," she answered shortly, looking at Sylvia defiantly. " Leave us alone—you've got your own boy. We're making a night of it. It's no use looking shocked, my dear. God knows where we'll all be in a week, and I'm going to have my fun."

" Janet, are you crazy ? " stammered Sylvia.

" No—nor drunk either. You run along. I'm not chucking chances away."

" That's right, kid. Trust Daddy ! " said the Australian. " He's got that sweet stuff. Good night, miss ! "

He put a possessive arm around Janet, and she nestled into his side. They walked away and turned the corner. Sylvia stood rooted to the spot. Derek was waiting a few yards away. Even if he had not heard he must have seen everything. Sylvia could not speak. Anger, disgust, pity froze the words in her. It was Derek who made the first comment.

" I hope there are no M.P.'s around," he said, quietly.

" Why ? "

" Why ?   Well—they might pick him up."

Sylvia said nothing.   She felt he knew it was Janet who was in peril.

They began to walk through the streets, along by the riviera out of the town.   They were challenged by guards twice.   The moonlight lay on the white houses.   The olive groves covered the ground with a crochet work of shadows.   A million diamonds flashed in the bay.   The air was warm.   The tireless cicadas filled the valley and the hills with their shrill noise.   They found a lorry at last, and Derek insisted on accompanying her.   Presently the tents of the hospital came into view.   They got down from the lorry, passed the guard at the gate, and threaded their way through the moonlit orchard towards the hospital.   In the heavy shadow of a catalpa tree they paused, looking across the silver-grey foliage of the olive trees to the jewelled sea.   The warm air was slightly aromatic.   It was the moonlit scene on a stage, before the characters had entered.   Far off, even now, they heard the drone of a plane.   They listened, and when it had faded again Derek was the first to speak.

" Well, this is good-bye, Sylvia."

" Yes, Derek—for how long ? "

" Who knows ?   With luck it might be a few days, a week, or——"   He did not finish the sentence and kicked a stone at his feet.

" Anything can happen.   I know that.   I shan't forget this.   It's been wonderful, Derek," said Sylvia.

She lifted her face to his and smiled.   The shadows of the branches made a mottled patchwork over them. Slowly, confidently, he took her in his arms and kissed her. She made no resistance.   They clung to each other in desperate ecstasy.   They were the prisoners of circumstance, insignificant as the leaves trembling over them, but for these few moments, against the threat of Time, they were all that life meant in its most exquisite beauty.

" Sylvia, will you believe me when I tell you you're what matters most to me now ? " he said.   " Perhaps I shouldn't say this—but there's nothing less I can say, now it's good-bye."

She made no answer but laid her head against his shoulder. His face was dark above the white jacket.

" I'm glad you said it, Derek," she said very quietly, after a time in which the small sounds of the night were audible to them. A blue light clothed the mountains. The houses by the shore were like white cardboard, with strong black shadows. A few stars glittered over the peninsula.

" I'll be back soon," he said.

" Very soon, I hope. If not, it will be just the same when you do come."

" You mean that ? "

" I mean it. You, too, are what matters most now. Good-night, my dear."

" Good night, darling."

Her face, pale under the moonlight, was lifted briefly to his. Her eyes shone darkly. Their lips met, and then she slipped away, her uniform dappled with shadow as she went down under the trees.

He waited until she was gone from sight, and stood, so wonderfully alive that within him the whole beauty of this mysterious world sang like choral music. It was such a supreme moment of consciousness as he had never known before, might never know again. Here and now something imperishable seemed to be born within him. It was a sensation as brief as it was acute. Then he belonged to the earth again, to an olive grove in the Mediterranean moonlight. He slowly descended, greeted the sentry at the gate, and stepped into the moonlit road. With luck he might pick up a lorry ; if not he would have to walk all the way to Suda Bay. In a few hours, at break of dawn, they were sailing. It was the twelfth of May, 1941. It was a landmark in his life, come what may.

CHAPTER II

WINGED ICARUS

THE orderly came in to wake them a little before dawn, but Richard was already awake. As the tent flap was turned back the cold dawn wind blew in off the African desert. It was still dark. Grumbling bodies began to move around him. There was a smell of hot coffee. Richard was the first out, incompletely dressed. Then Kid Carter put out his tousled head. A streak of yellow broke over the dun hummocks to the east. In a quarter of an hour they had washed, dressed, and eaten, all processes simultaneously performed. On the drome the roar of engines warming up beat the air. The North African day began to leap across the desert. Kid Carter pulled up the zips of his fur-lined flying-suit and then pushed his yellow curls inside his helmet, strapped, with the microphone dangling.

" And we go from here to hell," he said to Knapps Farmiloe.

" One hell's as hot as another, so what's your grouse ? " asked Farmiloe.

" Day says it's a beautiful island. Ever read *The Blue Lagoon* ? In my distant childhood it was a favourite yarn," said Stanway, from the lofty experience of thirty-two.

" Look at that," said Richard, pointing to some clouds. " We can hide at twelve thousand if there are any Savoias around."

Their Gloster Gladiators stood in a row, brown against the brown desert. The engines were revving steadily. Mechanics came crawling out of the cockpits like disturbed ants.

" Ready to go, Sergeant ? " asked Richard, fixing his parachute harness.

" All ready—good journey ! "

" Thanks ! "

Richard stepped up to the wing, lowered himself into the

cockpit, and ran his eyes over the instrument panel. He
plugged in the microphone cord. Along the field the others
were in. He opened the throttle, moved forward, pulled
her round, and went taxi-ing over the bumpy field, centre
of his quintet. They turned at the end of the run, facing
upwind. Richard moved up to the point of their arrow-
head formation. They went forward, gathering speed,
until their tails lifted. The ground fell away. In a last
circle they gained height, unwinding the desert, the mountains, the aerodrome below them. The sun was up now.
It glinted on propellers, threw a rosy light over the mottled
earth, and put a leaden glaze on the sea, wind-wrinkled like
an elephant's skin. Mersa Matruh reeled away behind.
There was nothing in the sky. With luck they might be
unmolested until they reached Crete. What a shuttle!
Egypt–Greece, Greece–Egypt, Egypt–Crete—and then?
There might be no then! Crete sounded like a last-call job.
They were the remnant of the squadron that had come out
of Greece, all except Kid Carter, a desert pup of three weeks,
straight from Heliopolis, in the repaired plane that had
killed poor Tony.

" How much higher? It's damn cold," asked Knapps.
Richard glanced at the panel. Twelve thousand feet.

" We'll keep this. Stop talking. There may be Eyeties
cloud-hopping," he said. He looked around. Kid Carter,
Knapps, to his left ; Stanway, Preston, to his right. They
floated, shining in the blue-white air. Wisps of cloud
passed them like ghostly wraiths.

This was luck, of course. Perhaps he should say " man-
œuvred luck." Ever since the certainty that Sylvia must
have gone to Crete, he had been string-pulling for this.
Where in Crete? he wondered. He had a list of five field
hospitals, so far as they knew in Cairo, but it was all guess-
work in Cairo. If only he had known when he was in
Greece that she was there. He might have been near her.
In the chaos of those last hours at Athens no one had known
where anyone was.

Crete was going to be hot. He could not feel sure about
these old Gladiators. Against Italian 42s they were on the
level. His four 303 guns had the same range. But when
it came to their G-50s and German Messerschmitts—that

was another story. Well, the end was the end anywhere.
One should always remember that. Strange, if he went
out over Crete, perhaps over Knossos, of all places, since
they were putting down at Herakleion. A bit of a ruin
over his pet ruins. He laughed at the idea, at its neat
absurdity.

When they sighted Crete he gave instructions.

" Going down to eight. Cape Lithinos coming up.
Mount Ida beyond. Over the cape I shall leave you and
follow in at Herakleion," said Richard.

" What's in the wind ? " asked Knapps Farmiloe.

" This is my home. I've friends to call on. Carry on,
Knapps."

Over the cape he left them, coming down to four thousand.
The long valley of Messara lay below, green and gold in its
fields. To the west lay the Bay of Messara, amethyst-blue ;
to the south lay the long, precipitous, hostile coast. Two
British destroyers going west left a white wake. They
looked like water-beetles.

He turned up the valley, along the silver vein of the
Mitròpotamos, and found what he sought, the cliff face on
which stood the Villa Vouni. He came down to three
thousand and flew in, parallel. Never before had he
realised how completely hidden the place was on its narrow
ledge. He could see the terrace now and picked out,
because he knew they must be there, the brown pantiles
of the long roof and the path back over the plateau to the
old mule sheds.

He dropped now to two thousand feet. There was not
a sign of life. He wondered where old Anastasia was—
probably at Vori, with her married daughter. He circled
over the mountain peak, picked up the road going to Herakleion, where the mule path ran into it at Gortyn, and began
to climb rapidly again, flying north. The sun-crowned
range of Mount Ida, with its sprawling arêtes, floated below
him ; ahead shone the misty blue Ægean, with the island of
Santorin faint on the horizon. Herakleion, the port and the
mole, came into view. He picked up the aerodrome in
the Knossos valley. What a change across the centuries !
The legend of Dædalus had come true. The wings of
Icarus filled these skies.

A staccato hammering came to him. Machine-gun fire. He scanned the air. There was a dogfight running along the edge of a white cloud out of which seven planes appeared. Below, he saw blotches boil up on the aerodrome, along its edges, and near the hangars. They were bombing the place. A Savoia suddenly appeared at eight thousand, having delivered. He looked to the west again and knew he couldn't go into the fight. There were two Messerschmitts and a 42 mixing it with a couple of their Blenheims. His own range was only five hundred yards. He calculated they were at twelve thousand. A Blenheim was on the tail of the 42. He was coming down steep. The tracers went over. Suddenly the Italian went into a flat spin; the black-edged white smoke proclaimed the kill. He fell into a head crash and went earthward.

Richard made a flat climb and circled, coming in again at twelve thousand. The fight went westward out to sea. The Messerschmitts were giving the Savoia cover. The two Blenheims hung on. This was a hot place. It was all he expected. There was no sign of the Gladiators. They must be down.

He banked tight, went down, and in a few minutes fishtailed in on the field. He taxied to the offices and saw fitters and riggers busy over a mess by the hangar. Someone had got it. The ground was pitted with bomb craters. He had to pick his course. He pushed back the top of the cockpit as a fitter reached him, and unbuttoned his microphone.

" Are my boys in ? " he asked as he climbed out.

" Three, sir. One got shot up coming in."

" Who ? "

" I don't know, sir."

" Is that it ? " asked Richard, nodding towards the mess. He could see now it was a Gladiator, her nose utterly smashed. The fitter nodded.

They walked across the field. Two figures came towards them. They were Knapps and Stanway. That left Preston and Kid Carter.

" It's the Kid," said Knapps, not waiting for the question.

" How bad ? "

" Washed out," said Knapps. " It's a miracle how he

brought her in at all. He came down six thousand in a tail spin and then flattened her out."

" How did it happen ? " asked Richard. Young Kid Carter, three weeks out. It was wicked. He could see that tousled hair, always too long, and the boy's mouth under the perky nose. God Almighty, a baby, a mere baby caught in this bloody business.

They approached the Gladiator. She had crashed, her nose buried in the hard soil. Half a wing had been shot away ; the cockpit cover was lacerated with bullets. There was a wet brown trail where they had lifted the body out and carried it to the stretcher.

" Why didn't the little fool jump ? He was at ten thousand when the Jerry bored in ! He would try to bring her down ! I saw him going and thought he'd jump," cried Stanway bitterly.

" P'raps he couldn't get out," said Knapps.

" He hung on, trying to bring her in," answered Preston. " Well, he brought her in ! "

" I'll tell you why," said Richard fiercely. " The Kid had had it drilled into him planes are scarce—that's why he didn't jump."

" To save that bitch thing," commented Knapps.

" It isn't saved," said the sergeant. " It's junk."

" A bloody good thing ! " cried Knapps, turning away. He saw Richard had gone to the stretcher and was stooping to raise the cover. He hurried over.

" No, I wouldn't, Dick," he said, putting out a restraining hand.

The two men stood up and looked at each other through a moment's silence.

" Anyone get his dog-tag ? " asked Richard.

" Yes, and he was carrying a wallet."

Someone handed him a sticky, wet wallet. It was against Regulations. Richard opened it as he walked across towards the office. A couple of letters, a little leather photo folder : father, mother, a girl—a sister ? She looked like none of them. " Love to Jack—Kitty." A clipping from a Yeovil paper about a brother, Lieutenant Carter, R.N., lost in H.M.S. *Bingham*. Here was his service paper. Richard glanced over it. John Cunningham Carter. Born May 14,

1920. Good God ! It was the boy's birthday. Twenty-
one. All over at twenty-one !

He greeted the squadron leader and sat down at a desk
and made out his report.

§ 2

The next day, while crossing a street, half of it a heap of
rubble, Richard heard someone calling him in Greek. He
stopped, and old Papapoulos, a caretaker at Knossos, came
hurrying up, crying in his delight. The old fellow was
almost inarticulate with emotion, then, recovering he began
to pour out his news. In the torrent came Morosini's name.

" You've seen him here recently ? " asked Richard,
startled.

" *Ochi, Kirie !* I've not seen him. But my niece, she
works at the hospital, and she has seen him ! He was shot
down on Tuesday."

Half an hour later Richard had found the matron. She
looked tired out, but patiently found a list and scanned it.

" Lieutenant Cesare Morosini—an Italian ? " she asked,
holding her finger on a line. " Yes—he came in on Tuesday.
If you'll wait I'll find out about him."

She left the room. A typewriter clicked somewhere.
Aides brought in papers and placed them on the desk. The
matron came in, accompanied by a Sister.

" Yes—he's in 6A. I don't know whether he'll know you.
He's in a very critical condition. You must be only a few
minutes," said the matron.

He thanked her and followed the nurse.

" Will he recover ? He crashed, I suppose ? " he asked
her as he went along the corridor.

" Yes, in the sea. They found a plane floating somewhere off the coast. There'd been a raid early that morning.
He was unconscious for two days. You know him ? "

" Yes—we worked here together before the war."

" Sometimes he talks in English, sometimes Italian. Compound fracture of the leg, broken pelvis, internal injuries,
concussion, and bad burns." She stopped and looked at
Richard. " Perhaps you should know—he won't see again."

" Oh," said Richard. They walked on. " Will he——? "

G

She knew his question and answered him at once.

" It's surprising he's lasted this long."

A screen was round the bed in the long ward. There was nothing to be seen but a mouth and half a nose under the bandages. He lay swathed like a mummy.

" There's an English friend to see you, Lieutenant," said the nurse.

" Cesare ! " called Richard softly, fighting to keep the break out of his voice.

" *Caro mio !* You ! " said a voice not recognisable to Richard.

" I heard you were here. I flew in yesterday. I've just heard."

" *Sono finito. Come sta ?* " said the voice.

"Oh, I'm all right, Cesare. I'm sorry to see you like this."

" Here we are again. Where did you come from ? "

" Mersa Matruh yesterday ; before that, Greece—a bad show. We were sent over in November, from Libya."

Morosini lay still, not speaking for some time. Richard waited. There was nothing he could say to this poor wreck. The nurse looked at him, as if to bring the scene to an end, but Morosini began to talk in Italian, very faintly, Richard leaned over him. He could not understand, perhaps he was delirious again. Then, in English, the shadow of a voice said :

" You'll tell Sylvia ? Where is she ? I think of her all the time."

" She's here, Cesare. She was in Greece. She was somewhere around Larissa, nursing. Her unit was evacuated here. I found out this morning she's at Canea. I'm trying to get over there to-morrow. She'll be grieved to hear what's happened."

" Dear enemy, eh ? We are all here together again," said Morosini, and, after a pause, " The old guitar's at Vouni. I left it, you remember ? "

" Yes, I remember."

There was another long pause. The nurse looked anxiously at Richard.

" I'm going now, Cesare. I'll come again," said Richard.

" Richard. Are we alone ? It's this darkness I hate— such darkness, and I always loved the sun."

Richard glanced at the nurse, who nodded and tiptoed away.

"Yes, we're alone, old boy."

"When you see Sylvia, give my love to her—tell her—it was to the very end."

"I'll tell her. She'll come and see you."

"No—no. Not that—please, Richard. You understand? Not now. *Carissima Sylvia, è miglio che tu non mi veda,*" he murmured. "Good-bye, Richard."

Richard bent over him. There were only his lips to touch.

"*A rivederci,* Cesare," he said. Then he straightened himself and with a set face left the ward.

The nurse was waiting. They walked towards the exit together.

"Is he blind permanently?"

"Yes—and terribly burned. We don't know how he lives."

"How long, do you think?"

"A few days, perhaps. We are surprised now."

"I'll come to-morrow—about twelve. Thank you, Sister."

"Good-bye. I'll be on to-morrow morning. Ward 6A. Nurse Comiford.

He went out and, sitting on a wall in the hot sunshine, lit a cigarette. His hand trembled as he lit it. He had seen so much that he didn't think anything could affect him now, like this.

§ 3

Sylvia lay in bed. She turned over and looked at her wrist-watch hanging on the rail. It was nearly noon, and the sun streamed into the dormitory. One of the nurses was dressing. Janet was still fast asleep. She had thrown off the single cover and lay clad only in her knickers and brassiere. The day was hot. Yesterday they had worked fourteen hours at a stretch, coming off duty at 6 A.M. They were all so tired from long arrears of sleep that they seemed to wake as fatigued as when they went to bed.

Sylvia lay contemplating the wire network of the bunk

above. She tried to remember the day, the date. All the days seemed alike. Bed-making, body-washing, wound-dressing, the smells, the sights, the sounds of a hundred men, maimed, sick in body, sick in mind, some brave, some whimpering, but most of them so quiet and patient. The odours of ether and antiseptics, mixed with that of gangrenous wounds, were always about one. At two o'clock an ambulance had come in full of wounded from a night raid at Suda Bay. Hypodermics, cauterisation, patients in and out of the operating theatre, overworked surgeons, irritable and exacting—one in particular, vain and touchy as a *primadonna*, but a great surgeon—she thought of all these things in turn, lying there in her bunk. For some reason a house surgeon at Bart's Hospital came to mind. She could see him taking off his rubber gloves, the moisture on his brow, the noise of water running at the sink, the steam from the sterilising trough. " When it comes it'll be a long war—ten years. A surgeon's harvest from our point of view. I remember the last. Well, well, well ! " They called him Jeremiah Jones.

Sylvia looked at Janet Farr. She was humped up over the bed and not a pretty sight. Her breasts were too heavy, her legs too fat. Her huge buttocks rose like a camel's hump. The Dutch masters, Rubens, in particular, would have loved her for a model. She lay on her side, her shock of coarse hair clouding her brow. Sylvia noticed how wide were the nostrils of her stumpy nose. It was a body that made the thought of animal passion nauseating, of love ridiculous, and yet Janet had all the desires, intenser perhaps than those of other young women. How unfair life was !

Neither of them had made any reference to that night at the cabaret. The next morning Janet had been prompt on duty, although she had not come into the dormitory except to change hurriedly. All that day she had had a truculent air. The nurses as well as the nurses' aides were afraid of her. She was a glutton for work and went about it with a kind of fury. She was never tired, never flustered. She could handle obstreperous men, as ready with her tongue as with her hands. Most of the patients were awed by her. She knew some of them loathed her and could resort to all manner of tricks not to fall into the hands of " Bloody

Awful." She had had a first-class training in a large Leeds hospital and was highly qualified. By sheer force of character and a fanatical zeal for nursing she had got out of a factory and by desperate effort had taken herself through her training, advancing from a scullery maid. Odd, ruthless creature that she was, Sylvia admired and loved her. She possessed an unshakable loyalty, a lion's courage. Under the hardness lay a nature that was eager to be recklessly romantic, with the bitter knowledge that unfulfilment was her lot.

Sylvia sat up and called her. They were on duty again in half an hour. Janet opened a pair of heavy eyes, but made no movement.

" It's twelve o'clock ! " said Sylvia, standing up over her.

" I could stay here for ever," answered Janet, yawning. She had small, strong teeth. Teeth, hands, and feet were perfect, Sylvia had noticed.

Someone came down the dormitory and stopped opposite their bunks. It was Peggy Farrell, one of the aides.

" Oh, I'm glad I've found you," she said to Sylvia. " Your brother's here—in the matron's office."

" Who ? " cried Sylvia, wide-eyed.

" Flight-Lieutenant Day. He is your brother, isn't he ? "

" Of course he is. But Dick—here ! I can't believe it ! " cried Sylvia, snatching up her sponge-bag.

" Come and see—and hurry, or you'll be losing him. All the ward's out," said Peggy Farrel coyly. She was like a pretty doll. The men spent their time trying to catch her hand ; she spent hers just not letting them.

" Tell him I'll be there in a few minutes," called Sylvia, running to the washroom. Richard in Crete ! It was something she had never imagined.

In ten minutes she was washed and dressed. She ran down to the hospital and into the matron's outer office. He was there.

" Dick ! " she cried, rushing into his arms.

He kissed her and, after holding her to him for a few moments, pushed her out at arm's length.

" Let's have a look at you," he said, his eyes going over her critically.

He was prepared for a change, knowing what she had gone through, but not for a change so thorough as this. He had left a girl in England, pretty and vivacious. She was now a matured woman. There were lines of fatigue under her eyes. Her mouth had a firmness he had never seen before. The lines of her face had hardened. Her figure had tightened and seemed bigger-boned. It was a shock and yet he felt, in some way, she was immensely improved. She had become his equal. The kid sister he had loved and treated inconsequently had vanished. It was an astonishing transformation. He knew in that moment in what a furnace of trials she had been tempered.

" Well, you look healthy ! " he said at last.

" Let's go into the grove," she said. " I'm on duty in an hour."

They found a spot under some olive trees, beyond the tents. She wanted to know everything and plied him with questions.

" It's unbelievable ! To think Fate should bring us back to Crete like this ! " she said. " Do you know, whenever an Italian plane comes over I look up and wonder if Cesare's in it. How odd, if he should bomb us and not know ! "

This was his opportunity. He told her of their meeting at Herakleion.

" I went back this morning. He wasn't there. They told me where they were burying him. I hurried up to the place and got there just as they were shovelling the soil in. I went over and took some flowers out of somebody's garden —zinnias and roses of Sharon—and threw them in for you and me. He gave me a message for you as I left him yesterday morning, ' Give my love to Sylvia—tell her it was to the very end.' "

Richard's arm went round his sister, and she pressed her face against his shoulder, hiding her tears. In a while she began talking again. He asked her now about her own experiences. He found, for a few days, that they had been very near to each other in Greece, when he had flown over Larissa.

They talked quickly, then they got up from their shady place and began to walk back towards the hospital.

" When shall I see you again ? " she asked.

" Very soon—I'll be over in a day or two. This is a sneak trip. They're very jittery here at Maleme. We've no planes to speak of. And there aren't any coming. There are only four Bofors and some machine-guns to keep Jerry off. Hanson wants to mine the aerodrome, but they won't let him 'cause they want to keep the ' recco ' sweeps going as long as possible. Retimo and Herakleion are no good ; they can't spare us ground crews. Well, if Jerry gets Maleme, we can wave the place good-bye."

" Do you mean Crete ? "

" Yes. They should have gone ahead with the field at Messara, and then we'd not have had all our eggs in one basket. I say ' they.' The trouble is no one ever knows who ' they ' are. Beamish—he's our wing commander—got here a month ago, and he knows it's too late now. The ' reccos ' over Greece all bring the same story. They're getting a terrific wallop ready for us. We've had a bad plastering these last three days at Maleme, Retimo, and Herakleion."

" I know—you can tell by the wounded ground crews they're bringing in," said Sylvia.

" It's always the same story : no fighters, no anti-aircraft. What's left of the 3rd Squadron has to be out doing reconnaissance. They're watching for invasion concentrations. Thank God for the Navy—or we'd get our ticket," said Richard. " If they do land, they'll find a hornets' nest. But the air worries me. We're losing it."

Sylvia went to the gate with her brother.

" Good-bye," he said, taking her in his arms. " I'm proud of you ! "

" I'm proud of you. I'm proud of everybody, Dick. They're so splendid," she replied.

" I'll try to get over in a day or two. I'll wangle Maleme if I can."

He kissed her. She watched his lean, tall figure go out past the guard.

He had almost reached Malene aerodrome when he heard the motor horns break out into their raucous air-raid warning. He began to run then and heard, in the sky above, the drone of engines. Men were running out of the buildings and the mess tent for the slit trenches. He wondered if it could be as bad as that. Two Blenheims were taking off. His Gladiator stood in the far corner. Almost as he reached the edge of the aerodrome the first stick of bombs came down across the field. He saw a Blenheim heel over and two tents flatten under the blast. Then four Stukas with their hellish scream came down and laid a course of fifty-pounders.

He hesitated for a moment, wondering whether to make for the slit trenches in the bare mountainside, or to attempt getting his plane up. The sky was full of Jerries—Stukas, Messerschmitts, and Heinkels. They were coming in from the south to avoid flying into the sun, and he guessed they had circled out from the east where they had just plastered Suda Bay.

He reached the Gladiator. There was a crew near, scurrying away from the toppled Blenheim on which they had been working. Two bodies on the ground told the tale.

" Come over—I'm taking off ! " he yelled.

The fitters turned in their flight. Another explosion over the field sent the red earth flying. The Gladiator rocked. The men came over to him, one with a bloody face. Richard climbed into the cockpit. They helped him to start and turn. Four or five Blenheims were up, mixing it, at about four thousand. The bombs were raining down. The Bren gun from across the hangar got a Stuka as it came in level. It crashed, somersaulted three times, and burst into flame over by the barley field.

Richard revved up his engine. At the best he might save it, for nothing on the ground would survive. There were half a dozen fires blazing. The Bofors had more than they could deal with. The machine-guns barked, but the Stukas came in constantly. He began to climb, putting her nose up. Great coils of smoke piled up over Suda. He couldn't count the Heinkels in the sky—forty, fifty, sixty, perhaps. Below him the bombs were bursting in swift concentric rings of destruction. If he ran into fighters he was lost. He was at two thousand now, and with relief saw the sweep going west. The Blenheims were hanging on their tails.

He headed due east. There were no planes now over Suda, where the pall of smoke spread over the bay. He was

over the sea, Retimo sprawling along to his right. As he
came in over Cape Stavros he saw a small convoy ploughing
west, with a couple of destroyers cavorting protectively round
it, the white wash vivid on the blue-green sea. Herakleion
and the Knossos valley, with hospital and the familiar Palace
of King Minos, flowed towards him. He was at eight
thousand and began to go down when, out of a cloud, came
two ME 109Fs. They were over him. Richard did an
Immelmann and heard a cannon shell burst at his side. In
that second he saw he was not alone. Coming in at ten
thousand was a Blenheim, with a Hurricane behind. One
of the ME 109Fs had got below him and was coming up
under his tail. Richard half turned, evaded his pursuer,
but in the instant saw the other plane coming in on a dive.
Then something hit his elevators. He was a lame duck.
Then seconds later there was a terrific burst in the engine.
This was it. The plane rocked. He pushed back the cockpit cover, half asphyxiated with cordite smoke. Levering
himself from his seat, he jumped for it and saw his plane
spiralling below him. Then he felt the tug of his harness
and he began to float down.

As he descended he wondered briefly if they would shoot
at his parachute. Larry Dean had gone that way ; a filthy
swine had riddled him. No, they were leaving him alone.
The Blenheim had gone in and the ME109 was turning
away. He heard a burst of gunfire. The earth slowly
floated up as he watched his drift. He was in luck ; instead
of going seaward, he was floating in towards the aerodrome.
The town lay below him ; in the valley he could see the
site of the Palace of King Minos, the harbour, the hospital,
the tents, the aerodrome. It would have been like a dream
but for the hammering of anti-aircraft fire and gun bursts.
The fight was running west. He wondered where the old
Gladiator had found its grave. Then he felt stickiness down
his right arm. He looked and saw a wet brown patch
spreading, and realised he had been hit.

CHAPTER III

AIR AND WATER

THERE was no peace for the island from that hour on. All through the day the sky rained bombs. They flew in in half-dozens, in flights of ten, twenty, thirty, and unloaded their bombs. On the seventeenth the pattern was plain. They left the town and Suda Bay comparatively alone. The target was the Maleme aerodrome. From dawn to sunset there was no let-up from those Savoias, Dorniers, Heinkels, ME109s, Stukas, The machines in the field were knocked off like sitting pigeons. The ground crews kept running to and fro from the slit trenches. The position of that scanty air force had become impossible. There were only a dozen planes left in the whole of Crete on the afternoon of the eighteenth, when the order came through for them to get out. There was no petrol left; the stores had been bombed and had gone up in flames. The remaining planes would soon be grounded. They had to go at once.

The next day the few survivors flew south to Egypt. Crete, wholly without air cover, dug in and waited for the drama to develop. The nature of the next phase was known. The " reccos " had reported the massing of planes, transports, and gliders in Greece for the invasion. At all costs Maleme aerodrome had to be held. If they could land there Crete was lost. More New Zealand troops were rushed to strengthen the defence.

On Sunday midnight the bombing started again. Sylvia, at work in the wards, heard it all around her. Suda Bay, Canea, Maleme. They were surrounded by terrific detonations. The place shook. At dawn, her duty finished, she was about to cross to the dormitories when a strange reverberation filled the air. The whole sky seemed to beat with a rhythmic thunder. The bomb flashes no longer lit the sky. Something else was coming in with the dawn, whose faint purple light spread through the sky. And then she saw what it was. She stood spellbound with the beautiful terror in the sky. There, steadily coming in, was the German armada. From the north-west it came, a black cloud of locusts, steadily floating on a mounting tide of thunder. Thousands of them. Their roar filled the air in one ceaseless crescendo. They were dropping now, growing larger, darker. Heinkels, Dorniers, Stukas. Around her she heard the sounds of people running, saw shapes fleeing across the orchards and the fields to the slit trenches on the foothills. The invaders were at less than four thousand feet now. Nothing could survive the annihilation they threatened.

They were over now. The Bofors and the machine-guns began to crackle around the aerodrome, from the river bed, the slit trenches. The air trembled under the thunder of those myriad wings. And then the skies spilled their wrath, and the living earth became one flaming hell.

There was a pattern to it. They came in, reckless of all opposition. Sylvia saw the tracers streaming from the machine-guns across the valley. It was all so pitifully inadequate, so contemptuously ignored. The Dorniers were right over now. She could see the fat bombs tumbling out of their bellies. The dawn was illuminated with flashes and punctuated with the hideous blast as the bombs struck. The red earth rose in fountains.

Then the fighters roared in, lashing the field, the olive groves, with streams of bullets. They sought out the machine-gun emplacements. They trailed the slit trenches and pits, blotting out the fire beneath them. A lurid light mingled with the growing dawn. The olive groves were on fire. And then the tornado passed. The bombers went down the sky; the fighters drew off; the crackle of ground fire died. The straffing had lasted three-quarters of an hour. Dazed men came out of the trenches, still deaf from their ordeal. They looked around them on a scarred, blazing world. Stretcher parties went out, and the wounded began to pour in. Sylvia knew there would be no rest for her this morning. She ran into Janet in a corridor, a set-faced Janet marshalling the aides with complete self-possession.

" I thought we'd get it every minute," said Sylvia.

" We may yet," commented Janet.

The sky was quiet again. The silence carried a threat. Within three-quarters of an hour the *Luftwaffe* returned, now in full daylight. This time it was a fuller fury. Under the great bombers, the Stukas wove in and out, following the waves of Dorniers and Heinkels. Their screamers brought a new note to the hellish uproar of bombs, guns, machine fire. They bore down fearlessly upon their targets, drawn by the fires that rose over the wreckage of buildings, tents, and blazing olive groves. After them came hordes of Messerschmitt fighters. They flew in level ; they hedge-hopped, strewing death over the fields and groves, pouring machine-gun and cannon fire into the narrow trenches. The pattern of it never failed in the diabolical pandemonium of their onslaught. They came over again and again, wave upon wave, in a terrible repetition of bombers, dive-bombers, fighters. For an hour this continued, while the soldiers in the trenches crouched and flattened themselves under the rain of death. To look up was fatal. A white face became a target.

And now a second lull. Was it all over at last ?

Sylvia and her fellow nurses had survived. The hospital, in the middle of a red hell, had miraculously escaped, except for damage from fragmentation bombs. Wounded lay outside in the olive groves, along the walls on the ground, in the shelter of buildings and tents. There were no more beds, no more space. They went from man to man, hypodermics for some moaning in their agony, the operating tent for others. The queue lengthened even while the bombs rained down. But now a lull.

It was of short duration. Again the air reverberated. This time it was louder. It was as if the floor of heaven were being thumped by a tremendous engine.

" Christ ! Look at 'em ! " shouted a man on a stretcher as they carried him out of the olive grove.

They looked up. In the bright morning sky came a new armada. It came on, scarcely four hundred feet above the earth. It blotted out the sky. The whole sunlit ground passed into its shadow. The noise was terrible, so that a human voice could not be heard. It came from giant planes, Junkers 52s and Wulf transports. Then traps opened, and out of them fell men in clots of thirty. They came down in

chutes that opened and fell quickly, dumping their human
freight in a few seconds. The sky was like a field of white
flowers bursting into bloom. Down they came, and amid
the white there were red and blue parachutes. The rifles
and machine-guns played over them. Many came to earth
as corpses, or fell limp, or suddenly crumpled up as they
disengaged their harness. A withering fire spread over
them. They lay in collapsed heaps or twisted in their death
agony.

The carnage spread as the shower of human bodies
dropped through the air. A few landed and scuttled for
cover. Sylvia had a confused glimpse of these survivors
with the goggles over their faces, the high boots, the belts
of ammunition round their necks, the grenades and boxes
strapped to their chests. Down they came, firing tommy
guns and throwing grenades. Some of the chutes caught
fire, and the soldiers plummeted to earth, or became living
torches, or were roasted alive under the flaming covers that
collapsed over them. They were dying in droves, but they
still came down, and, in clusters, began to take cover from
the deadly cross-fire kept up by the New Zealanders. Some
men landed in trees and dangled until a bullet stilled their
agitation. Some fell on the housetops of the village. There
were desperate hand-to-hand encounters. A swarm of
Maoris, venting their bloodcurdling war-cry, went in with
bayonets where a concentration of Germans began to make
a stand. The white walls of the houses dripped with red
blood. Up in the hills, in the groves, along the trenches
the fight went on. The Cretan civilians streamed out, along
the roads and over the plain. Old men, young men, women,
boys, with long knives, sickles, yagathans, anything with
which they could slaughter the invaders, plunged into the
carnage. The desperate fight covered the countryside.

But now came another invasion. Great black gliders,
towed across the Ægean and released near the coast, began
to float in, sinister, silent. Some landed on the water and
chugged in with outboard motors ; some glided down upon
the open fields, across the aerodrome ; others fell in the
groves, on the slopes and foothills. There were tremendous
crashes as some of the gliders were rent in mid-air and
spilled their human freight. Others collided with trees

and crumpled up, a mass of splintered wood and torn bodies. But still they came, skidding along the earth and coming to a stop, hidden in a cloud of brown dust.

The transports were still coming also, putting down, discharging their living freight, and taking off again for a new load. More and more gliders came and came ; more and more black and brown ants swarmed out of them. They were swept by fire, but here and there pockets of them became entrenched. Some of them had settled in the riverbed by the edge of the aerodrome, others in the craters their bombs had pitted. The machine-guns could not get at them. There was lively fire coming from the north end. The road to the town and the town itself had been held, but the invaders were covering the aerodrome, and the transport planes continued to land there. The men out of them worked fast, heroically, reckless of death. The smaller gliders carried companies of twelve, complete with machine-guns, mortars, tommy guns, and grenades. They leaped into craters and fought desperately.

Sylvia, in the midst of all this, was suddenly blown off her feet. There was a rending explosion. A black cloud settled down on the hospital ; then came a series of small explosions, smashing the place to atoms. It had been deliberately attacked.

Sylvia raised herself, half buried in debris. Men, wounded and dying, lay around her. Something soft weighted her down. She pushed, and the soft thing yielded, slithering down a pile of rubble. It was one of the sisters, decapitated. Sylvia lay stunned for a time and then began to struggle up, bleeding and bruised. There was no doubt about it. They had deliberately attacked the hospital. They were now being gunned and dive-bombed by Stukas.

Sylvia and two other nurses struggled out of the ruined ward. Some of the patients were being taken to the slit trenches. Others sat helplessly in their beds, open to the sky while the Stukas flew over them. Sylvia, recovering, began to help with moving the wounded to the trenches. Janet passed her, carrying on her shoulders the heavy limp body of a New Zealander. She walked sturdily on, her face and uniform black with dirt.

For half an hour they worked, rescuing the wounded. The dive-bombing had ceased. The hospital existed no longer, its tents ripped open, its building flattened. Seven nurses and aides were dead. Many of the others were wounded.

But the end was not yet. Paratroopers suddenly appeared, as if out of the earth. They drove wounded men, nurses, doctors before them with tommy guns. They had taken the old jail. They were now taking the hospital. The flag was still flying from its mast. They hauled it down, and the swastika fluttered in its place. A Messerschmitt pilot, shot down over Canea, and convalescing in the hospital, ostentatiously saluted it. " You bloody swine ! " exclaimed one of the junior surgeons. A paratrooper turned his tommy gun on him. The surgeon crumpled at his feet, and the paratrooper then drove his prisoners on.

They were being rounded up in a corner of the grove. In a few minutes the purpose was clear. The paratroopers wished to join up with others established at the end of the village. They began to drive the staff from the hospital and the field ambulance, together with the wounded who could walk, as a cover for their advance. They had only gone a few hundred yards when firing came from the New Zealanders in the bushes, picking off the paratroopers. The Germans drove their captives on more ferociously. The firing increased. Some of the wounded fell under it ; some of them, despite their guards, called out to their hidden comrades, directing the fire. One by one the Nazi guards fell. Then, in a panic, they deserted the human shield they had been driving up the road and fled. A New Zealander came out from his cover and greeted the rescued party. Late that afternoon a New Zealand force recovered the 7th General Hospital, but it was too wrecked and exposed for further use.

That evening a new hospital was set up in one of the few buildings standing on the outskirts of Canea. The air attack had ended and failed. Nearly three thousand airborne Germans had been dropped on Canea and Maleme. One-third of them was dead. Patrols were out rounding up the survivors. The aerodrome and the groves were littered with the wreckage of gliders and crashed transports.

But as sunset came danger remained. The enemy were entrenched along the dry bed of the Tavronitis River, and they occupied pockets around the aerodrome. With superior equipment and continuous reinforcement from the air, they defied all efforts of the patrols to dislodge them. At sunset the New Zealanders withdrew to positions on the eastern end of the aerodrome. The costly battle had not won Crete, but the enemy were entrenched at the most vital spot in the island. Maleme aerodrome was now a No Man's land. If the Germans succeeded in holding their grasp and dominating the aerodrome, then the end was in sight, for the aerodrome was an essential base for their over-whelming air power. They had well-nigh won the first round. The skies grew quiet except for bombing over Suda Bay. The *Luftwaffe*, badly shaken, withdrew to lick its wounds.

Up in the hills, along the mountain roads, across the valley, in the olive groves and the streets of Canea, the fight went on. The evening quiet was marred by sporadic gunfire as the tough New Zealanders, aided by the Greeks, mopped up the tenacious paratroopers. A waning moon silvered the scene of carnage.

§ 2

It was still dark on the morning of May 22, when Derek Whatley went to the bridge of the cruiser to which he had been transferred. He had cat-napped in the wardroom, fully clothed. The sea was calm; the moon had gone down. There was even quiet in the air. For two days the sky had been thick with planes, while Crete had taken terrible punishment from the bombers, and incessant waves of transports and gliders had swept down upon the island. Canea and Suda Bay had been the main targets, but Maleme aerodrome was the vital prize they sought. So far it seemed, to have withstood capture. Yesterday had brought a terrible holocaust of wrath from the air. Heinkel bombers and Stuka dive-bombers had come out of the sky to annihilate them. High-level, low-level bombing, torpedoes, mines, every form of attack had swept them. In that fierce tornado Messerschmitts had come skimming in at deck level, with cannon and machine-guns sweeping the anti-aircraft crews and laying a bloody trail across the decks. The destroyer *Juno* had been sunk under a stick of bombs, the sea boiling over her. One minute she was splendid and powerful. The next minute she had gone. The noise of battle rent the skies, into which the fleet threw everything it had, desperately attempting to hold off pilots who came down in death dives, heroically indifferent to the fire that met them. Every ship had its dead gun's crews, its riven decks and smashed turrets. Bomb explosions covered them with fountains fifty feet high. Misses, near misses, shook them from bow to stern. Bomb blasts blew men across the decks and flung them skyward and overboard like leaves in an autumn gale. The fleet twisted and turned in desperate evasion of incoming bombers. From dawn to sunset the hellish contest went on. With darkness, the baffled *Luftwaffe* withdrew. It had failed in its purpose. The Mediterranean fleet, reduced, maimed, exhausted, still guarded the Cretan shore.

Last night the Germans had made a desperate attempt at invasion by sea. Towards midnight the *Janus's* searchlight had picked up the enemy convoy. The British flotilla was steaming north. Cruisers, *Dido*, *Orion*, *Ajax*, with the destroyers *Janus*, *Hasty*, *Hereward*, *Kimberley*, broke in with their beams of light. There on the grey sea, led by the Italian escorting torpedo-boats, lay fourteen Greek caïques, loaded to the gunwales with troops and equipment.

Instantly the still night had burst into a pandemonium of gunfire and incendiary shells. The Italian torpedo-boats caught the first blast. The sweeping searchlights netted them. In a few minutes they had been shattered and sunk. The hapless caïques now received attention. There had been something terrible and sickening in that steady massacre. The guns roared ; the night was lit with their flashes stabbing the darkness. A red hell began to glow and light the sea's face as caïque after caïque took fire and burned until gunfire sank them below the waves. Herded, rammed, blasted with shell fire and pompoms, the red battle drifted off the Cretan shore. Slowly the glow faded ; the curtain of quiet fell on a sea strewn with the bodies of men, the flotsam and jetsam of the annihilated convoy. The search-lights swept a full circle, finding only two hulks whose fires were dying down.

They were developing north-west now. Cruisers *Naiad* and *Perth*, with anti-aircraft ships *Carlisle* and *Calcutta*, and the destroyers *Nubian*, *Kandahar* and *Kingston*, were in contact. The battleships *Warspite* and *Valiant*, with light forces, were distant to the west. What would come with dawn to-day?

God, how tired they were! For almost two long years of continuous service, the day-long, night-long wearing vigil in the Mediterranean had been maintained. Its control had so nearly slipped from their grasp. Malta bombed and Suez bombed, there was scarcely a mile of this vital artery not under menace from land-based bombers in arrogant numerical superiority, and from submarines creeping out of the myriad lairs on the enemy coasts.

For two months now the war had grown more and more intense. There had been the clash with the furtive Italian fleet in the Cape Matapan battle at the end of March, following the task of conveying the British army from North Africa to Greece; then came the evacuation of the retreat-ing forces. For months along " Bomb Alley," between Alexandria and Tobruk, they had kept open the vital sea route, while across the whole Mediterranean, from Gibraltar to Jaffa, they had somehow kept the convoys going, under the running attack of the *Luftwaffe*. Between Sicily and Pantelleria they had run the gauntlet, while bombed Malta wondered if the life-line would snap. Somehow it had not snapped, thanks to the indomitable courage of these men, a brotherhood the like of which the seas in all their history had never known before. But, O God, how tired they were; there was no respite, not even in the harbour where they went for more fuel and ammunition. The ships, too, were worn. The guns wanted new rifling; even metal tired under this incessant strain.

A muffled bell rang. A signal from the wireless-room was passed to the officer of the watch. They were all at action stations. All night no one had left the guns. They were ten miles off land. There was a slight swell. The

calm night, the quiet sea seemed menacing after the slaughter
of the midnight. It was almost dawn. Then over the sky
swept a blade of light, two blades, four blades. They were
from the cruisers *Naiad* and *Perth*. Between them they
had picked up a fleet of boats, low Greek caïques, their
decks crammed with men. Together with the destroyers
Nubian, *Kandahar*, *Kingston*, and anti-aircraft ships *Carlisle*
and *Calcutta*, they opened a murderous fire on the helpless
invasion fleet. It was a horrible massacre of almost defenceless boats, but it had to be done. Those boats carried
deadly equipment and reinforcements to Crete, whose
survival hung in the balance. When the ghastly work was
done the sea was again strewn with struggling soldiers.
They leaped from the decks of the caïques, burning and
shattered by relentless gunfire. They swam in oil and
choked and drowned. They drifted in the tide, they lined
the beaches of Crete with their inert bodies and staring
eyes. Of five thousand proud young Germans only a boat-
load survived, to land half crazed with hunger and thirst.

The dawn came up, beautiful and calm over a sea of
pearl. The headlands of Crete caught the rising sun, and
afar the White Mountains lifted their glittering peaks of
snow under the brightening dome of heaven.

" God Almighty, look ! They're here again," cried the
officer of the watch.

A morning mist had lifted off the horizon to disclose two
more vessels of the invasion fleet running the blockade.
Instantly the guns were trained, and the calmness of the
dawn was shattered. The doomed ships lasted but a few
minutes. The last of the invaders were struggling in the
sea.

" We'll get it to-day ; you'll see," said Torps as Derek
Whatley came into the wardroom to get something to eat.
" They'll bomb us like hell. If they don't get rid of us
their game's up. What's the news on Crete ? "

" Pretty bad," answered Richards, the navigator. " Retimo
and Herakleion are cut off. They're fighting all along the
coast road, and there are pockets of paratroops up in the
hills. Those gliders came in again on Maleme aerodrome
like a snowdrift yesterday. They're clinging to the coast
end, and they've dug in up the Tavronitis River bed."

" They've got the hospital and field ambulance——"
began Fielding.

Whatley spun round as he helped himself to coffee.

" Where—what hospital ? " he asked, trying to keep his
voice steady.

" Over by Maleme. Those bloody swine bombed it, the
wireless says, and took the staff and wounded prisoners.
They were herding them along as a screen when the cross-
fire up the valley became too intense and they had to quit."

" What became of the wounded and the staff ? " asked
Whatley.

" I didn't hear. You don't have to pity those swine we
dished this morning ! When you think what they'd do if
they got ashore it's good to see the vermin drown. I
haven't forgotten those poor devils left in Greece, and how
their Stukas pulped 'em on the beaches. The Old Man
said it made him sick this morning to be drowning 'em by
the thousands. The hell he was ! It's given me a damn
good appetite for breakfast. ' Every little Nazi dead means
a safer sleep in bed.' Those are my sentiments, gentlemen ! " Fielding cut himself a chunk of bread and covered
it with marmalade.

Whatley said nothing. He never argued with Fielding,
always rowdily belligerent. He was thinking of Sylvia.
They had bombed the hospital and driven the survivors
ahead of them as a screen against the cross-fire ! She
might be alive, she might be dead, she might be a prisoner.
Weeks would elapse through which he would be tortured
by uncertainty. They were not going back to Crete for
some time. They were to refit and refuel in Alexandria if
they came out of this. His hunger, intense up on the deck
a few minutes ago, had vanished. He forced the coffee
down and made himself eat.

The doc. came in. He was only twenty-four, but looked
older. There were heavy black rings under his eyes. His
left hand was bandaged. He had been treating thirty men
in the last six hours, emergency amputations, fractures,
bomb splinters, minor wounds, cases of blast and concussion. Three of a gun crew had been killed outright ;
seven had died of wounds, two of exhaustion. He had seen
things no operating theatre at Guy's had shown him.

He sat down and ate steadily and silently. He had hoped for experience when the war broke out. He was getting it. Strangely enough, what shook him most was to see how bravely men died ; not a whimper, only a steady, quiet look.

" I hope we get through to Alex pretty soon—or there'll be no survivors of the H.A. guns. There are three gone west and twelve knocked out," said the doc.

" When do we get to Alex ? We're getting pretty low in the magazine," asked Fletcher, the gunnery lieutenant.

" We might go back to Suda—if we catch a convoy," said Whatley.

" Not a dog's chance. It's too unhealthy. They prefer bombing the place to ashes. If you want my——" began Fielding.

He did not finish the sentence. Overhead the high-angle guns banged away.

" What now ! " exclaimed Fletcher, jumping up.

They left the wardroom and rushed up on deck. Their question was answered at once. A cloud of planes came up the sky, facing the sun. The level rays glinted on propellers and prows. It was a terrible and beautiful sight to see these sinister birds roaring through the sky to tear at their enemy below. They came on, clouds of them, in unperturbed formation. There was no one to challenge their approach, to break up their formation. Contemptuous of the H.A. guns, they were the lords of the air, recklessly brave in the lust of destruction.

" God ! What a packet of trouble," said the gunnery lieutenant quietly sweeping the sky with his glasses, as Whatley came on to the bridge.

The flagship was making her signals. The cruisers were to deploy. The yeoman of signals reported the orders. " Revolutions for thirty knots," said the captain. The engine-room telegraph jangled ; the needle vibrated toward " Full Speed " as the ship flew through the water, which came curling over her bow. The *Gloucester* ahead left a foaming white wake.

The cruisers were changing course again. To port came the destoyers *Hasty* and *Greyhound*. The anti-aircraft ship *Calcutta*, steaming slowly, took security from submarine attack behind her destroyer screen, *Hereward, Kimberley,*

Nubian, Kandahar. The four-inch H.A.s and the pom-poms began to fire ; the first bombs came whistling down. Great fountains of water majestically climbed the sky and collapsed in seething foam.

The battle was on. The eagle and the lion were matched. Heinkels, Savoias, Macchis, Messerschmitts, Stukas, all the devilish brood of the sky was there ; high-level bombing, low-level bombing, dive-bombing, gunning, every known form of attack was tried. The Stukas came down in per-pendicular dives ; the Messerschmitts swooped, levelled out, machine-gunned the anti-aircraft crews, or cannoned the decks and shot up the bridge. The noise of bombs, the scream of engines, the racket of pom-poms and H.A. guns drowned out the throb of the ship's engines. The sky bellowed and shook ; the sea boiled and spurted ; men cursed, mangled amid twisted steel or riven decks. Planes crashed and burned fiercely on the decks or plummeted to the sea. Under this deadly rain the fleet twisted and turned, each ship swinging away from bombs, blurring the target with erratic courses, while into the sky their guns threw a deadly barrage of shrapnel. It developed into a long-drawn battle of returns and retreats, of attack on bow and stern, starboard and port, at all levels, in ever-changing formations and devilish flurries. All through the morning, the noon, the afternoon, the birds of prey curved and swooped. With ships badly mauled, or on fire, or reduced in manœuvring power, the battered fleet fought back.

The casualties mounted. The cruisers *Gloucester* and *Fiji,* bombed out of action, sank beneath a last concentra-tion of bombers. The *Greyhound,* lamed and helpless, slipped below the waves. The *Kelly* had been capsized by a direct hit from a thousand-pound bomb. Men floated by, clinging to wreckage, for most of the boats had been smashed. Nor were they safe as they struggled in the water, for the merciless fighters flew down and machine-gunned them. It was perilous for a ship to pick up sur-vivors ; she became an easy target for the swift aircraft. Southward now the harassed fleet fought its way towards Alexandria. Later, the *Kashmir* foundered.

Derek Whatley had no time to speculate on their chance of survival. There was no moment of relief from this flying terror. He was going to the control tower when a terrific explosion shook the cruiser from bow to stern. A bomb had struck her directly. At once she began to list. Another plane bore in on her, and she lost her power of manœuvre. She quivered again from end to end and began to settle rapidly. The order came to abandon ship. Under a hail of machine-gun fire they leaped into the water. The battle still raged around them. Their ship went down, with successive explosions, in a fearsome maelstrom of onrushing water.

Derek began to float as his Mae West inflated. The chance of rescue was slight. Ships that attempted it were in terrible peril. There were men all around him, swimming, clinging to wreckage. Their rafts had been lost in the evacuation from Greece. He felt strangely calm in the midst of the hell that raged around him. The battle began to drift away. If he was not machine-gunned by a diving plane he could last some time in this warm sea. A current was taking him away from his companions. Their struggles were subsiding. He heard men singing defiantly on a raft. Some actually cheered as a destroyer dashed past on her course. Then slowly, aware of the utter futility of his effort, with little hope of being picked up, Derek Whatley began to swim away from the sun in the direction where he thought Crete might lie.

How very odd that this might be the end. He felt so calm. He thought of his mother and their lovely old farm in Sussex set amid its orchards, of the playing fields at Dartmouth, and of Sylvia, her face as clear as when they lay on that bank at Mournies, in the shade of a catalpa tree. Was she alive, a prisoner, or free ? Ill fate had prevented his getting a note to her. Sylvia Day, a lovely name for a lovely person.

The sun was falling rapidly. His own shadow on the water lengthened. It was very calm. But in the sky overhead the transports were still flying to Crete. Could it hold out against this ceaseless invasion by air ?

He swam on. There was no sign of land. Once he saw a small boat and hailed it with some misgiving, for it might be an enemy craft. Either it did not hear him or chose to ignore him. The light left the water. In the sky the emerald, gold, and crimson of evening spread in glory, then faded in the darkening purple of night.

CHAPTER IV

RETREAT TO SFAKIA

THE new hospital in Canea was an improvised affair. All the equipment at Maleme had been destroyed or seized by the enemy. Only half of the staff had survived the blitz or escaped being made prisoners. The night, with its blackout, added to the general confusion. The wounded lay on bare floors. There was not a window left in the villa. A bomb crater stood in the middle of the drive. The water supply had failed.

All through the night a few nurses and aides, tired, hungry, dirty, but still indomitable, laboured on. The roar of explosions at Suda Bay never ceased in the long night. Street fighting was creeping through the suburbs. Before dawn the noise and flames of the bombing of the fleet added fresh apprehensions. Herakleion and Retimo had been put out of communication. Paratroopers had seized the cables and cut great lengths out of them to prevent repairs. Radio sets were almost non-existent. Dispatch riders fell under the fire of snipers. Swooping planes machine-gunned the motor-cyclists along the one coastal road.

By the morning of the twenty-second the lines of communication over the island were shattered. Headquarters was cut off for six hours; there were no telephones left intact between Canea and Herakleion and their adjacent aerodromes. The pattern of the war became clearer and more deadly. All through the twenty-second the incoming gliders never ceased to settle on the beach and the aerodrome at Maleme. They settled in the face of withering crossfire, in the midst of a shambles of their own transports and gliders. But down they came, and the location of defensive fire now being known, their Stukas and Messerschmitts systematically sought out and obliterated these machine-gun pockets.

The number of transport-borne troops steadily grew

The beach landings were now covered by German fire. In the bed of the Tavronitis River they were soundly entrenched and resisted all efforts to drive them out. Troop transports came circling in from the sea and settled on the aerodrome, now defended by two Australian battalions that had been brought in from beyond Suda Bay. A withering fire failed to check the suicidal heroism of the German pilots. Their transports crashed and spun and went up in fire, but down they came amid the splintered and flaming wrecks of their forerunners. The paratroopers who descended on the second day were prepared for everything. Doctors were equipped with complete medical units, even with stretchers on wheels. Pilots with coloured flares gave direction to the downpour of arms, machine-guns, mortars, tommy guns, hand grenades, anti-tank rifles, field guns, and wireless sets. Nothing was omitted. Nothing could stop them.

Sylvia's knowledge of Greek drew her into constant service as an interpreter. The Cretans were fighting magnificently, men, women, boys. There was no quarter asked or given ; there were no rules of war. Women who had seen husbands and sons butchered fought with demoniacal fury. Some, lacking weapons, leaped from doorways and roof tops and strangled the surprised enemy with cords. They had fired a field of barley, roasting alive the lurking invaders. But it was in vain.

On the evening of the twenty-second, a New Zealand captain was carried in, his right arm gone, his leg shattered. He had led a desperate attempt to retake the aerodrome. Two New Zealand battalions had gone out in the early dawn. One of these, composed of Maoris, made for the river bed of the Tavronitis, the other for the aerodrome. Their line stretched for three miles, from the sea coast to the main road. They lay in the olive groves and fixed their bayonets, while Jerry's tracer bullets sent a shower of flame through the trees. In Maleme village every house was a nest of Nazis. The New Zealanders, with the Maoris attacking and shouting blood curdling war cries, routed out the Germans in the houses. In was close fighting with bayonets, hand grenades, Bren guns. They swept on from house to house, until the Nazis tried to flee.

Maleme village had been cleaned out, but with full day-light the stukas came. Everything that moved, troops, civilians, animals, fell under murderous fragmentation bombs. The defenders hung on desperately. But it was all in vain. Maleme aerodrome was firmly in the grip of the invaders. They could now sweep in with Junkers 52 transports and gliders. All day they came until some twelve thousand soldiers had landed on the aerodrome, and some thirty-five thousand were in Crete.

" We couldn't do it, Nurse. The boys fought like fury, and went down like ninepins under those devilish dive-bombers. We got back to the groves and oat fields and vineyards—wherever we could get cover from air attack. You never saw such slaughter ! The boys were marvellous —marvellous, God bless 'em ! *Kia ora !* "

He smiled, lay back against the wall. The smile faded. He was dead.

§ 2

The outlook grew blacker hour by hour. News trickled into the makeshift hospital. On the twentieth, the King of Greece and his party had left Mournies, around which paratroops had begun to descend, and had gone up into a village in the White Mountains. At every few yards of that journey, accompanied by his Prime Minister, his cousin Prince Peter, and a New Zealand guard, the King had to seek cover in wayside bushes from German planes flying low overhead, gunning everything alive. They arrived at the mountain village and stayed overnight. A strange sight met the eyes of the royal party the next day. Below them lay the valley and coast, with golden wheat fields, silvery olive groves and vineyards, spotted for miles with falling parachutes, until they lay across the landscape like a snow-drift. The sky overhead was smudged with bursting shells from anti-aircraft fire, and alive with Junkers transports and bullet-nosed gliders flocking in from over the sea. The fight was sweeping over the valley and up the hills.

Towards noon a telephone call from the S.N.O. at Suda Bay sent the royal party hurrying on. It was not safe.

They must make their way over the mountains to the south shore where the navy would be warned to look out for them and take them off the island.

They climbed again all day, and at sunset slept in the open on the crest of the White Mountains. It was bitterly cold ; a wind blew over the unmelted snow. Before dawn they were awakened by distant gunfire. In the darkness they saw the flashes of gunfire out at sea, and as the dawn broke they watched the British fleet blowing the caïques and transports to atoms and then battling with the cloud of enemy planes seeking the navy's annihilation. Breathless, they watched the terrible spectacle on which the fate of Crete seemed to hang. Then, unable to linger, the party renewed its frightful journey over those savage heights.

The news of the King's flight over the mountains, urged upon him lest the Germans should capture so valuable a hostage, was brought to Sylvia on the evening of the twenty-second by Janet Farr, who suddenly appeared as from no-where. When the Germans had captured the hospital and driven them up the road towards the groves, Sylvia had looked for Janet in vain. She had concluded her friend had been killed or captured. Now, just as Sylvia came out of the room where the New Zealand captain lay dead, she encountered Janet.

She was an astonishing apparition. Her nurse's uniform was torn and stained with blood ; her hair, always unruly, lay, a matted shock, over her shoulders. One eye was bandaged ; the skin had been torn off her nose, and the black blood had clotted upon it. Her lower lip was twice its normal size. She stood there smiling, a frightful object, but the same stocky defiant woman. She briefly told her story. She had been knocked out in the blitz of the hospital and later found herself a prisoner and set to attend some Germans. That night she stole a revolver from the kit of a wounded man and, creeping up to the guard, shot him and ran across into a barley field. She wriggled through this when suddenly she was challenged.

" I thought I was going to get it. I held the revolver on my hip, ready to shoot. ' Come on in, miss ! ' said a voice. Would you believe it ? I stumbled on a machine-gun nest of Aussies ! I stayed the night there, on the edge of the

aerodrome.   Then at dawn they got me back to a first-aid
post in a vineyard.   Sylvia, you never saw such equipment
—beautiful—Nazi stuff, all of it."

"Whatever do you mean?" asked Sylvia as Janet
blurted out her story.

"Oh, it was great fun!   Those Nazi paratroops have it
all worked out.   Their chutes have different colours for
different things.   Ammunition's red ; food's blue ; medical
supplies, pink.   When the men get down they use ground
strips to tell the carriers what they want.   Our boys got
hold of the code.   They signalled pink, and down came a
packet of medical supplies.   Sylvia, you won't believe how
those things came !   It was like ringing up heaven for
supplies !   I worked like a nigger in that vineyard—that's
where I got it—this," said Janet, pointing to her eye.
"They found us and bombed us out and——"

"Is it very bad?" asked Sylvia.   She saw how waxen
Janet's face was under its dirt.

"It doesn't hurt so much now.   We advanced into
Maleme village just before dawn.   My God, you should
have seen the boys—bayonet work, most of it, till the
Heinies squealed.   We'd have it now but for those Stukas
coming in.   That finished us.   Where are our planes?
Where are they?"

"We haven't any.   The last few were told to leave on
Friday.   They'd have been annihilated.   There weren't ten
left.   Dick said the sky's theirs all over the Mediterranean.
We just haven't the planes.   How did you get here?"

"When we were driven out of Maleme—I'd set up a post
there and did what I could—we fell back to the hills and
worked our way to Canea.   This won't hold long.   They've
got the aerodrome and the shore."

"I know—we're drawing out now.   Palairet, our Minister
to Greece, left yesterday for Sfakia, the other side of the
island.   The King of Greece went the day before.   There's
been a naval battle.   Suda Bay's a shambles.   Retimo and
Herakleion are cut off.   They've had to send troops to protect divisional headquarters.   We're choked up here ; we've
no supplies.   There are only twenty of us.   Dr. Lane's our
only surgeon."

"God, what a show !   You should have seen the aerodrome. It was an inferno of crashed gliders, shot-down transports. We must have killed two thousand of 'em, and still they come. It rains Nazis—and now there's nothing to stop them. They've got the 'drome. There's a traffic jam over it."

She leaned back, faint and breathless, and looked at Sylvia.

" Don't look scared. I'm all right. And what do you think ? In one of the nest holes I tumbled on my sergeant, Freddie."

" Your sergeant ? " queried Sylvia.

" Don't you remember ? The Aussie I spent the night with. I know we don't mention it. You think me dirt——"

" No, Janet—I——"

" Never mind," said Janet, patting her arm. " But don't ask me to repent. I'd do it again. He's a grand lad— or was."

" Was ? "

" He was knocked out when we were fighting our way out of a garage. I saw him go over like—like a rabbit," said Janet fiercely. " So I shan't be made an honest woman now."

Her eyes watered ; her swollen lip quivered.

" Oh—Janet, I'm sorry," said Sylvia.

" I got him—the Nazi who brought him down. I got him in the belly ! That was good," said Janet huskily. " I suppose I've broken the code, but nursing isn't enough. When I saw those Greek women sailing it, with nothing but their hands and stones, I had to go in with them."

" You've been fighting ? "

" All day—look ! " she said defiantly. She lifted her blouse. Under it was a pouch and a revolver. " Good German stuff, all of it."

" Take them off. You're going to be nursing all night. Can you ? " asked Sylvia, looking at the white blood-caked face in front of her.

" Yes—when I've eaten and got some of this filth off. P'raps I'll scare the boys."

Sylvia put her arm around her and pushed her along.

§ 3

On the fourth day some sailors, picked up in an exhausted condition from a raft, and badly wounded, were brought into the hospital. From them Sylvia learned details of the battle at sea. Derek Whatley's ship had gone down, she learned. She locked the anxiety in her heart and worked on fiercely. There was Richard, too. How had he fared?

In the afternoon a wounded pilot came in. From him they learned that British aircraft, scraped together and thrown in from North Africa, was attacking Crete. It was a desperate gamble. Blenheims, Hurricanes, Marylands, and Wellingtons mostly; they were terribly handicapped by the distance from their bases. It was some two hundred and fifty miles. They fitted extra fuel tanks to some planes, sacrificing armour and ammunition. With this extra tank load they lost speed, climbing power, manœuvrability. The Messerschmitts played round them. But they came; they bombed the aerodromes, the Junkers transports, the gliders, the ground crews. Other planes, their fuel exhausted after only some ten minutes over the target, were fought until the last moment, when the pilots were ordered to abandon their machines and bale out.

All through Wednesday, Thursday, Friday, there had been no lull in the fighting. The furious downpour of bombs and bullets never ceased. Fires blazing through the day cast their lurid glare by night. On Friday the attack moved heavily over Canea. On Saturday morning the town was a blazing ruin. They moved out of the hospital in the dead of night, to the east of Suda Bay.

The next day the battle reached a crescendo of fury, with British, Australian, New Zealand, and Greek troops desperately attacking at Galatas village. They retook it, but all their gallantry was in vain. Worn out, outnumbered, ill equipped, and defenceless under the systematic air bombing, their force spent itself, and their lines broke in two places. They fell back towards Suda, leaving Galatas a cemetery of Germans. At midnight on Monday four British Commandos were landed. It was a last desperate throw to save Crete. But it was too late. Retimo and

Herakleion, now isolated, fought on. Up in the hills, in the villages above the coast, the fight still raged, but the position was cracking. The Cretans watched the defenders beaten back. They saw them go sadly, waved to them valiantly, and awaited the Nazi vengeance that would be visited on them for the crime of defending their own homeland.

Tuesday, the twenty-seventh, saw a last wild bayonet attack by three British battalions holding up the Germans advancing on Suda. The shock drove back the enemy for a time, but they came on again. Towards noon the decimated staff of the hospital was called together and addressed by the commanding medical officer. The position was hopeless. The battle of Crete was lost. Orders had come from headquarters. A withdrawal was to be attempted by the only road open, over the White Mountains, to Sfakia on the south coast, where the navy would attempt an evacuation. The journey was so severe that no one badly wounded could attempt it. They would remain and surrender to the enemy.

" We have done our duty. This last duty is the hardest of all, but we shall not flinch. A medical unit will be sent out with the retreating troops over the mountains. God bless you all ! "

In these last days an idea had grown in Sylvia's mind. It was now fully developed. Her future was clear and imperative. She sought out the medical officer. She could speak the language ; she was young and strong. She wished to be in the unit crossing the mountains. The natives could be called upon for assistance. After the interview she went to Janet.

" I'm leaving with the unit for Sfakia. We start to-night. The navy's going to attempt an evacuation at Herakleion as well as Sfakia, but the road's closed. We must surrender here or go over the mountains," said Sylvia.

" I'm coming with you," replied Janet, her face grim with resolution.

" Matron may want you to stay, Janet."

" I shall come or I shall desert. Do you see me nursing Germans ? "

" But our own men ? "

"Others can look after them—I'd be in trouble in ten minutes here. When do we leave?"

"Soon after dark. Janet—I want you to come. But you must get permission."

"I'll get it. Leave it to me," said Janet, and left her.

Sylvia sank down on to a box. She was utterly tired. She knew better than most the ordeal that faced them in this retreat over the mountains. But her fatigue was more mental than physical. Death and ruin were all around her, but the heaviest burden of all was this gnawing anxiety concerning the fate of Richard and Derek. They were, to her, the two dearest persons in all the world, and at this moment she did not know whether they were alive or dead. They were all going down in the maelstrom. The darkness had now completely engulfed Europe. Richard's one hope had failed them. The United States had not come in. She made generous gestures of help, but vitiated by argument, stood aside while civilisation was rocked to its foundations.

Calamitous news poured in over the radio, on which they depended for much of the information upon the battle here in Crete. The eastern end had been overrun by Germans; H.M.S. *Hood* had been sunk by the *Bismarck*, with a loss of twelve hundred lives. The pursuit of the German battleship was still on. The Rome radio made fantastic but harrowing claims of British losses in Crete—five battleships and cruisers sunk, ten destroyers, six transports; all ships in Suda Bay obliterated. If half were true it was calamitous.

Janet Farr marched in and interrupted her gloomy thoughts.

"I've got it! I'm coming with you," she said joyously. "I've just heard we've sunk the *Bismarck*! So that score's settled. And Ethiopia's surrendered. Gosh, I'd like to be in Rome when the Emperor Highly Salacious makes a return call on that pip-squeak Emmanuel. It looks as if we've squashed the Iraq rebellion. Don't look so serious, Sylvia. Our turn's coming!"

Sylvia looked up at her friend's battered face, and a feeling of shame came over her, confronted by the unquenchable spirit of this tough little *gamine*.

§ 4

That night Freyberg's weary army began its painful trek south, over the cruel White Mountains, down to the sea at Sfakia. The ranks were intact and disciplined still, but the knowledge of defeat was heavy upon them. Not all their valour had prevailed against an enemy who was courageous, marvellously equipped, and who had dominance of the air. It was the air, filled with those murderous planes, screaming, dive-bombing, gunning, and troop dumping, which had sealed Crete's doom.

It seemed as if Nature sought to offer every obstacle to that weary army falling back across those thirty miles of precipitous cliffs, deep gullies, torrents, snow-lined ravines, and rugged paths winding over barren razor-sharp rocks. Behind that long line of men the tenacious enemy kept up a harassing fire. Over them the diving planes swooped, bombed, and gunned the long defiles. There was no cover from that deadly pursuit ; the only friend was the darkness of night, and night was not safe along that winding cruel road. The enemy planes dropped amber flares. They fired the olive groves. A blazing inferno lit up the sky. Some of the men, wounded too badly, or too weary, had not attempted the journey. Others who had hopefully started began to straggle. The long line lost order under the incessant blasting. An army of stragglers, five or six thousand strong, from broken units, was interspersed among the regular formations and created general disorder. Wounded men, bandaged, bleeding, some without hands or arms, or crippled in the feet, staggered on and then collapsed and lay, broken in body and spirit, by the stony roadside. Men, unwounded, dropped in their tracks from sheer fatigue. Some had voice and spirit enough to curse impotently the planes that dived to kill them. The rear guard, fighting back in turns to give cover to the retreating line, found themselves overrun by fresh German machine-gunners brought up from the plain in motor lorries. All through that red night, all through the scorching day, the weary army trudged on, climbing, scattering in rocky gullies and woods when a Stuka roared over. At night some tried to rest, but

H

at an altitude of seven thousand feet the intense cold bit through their light uniforms. Hunger harassed them also, and thirst, until they came to torrents and slaked their throats with the slaty grey water from melted snow. Foot trouble added to their woes, for the wicked limestone crags and sharp stones cut their boots to ribbons, and their flight from bombing into the cruel, spiky bushes tore their clothes to tatters. Blistered, bleeding, scorched by the sun, frozen by the night air, they trudged on, now risking death in a defile between mountainous walls, or wading knee-deep in icy mountain torrents. Parched and pouring with sweat by day, bitterly cold by night, beneath them the razor-sharp stones, above them the murderous sky, the sick, beaten army struggled on.

Overhead, the planes never ceased to hover, to swoop screaming, with the threat of death on their hapless target. Again and again the winding line scattered for refuge among the trees and rocks. Then the trek was resumed, the living stepping over their comrades strewing the road, whose bodies, amid the clutter of discarded equipment, marked the trail through the mountains. When they came to the isolated villages there was such help as willing hands and the poor resources, long exhausted, could provide. No threat of the Nemesis to come for this help to the defeated deterred the grim islanders. They bound the wounds, gave shelter, brought wine and food. There were upland plains in which the little white villages, lying amid the ripening fields, seemed like a vision of Paradise, until that straggling line of khaki drew down upon it the merciless fire of dive-bombers, and the valley rattled with the noise of machine-guns and pursuing motor trucks. The craggy walls of the mountains echoed back the crash of bombs.

They began to descend now, and the human crocodile wound to the plain, an unending line from the high cliffs to the wooded ravines. Dazed, staggering, the steady stream flowed on. It had flowed thus, over mountain and valley, for one hell-smitten night, one torturing day. There was one more night before they came to the shore and whatever fate decreed. They had crossed the barrier, English, Australians, New Zealanders, and Greeks, no longer in orderly units, but a broken stream. They had passed a great chasm in the darkness, had reached Askipho in its great plain, while behind them the rear guard held the mountain pass. The plain was safer, covered by defensive fire. The hope of liberty began to glow. One thing the triumphant enemy had failed in. He had not been able to convert the tragic retreat into a rout.

There were strange meetings and reunions on that deadly trail, as when a rabble of Italian prisoners, captured by the Greeks in the Albanian campaign, now released, made a sage-green counter-current as it struggled northward through the mountains, flamboyantly covered by white flags. They were seeking their Axis ally. And with what surprise the New Zealanders saw again the two companies of tough Maoris they had left behind, encircled at Canea. Somehow they had fought their way back, carrying their wounded with them.

Sylvia's small unit fought on over mountain and valley. Six mules had been found, but the going had been so rough that even these animals floundered and, panic-stricken by the bombing, had had to be discarded. Two small motor lorries, loaded with medical kits, came through miraculously. There had been a tense moment when a Stuka came diving down on them. Just as they crouched for the bombing, certain the end had come, the pilot pulled out without releasing his bombs. He had seen the Red Cross markings on the lorries. They watched him climb again. Their fears returned when they saw that he continued to hover over them.

" My God—I've seen one decent Nazi at last ! Look ! cried Janet.

Sylvia and her companions looked up. The Stuka was circling in the sky over them.

" Is he going to bomb us?" asked Sylvia.

" No. Look at him ! Do you see what he's doing ? Can you believe it ? " cried Janet.

They watched breathless, and the incredible fact became plain to see. He was actually guarding the Red Cross unit, warning off all approaching aircraft.

" Sir Galahad Goebbels ! I'd kiss him if he came down. If he'd think that any reward," said Janet, gaily.

They halted the lorries. Three badly wounded Aussies,

caught in a raid, lay bleeding terribly on the roadside. All the time they tended the men, lifting them into the over-burdened lorries, their protector hovered over. They lost him at sunset. He came down and went off with a wave of his hand. They waved back.

Dawn was breaking when the small group of nurses, stumbling along on foot, almost unconscious with fatigue, caught their first glimpse of the sea, sparkling in the sunrise. Sfakia, white and rambling, squatted on the coast by the blue Libyan sea. Planes flying overhead guarded the slim grey shadows on the silver horizon. The British navy was back again, to evacuate the waiting army.

§ 5

They did not descend to Sfakia, but bivouacked in the caves on the mountainside. It was not safe to cluster in the narrow valley. The navy was taking off the troops by night. The moon had waned and they operated by star-light, taking off the men in barges, out to the waiting war-ships. They took only the organised forces, and a strong guard held back the thousands of stragglers who began to assemble on the beach and in the valley. The navy shuttled between Egypt and Crete, loaded to their gunwales with soldiers. On both journeys they ran a fierce gauntlet of enemy planes. Hurricanes and Blenheims, ill spared from Africa, went into an unequal fight and desperately held off the straffing Messerschmitts. In two nights and days fourteen thousand soldiers had been evacuated. But the toll in ships, attacked by bombs, E-boats, mines, was heavy. It became too heavy as the German attacks grew in weight. From the cave in Sfakia which he had used as his last head-quarters, Freyberg handed over his command to Weston, of the Royal Marines, and withdrew. He had succeeded in bringing far more of his shattered army to Sfakia than he had ever dared to hope.

On the night of May 31 the Mediterranean fleet attempted its last salvaging trip. Losses in ships had brought the margin of safety too low for further operations, following the Greek evacuations and the Crete battles, if the navy

were to retain its control of the sea. With a final effort it
evacuated four thousand more men.

In the afternoon of that last day of sunny May, word
came to the Red Cross unit that it was to be evacuated at
22.00. Towards sunset they moved down from the hills.
Word had gone round that this would be the last attempt to
take men off the beach. The position had rapidly degen-
erated. Up in the hills English, Australian, and New
Zealand rear guards fought desperately to hold off the
Germans closing in around Sfakia. The village was being
bombed with increasing ruthlessness. Four Commandos,
about a thousand men in all, led by Colonel Laycock, after
a first abortive sea trip from Alexandria, had succeeded in
landing on the night of the twenty-sixth. They had no
artillery or mortars, only tommy guns and Bren guns. They
went off up into the hills and fought rear-guard actions, to
protect the work of evacuation on the beaches. Often they
were surrounded. Once, with three light tanks, they fought
their way out of an ambush. They stayed on to the very
end and lost six hundred, three-quarters of their strength.
Many of the remaining men were left behind on the beach.

Out at sea and all along the coast, and on all roads by
which the men were attempting to reach Sfakia, Messerschmitts flew low, machine-gunning small boats or mowing
down the stragglers. Towards noon on May 31, after fifty
bombers had pounded the village for two hours until it
was a heap of ruins, news came that Germans were infil-
trating down a narrow valley, by-passing the rear guards.
Volunteers were called for from the New Zealanders to go
up into the valley and hold the Germans. They went two
thousand feet up into the hills, carrying their own water
supply in gasoline tins under the scorching sun. They had
no illusions about their mission. They were to hold the
pass while their comrades on the beach were taken off.
For them there was nothing but death or surrender. Along
the crests above the valley, the Royal Marines and Commandos supporting, these rear guards fought on until, of
their force of two thousand, some fourteen hundred were
killed, wounded, or captured. Dive-bombers, an enemy
equipped with machine-guns, mortars, rifles, pressed in on
the gallant defenders. The end was in sight. Thousands

of men knew they would find no place in the boats running to and from the overcrowded ships standing off the shore. Their long, painful trek over the mountains had come to a dead end. They could only lie on the beach and surrender to the oncoming Germans, or take to the hills and wage guerrilla warfare for as long as ammunition and strength lasted.

Early in that last afternoon Sylvia was ordered to go down to Sfakia, from the foothill where her unit operated. They had been moving the wounded down and evacuating them. Before leaving she had decided upon a course of action that had been growing in her mind from the moment she realised that thousands of these gallant fellows could never embark. She had no illusions about the terrible revenge the Germans would wreak upon the Cretan civilians who had fought the invaders of their soil so fiercely. She knew, despite wholesale executions and the destruction of their homes, they would never cease fighting. The war would not end with the British withdrawal. The Cretans would fight on until the Allies came back. Meanwhile the Germans must be harassed and smitten without cessation. She saw clearly how she could help in this protracted campaign.

A sense of elation succeeded to her former despair. She knew these people ; she spoke their language. She had a headquarters that might prove invulnerable for a long time. Thousands of British lads, assisted by Greeks and Cretans, could carry on a guerrilla warfare in these bewildering mountains. They could be saved from capture, from the soul-rotting prisoners' camps.

She would need help. Instinctively she thought of Janet Farr, who had the temper for so desperate an enterprise. Yes, Janet should have the opportunity.

Shortly before her mission to Sfakia, Sylvia found Janet and drew her aside.

" You know we're leaving to-night ? Janet, I'm staying behind. There's something I can do better than nursing," said Sylvia. " I'm not going to Alexandria."

" Are you asking me to join you ? "

" Yes—if you really wish to, but anything might happen to us."

" I've been hoping you'd ask me," said Janet quietly.

" I've known for days you were planning something. I want to stay and fight 'em. I'm with you all the way, Sylvia. What do we do now ? "

" We go down to the shore with them to-night. It will be dark. We can slip them. It will be too complicated if we ask permission, and we might not get it. Dick's villa is near Vori, east of Messara Bay. We can collect a few soldiers and make our way there over the mountains. The villagers will help us. The Nazis won't penetrate the south coast for some time. Up in the mountains we can get organised. We'll form an underground railway and get our men out little by little. If all goes well, in time we shall attack here again. If not—well, if not, does anything matter ? We'll go down fighting. We may be lucky and get some of the men not too badly wounded into hiding. Our men are scattered all over Crete now."

They were discussing their plan in detail when one of the nurses came across to them.

" You're wanted, Sylvia. There's a naval officer asking for you," she said.

" For me ? "

" Yes—he's come up from the beach and seems in a hurry."

It was one of the evacuation officers. She crossed the grove in which she and Janet had been talking and went into the hut they had made an office.

" Derek ! " she cried, standing still in amazement.

" This surprises you, eh ? " he laughed.

It was odd how they both felt a little constrained. The moment was too great for them, except to look at each other, overwhelmed.

" I heard a Red Cross unit had got over the mountains from Canea. I had a wild hope you might be in it," he said.

" I heard your ship had been sunk, but I've never given up hope ; I——"

He saw she was trembling, and with one step he was by her, his arm around her.

" You've had a rotten time," he said.

She put her head against his shoulder and stood there, not moving for a few seconds. He kissed her, smiling at her.

" Let's go outside—into the orchard. They'll be coming in here," said Sylvia, releasing herself. " Oh, Derek, Derek, I can't believe it ! How did you get here ? "

" That's quite a story, darling. Listen. I've rushed up here and I must be back quickly. I am the S.N.O.'s assistant. You know we're drawing out to-night, the last trip ? "

" Yes—we're warned for eleven p.m. I'm going down now with some of our wounded in the truck."

" Good—I'll go down with you."

They looked at each other again in speechless joy. The he took her in his arms and kissed her passionately.

" Derek, we must go ! " she said, straightening her cap. " Do I look a wreck ? "

" You look wonderful. It was pretty bad, I hear."

" Yes—a bit of hell. They straffed us day and night. Derek, you haven't told me about yourself. Was your ship sunk ? "

" Yes. I'll tell you going down."

They went outside. It was ten minutes before the ambulance and its six badly wounded men were ready. The driver went slowly over the rough mountain road leading to the plain. Sylvia was inside the truck with the men. Derek sat beside the driver, so they had no opportunity to talk. When the truck arrived at its destination, an old house partly protected by an overhanging cliff, and she had disposed of her charges, Sylvia ordered the truck to return, saying she would walk the two miles back. The house had a long garden. An olive grove ran down one side of it. Soldiers were sleeping and lying there in their exhaustion. They found a solitary corner in the shade of an olive tree and sat down on the ground. The air shook with a continuous blasting around them. The bombing was so incessant that no one found it unusual any more and developed a fatalistic indifference. If one's name was on the bomb or bullet, then that was the end. There was nothing more to do.

When Derek had satisfied his curiosity regarding Sylvia's experiences, he narrated his own. He described how night fell as he floated in the sea.

" I think I must have become insensible or dozed. Then

I found the dawn had come. There was no land in sight. I was very cold now, and hungry, and wondered how much longer I could last. I had kicked off my shoes. The Mae West supported me splendidly, but the lapping water had badly chafed my neck and face, and the flesh under my arms was raw where the jacket had rubbed. I had been floating and swimming in an effort to keep up the circulation, for almost an hour after sunrise, when I saw a small boat with a sail, bearing down towards me. They must have seen me. There were seven people in the boat. Two women, four men, and a baby. The baby had been dead for twenty-four hours, but the poor mother wouldn't give it up. The boat belonged to the two Greek fishermen who were sailing it; the two women were their wives. The other two men were Greek soldiers they had picked up out of the sea from a sunken boat that had been gunned by a Messerschmitt, killing and drowning all but these two. It took a long time to learn all this. I don't know Greek. There wasn't room for me in the boat, so one of the soldiers went overboard and clung to the side, and they hauled me in to rest. An hour later we sighted land, a long peninsula running north. Half an hour after that we turned south into a deep bay and hugged the precipitous shore. The German Junkers 52s, Heinkels, and Dorniers, and gliders were swarming over the sky, eastward. Some of them tried to bomb us, but they were too intent on their trip to halt and get us. The sky thumped with them. About noon we decided to try our chance at a landing. We found a small cover and beached the boat. There was a hellish swell running that almost capsized us. We hadn't been out of the boat five minutes when the swell caught it and stove it in on a rock. The next two hours were pretty terrible. We literally clawed our way up the steep rock face. We hauled the women along. That mother wouldn't let go of her baby. We saw she was crazed. She died that night in a goatherd's hut.

" But to go back. We came out on the top of the cliffs, and a beautiful sight met our eyes. There, locked away in the mountains, was a small valley, with meadows of wheat and green with maize and vines. There was a small village and a road that wound out of the valley. We'd have made for it at once, but we'd no idea where we were or whether the Germans were there. So one of the boatmen went ahead. He came back in an hour. It was all right. A German patrol had been there, but had left again. The village was five miles up in the mountains, west of Kastelli, where a road ran east to Maleme and Canea. I had immediate hopes of getting back to Canea, but these were soon dashed. Kastelli was held by the Germans. I knew then things must be pretty bad and that perhaps Maleme had gone.

" We stayed two nights in the village. I was quite worn out. I was too exhausted to worry whether the Germans came, or whether I should be handed over by the frightened peasants, who knew that the death penalty would be visited on anyone harbouring an Englishman. The second day, about nine in the morning, I learned that the road to Canea was impossible. The Germans held Maleme, and Canea was cut off. The King of Greece, they said, had gone over the mountains to the south coast, and British troops were already beginning to make their way up the mountains in the hope of reaching Sfakia on the coast, where an evacuation was to be attempted.

" Those Cretans were splendid fellows. They fed me ; they brought me a pair of boots, too big for me, thank goodness, for my feet were lacerated and swollen after clambering up those cliffs. The question now arose how I could get over to the south coast. That afternoon they produced a young man who was willing to guide me by mule paths over the mountains. He had worked on a farm in Ohio as a boy, with an uncle settled there, but had returned to his parents, who had olive groves near Kastelli. He spoke a little English, though I could understand him only with difficulty. His name was Themistocles Diamantopoulos. He had the appearance of an absolute thug, and a diabolical grin. He squinted badly and boasted he had disembowelled three Germans with a jack-knife, whom he had trapped on sentry duty in Maleme. I could quite believe it.

" They rigged me out in some indescribable clothes that already had other occupants, and early on the twenty-sixth I set out with Thermistocles. We had to go very carefully. Paratroops had been dropped all over the northern slopes of the mountains. Some had been killed at sight; others had collected and made defensive nests, supplied by aeroplanes that were in wireless communication with them. Whenever we came upon a house or a small village I lay in wait while Themistocles went ahead to find if the coast was clear. We climbed all that day until it was too dark to go farther. I was absolutely exhausted. We had gone through ravines and climbed up dry river beds. By great luck we came upon an isolated hut occupied by a woman and five children, to say nothing of the animals that lived on the floor. Her husband, his two brothers, and her three elder boys were all away, fighting. She didn't know whether they were alive or dead. She gave us some coarse bread and wine and sent some of the children to sleep in an outhouse so that we could have their beds. I'd never have thought it possible one could sleep in such beds! The fleas tried to push me out, but sleep we did. In the morning that poor woman insisted on dressing my feet, which had begun to fester.

" We started off at dawn and crossed the mountains at about seven thousand feet and then came upon a lovely sight, the plain of Omalos. Themistocles found a house on the edge of the village. The old man said German motor-cycle patrols had been through. The sky had never been free of planes. A glider which had gone adrift had crashed in a forest, killing all its occupants. They had cremated the bodies, afraid the Germans might accuse them of killing the men. Not a sign of the crash remained. The old man hid us away in a back room and sat up all night to guard us, he was so frightened of patrols. His grandson knew the paths through the mountains to Rumelli, from which a coast road ran to Sfakia. So that dawn three of us set off. I had a mule this time, for my feet were in a terrible state, and I was in agony with every step. We finally got to Rumelli, and there the boy left us. I'd like to see that kid again—he was fourteen and looked like a little faun. I never saw anything like it. He killed mountain hawks with a catapult and ate them raw. His name was Charmides. He was as beautiful as Socrates' boy friend, but that old bore would have found him a little savage.

" From Rumelli to Sfakia was easy, but we had to keep

off the coast road ; the Germans were gunning it. They knew we were collecting at Sfakia. When I got there our destroyers were already coming in. I reported to the S.N.O. and I got a rig-out, and here I am. I've been here three days. I met Torps yesterday. He was picked up with some of our fellows by the *Kashmir*, but she sank later on the way to Alexandria, and they had to be transferred. The King and his party are in Cairo now. I hope we get out to-night without being bombed to pieces. A lot of these poor devils are going to be left."

He was silent for a few moments. Then he took hold of Sylvia's hands and smiled into her eyes.

" Fate has been very kind to us—to meet like this, to be sitting here. Darling, I'm going to ask you something."

Sylvia looked at him, aware of every line of his face, of the clear, boyish eyes that belong to the seagoing breed. A tide of gratitude and pride flowed through her.

" To-morrow we shall be in Alexandria. Will you marry me then ? I can arrange it quickly. Nothing can touch us then, really," he said.

She saw the hope, the certainty that shone in his eyes and felt the firm strength of his hands holding hers. It was hard to find words.

" Derek darling, I'm not going to Alex. to-night. I'm staying here," she replied quietly.

" Not going ? But we're taking your unit off. You said so yourself ! "

" The unit's going, yes. But I'm not going with it. I'm staying here because there's so much I can do here. It doesn't end with to-night—or any night. We're fighting on. I know these Cretans. A lot of our men too—they won't tamely surrender. They'll go up into the hills and fight, somehow."

" But, Sylvia—you're a woman ! Don't you realise the kind of fighting it'll be ? There'll be no mercy. It's madness ; it can't succeed. What can you do ? What——?"

" I speak Greek ; that is a lot. I know some of this country. I'm not without a plan. I shall——"

He pressed her hands in his and leaned towards her.

" Darling, you can't do this ! It's crazy—and they won't let you," he exclaimed.

" They can't stop me. It isn't madness, Derek. I'm determined to do it. I shall go to the Villa Vouni and organise from there. Janet Farr's staying too."

" That creature ! "

" Derek, please ! I admire Janet tremendously. She's fierce and coarse, perhaps, but she's the bravest women in our whole unit. She's the courage of a lion. She's been wounded ; she's probably lost one eye—she didn't let us know for some time. She fought her way out of Maleme."

" I'm sorry, darling. But it doesn't make the whole thing less preposterous, whether there's one or ten of you," protested Derek. " The Nazis are going to play hell with this island. They'll kill or starve everybody in the place. Look what they're doing to Greece ! They're dying like flies and shooting up the wretched civilians on the slightest pretext. It's wonderful of you, my dear, to wish to do this, but you can't stay here."

" Derek, I've made up my mind. I'm staying, come what may. Darling, I want your help ; I want it terribly."

" My help ? "

" Yes. When you get to Alexandria, get hold of somebody—somebody who can do things. Get General Freyberg, or your own chief, or King George—anyone who has authority. They must help us to keep going. Boats must come to take off some of the men, the sick and wounded we shall collect. We'll want food, guns, ammunition. They can send it over by plane and drop it at places we shall tell you of, or by boat, landing it at night, in places we shall signal to you. I've written it all down, with a plan of the Bay of Messara, and I've marked the coves we shall try to use. We'll signal with our flashlights or lanterns when it's safe for you to come in. Please, please, Derek, you must do this for us ! I want you to find my brother too. They should send him here to help us—if he's alive—he knows the country and the people so well. To-night I shall give you a list of the things we'll need. I shall go to the villa and make that my headquarters. There are enormous quarries we can use near Gortyn, where we can collect our men. We have a secret path to the villa. The Germans will never find us—or not for a long time. I've got the whole thing mapped out in my head. You must help me !

These Cretans and these men of ours are so wonderful, I won't leave them, Derek, that's why I can't marry you now. When it's all over, when Crete's ours again, then we can be married. Now I want to remain here and do all I can for the men who can't get away to-night."

"They're thousands—you can't handle thousands of desperate men," said Derek.

"I'm going to try, and you're going to help me."

He made no reply, but stood up, helping her to her feet.

"Darling, I must go. I ran off duty to find you. You won't change your mind?" he asked.

"No, Derek. Nothing can change my mind. Will you help me?"

He saw her determined face staring up at his.

"Very well—under protest. You're coming down with your unit to-night?"

"Yes—I shall come to the boats with them. I may have to slip them."

"Slip them?"

"I may ask permission to remain, or just desert at the last moment. I haven't decided yet what course to take. How shall I find you?"

"That will be easy. I'm embarkation officer and will be the last to leave, with the S.N.O. You're moving down at twenty-three o'clock. I'll be on the look-out for you."

"Thank you. It's good-bye?" she asked as they went down the grove.

"Till to-night. Good-bye, darling."

They looked at each other in silence for a few moments. The bombing and the gunfire sounded all around.

"I'm angry with you—and I'm terribly proud of you, darling," he said. Taking her firmly by the shoulders, he kissed her and then hurried away.

All that night the boats ferried to and fro between the destroyers and the beach. Only the bright stars lit the cloudless sky. In the darkness along the shore, soldiers stood patiently in line, three deep, and filled up the boats as they came in. Around in the hills a last desperate stand was being made. At any moment the enemy might break through and come pouring down to the shore. Mercifully, they had failed so far to drop flares and bomb the coastal boats, but the noise of planes filled the dark sky. Otherwise there was a strange, funeral silence among the men massed along the beach. They were tired, hungry and dispirited, and in some cases tormented by thirst. Before them lay liberty, food, sleep; behind them, at the best, the prison camps of Germany.

Sylvia waited with her contingent until the very last. She had announced her plans, deciding against secrecy. She faced strenuous opposition, and finally declared her absolute determination to follow the course she had planned. Janet Farr stood steadfastly with her. It was nearly one o'clock when she watched the unit embark and fade away across the dark water, and it was with a pang she saw her comrades go. They had been through terrible scenes together, in Greece, and again here in Crete. Their ranks had been thinned by violent deaths and capture. Some of their wounded had been left on the hills and in the villages during the terrible trek over the mountains.

And now it was all over. The guards were being withdrawn. Only once did the perfect discipline collapse, when a wave of desperation swept over some of the men who saw their last hopes vanish with the retreating forces. The men who had lost their companies, and had come down from the caves in which, starved and thirsty, they had taken refuge through the day, now, without officers and direction, broke into disorder as they saw the last guards preparing to depart. This sight of the door closing on the trap was too much for them. They surged through the orderly ranks and rushed into the water, storming the boats. It was futile, tragic. Three of the boats were swamped.

The moment of madness passed as swiftly as it had come. The last boats drew out silently into the darkness, and the remaining men stood on the beach, peering across the dark water. Then slowly they began to dissolve. Some lay down in weariness to await the dawn and the Germans; some, still unbroken in spirit, trudged towards the hills, nursing their arms, to make a last stand or to creep along the coast, still hoping for a chance boat that might pick them up.

Sylvia and Janet waited until the last boat had gone.

They had seen Derek intermittently as he organised the boat parties. Then towards two o'clock he came back to Sylvia. There was little said between them in those last tense moments. Locked in each other's arms, that agony of separation, sweeping the whole world of the hopeful young and the prayerful old, was theirs in all its inarticulate intensity. Then, with a last brave word, he was gone. The boat slid over the gravel into the dark night.

CHAPTER V

THE BRAVE BUT ONCE

SLOWLY, out of the chaos, Sylvia evolved order. As the men melted away into the hills or waited along the beach to surrender to the incoming Germans, she carefully selected some thirty who were willing to make the attempt to reach the Villa Vouni. The journey took them three days by the coastal road to Tymbaki, at the entrance of the Messara Plain. They travelled by night, hiding in caves and woods during the daylight, for the coastal road was being watched and ceaselessly bombed. They suffered terribly from fatigue, hunger, and thirst. Help was given them in the villages through which they passed, but the absence of all the men and the draining off of all the supplies had left these poor peasants on the verge of starvation.

One fear Sylvia kept to herself, that the Villa Vouni might have been discovered or destroyed, or that the final track up the mountain might be barred by the enemy. They were too exhausted to attempt the painful detour that would then be necessary. But all had gone well. Exhausted, they had reached the Villa Vouni, leaving behind ten stragglers who had collapsed *en route*. Careful instructions had been circulated to the forces at Sfakia, and Sylvia had succeeded in enlisting a number of Cretans who would act as guides to any who felt inclined to attempt the journey rather than surrender. The grapevine also sent word through the mountain villages that a headquarters were being established in the labyrinth near Gortyn, from which guerrilla warfare would be carried on.

Sylvia and her party arrived at the Villa Vouni on a late afternoon in June. They had almost lost count of time in the nightmare of these last days. Their whole world had been shattered in less than two weeks. It was now June 4. On May 19 they had slept in the hospital at Maleme. Canea, Suda Bay, Retimo, Herakleion had all existed then.

It was decided to place the men temporarily in the stables and after they had rested for a few days to get them by the secret track down to the labyrinth of the Minotaur and there arrange the defence of its entrance against possible attack. The first requirement was the establishment of a commissariat. Fortune favoured them. On the morning of their arrival at Villa Vouni, Sylvia was astonished to see old Anastasia walking along the terrace. In the mysterious way of these mountain villagers, the old crone had heard of Sylvia's arrival, and, always practical, she had come with a mule laden with food, accompanied by three elders of Hagi Deka. A war council was held, and the problem of feeding the refugees began to be less serious.

There was no doubt of the spirit of these resolute Cretans. They were not to be cowed by Nazi ruthlessness. Already stories of the wholesale shootings, the burning and bombing of entire villages in retribution for assistance given, came in from all sides. The beach at Sfakia had been terribly bombed on the morning Sylvia had left. The prisoners were rounded up and driven back again over the dreadful road to Canea, to the internment camps at Maleme.

Retimo had surrendered. By some blunder, messages had failed to get through, and the Australians had gone on fighting for three days after the battle for Maleme had ended. Finally, the advance of the enemy, massed in trucks, tanks, and armoured cars, told them that they stood alone. Surrender became inevitable on May 30, but one hundred and fifty officers and men had elected to go on fighting. They had retreated somewhere up in the hills and were now making their way south.

Herakleion had been successfully evacuated by the British Navy on the night of May 28, but there were rumours that the fleet, loaded with men, had been trapped and bombed out of existence in the Strait of Kaso, *en route* to Alexandria. This dealt another blow to Sylvia's hopes for Richard's safety He had flown off to Herakleion a week ago. Had he survived the air fighting, been among the planes withdrawn the next day to Africa, or had he been trapped in Herakleion, sharing the fate of the evacuated forces ?

Anastasia remained at the villa. Four of her sons and ten of her grandsons had been fighting in Crete, their fate unknown. Three of her grandsons had disappeared in Greece.

" Do not despair, miss ; we shall drive them out yet. We have hands, teeth, and knives ! " said the old woman fiercely. " Now what can I do ? "

Their first task was to camouflage the terrace, the only thing visible from the air. They cut posts, built a pergola and covered it with branches of cypress. Sylvia appreciated now the cunning with which this old monastery had been planned. It was almost impregnable and invisible. They lit no fires during the day, afraid that the smoke might betray them to planes flying over. They drew in all the stores they could obtain from farms in the plain of Messara.

Within three days the news of the headquarters established by Sylvia had gone through the countryside. Help poured in. Stragglers also began to appear, brought over the mountain paths by the natives. Down at Tymbaki and Eremopoli, on the coast, watchers had been warned to look out for British destroyers that might come by night. Four men from the Signal Corps had been stationed at advantageous spots along 'the coast. They had pocket torches and were told to signal P.S.B.—Please Send Boat—at the sign of any friendly ship. Some kind of contact had to be established with North Africa. Guns, ammunition, medical supplies, and clothing were urgently needed. So far, they were using captured material dumped by German parachutes. Sylvia anxiously awaited some sign that Derek had got through with his message.

" I'm getting scared, not because we're so weak, but because we're getting so strong ! " said Janet Farr early one morning, at the end of a week. She had just come back from the labyrinth now called Fort Minotaur. " Thirty more men came in last night. They're still coming over the mountains. If we can't ship some of them soon we'll have a famine on our hands. Besides those Aussies are so restive. They want to go out after the German patrols, and I can't make them understand we're to lie doggo for some time."

She threw herself into a chair in the living-room, and, looking at her, Sylvia burst out laughing.

" What's the joke ? " asked Janet, lighting a cigarette made out of chopped green tobacco leaves. It gave forth an acrid smell.

" What horrors we must look ! " said Sylvia.

They were wearing peasants' trousers and boots and ragged Cretan jackets, frogged and embroidered, found somehow by old Anastasia. They had cropped their hair. Their skins were reddened and chapped by the fierce sun and the mountain winds. Their hands were grained with dirt, the nails broken.

" I never had what's called feminine charm," said Janet, puffing hard, one leg cocked over a chair. Her head was still bandaged ;   a black cap covered her left eye.

" I am an animal, a good healthy animal—except for this wonky eye. All these men make me alive, as I've never been alive before. They do something to me. If I weren't an ugly duckling, I'd be a riot. But you—their poor tired eyes just roll when you come round. What a gift ! "

Sylvia had taken off her boot and was hammering a nail in it. She looked up.

" Janet, sometimes you scare me. I hope, for the sake of discipline, there isn't going to be——" She hesitated, searching for the right words.

" Any more nights with the sergeant ? " said Janet.

" It's a little blunt—but that's what I mean."

Janet stood up and looked out across the valley for a few moments. Then she turned to her friend.

" Sylvia, God knows I'm a mess, but I'll always be honest with you. I'm giving no promises, but I'll take care, whatever happens, you don't know about it."

" That's not enough," said Sylvia quietly, putting down the hammer. " We are two women among a lot of desperate men. There's a principle involved. What you do with yourself is no concern of mine, but what you do while I'm in control, and responsible, is."

Janet Farr looked at Sylvia and smiled a little pathetically.

" Thanks for the warning. I suppose I seem to you just like a dirty little rabbit. Perhaps I am. I came out of a warren and I know well that what you emerge from counts in the long run. Sylvia, I'm so desperately afraid I'm going to miss everything. I never had a real lover, you see. I'm a man's woman, with none of the assets. If you're born poor, it's bad ; if you're born poor and ugly, it's worse ; but if you're poor, ugly and old, God help you, what have you ? "

" I don't agree at all," said Sylvia, lacing her heavy boot. " In the first place you're not ugly—when you smile you are beautiful. Men don't always want beauty ; they want character and sympathy and——"

" Not the kind of men I seem to attract. Sylvia, you're a darling. I don't know why you bother with me, but I shall never forget all your kindness, and if I let you down——"

Sylvia went across to the window and put her arm around her.

" You're not going to let anybody down, so why talk about it ? You're the bravest thing that ever walked on two legs."

Janet looked at her friend dumbly. There were tears in her eyes. Then she threw away her cigarette and hurried out of the room. Sylvia watched the lumpy figure walk down the terrace. Strange that Janet, who could handle men in the mass as well as any drill sergeant, and was feared and respected by them, seemed unable to manage her own personal relationship to them with more self-discipline.

There was a tap on the door, and in response to her cry two men walked in, Captain Pierce and Lieutenant Walker. They had trekked over the mountains with a handful of men, and Sylvia had given them command at Fort Minotaur. One was English, one Australian ; they were experienced, resourceful, and always in good spirits. They reported they had made the entrance to the fort almost impregnable. As a last resort the outer cave was mined and would collapse on any invaders. The mountain path from the inner cave up to the secret exit, leading to the stables at the villa, had also been mined, and the mule track that led to the Messara valley was covered by a retrieved machine-gun. Villa Vouni was stoutly defended.

Sylvia thanked them and walked out with them. She had ordered two mules saddled, and her orderly for the day, a cheery New Zealand lad called Macpherson, stood waiting. Every morning they went over the mountains towards the Herakleion-Gortyn road. The German patrols covered it, and planes flew over it, but soldiers were still hiding in the woods and caves during the hours of daylight and journeying along it by night. Sylvia had collected quite a number of exhausted men in these excursions along the mule tracks. The chief danger came from the reconnaissance planes that were sweeping the island.

It was not safe to go into some of the villages ; the Germans were already in occupation. Other places had been razed to the ground. Gradually stories came in of the terrible vengeance visited upon those who had aided British or Greek soldiers. The males were all summarily executed ; in some instances they were compelled to dig their own graves and were shot on the edge of them. Mournies, Lakko, Kandanos, Skenes, the shootings and burnings in these and other villages spread terror among the islanders. Priests were seized in their churches and received the same summary treatment. The search for hidden arms was pursued with a ruthlessness that often resulted in the physical torture of peasants under examination. A few hoped to escape vengeance by painting swastikas on their doors, but these were only a cowed minority.

A new desperation seized the Cretans. They left their villages, and with a few belongings took to the hills. They acted as spies ; they sent waves of fear through lonely patrols by suddenly pouncing on them and killing them. They shot from hedges and caves ; they dropped on their victims from roofs and trees, armed with knives or with cords, with which they strangled the foe.

The merciless warfare went on by day and night. Many an old peasant faced the firing squad for harbouring a fugitive, but vengeance would swoop down, and small companies of Germans disappeared in the hills for ever. The ungathered parachute dumps of arms and munitions had helped to arm the islanders. Their secret telegraph system worked in the strangest manner. Sylvia received constant warnings of enemy movements, of scattered fugitives trying to make their way towards Fort Minotaur. Each day she went out and brought in some sick or wounded lad who lay in hiding. The collection of wounded at the fort had progressed so rapidly that a grave problem of disposal was arising. Unless communication was soon established with North Africa the nursing and feeding of these men would grow beyond her limited capacity. Four hundred soldiers were already based at the fort. Two-thirds of these went out in sorties against the enemy. Some fifty of them were wounded or too ill for such excursions. These would have to be evacuated at the earliest opportunity.

Sylvia used the hidden track through the stables, but when she went out to rescue wounded men or the sick, following information that came to her, she did not go down through the cave to the fort. She took a path across the mountain, and then descended the ravine and crossed the stream to the opposite face of the mountain, visible from the terrace of the Villa Vouni. She then followed a zigzag path up the face of the mountain that was covered by a stunted pine forest. This path, well hidden from planes overhead, then diverged in various directions, to the villages scattered between Mount Ida and Mount Jukta, a terrain the Germans had not yet penetrated.

This morning she set out for the Grotto of Kamares, reached by a punishing mule track that led from Vori, via Grigoria, to the tiny village of Kamares itself. From there a guide would take them to the grotto in which two wounded men had been hidden and cared for. The party consisted of Janet, a Greek boy, Nikephoro, with two mules, and four stretcher-bearers, New Zealanders. They were all armed, including the boy, who had fought fiercely in Retimo, from which he had come with the Australians who took to the hills when the forces surrendered. It was not yet eight o'clock, and a mist lay over part of the mountains. Later the burning heat of the June sun would add to the ardours of their journey.

At Vori they halted and learned that the priest and ten villagers had been taken away. Their fate was unknown. A German plane had crashed near the village. They were accused of killing the pilot because his body had not been found. The plane had burned itself out.

Four Australians came out of hiding. They had come over the mountains from Retimo, part of the force which had gone on fighting after the rest of the island had been conquered. From one of these, who had escaped previously from Herakleion, Sylvia learned that the Navy had successfully

evacuated the garrison there on the midnight of May 28.
He had been in the hospital at Knossos. The Germans had
occupied the road between Knossos and Herakleion, and the
inmates of the hospital had to be left behind. He had got
out, disguised in peasant's clothes brought to him by an
old laundry woman, and had boldly walked right through
the guards. Unfortunately, in the darkness he had taken
the wrong direction and found himself beyond the Germans
guarding the valley. After several days of climbing he had
run into three other men who had escaped from Retimo.

" What was Herakleion like ? " asked Sylvia.

" Why, miss, when I last saw it, it was just a heap of
rubble. They'd given it a terrible plastering, but the
harbour wasn't blocked."

" Did you see any air fighting ? "

" Not after May 24. They withdrew our airmen. There
wasn't one left there. We hadn't a dog's chance, miss.
The air was thick with the Nasties."

" Did they bomb the hospital ? "

" No, miss, they left us alone."

" There were some excavations up the valley, at Knossos
—the Palace of King Minos—do you know if they were
bombed ? "

" No, they didn't bother with those ruins, miss. I suppose they thought they were wrecked already," replied the
wiry Australian, smiling. He looked around cautiously and
then said quietly, " Excuse me, miss, but can I have a word
with you privately ? "

" Yes," answered Sylvia, a little surprised by his furtive
manner. She sent the mule-boy over to the waiting
stretcher party in charge of Janet, who rode another mule
with medical supplies. " Well ? " she asked when they
were alone.

" We're worried, miss, about a young Nazi we found this
morning up in the forest. He's only a kid, poor devil, and
it looks as if he's dying. He must have 'opped out of a
plane and he's an awful mess, and off 'is 'ead. We've been
sleeping in a goatherd's hut—a nice smelly place, too, but
they're afraid to bring us into the village in case the Jerries
come. This morning, as I went up into the wood—to—
well, on a visit, like, miss—I 'eard someone moaning and

began to look around. And there he was, lying in some bushes. I looked at him, but he didn't seem to know me. So I fetches my pals, and we gave him something to drink —which was all we had then. We'd just come down for some food when they said you were here. We haven't told 'em, miss. Nazis don't get much of a shift when these Cretans get hold of 'em, and I don't blame 'em either, seeing how the Nazis have been shooting 'em up and blowing their homes to smithereens."

" You say he's a Nazi ? A pilot ? "

" Yes, miss. We found his parachute lying near. Looks as if he came down with a bang. He's an awful sight, all over blood and muck. He's been there some time, I'd say, by the things that 'ave got into his hair."

" Can you lead us to the place now ? How far is it ? "

" About half an hour, miss."

" Very well—show us the way."

Sylvia called up her party and told them of the wounded pilot. She talked a few minutes to three of the old men of the village, gathering their news. Then, with the Australians, they set off, climbing out of the village. The path disappeared at times. It was scarcely a mule-track, and crossed a barren limestone gully. Round the corner they found a rocky plateau covered with wild thyme and sage bushes. In a slight hollow, with his face half buried in the tufts of coarse grass, they came across the body of the young German.

Sylvia stooped and turned him over. He moaned, but seemed quite unconscious of her. At a glance she saw he was in a pitiful state. His black wavy hair was clotted with blood. Flies and insects were crawling over it. His brow was cut, and a long wound, still open, ran from his temple to his ear. Evidently he had had a violent fall and had been dragged over the razor-sharp crags. His tunic was lacerated. He wore the uniform of a lieutenant of the *Luftwaffe*.

Janet's hands went over him quickly as Sylvia examined the boy's head, wiping the insects away from the wound. Blood had been running from the nose.

" Fracture of the skull," said Sylvia.

Janet's hand gently explored under the opened tunic.

" And two ribs," added Janet. " He must have had a bad fall."

She slowly examined the boy's legs, cutting away his long boots. " The right leg's broken—compound fracture," she said after a while.

She gave orders to the stretcher-bearers. They made a splint. Very carefully they moved the inert figure on to a stretcher.

" This is going to be a difficult job," said Sylvia. " There's another complication, too. He's a Nazi. We can't move him to the fortress—it's easier to get him back to the villa, and better for many reasons."

" But you'll have to nurse him there if he lives. It's going to be a complicated job," said Janet.

" Well, we've got to attempt it, that's all. We'll cut out the Kamares trip to-day."

" All this for a little Nazi who's probably bombed a few hundreds of our boys out of existence ! It doesn't make sense," said Janet, bitterly.

" None of it makes sense, but we do our best in a crazy world," observed Sylvia.

The stretcher-bearers moved slowly down the mountain-side. There was a gruelling journey of three hours before them. The sun was now high and fierce in the mountain air. The ravines were noisy with cicadas in the carob trees. It was four o'clock when they reached the villa ; the party was exhausted.

" We've lost a day all because a little Nazi didn't fall hard enough," said Janet. " And if he lives he'll breed for the next war. That's a thought ! "

§ 2

The wounded youth was placed in the room that had been used by Cesare Morosini. They stripped him, and in his pocket found a wallet and papers. There was an army identity card, with the same name and number as they found on the disc round his neck. He was a junior pilot officer, aged twenty. His home was in Vienna.

"Well, that's something. He's not a German; he's an Austrian," said Sylvia.

"I don't see what's the difference. Nazis are Nazis, and nasty wherever they're born. I wonder we haven't found a monocle in his pocket," said Janet cynically.

"Perhaps it was knocked out of his eye," suggested Sylvia, as she helped to wash their patient. "You'll admit he's a handsome lad?"

They looked at the bruised, naked body. He was shapely and well developed. The face of the unconscious youth was handsome. He had a full young mouth, a fine nose, and a good brow. A fractured skull, a broken leg, two broken ribs, and bad contusions were the sum of his injuries, unless there were internal ones as well. He was delirious and from time to time muttered in German.

"Do you know German?" asked Janet.

"A little—but I don't know what he's saying."

"Thank God I don't know any, so he won't corrupt me with his *Mein Kampf* stuff," said Janet, now dressing the wound behind the ear. "You know, this is going to be a long job—if he pulls through. We've got our hands full."

"What else can we do?"

"We might get fond of Little Waltz Dream. That would be a real triumph for Herr Schickelgruber!" commented Janet acidly. "Well, he's here for quite two months—if we last that long—or if he does. Poor Heinie! With his uniform off I hate him less. But I still say it's a pity he didn't have a harder bang."

§ 3

They kept their patient in a darkened room and never left him alone day or night. Harry, the Cockney marine, became the ward orderly. "Gawd luv a duck! To think I'd be washing a bloody 'un!" he exclaimed.

One morning he came hurrying in to Sylvia, with eyes wide open with excitement.

"He's conscious, miss, Blimey, he's talking English as well as you and me! Wants to know where he is, if he's a prisoner in England—'ow d'you like that!"

Sylvia followed the orderly back to the room. She found the young Austrian fully conscious.

" Where am I ? " he asked as Sylvia stood over him.

" You are in Crete—in my house."

" A prisoner ? "

" Yes."

There was a silence. She saw the muscles of his face work, then tears welled into his eyes.

" I do not wish to be a prisoner. I would rather die," he said in a choked voice. " Please shoot me."

Sylvia laughed at him.

" We don't shoot prisoners. And at twenty life should be worth living. You are not to talk."

" What is the matter with me ? Why am I here ? " he asked brusquely, the tears on his cheek.

" You made a bad parachute landing. We found you on a mountainside with a fractured skull, a broken leg, and two broken ribs. You must have been there for a long time. It was lucky we found you."

" I do not think so," said the youth, coldly.

" You are not to talk. The orderly will give you any-thing you need," said Sylvia firmly, stemming her anger at the graceless young cub.

She stood for a few moments outside the room, mastering her anger. She would do her duty, but there could be no sentiment with a youth like this. The poisoned generation, someone had called these young Nazis. She began to see it was true. One had to be ruthless with them. It was the only code they knew. She had always felt somewhat sentimental towards the Austrians. They were a civilised race—the home of Schubert's songs, Strauss's waltzes, Franz Lehar's operettas, of " The Blue Danube," " Tales from the Vienna Woods," of gay Vienna itself. Well, that was all nonsense. This sprig showed that. He was one of Adolf's dreadful brood.

Sylvia walked along the terrace towards her office, worried and tired. The number down at Fort Minotaur had swollen to six hundred and sixty, of whom a third were unfit and should be evacuated. Yesterday ten men had been killed in a clash with a German patrol in the valley. Sylvia herself had narrowly escaped. Enemy planes had been over the villa on three consecutive days, and she was apprehensive.

There was still no word from Egypt. It was ten days now since Derek had left. Three lots of men had been taken off the coast at night by visiting destroyers that lay off in the darkness and sent boats to the beach. Not one of these had brought any message. She had sent urgent appeals to them. Medical supplies, guns, ammunition; the Cretans as well as her own people were in urgent need of them. The Germans had conquered the coast, but inland, among the mountains, the spirit of resistance was strong. They had not dared yet to advance into a wild country that lent itself so readily to ambushes and guerrilla war. With outside help Crete could never be wholly subjected to Nazi domination. It might become a running sore.

Sylvia was working at her desk, compiling a list of the things most urgently needed, when footsteps behind her made her turn. What she saw left her speechless with amazement. It was Richard, out of uniform, standing there, smiling at her.

" Can I see the commandant ? " he asked, grinning.

At a bound she was in his arms, kissing him.

" Where have you come from ? " asked Sylvia, when at last she could find words. Richard looked bronzed and well.

" I landed at Tymbatsi last night. We came in on a destroyer and took off twenty men. I've brought in some supplies for you from Alexandria. Let's go out. I see you've done some camouflaging."

They walked out on to the terrace and sat in the shade of the pergola, where so often they had lunched when last they had been together at Villa Vouni. Little by little she obtained the whole story of his adventure since they had parted in the hospital compound at Maleme.

He told her how he had been shot down. The next morning their only remaining plane had been withdrawn. Knapps had been killed; Preston had crashed badly and was left in the hospital at Knossos. Only Stanway had flown back to Africa. On the night of May 28 the navy came in.

They did a grand job. They'd come through hell to do it. They took off about four thousand of us between midnight and three o'clock. We caught the Nazis napping. They had bombed the life out of us the night before. There's nothing left of poor old Herakleion—everything's a heap of rubble, even the Venetian walls. There'd been terrific street fighting, and we'd cleaned up all the Nazis. But they'd got a ring round us we couldn't break. We didn't know what was going on elsewhere, though we guessed it was pretty bad when we got the order to be evacuated. The road to the hospital and Knossos was quite cut off. Our ships had had a hell of a journey to get to us. They'd come across from Alex.—three cruisers, *Dido*, *Ajax* and *Orion*, and about half a dozen destroyers—*Hereward*, *Hotspur*, *Kimberley*, *Jackal*, *Decoy*, and *Imperial*. They came through the Kaso Strait at the east end, at sundown, but they were picked up by bombers and had a bad plastering. Still, they got in before midnight. We were all ready. We had called in our fellows from the aerodrome, and all the garrison were lined up, kit complete. Chappell, the brigadier, and MacDonald, the S.N.O., did a grand job. We almost tiptoed down the jetty, which, thank God, was intact—you remember?—the one we sailed from with poor old Cesare—scared to death that Jerry might drop flares and show us all up to the Stukas. Well, he didn't, for some odd reason. The destroyers came right in, and we went up the gangways as if we were leaving Dover for a holiday. They ferried us out to the cruisers, where we were packed like sardines. Then we moved off in the darkness—and that was our farewell to Crete.

" We were all terribly sick about it, but we hadn't gone far when the *Imperial* began to drop behind. She'd had a bad hammering from the bombers. We took our men off and sank her. Dawn broke just as we approached the strait. Then hell let loose. The Nazis and the Eyeties came winging in with everything they had—Dorniers, Heinkels, Stukas, Macchis, Messerschmitts—God, you never saw such a swarm ! We fought 'em with every damn thing we had—Bredas, pom-poms, machine-guns. The boys even took pot-shots with their rifles. But you couldn't stop 'em. The sky was thick with 'em, dive-bombing and machine-

gunning us. We shot 'em up ; we saw 'em burst into fire
and crash, but it seemed to make no difference. They just
kept on coming in. Those boys have guts, I tell you. The
poor old *Orion* got a bomb right amidships, her second and
worst. It tore through her steel deck and went down into
the stokers' mess deck, where it burst. You can imagine
the scene ! The boys were packed in all over the ship,
and it made a pulp of 'em. Then she caught fire. Luckily
I was aft or I shouldn't be here now."

" You were in her ? " cried Sylvia.

" Yes—but it wasn't her call, evidently. Even the magazine had flames round it, but they got them under, and the
old ship swung about, her main control position gone. We
were all in darkness except for flames. You never saw such
a sight—a great gaping crater, with jagged spikes of steel,
blown up vertically into cruel combs, fragments of bodies,
blood running. Everything caught fire with the heat. Men
like torches jumped overboard, and on top of all the noise
of planes diving, guns firing, bombs blasting, there was a
kind of fireworks show from pom-pom shells popping off
in the blaze, shooting great flickers of light over the inferno.
It's funny how you see these things and don't feel 'em at
the time."

" Were you hurt ? "

" Not a scratch, but I stank for a week, it seemed to me.
You never get rid of the smell of a blasted ship—paint,
flesh, red-hot steel, charred fittings, stinking smoke. They
got the hoses going somehow. Every second the hellish
racket was punctuated by the popping of those loose pom-
pom shells. And I remember the sizzling and the steam
where the sea water poured in over the red-hot plates.
After a time they got her emergency steering going, and the
gallant old *Orion* stopped bouncing around and took up her
position again. All day those bastards hung on to us,
bombing and machine-gunning, all the four hundred miles
across, until we saw landfall in the red Egyptian dusk. We
hadn't been in Alexandria a couple of hours when another
of our squadrons came in. I heard it had brought back the
first lot of men from Sfakia, so I immediately asked what had
happened to your unit at Maleme. I heard you were
awaiting evacuation. So I never left the docks until finally

your unit came in. I found the M.O., and he told me you
and Janet Farr had insisted on remaining. That knocked
me back a bit, but anyway you were alive, and I guessed
what you were up to. Then I ran into the S.N.O., back
from Sfakia, and who should I find in his office but your
Derek Whatley ! He jumped out of his skin when he heard
who I was, and I jumped out of mine when I learned he's
going to be my brother-in-law."

"I've to tell you about that," interrupted Sylvia.

"I like him a lot—he's a great lad. Well, he then told
me your plans and showed me your instructions. We got
busy then. Finally I had to go to Cairo—you know what
it is when you want to do something they've not thought of.
But I wouldn't be shaken off. I got permission to come
back here and do all the damage I can. They're backing us."

"How ? "

"I've brought a lot of stuff. We've hidden it at Tibaki.
We'll get it distributed—rifles, ammunition, medical supplies. Every destroyer coming over to pick up men will
bring supplies. When we can organise safe dumps they'll
fly it in. Have you heard of Colonel Mandakas ? "

"No."

"He's a Greek colonel who's here, organising guerrilla
bands in the mountains. He knows every inch of the
country, and his spies cover the place. We must make
contact with him," said Richard.

"So far we've been completely isolated. Some boats
have come in at night in reply to our signals along the coast,
but we have to be frightfully careful, for the Italians are
patrolling. Two nights ago twenty of our men were decoyed
on to an Italian destroyer. Do you know what I want
most ? A new battery for the radio—we've no idea what's
happening in the outside world."

"It's funny you should say that," said Richard, laughing.
"I've brought you a short-wave set, complete with batteries,
and also a supply of electric torches for signalling."

There was silence between them for a few moments.
In the hot noontide the cicadas were singing loudly. Far
below lay the valley with its patchwork of cultivated fields
of maize and wheat, its vineyards and olive groves. It was
so peaceful a scene that it was difficult to believe that this

was a land in the grip of a ruthless enemy, and that everywhere, in towns and villages, in mountain huts, coves, quarries, ravines, forests, and fields, a desperate battle went on, furtive and secret, giving and receiving no quarter.

"Do you remember when we last sat here?" asked Sylvia. "It doesn't seem possible we should be here again."

Yes. Poor Cesare was with us. We had a dismal farewell meal before going down to Herakleion. Do you remember that afternoon when some planes flew over and he recognised them as Savoias? They left us alone then; they wouldn't now. You're wise to camouflage this terrace. I wonder how long it will be before they spot us here. I'm glad you've had good guards posted. Who's doing it?"

"An English officer and an Australian, Captain Pierce and Lieutenant Walker," said Sylvia. She described to him their organisation and their camp headquarters at the fort. Finally she told him of her excursion one morning and the young Nazi they had found.

"You've brought him here? Was that wise?"

"There was no choice," replied Sylvia. "It was not at all certain he would live. He couldn't be moved all the way to the fort—we can only deal with slight cases there. Besides, we've no prisoners, and it wouldn't be wise to have him see what's going on there. So we brought him here. He was unconscious for two days. As soon as it's possible to move him we'll send him across, but that's going to be some time. He's got a fractured skull, a broken leg, and two broken ribs. He's lucky the natives didn't get hold of him."

"What's he like?" asked Richard.

"He spoke for the first time this morning. He's an Austrian, twenty years old. He speaks quite good English, but I haven't talked with him much. He must be kept very quiet. From what he did say, he's pretty hostile—didn't want to be taken a prisoner—wanted to be shot! He'll *heil* Hitler the moment he gets his arm up."

"They're all like that. They're certain they've won the war, and damned arrogant."

"They've good reason—look at this show. Dick, what is the matter with us?"

I

" We're slow starting. They've been preparing for years. And we stand alone. Well, they didn't have it all their own way here. Churchill spoke yesterday in the House. We lost about 13,000, including 2,000 who are still at large here. About 14,000 were evacuated. We British lost 7,000 out of 14,000, the New Zealanders 2,600 out of 7,000, the Australians about 3,000 out of 6,500. That's not counting Greeks and Cretans. Compared with Crete, Dunkirk was a side show, according to fellows who've been in both. We lost twelve per cent. there and fifty per cent. here. The Germans have lost over 12,000 and we drowned 5,000. It was pretty equal. In one sense, it was more than equal. We've bled the *Luftwaffe*. It'll never be itself again, I think. There's not much left of those paratroopers and gliders. We bagged a couple of hundred fighters and bombers and two or three hundred troop carriers. I heard they were on the verge of quitting at one time. We've thrown their whole timetable out of gear, so I don't admit we've been defeated. Territorially, yes—this island's gone for the time being. They'll go for Egypt now, but they've had a terrible mauling. They can't repeat the Crete show. I don't want to boast, but I think we've saved the Middle East, though I can understand the Greeks feel bitter about the island going. Look what the R.A.F.'s done—we were never a squadron ; we were only a fragment of the 36th at Maleme and Herakleion. We've fought in Greece ; we've held Rommel ; we've protected convoys to Tobruk and Malta, and fought in Iran and Iraq and Palestine. We've done a hell of a job. I'd like to wring the damn necks of some of those cackling M.P.s and commentators at home. We've made Hitler unleash everything he had, first in Yugoslavia, then in Greece, now here. We've upset all his plans for this summer. He's attacking Egypt ; he's bombing Alexandria and Suez. He'll hope to attack Cyprus and Syria, and he's designs on Iraq, but we've drawn his sting. There's another point a lot of those grousers miss. We've weakened the *Luftwaffe* at a time when they can't afford it. Plane production's coming along in England and America. It's going to be stupendous. They've learned one thing here, whatever it's cost us. They're never again going to have it their own way. Crete has been their graveyard.

We've had about fifty planes in all the Middle East against their whole *Luftwaffe*, based on nine airfields only a hundred miles from Crete. When some of us hopped over here we'd only ten minutes' fighting time in our petrol tanks. Most of us knew we were doomed. But it had to be done. I know there've been blunders. I think we should have mined Maleme aerodrome in case we couldn't hold it. That may have lost us Crete. When the Nazis got that aerodrome they poured their men in. But it was touch and go, and they've not kicked us out of the Mediterranean yet —nor here. We'll be back one day. Meanwhile we'll make it as hot as hell for them!"

"I'm glad you feel like that," said Sylvia, her eyes shining. "Then you believe I did right to refuse to leave —and Janet?"

Richard put his arm round her shoulders and hugged her.

"Of course you did. I'm proud of you, old girl!"

"You're staying?"

"Yes—and I'm to let 'em know what we want, and if at all possible we'll get it. How many more men do you think we can get out? They think it's wiser to let it be a Greek show for the present."

"Perhaps a thousand—some are scattered, and we haven't got into touch with them yet. They're fighting everywhere. The Cretans are wonderful. We get offers of help every day. And Janet's a tower of strength."

"Where is she?"

"She's working at Fort Minotaur. She'll be back to-morrow."

"Fort Minotaur! That's a good name for the old labyrinth. Shades of Theseus!" laughed Richard.

There were footsteps on the terrace. They looked up.

"Heavens! If it isn't old Nasty!" exclaimed Richard, jumping up. The next minute he stood embracing the old crone, who shed tears of joy over his return.

CHAPTER VI

CALL OF THE BLOOD

JUNE passed. Conditions on Crete became more critical. They were well organised now. Colonel Mandakas' forces began to operate through the Klephts, a secret society of patriots banded together to destroy the enemy. They took an oath that the foul invaders should be drowned in their own blood. In every village their agents operated. Odd Germans disappeared ; patrols vanished. It was in vain that men were arrested and shot over their own graves, that houses were fired, crops destroyed, and a reign of terror instituted. Mandakas' forces numbered about five thousand Cretans. To these were joined the British and the Anzacs, over a thousand, who co-operated and fought in guerrilla engagements.

The mortality was high, but the fierce resistance to the Germans never faltered. There could be no massed attack. It was a furtive warfare, of small, mobile groups falling suddenly on outposts, guards, patrols, so that the inland valleys and mountains became a deadly terrain into which the enemy ventured nervously. He was safer in the air, from which he reconnoitred and bombed. He devastated whole villages in retribution, but the enemy against which he fought remained elusive and mobile. Its secret communication system worked so rapidly that he was driven to frenzied rage, which produced his subsequent cruelties.

It was not only the men who fought. Janet Farr had joined forces with a band of Cretan Amazons. She was now talking Greek. She was everywhere, took tremendous risks, and had developed into a deadly shot. She was less and less at Villa Vouni. Finally she ceased to sleep there at all and made her headquarters at Fort Minotaur. Each day she went out from there with the guerrilla parties before dawn. The men swore by her.

" I suppose you know ? " asked Richard one day, when

Sylvia spoke of Janet, who had not been up to the villa for almost a week.

"Know what?" asked Sylvia, very tired after convoying another batch of wounded down to the shore.

Richard laughed. "Well, it's none of our business anyhow," he said. "She's doing a great job."

"You mean Janet's—— There's a man on the scene?"

"Yes—a New Zealander. I must say they're very open about it."

"Open! Dick, don't you see it's outrageous?"

"What can you do about it?" asked Richard. "It's her affair."

"But it isn't. It's ours! She can't behave like this!"

"Well, she does, and I don't see what you can do."

"I can send her to Alexandria," said Sylvia, angrily. "Unless she marries the man."

"With a Greek priest, if he'd do it? And could you send her back? You're not her senior, and anyhow there is no question of rank here; we're on our own."

"Then I shall send the man back. We can't have things like that going on!"

"My dear girl—do be practical. Do you suppose our lads aren't looking at the Greek girls? Leave it alone."

"I can't acquiesce in anything like that. I shall speak to her," said Sylvia firmly.

"Very well. It's on your own head," replied Richard. "I don't envy you the job."

A few days later when Janet came to the villa Sylvia made her protest. But it was useless. Janet was adamant.

"We've been over all that before. I'm leading my own life," said Janet stoutly.

"Are you going to marry him when this is over?"

"No. It's purely a physical matter, and I know it might not last."

"Janet, you distress me."

"Perhaps I do. I'm not a nice girl, I know what I want. I'm taking what I want. You can't change me, Sylvia. Bill and I click. That's all there is to it. Let's drop it."

She looked at Sylvia defiantly, and then tears came into her eyes.

" I wish you'd never made a friend of me. I knew I'd
hurt you, Sylvia," she said gently.

Sylvia's antagonism vanished instantly. She knew the
coarse honesty and courage beneath her lonely pugnacious
spirit. She put her arms round Janet and kissed her.

" I'll never understand you," she said, " but I know I'll
never cease to be fond of you, even when you frighten me
most."

§ 2

It was Sylvia's habit, when at the villa, to visit her
patient for a few minutes before the evening meal. He had
improved rapidly, although imprisoned by the broken leg
in its splints and his fractured ribs. The scars on his head
had healed well, and he had escaped the dangerous compli-
cations incident to this form of fracture, but his convalescence
was going to be a long job, and the idea of getting him down
to the coast could not be considered for some time.

Gradually the youth softened in his manner, though he
remained a violent Nazi, whose God, Hitler, it was sacrilege
to assail. Sylvia, aware that any form of mental agitation
was dangerous, carefully avoided political discussion, and
when he attempted to proselytise she firmly stopped him.

" I regard you as a complete case of the corrupted mentality of German youth. We should never agree, so don't
let's discuss it, Franz," she said quietly.

He smiled. It was a smile of singular radiance which lit
his dark eyes and handsome young face. His voice, too,
had charm. Janet called him " The Teuton Menace."

" But, Miss Sylvia, the day will come when you will have
to face reality! We are the New Era. Why are you
English so obstinate? Europe is ours, to-morrow the
world ! "

" Franz, you've been handing out that parrot talk a long
time, but nobody seems to want you to own the world.
You're not exactly loved in Norway, Holland, Poland,
Czechoslovakia, France, Belgium, Greece, Yugoslavia, or
here. And now you've marched into Russia, where you're
blasting your way into the hearts of the people ! "

" But they are barbarians—we are saving the world from Bolshevism."

" Bosh ! You forget you allied yourself with Russia to start a world war and carve up Poland between you. It doesn't make sense. Your Hitler foams at the mouth over Bolshevik Russia, then he allies himself with it ; now he makes war on it. You chant about purity of the blood, and you make an ally of the Japs ! "

" Our racial purity—— "

" Franz, I refuse to discuss the matter. As your nurse, I forbid it."

" But you do discuss it ! " he replied, teasingly.

" You irritate me, and I forget."

It was some time before Sylvia realised there was a degree of impishness in his nature. His views horrified her. She had not believed the Nazi corruption had become so ingrained in the character of its youthful disciples. It was a faith that seemed likely to survive military defeat, even if these young Nazis could imagine such a possibility. It depressed her because she could not see any way in which the consciousness of monstrous error could be brought home to minds that had no fundamental basis in truth. This blind, passionate worship of the perverted messiah of the Nazi faith was a corruption of the spirit no conversion could assail. It seemed something that could be eradicated only by the death of the person in which it had spread its cancerous creed. Here was a boy, well bred, well educated, brave and intelligent, yet dead to the fundamental decencies by which men of honour and tolerance could live. She was appalled by the nature of the nightmare Nazism had brought upon the world, when she heard this youth affirm his sincere belief in the preposterous and wicked credo of the charlatan from Berchtesgaden.

Little by little, along with is appalling political doctrine, she learned something of his life. There had been a moment of complete surprise, when, following her comment upon the excellent English he spoke, he revealed that his mother had been English. Not that she had taught him his English, for she had died in giving birth to him, and she was only a legend, but his father had seemed anxious to continue the English connection. Franz had had an

excellent Scottish governess and had spent frequent holidays
in England with his maternal grandparents. His father, for
some reason, did not play nearly so large a part in Franz von
Kleber's account of his life and his home as did an old
Austrian great-uncle, a bedridden old general who had lived
to be eighty and had dominated the boy's life until he was
fifteen.   Grossonkel Rudolph, and the old castle at Garstein
where he lived, almost monopolised young Franz's account
of his boyhood in Austria.   From this dominating old man
Franz had imbibed all the Kleber traditions.   Franz's own
father had married again, a Hungarian whom neither Franz
nor the old general liked.   In the end, Franz, with his
governess, spent most of his time at Schloss Garstein instead
of at his home in Vienna.   This plan suited Franz's father,
who was free to move about with his pretty young wife.
Grossonkel Rudolph died during young Franz's first year
at the military academy at Wiener Nieustadt, to which he
had gone in fulfilment of the general's desire to continue
the von Kleber military tradition.   On the death of the old
man it was found that he had passed over his nephew and
left the Schloss and estate in trust to young Franz.

"One day you must see it. It's grim and strong and
beautiful, among the mountains, with the sound of running
water everywhere," said Franz von Kleber. "You would
love it."

Sometimes he talked of his father, who was now a colonel
on the staff with the German army in Paris, but he gave
Sylvia the impression that he had little respect for him.
The dictatorial old great-uncle still dominated the youth's
heart.   He had not cared very much for the life of a cadet,
and he was bitter about the state of Austria.

"We'd gone to pieces. We'd nothing to live for. We'd
been robbed of our soil. The Socialists pulled us into the
gutter with them. There was no hope for us until the
Fuehrer came. I was there when he marched into Vienna !
It was wonderful, wonderful ! " he exclaimed, with shining
eyes. "You couldn't openly join the Hitler Jugend, or the
Schwarzekorps—but you could after that ; you could wear
the uniform ! We'd been drilling secretly. We knew the
day was coming when that creature Schuschnigg would go.
I was at the academy at Wiener Nieustadt when the Fuehrer

came to review us. The place went mad ! I knew then
what I wanted to be. I wanted to fly. We were allowed
to learn ; we——"

" Yes, but I'm not interested in Der Fuehrer, Franz—
and you're getting too excited. I'll see you to-morrow,"
said Sylvia, cutting him short. " Good-bye."

" Ah, that is how you punish me ! Auf wiedersehen," he
replied gaily. " Heil Hitler ! "

" I forbid you to say that. How dare you here ! "

" Heil Hitler ! " he repeated. But a thousand devils
danced in his eyes as they laughed at her.

It was difficult to be angry with him for long. He had
a quite preposterous capacity to charm, with his dark neat
head, his dancing eyes and alluring smile. Even Helen, the
Cretan maid of all work, who for a fortnight had refused to
go into the room of the hated Nazi, finally succumbed to
him, although they could not exchange a dozen words.
Richard, after a somewhat cold interview, admitted he was
a youth of singular attraction.

" They've shot the poison into him all right," he said.
" What are we going to do with 'em all ? When we've
walloped 'em, they'll still contaminate the earth. These
kids are fanatics. They've been nurtured on vitriol and lies.
Did you hear him bleating about the German blood—that
nonsense about the *Herrenvolk*, the Reich that's to last a
thousand years, German *Lebensraum* ? His German blood !
My God, the little bastard's half Austrian and half English !
The terrible thing is, like a lot of these kids, he believes it ;
he's proud to sacrifice his life for it. He's not a corrupt,
rotten little cuss like Goebbels, Goering, and Ribbentrop.
What can we do with perverted minds like his ? Here we
are mending the crack in his skull, but you can't get at the
crack in his brain. We should really pitch him over the
terrace ! "

" You wouldn't do any such thing ! " said Sylvia.

" No. Funny, isn't it ? I'd cheerfully shoot him in the
air and on the ground, but I can't shoot him in bed, where
he's the same nasty little Nazi."

" Somehow I can't think he's nasty—though he infuriates
me," said Sylvia. " What do you think he said when I took
him in the radio yesterday ? He listened to the English

programme to find out just what kind of lies we were
telling ! ”

“ Don’t let him have it.”

“ Ah—I’m not sure about that ! Curiosity may get him,
and he’ll hear a lot he’s never been allowed to know.”

“ He won’t believe it,” commented Richard.

“ Well, I’m trying it,” said Sylvia. “ You never know.”

Listening to the radio certainly had one effect upon
young Franz Kleber. He became aware of the almost
universal hatred the Germans had succeeded in creating for
themselves.

“ I don’t understand it,” he complained.

“ That’s just what’s the matter with you Germans—and
you never will. You want to shoot people and rob them
and occupy their countries, and you expect to be loved by
them ! Now, Franz, I’m not going to argue with you any
more—it’s bad for you and we get nowhere,” said Sylvia
one afternoon.

“ But you want me to listen-in, don’t you ? ” asked Franz,
with a twinkle in his eye. “ You want to corrupt me ? ”

“ I’m quite indifferent as to whether I corrupt you or not.
You’re a horrid little Nazi—and you can remain one ! ”

“ Really horrid ? ”

“ In some ways.”

“ Why are you so kind to me ? ”

“ You were wounded. We do not ill-treat wounded
prisoners.”

“ Ah—please, I want to ask you something.”

“ Yes ? ”

“ I am your prisoner ? You know I might escape ? ”

“ Not with that leg—and let me warn you. If you fell
into the hands of some of these Cretans you’d be——”

Sylvia drew her finger across her throat.

“ I am very curious. Can I ask you something, Miss
Sylvia ? ”

“ You can ask me anything, but I may not answer you.”

“ You’ve been very kind to me, more kind than any
wounded enemy could expect. I am very grateful, and
I am worried for you.”

“ For me ? ”

“ Yes. You are a nurse with the British Army—you and

Miss Janet. But you are nurses no longer. You fight. You are the centre of opposition and spying. When we come here you will be shot. You have violated your non-belligerent status as a nurse. Your brother might be treated as a prisoner——"

" I don't know how much you think you know, but I was prepared to take a risk when I brought you here."

" That was very gallant of you. You are my enemy, but I admire you, although it makes me sad to know what must happen to you. And please do not think I am spying. When my bed is wheeled out on to the terrace I cannot help seeing things—the camouflage you have made, the coming and going of people—British soldiers, Greeks, even priests——"

" Yes, even priests, Franz. One came here this morning. He told me how his bishop has aided his countrymen and been condemned to death. They've condemned to death the Archbishop of Crete also. He's in prison in Athens, though you've reprieved him because of his age—he's nearly eighty. There's another bishop, fighting with the guerrilla forces in the mountains—he's seen all of his children and grandchildren slain before his eyes in savage reprisals you Germans took at Mournies."

" Priests shouldn't fight."

" Perhaps not, but they are patriots and men first. There was a brave little priest who held a service in Herakleion Cathedral—what's left of it—for the men who were going out to die as guerrilla fighters. He was seized at the altar, stripped naked in his own church, put to hard labour for four days on the roads, and finally, after a trial, made to dig his own grave and shot."

" I do not believe it."

" I'm not surprised you can't. But these things have happened, are happening ! A few weeks ago you shot every living male in Mournies and burned Lakko to the ground because it had harboured some of our strayed soldiers."

" That is war."

" It is Nazi war, yes. But I don't want to argue. When my unit was leaving I decided I could do most for our own soldiers and these poor people by remaining. I speak Greek ; I had this place to retreat to, for a time at least.

Janet Farr volunteered to stay with me. We took off our uniforms ; we joined the guerrilla army ; we are fighting, come what may, with these people who have had their country invaded, their husbands and sons killed, their homes destroyed. You Germans will do the same when we invade Germany—and if you don't you'll add the contempt of the world to the hatred of the world."

Franz von Kleber looked at Sylvia's earnest face. The passion in her voice was something new. She was always so calm.

" Miss Sylvia, you don't believe Germany will ever be invaded ? We have won the war ! You have not a soldier in Europe. In a month or so we shall be in Leningrad and Moscow. Russia will be utterly crushed, like Poland, Holland, Belgium, France, Greece."

" We needn't argue that, Franz. I have my own faith. But there is something I must say to you, since you have raised the subject. As soon as you can be moved you will be sent to Alexandria."

" But we shall be there—Egypt will be ours in a few weeks ! We're bombing Alexandria and Suez now. You admit that on the radio. You've been thrown out of Libya ! "

" Then you'll be sent somewhere else. You will try to escape. It is useless to ask for your parole—you would not give it, I know. I respect that. But should you escape, are you going to utilise all you have seen here while we have been nursing you ? We could have kept you down in the village—at a risk to yourself and less to ourselves."

" I know that, Miss Sylvia. You are all my enemies, but I admire your bravery and what you have done for me here——"

He paused while he could control his voice, and his hands smoothed the coverlet in a helpless gesture of frustration. Then with steady eyes he looked at Sylvia and said :

" If I escape you—whatever happens, I give you my word of honour that not one iota of what I have seen or heard here will leave my lips, though I hope to fight you again."

" Thank you, Franz. That will make it easier for both of us," said Sylvia.

" You will not take my advice ? " asked Franz, smiling.

" What's that ? "

" To escape now, while you can. We shall be here soon.
Our planes are always over—and, Miss Sylvia, there's no
need for that funny Cockney soldier to stand on the terrace
ready to shoot me, when I'm out there, in case I signalled
to our planes."

" We cannot take the risk, Franz."

" I have given you my word of honour. I am not even
counting how many soldiers you and Miss Janet are convoying down to the coast. I am curious, of course, to know
where you go to early each morning, where Mr. Richard
has his headquarters, where you hide all your stores. It's
somewhere behind in the mountains—in those caves, I suspect. I lie here and wonder just where you are at some
particular moment and pray our fellows haven't trapped
you, or——"

" Oh—so you're that much on our side, Franz ! " exclaimed Sylvia.

" I'm expressing a purely private opinion—not that of
a soldier," said Franz earnestly, and with such haste that
Sylvia had to laugh.

" I hope you would not command my shooting party—
sentiment might bungle it ! " she said lightly.

" That is a terrible thought ! " he protested. " But—
I should be a good soldier."

" Despite your mother—that was a very German
moment."

" I do not understand."

" You couldn't ! " said Sylvia. " There's where we
English have you beaten."

He looked so puzzled and hurt that she smiled at him and
rumpled his black hair, too long just now, and very thick
where it swept back from the widow's peak on his brow.
He caught at her hand and, suddenly holding it to his
mouth, kissed it in a gesture of gratitude.

" Now I'm going," she said.

" Oh, please stay a little longer ! " he pleaded.

" I have a lot to do."

" You're going to the beach to-night again ? "

" That's an improper question, my enemy. What makes
you think I go to the beach, and why ? "

" Very well, you do not go to the beach, Fräulein Day."

" Thank you, Herr Leutnant Kleber. Do you want any more books ? You've almost exhausted the library."

" Oh, I've something to show you ! "

His hand searched through several old copies of the *Tatler* among the magazines, precious reading fare, that the coast-running destroyers brought in with more serious stores.

" There's a portrait here of your detestable friend," he said, picking out a *Tatler* and turning over the leaves.

" My detestable friend ? "

" I think he's utterly detestable. The lies the man tells ! He infuriates me ! You British lap him up. There—look at him ! "

He passed the *Tatler*, opened at the full-page portrait of a middle-aged man seated in front of a microphone. Sylvia read the text underneath.

" Mr. Randell Dunning, the well-known novelist, is perhaps our most popular news commentator. His nightly summary over the B.B.C. has gained for him an immense and admiring public. His weekly broadcasts in the North Atlantic service have constituted him England's voice in the American continent, and his nightly broadcast in the European service has made him Dr. Goebbels' most formidable adversary. Mr. Dunning's tremendous industry at the microphone has not prevented him from writing another of his novels. The latest, *We shall Look Back and Wonder*, is again in the front rank of the best sellers.

" I never imagined he looked like that. I expected he was short, plump, and fair, and he's tall, dark, and thin. Quite handsome—and very good at his job. You'll admit that ? " asked Sylvia, putting down the paper.

" He infuriates me beyond words ! This portrait doesn't flatter him—he's even better looking, the beast ! " said Franz.

" How do you know ? You've never seen him ? "

" Oh, yes, I have ; I know him ! "

" You know him ! " asked Sylvia, incredulous.

" Yes," replied Franz with an intriguing smile. " He got me into awful trouble ! "

" How—in Germany ? "

" No, in England."

" But that must have been before the war. You were a mere boy then ! " exclaimed Sylvia, mystified. " I don't understand."

" Well, it was only two years ago—I was eighteen. I was staying with my grandparents. I used to go every year for a month. Their home's at Market Harborough, in Leicester-shire. They're great hunting people. My father as a young man went out with the Quorn—that's how he came to meet my mother—who was very young and pretty then. Well, the last time I was at Grandpa Cameron's——"

" Cameron ? "

" Yes—my mother was Carlotta Cameron. The last time I was there, in July, '39, there was a tennis tournament at Market Harborough, and I entered for the singles. I might say I'm considered quite good for my age ; I won twice at the Innsbruck tournament. I did pretty well at Market Harborough and got into the semi-finals. Nobody thought I had a dog's chance then because I was drawn against Randell Dunning."

" So that's how you met him ? "

" Yes. I didn't know then he was a famous writer, but everybody told me he was a terrific tennis player and my number was up. Well, to everybody's amazement, including my own, I won ! It was very odd ; he seemed to have gone right off his game. I must say he was very nice and sport-ing about it. When we went down to the courts together —we met in the umpire's tent—he asked me if I was English or Austrian. You see, I never use the ' von ' in England. I told him I was half Austrian, half English He said, ' You're not *Von* Kleber, are you ? ' I told him I was. ' Your mother's name's not Carlotta, by any chance ? ' he then asked me. I told him my mother, who was dead, was named Carlotta—my grandmother had had a great friend, an Italian girl, and had named her after her. I asked how he knew my mother's name, and he said he had once known a Gräfin Carlotta von Kleber in Tunis. Wasn't that funny ? What a silly little world ! It was my mother ! I showed him her portrait, and he recognised her. I carry it in this ring. Look ! "

He pulled off the clumsy signet ring that Sylvia had noticed on his finger. She saw now the reason for its size. The crest was engraved on a lid which opened. Inside there was an exquisite coloured photograph.

" But she's beautiful, Franz ! " exclaimed Sylvia.

" Yes—poor Mamma, I believe she was. Grossonkel adored her and said she was lovely and high-spirited."

Sylvia passed back the ring. He closed the lid and put it on his finger.

". You know, he couldn't get over it ! " continued Franz. " I'm sure it put him off his game. Everybody said he wasn't a bit on his form. He asked me to have lunch with him in the pavilion afterwards. He was really charming— I've got to admit that. He wanted to know all about my mother. He asked me dozens of questions—how old I was, where I was born. He'd met her in Tunis, he said. I rather suspect he must have been a bit in love with her—do you wonder ? Well, he was very nice to me. We had lunch together, and the next two days, at the tournament, and when I won the open singles he was delighted and gave me a gold wrist-watch to commemorate it—and that raised what you call a shindy ! "

" How ? "

" Well, it was my uncle James who made the fuss. He was annoyed because I lunched three times with Randell Dunning and not with his party—his daughters, Emily and Grace, are lumpy, and frightful bores. He said it was a great impertinence for Randell Dunning to take me to lunch like that three times. He said he didn't believe a word about Dunning's having known my mother. I asked him why he should invent such a story. He couldn't answer that and mumbled something about my not allowing myself to be picked up by strangers. Then I did a silly thing. I showed him the wrist-watch. There was quite a scene. I might have been a naughty girl who's looted it off a silly old man. In the end he insisted that I return it. It was unthinkable for a mere boy to accept presents from strange men. So I sent it back to Randell Dunning, who had given me the address of his club in London. He'd asked me to dine there with him. I didn't, of course. He wrote me quite a pleasant letter when I sent back the watch, which

I felt was a rotten thing to do. And that was the end of it. I must say I liked him then, but I dislike him now. He is simply monstrous about the Fuehrer and Germany. I hate the sound of his voice. He talks about us as if we were hooligans. I expect he gets a lot of money for his lying propaganda."

" I think you behaved rather badly to him," said Sylvia.

" It wasn't me—it was Uncle James. Perhaps he was right."

" Right! I think Randell Dunning was very friendly. You say yourself you felt bad about the business."

Franz von Kleber made a grimace. " I shouldn't want to know him now," he said. Then, to hide his embarrassment, he began to dial the radio. It was time for the Berlin official bulletin. The German station came through, loud and triumphant.

" I'll leave you to your daily dose of poison ! " exclaimed Sylvia. " But at seven I shall want the radio."

" For Randell Dunning? Oh, don't take it. Come in and listen. I like to hear what he has to say ! "

Sylvia laughed. " You know you admire him enormously, and you won't admit it."

" I detest him ! There's something in his voice that always infuriates me, apart from his inability to speak the truth ! "

" You may be incapable of understanding it, Franz. A Nazi education must make that impossible," replied Sylvia.

" You do hate us, don't you ? "

" A frank question merits a frank answer. There is nothing personal in this. I am living for the day when the Nazis and all their devilish works are obliterated from the earth. I will give my life for that, if necessary."

" I will give my life for the Fuehrer, if necessary," said Franz quietly. " Isn't it strange, Miss Sylvia, we are such implacable enemies, and yet I feel—I hope you feel, too— we are—we are——" He hesitated for the words he wanted, singular in one whose English was always so fluent. " We are very good friends. May I think that, please ? " he asked, giving her one of his warm smiles. " And it has nothing to do with gratitude, though I feel that also," he added.

Sylvia made no reply for a few moments. She felt how sad it was, how perverse of life, that one who had such attractive qualities, mental and physical, should have been corrupted by the monstrous Nazi faith. For faith, she learned from him, it was. It burned with a steady flame such as lit the inward life of a saint. It made him count the price of death as nothing, if thereby he might fall a soldier for the leader from whom he drew his faith. There were hundreds, thousands, hundreds of thousands of young men like Franz, who were fighting and dying courageously in the service of a creed that was conceived and preached by base men operating through fraud and force. Sometimes she was appalled by the complexity of truth. It should be a clear, vivid thing that no perversity of mind, wilful or unpremeditated, could obscure. But it was not so. Clever men could make it seem Janus-faced. It could be tricked out with tinsel crowns and imitation jewels so that its false brilliance deceived the single-minded. Skilful men dressed it in glittering words, cloaked it with sham loyalties, and made their blasphemies sound like the voice of God. How otherwise could this generation of German youth, so clean, finely tempered, loyal, and courageous, march, with shining eyes and singing voices, beneath a banner that betrayed the eternal verities? It was a terrible price for the young to die nobly for a righteous cause. It was a still more terrible price for them to die vainly for the twisted mind of a perverted creature, who, in the name of patriotism, called them to a supreme sacrifice for a supreme falsehood.

All this—the pity, the wickedness of it—passed through Sylvia's mind as she stood looking at the eager face of the youth in the bed before her. Sometimes she was of a mind never to refute his belief, aware that, in breaking his idol, could she achieve it, she would break the faith that inspired him. Yet she felt she must speak the truth as she believed it. All over the world other youths, as fine in their courage, as selfless in their faith, loyal to the pattern of life in which they found themselves, were fighting and dying to sustain a way of life they believed in. No heroics stirred their nature. Many of them were cynically suspicious of the politicians who gave them slogans for the way of death, or promised them such glittering rewards in the future.

Their fathers, decorated in a war to end all wars, had sung in the gutters of prosperous cities or cluttered up the corridors of labour exchanges. These, too, might receive the same spurious coinage for the gold of their youth. That would await the proof. For the present they made no bargain and suppressed their reproaches. The fires of a hundred cities, the rape of a dozen nations, the ravaged faces of their homelands were cause enough for their dogged, unconquerable spirit. The Johns and the Franzes, these victims of destiny, were to put to the proof before the bar of history whether man could live and flourish in a world subjected to the doctrine of a single mind. So far it might seem the dictators were winning, but the stars in their courses proclaimed an eternal law. The eclipse of truth was temporary ; a dark world would shine again. Believing this, Sylvia beheld in young Franz the banner-bearer of a doomed generation, and not all his bright faith could redeem it.

" You make me very sad," said Sylvia at last, as his eager young face searched hers, curious over her delayed answer to his appeal. " I am glad to have you for a friend, Franz —though nothing but tragedy can come of it."

" Tragedy—why ? "

" We shall defeat you, or you will defeat us. Two conceptions of life—your Nazi and our democratic—cannot exist in the world together, nor can they ever compromise. That means the elimination of one of us. Franz, we mustn't keep returning to this subject—it's useless."

" But you do hope for my conversion, don't you ? " he asked, with smiling eyes.

" Perhaps that is foolish of me. Good-bye ! I've a lot of work to do."

" Good-bye. I believe nothing that you hope for me can be foolish," he said soberly, his eyes following her to the door.

Sylvia made no comment, smiled, and left the room.

On the way to her desk she wondered from whom Franz had derived his charm, from his Austrian father or his English mother. One day she would seek out Randell Dunning and learn something about Carlotta von Kleber.

CHAPTER VII

WINDS OF AUTUMN

IN August the situation of the guerrilla forces grew more critical. The Nazi control became tighter. Their airplanes patrolled the south coast, and in conjunction with the Italian navy and air arm made contact with the British ships coming from Alexandria extremely hazardous. The precipitous coastline had very few possible landing-places, and over these the Nazis kept a ceaseless watch. All contact with the sea had to be made in the darkness. Evacuation parties had been captured on three occasions. This resulted in some ninety men being taken prisoners and the loss of about fifteen in the fighting that ensued. Italian gunboats hung off the coast at night and decoyed embarkation parties, until experience taught the British that all vessels approaching and answering signals must be investigated.

Despite all these dangers and difficulties over six hundred English, Australian, New Zealand and Greek soldiers had been evacuated. Those remaining now were determined to harass the Germans as long as supplies of arms and ammunition would last. There was now another source of supply for the resisting forces. Planes were coming over from Egypt at night and dropping stores on places in the mountains where they observed the agreed signals. The infuriated Nazis, despite the Draconian measures they took with the population, had never succeeded in penetrating or reducing the mountain area. They reconnoitred and bombed ; they took hostages and shot them ruthlessly, but the interior remained rebellious. Colonel Mandakas and his forces still kept to the mountains. In conjunction with Pierce and Walker and Richard, they harried the nervous German patrols and at every opportunity swooped down upon the towns and villages.

They took bold measures to check the Nazi habit of shooting hostages. A special Commando was formed of hand-picked English, Australian, and New Zealand soldiers, with a sprinkling of Maoris and Cretans, whose special task was the seizure of unsuspecting German soldiers. When fifty of these had been captured, a list of them, with their names and rank, was sent to the German commanders, with the statement that, for every Greek hostage shot, a German soldier would die. One Nazi commander had not believed the threat and shot five hostages, three old men and two youths, after a raid on a German outpost. The next morning at dawn there was consternation in the Nazi headquarters when the bodies of five Germans were found neatly deposited on the graves of the executed hostages. This was repeated four times. The shooting of hostages ceased.

All Crete rang with the story of six women guerrilla fighters from Herakleion who had been sent as prisoners to Athens. They had survived the bombing of the town and were members of a band of resolute women who had carried on the fight among the ruins. After five weeks' ferocious fighting they had been caught, attired in men's clothes, complete with rifles and bandoleers. They were sent to Athens and brought before Field-Marshal Wilhelm von List, who pompously addressed them and said, despite an offence meriting death, Fuehrer Hitler had decided to honour them as prisoners of war. He then held out his hand to the prisoners, who ignored it. " Hitler cannot honour the women of Crete ! " exclaimed one of them, Maria Georgidalakai, whose head was bandaged. " My husband died fighting you—we, too, would die fighting you. We fight for the love of our country and the shade of Venizelos ! " She went back to the Ambelokybe Prison with her companions, and died there of her wounds. A Maria Georgidalakai company of Cretan women had sprung up to honour her memory by carrying on the fight.

" God help the Nazi who falls into their hands," said Janet Farr one day, who had been with them in an outpost raid. " I've never seen such knife work ! "

Towards the end of August there was almost a major disaster to the guerrilla ranks. Watchers on the White Mountains had reported a large convoy of British ships. On this same morning the Germans, for some reason, were

practising parachute landings. The hasty conclusion was
drawn that the British were making a sea and air landing.
The great day had dawned! To assist them a double raid
in force was made on the German aerodromes at Maleme
and Herakleion.

Richard was in the Maleme attack. At the start all went
well. A hangar and twenty planes were destroyed. Three
hundred Germans fell in the fighting. But the error soon
became obvious. The convoy was not destined for Crete.
A desperate retreat had to be made, with heavy casualties.
Richard's company had been almost surrounded and fought
its way through to the hills, losing fifty per cent. of its
forces. Janet Farr, besieged in a cottage where she attended
the wounded, had held out for an hour before being relieved.
The guerrilla army paid heavy for its faulty conclusion.
The next day the Germans bombed four villages to ashes
in retribution.

All communications with the outside world was not yet
cut off. Even mail came in the parachute parcels or by
boats that sneaked in at night. One day there was a small
package for Sylvia. In it she found a letter from Derek
one of seven she had had, and an engagement ring, gold,
with a small diamond, which he had bought in Alexandria.
" I am back here again. If my luck holds in the next few
days I may be on a visiting destroyer. God bless you, my
darling," he wrote.

Sylvia acted upon the hint. She went down to the coast
every night for two weeks. Three destroyers took off men
in that time, but Derek was not in any of these ships. She
sent back letters with each boat. One was for Grandma
Day. Richard had received a letter from her when last in
Alexandria. She had a houseful of London refugees from
the bombings and was vigorously carrying on at eighty-three.
She found the voices of " ten Cockney guttersnipes " very
penetrating. The telephone service is increasingly abomin-
able, but the spirit of everyone quite exhilarating. Rationing
has improved the figure of Father Duffy.

The news these days from North Africa was bad. Tobruk
was besieged; Rommel sat at the gateway of Egypt.

" If they get Egypt, shall we be able to hold out in the
Mediterranean ? " Sylvia asked Richard after a very gloomy

review of the position over the London broadcast. " The
House of Commons is talking about a vote of confidence—
they sound jittery."

" If Egypt goes, our whole Mediterranean position goes
—Malta, Cyprus, Palestine, Iraq, the Persian Gulf, and
India possibly. I should say we were going to lose the
war but for three things : Churchill, the ordinary people of
England, and President Roosevelt. The past record of the
House of Commons—it's the same Baldwin-Chamberlain
lot in sackcloth and khaki—doesn't inspire me. My bet is
if Churchill challenges 'em to a vote of confidence, they'll
beat a hasty retreat," said Richard.

" Why do you say President Roosevelt ? Do you think
the United States will come in ? "

" They are in—though some of them don't want to believe
it. They've frozen all German assets. That tells Germany
where she is. And Roosevelt and Churchill haven't met in
the Atlantic merely to publish the Atlantic Charter. You
don't lease and lend up to the hilt and then let your friend
go under. Somehow we must hang on until America
weighs in. The Germans aren't in Leningrad yet. I don't
believe they'll ever get there—or Cairo, or London. The
Navy's still in the Mediterranean. It'll stay there, either at
the top or the bottom, and I believe at the top ! "

" You have a wonderful faith in England, Dick ! "

" I have ! " affirmed Richard, putting his arm round
Sylvia's shoulders. " I believe it's unconquerable because
of lads like Kid Carter, and frail young women like Sylvia
Day—and I'll add Janet Farr, the trollop ! They're bred
by the thousands in English towns and villages and
in far-off places like Canada, Australia, New Zealand,
and South Africa. Yes, my God, and in India, too, despite twisters like Gandhi. You should have seen those
Indian soldiers in Libya ! We're all right, Sylvia—we're
going to win, even if the Mediterranean goes, and us
with it."

" It's getting bad here, isn't it ? But I'm not pulling
out," added Sylvia hastily.

" It's going to get tougher. That reminds me—about
our young Nazi friend——"

" Franz ? "

" Yes, I see he's now wheeled out on the terrace each morning. When can we ship him ? "

" He's not fit enough yet—even if we were sure of a boat. Why ? "

" I've noticed that planes are coming over pretty frequently now. He might signal to them."

" He gave me his word of honour, Dick. You don't trust him ? "

" No—I wouldn't trust any Nazi—no matter what he swears to. I know 'em," said Richard bitterly. " They've had such a doctrine pumped into 'em that a black lie's a white deed for Hitler. Keep him off the terrace."

" Very well—you are probably right. I confess I've come to like Franz ; he's changed a lot. He was odious at first. Now he's beginning to be less virulent. Randell Dunning's been working on him. He pretends he doesn't believe a word and swears he hates him, but I notice he never misses him. He calls Dunning ' Liar Number One.' They once met in England, and although Franz won't admit it, he's rather fascinated by him."

" If Dunning can get under the hide of a Hitler brat, then he's ten times cleverer than I thought he was ! " declared Richard. " Well—I'm off ! You'll see me in a day or two. Oh, I've an apology to make—your roughneck Janet ! I still think she's a strumpet, but, by God, she's a brave strumpet ! She fights like a tiger and nothing can break her. I wish you had her with you on your boat-running job."

" Janet won't leave the guerrillas—and there's another attraction."

They looked at each other. They had avoided discussing Janet's foibles.

" The prize fighter ? " asked Richard. " Yes, I suppose that's it."

" Prize fighter ? I didn't know Boswell was a pugilist."

" Boswell ? My dear, Boswell, was her New Zealand flame. He was killed a month ago, poor devil. She's replaced him with a boxer, a pug-nosed beau with a triangular torso. They're affectionately known as Pug and Mug. It would play hell with discipline if Janet hadn't got

an iron fist and scared the life out of 'em. Now, I'm off.
Take care of yourself ! "

He kissed her and, taking her hand : " I'm glad you got
the ring. Why don't you wear it ? I like your Derek
enormously. It's too bad he's not here."

With a swift hug he was gone.

§ 2

One of the refugees of the army from Greece, who had
lost a foot in the snows of Albania in those early months of
Greek triumph over the dismayed Italians, Dr. Polidori,
was pleased with the progress of Franz von Kleber. " Soon
he can begin to walk a little," he said to Sylvia, who had
asked him to come up from Fort Minotaur, where he
tended the exhausted men brought in from the mountains.
" But it is here that trouble might come." He tapped his
head. " So far all is well—we must see and hope that
there are no after-effects."

" But do you fear anything—epilepsy, or mental trouble ?"

" No, Miss Day, but a fracture of the skull may have
ultimate results. He is a very bright boy. He must not
be excited."

" When do you think we could move him—to Alexandria ? " Dr. Polidori pondered awhile.

" He could go now, but it would be unkind, even if the
journey were easy. Ask me in a month. You wish him
gone ? "

" There are reasons. He is our prisoner—and our
enemy."

" Yes, I understand. Sometimes we forget that, in our
professional interest. Well, we will see. Next week I shall
allow him to walk."

When the doctor had gone, nimble with his crutches,
Sylvia went to Franz's room. Harry had just finished
dressing him and had placed him in his chair. She greeted
him and asked the orderly to leave the room. Franz looked
at Sylvia.

" You have something serious to say ? " he asked, reading
her face.

" Not serious, but—Franz, you must not be hurt by what I am going to say. Your planes are coming over the house more and more."

" Yes, I see them. I am worried. They have found us ? "

" No, I don't think so, yet," answered Sylvia, " but it makes the position difficult—for you, for us. Franz, we have decided we can't allow you to go on the east end of the terrace. You must keep to the loggia."

As she spoke his mouth opened and closed again, but no word escaped him. He looked down at his hands. Something in his silence, the bent head, smote her heart.

" You do understand—how difficult it is ? " she asked.

" Yes, I understand," he said quietly, in a choking voice. He raised his face, and she saw his eyes were swimming with tears. " You can't trust the little Nazi—he might betray you, despite his word ? "

He tried to smile, but his mouth quivered. Sylvia felt just then how very young he was for all his masculine airs, his feigned self-assurance. She put her hand on his, moved to compassion by his emotion. With a swift gesture he raised her hand to his lips and kissed it.

" I do not complain. You have been very kind, more kind than you should have been. Perhaps soon you can send me away," he said. " I wouldn't mind that others do not trust me, but you—if only you could trust me. I would die rather than harm you ! "

" I believe you, Franz. We are victims of circumstance, that is all."

" Thank you, Sylvia," he said gravely. The boyish smile came back to his eyes as he looked up at her. Something within Sylvia made any more words impossible. She put a hand on his dark head and playfully ruffled his hair. Then she hurried from the room.

§ 3

The glory of the summer had waned ; the rich tints of autumn filled the valley and wooded hills. The barren slopes of the stony mountains were softened with a bloom

of purple and crimson furze. The maize and the wheat
had been gathered, the vines stripped. The brilliant roses
of Sharon in the hedges, the wild white clematis and purple
lysanthus flowered and withered. Colder winds blew off
the mountains ; the face of the azure sea was roughened by
the white-lipped waves that pounded angrily against the
fortress wall of cruel rock. The rains had begun.

The fighting in the mountains, through shortening days
and lengthening nights, grew more arduous under the
weight of indifferent Nature. The cold bit into the limbs
of men who slept in caves or in the partial shelter of the
rocks. It became more and more unsafe to visit the
villages. A cruel fate came to those caught in any act of
help or connivance with the guerrilla bands. Death stalked
the ravines, the mountain paths. The uneasy invader,
within the crumbled walls of the ruined towns he fortified,
watched with a nervous cruelty. Fear created panic ;
panic expressed itself in ruthless acts of repression against
the helpless, but hostile population. The guerrillas, quick,
intrepid, struck here, struck there. A knifed sentry bled
silently to death at his post ; a lorry, on a collapsing bridge,
fell with its flying bodies into the deep ravine ; a hangar
took fire ; a poisoned well spread panic ; nightfall made
every shadow a menace, every window a lancet of death.
By day and by night the ruthless, furtive fight went on.
Crete writhed, struck back, suffered famine, death, burnings,
and the refined tortures of Himmler's trained executioners.
Even worse were the irregular cruelties of sadistic boys
reared in the Nazi creed.

The Greeks, Cretans, Australians, New Zealanders,
Maoris, and English, a rabble it may have seemed, dressed
in oddments of uniforms, haphazardly armed, polyglot,
revealed a maddening insensibility to defeat. They lived
and moved like goats across the face of the cruel mountains ;
they descended like hornets upon the Nazi strongholds ;
they picked off the few and the solitary with deadly precision. Every bush and tree, every roof and window might
spit death and leave a man choking in his blood. Splendid
equipment, swift transport, command of the air, none of
these things, hitherto so triumphant could quite kill off this
monster that sprouted a thousand heads, a thousand claws,

with which to belch fire, to strike down. High rewards and the aid of cowards and traitors failed to overwhelm this quicksilver rabble in the hills.

But with the passage of time the quarry became marked. One by one the holes of the marauders were stopped. The battle took a new intensity ; cunning was matched with cunning, and when foe met foe there was no chivalry, no quarter. To kill was all.

Help was still coming from Egypt. Destroyers hugged the shore by night, and each time a few men, recovering from wounds, or sick, were taken off. They had ceased to straggle into Fort Minotaur now, and it was believed that all who had not been captured or killed had somehow succeeded in reaching headquarters. Thus far the Germans were baffled by this fortress in the mountains, the lair of the guerrilla fighters. They knew it existed ; they had some idea of its location, but all their strenuous efforts to uncover it and attack it had failed. They held systematic bombings of the area. They stopped all the roads, paths, and possible approaches towards the mountains where the elusive enemy lurked. Again and again they believed they had trapped the fighters and discovered their stronghold, only to find they had dissolved into thin air. Successive attempts to penetrate the fort had failed. The ravines and passes were too deadly for the single files that could traverse them. The labyrinth they sought was as impenetrable as it was invisible. Stung again and again by sudden sallies of intrepid fighters, the Germans gradually admitted the existence of a No Man's Land beyond their control. German guards at the headquarters and in the coastal towns and ports lived on a knife edge of apprehension.

Twice a week Sylvia made the journey to Fort Minotaur, loaded her string of mules with those too sick to walk, and led her convoy back through the ravines to the stables of the villa. There it rested overnight and the next night began the more perilous journey down to Messara Bay. Strong German patrols occupied Tymbaki and Eremopoli, and these ports and the Messara valley had to be avoided. But a chain of refuges had been formed in hidden places along the coast where native fishermen and their boats put off from secret coves when the approach of rescue craft was signalled. Sometimes the fugitives were detected. The natives were summarily executed, but as one brave Cretan fell a victim to Nazi fury, another sprang into his place. Steadily the evacuation had proceeded.

The Nazis knew their chief foe now, engaged in this business of getting off the British and Greek soldiers. The reward for the capture, dead or alive, of Sylvia Day mounted higher and higher. Next to Mandakas, if the size of the reward measured their fury, she was the chief enemy. Some of the Nazis, frustrated in all their attempts to lay hands on her, vowed she was a myth, but every village, by mountain and coast, knew the legend of Sylvia Day, who spirited soldiers away under the noses of the Nazis and who fed the guerrilla bands with arms and ammunition. " Here comes Sylvia " became a kind of affectionate catchword.

One late September afternoon she brought in her convoy from the fort. This time they had been within an inch of capture. One of the trails, which had seemed so safe in the past, and led through a fir forest down into a gully that had to be crossed before the last ascent, had been bombed from the air. Two men had been killed and five wounded in the convoy of twenty. The bombing had been too accurately timed and placed for it to have been haphazard. Somehow the Germans had found this section of the trail and had it under observation. Obviously it could not be used again. A long detour would now be necessary.

Something of the fatigue from this harrowing experience must have shown on Sylvia's face, for when she came late that night into the sitting-room where Franz Kleber sat reading, he questioned her at once.

" Something's happened ! What is it ? " he cried, alarmed.

Sylvia did not answer for a few moments. She sat down wearily in front of the table where Macpherson had laid the evening meal, in anticipation of her return.

" Your eyes are very sharp, Franz. Yes, something's happened. They've got on to our track. We were bombed an hour ago," she said.

" You are not hurt ? " he cried anxiously. He rose to his feet and, with the aid of his sticks, hobbled across to her and stood examining her face.

" No—but two of the boys were killed and five wounded. We can't use that route again."

There was a long pause. Macpherson came in with a tray of food. Sylvia began to eat hungrily. The heavy curtains had been drawn and the lamp lit. Sylvia glanced around.

" Odd to think how cosy we are here. I often wonder for how long. It begins to look as if——" Her eyes suddenly caught sight of a guitar lying on the side table. It was Cesare Morosini's guitar, still decorated with the blue, red, and white ribbons that had shook when he played it. It had hung for so long in his room, ever since that day he had forgotten it.

Franz saw her stare at it and noticed how she stopped speaking.

" You don't mind, do you ? " he asked. " I've been playing it."

" Can you play it ? "

" Yes—I'm very fond of the guitar. My father had an Italian valet. He taught me."

" That belonged to an Italian—a friend who lived with us here."

" Oh—then he's an enemy now. Perhaps you'd rather I didn't touch it. I'm so sorry, Sylvia," said Franz quietly.

She looked up at him and smiled.

" Not an enemy, Franz. He's dead. He died last May in the hospital at Herakleion. He'd been shot down. He was a—a—very dear soul, and gallant," said Sylvia.

Franz sat down at the table, opposite, and watched her eating. He noticed how pale she was.

" Was it very bad—very dangerous ? " he asked after a pause.

" Well—touch and go. They were waiting, obviously."

" But it was dark ? "

" Yes, almost."

" Then how could they know you were there ? They couldn't hear you ? "

" No—and it was in a forest." Sylvia's eyes met Franz's. " Someone must have given a signal. The bombing was deliberate."

Franz stared at her, then she saw the blood leave his face.

" Sylvia, you don't—oh, you don't suspect me ! " he cried, his face quivering.

" Good heavens, no ! Don't be silly ! You don't know where it happened. It was nowhere near here," replied Sylvia, smiling at him. " And, Franz, I actually trust you, anyhow."

There was misery in his face as he looked at her.

" Thank you," he said gravely. " You would be justified in thinking anything—after what we've done."

Their eyes met as he spoke. It was a confession. They both knew it.

" Won't you play me something on the guitar ? It's so long since I heard it," said Sylvia after a moment's silence, tense with embarrassment.

He got up and went over to the side table.

" I don't play very well," he said, picking up the guitar. " I played it chiefly for accompaniments."

" You sing ? "

" Yes—a little."

" Franz, why have you kept this from us ? "

" I'm not very good, really," he said, smiling shyly.

" Let me hear."

He began to strum the guitar. What memories came crowding back with those vibrating strings ! No one had touched that instrument since Cesare Morosini had played it. Could it be two years ago ? Then with a shock Sylvia remembered, by the oddest chance, that it was exactly two years ago to a day that they had sat in this very room while Cesare played. To-day was the second anniversary of the outbreak of war. She remembered so vividly that evening when they had heard the news and knew that their pleasant life in the villa had come to an end. She shut her eyes as Franz played. It was ghost music from another world.

" You do not like it ? " asked Franz, seeing she had closed her eyes. " Perhaps it makes you sad ? "

" No, go on—it is lovely."

He stopped suddenly. Sylvia looked at him. He turned his serious face towards her.

" There is something I think I should tell you," he said quietly.

" Yes ? "

"I have been watching the sky from the terrace these last few days. I do not like it. There are too many planes coming over."

"What do you mean?"

"I don't like it. They are making a special reconnoitre. Perhaps they have seen something—they keep circling around. One came down to two hundred feet to-day. I kept in hiding and watched."

"Italian or German?"

"Ours—a Stuka," said Franz, his young face grave. "Perhaps they suspect something. They may be watching. You must be very careful."

Sylvia did not answer for a few moments. The attack in the forest to-day had been only three miles away. Were they trailing her to the villa? Richard said they had charted all the mountain routes to Fort Minotaur. One day soon they might attack it, when they could safely bring up their patrols.

"Perhaps you are right, Franz. Thank you," she said after a pause.

Anastasia came into the room to clear away the tray. Sylvia waited until she was gone, then she turned to Franz, who was nervously strumming the guitar.

"Franz, what you've told me makes it even more necessary you should go."

"Go!" he exclaimed hoarsely. "Go? But, Sylvia, why?" he asked, dismay in his face.

"You will have to go soon—you are beginning to walk. If the Nazis get here it will be awkward for you."

"I was wounded; I was nursed here. It is very simple," answered Franz.

"I don't think so. It won't be enough. They will know you have seen things, that you know details."

"I shall not tell them a thing!"

"Are you a good German soldier? Would you fight for Germany?"

"Yes," said Franz desperately, white-faced.

"Then they would think it your duty to tell them everything—they would demand it. Friendship, gratitude would be nothing in their eyes. Don't you see why you must not be caught here? They would think you a traitor if you——"

" I would die before I would tell them a thing ! " cried
Franz passionately. " Sylvia, what do you think I am—
what sort of a wretch—what—what——? "

He trembled with passion, inarticulate, his eyes blazing.

" You are a good Nazi. For that reason you—— "

" Sylvia ! Please ! " he cried in an anguished voice, his
eyes full of angry tears. " *Lieber Gott !* I don't know what
I am ! I don't know ; I don't know ! "

He sank into a chair, his young body shaking. Presently,
without looking up, he spoke in a voice of anguish, his hands
nervously clasped.

" I came here a good soldier, a proud German soldier.
It would have been good to have died for the Fuehrer, for
my country, to have died with my comrades. You found
me ; you brought me here ; you nursed me. Oh, you
have been kind, very kind. I am not ungrateful, please,
please ! But it would have been better had I died. I have
been happy here—too happy. Little by little things have
changed in me. You have talked ; you and Richard and
Janet have told me things. I did not want to believe them ;
they seemed such monstrous things, such lies about us.
But I listened ; I could not help listening. Everywhere
I heard things, the same terrible things about us, about the
Fuehrer, Goering, Goebbels, Himmler, what we are accused
of in Norway, in Belgium, in Holland, in France. Harry,
too—he told me about our planes over London and, when
I pressed him, what they say of us, think of us, live to do
to us. And when it was not you, or Macpherson, or Harry,
or the papers I saw—then it was Randell Dunning—every
day, every day telling me we are beasts, vandals, murderers !
I knew he lied, he lied, he lied—it was horrible, but I had
to listen, though I hated him, and his voice tortured me.
Here you believed him, all of you. If I think he is speaking
the truth, that you are speaking the truth, what am I ?
I ask you, what am I ? What sort of people are we ? What
am I ready to fight for, to give my life for ? You cannot
know how terrible it is to hear, day after day, everything
I have known, I have worshipped, execrated and demolished.
I find myself wondering, questioning, doubting. Yes—I
have begun to doubt ! "

He covered his face and cried into his hands with the

K

unrestrained sobbing of a child. Sylvia knelt beside his
chair and put her arms about him, holding him, as if he
were a small boy, to be protected against his fears. She
knelt there, saying not a word, until his sobbing quieted
down. Presently he pulled out a handkerchief and held
it to his face.

"I am sorry to be so childish. Forgive me," he said in
a muffled voice. "I am overwrought."

"Franz, there's nothing to forgive. You must forgive us.
Perhaps we have done you an injury. It is always wrong
to tamper with loyalties, especially loyalties to one's own
country, one's own people. The tragedy of wars isn't
death—not even, I feel, the death of the young, terrible
though that is. The real tragedy lies in what we are
called upon to do honourably, though it may inflict cruelty
and wrong upon others no more guilty, individually, than
ourselves. That is part of the imperfection of the world,
the great mystery of life. All over the world you boys are
dying with great courage. Men and women everywhere,
on all sides in this conflict, amid much hatred and cruelty
and blind passion, have not lost the divine spark that lifts
us above the animals. They can make great sacrifices;
they can suffer nobly and, if need be, die for others. For
the rest—while we think we know where error and guilt lie,
some other tribunal must try us, some court less passionate
than ourselves—perhaps Time, perhaps God Himself, if He
will take pity on our follies. One day this terrible nightmare will have passed. Until then we can only each of us
do our duty as it seems to us."

"You have been very kind, all of you. But for you
I should not be here now, alive," said Franz, raising his
head and looking at Sylvia. "You must forgive me for
making this scene. It won't happen again. If you think
I must go, then you are right. But if I stayed and they
came and found me here, there would be no harm come to
you because of me. Will you believe that?"

"Of course I will. It's for your sake, not mine, Franz,
that I wish you to go."

"And you? Haven't you risked enough? Sooner or
later they will find this place. Why don't you go while
you can? This is a man's war—especially here."

Sylvia smiled at him and pressed his hand.

" I think it is a woman's war, too, as long as a woman can stand by the men she admires and loves—as long as she is a help and not a burden to them. It isn't a matter of being brave or noble ; it's just that one can't bear to be left out."

" You are so splendid, Sylvia," said Franz, his hand resting in hers, his grave eyes lit with unfeigned worship.

She laughed a little awkwardly, embarrassed by his candid adoration, and withdrew her hands, rising.

" Now, won't you play and sing something ? We've been much too serious ! " she said.

He looked up at her and smiled in a manner she knew so well.

" I would like to—but, please, not to-night. I think I will go to bed now."

" Very well, perhaps you had better," she replied.

He got his sticks and stood up.

" When—when do you think I should go ? " he asked in a carefully controlled voice that did not deceive her.

" As soon as possible, Franz."

" Very well. Good night, Sylvia—and thank you."

" Good night."

He left the room. The guitar he had begun to play lay on the table. Sylvia picked it up gently and passed her hand over it. Then she put it away.

CHAPTER VIII

WHO IS SYLVIA? . . .

SYLVIA returned to the villa after five strenuous days down on the coast near Tymbaki, where she had succeeded in embarking sixteen wounded men on a destroyer that had come off-shore by night. The excursion had been unusually tiring. The weather had broken, and the island was swept by torrential rains. With the end of September the long nights and colder days had come. As Sylvia changed her clothes, having arrived home wet to the skin, she thought of Franz, who had greeted her with a joy that followed his deep anxiety. She had been away much longer than usual, and Macpherson reported that after the third day Franz had grown increasingly worried over her absence.

Franz was one of the problems that could be deferred no longer. He would soon be able to walk without his sticks. The time had come for his departure, and Sylvia, while down at the coast, had made arrangements for his transfer to Alexandria. There would be no moon next Saturday, and they would attempt to run in a destroyer at midnight. It was necessary to have Franz in readiness down at the cave from which they rowed out to the destroyer. The news of this she would not break to him until they were due to leave for the coast.

In dry clothes, she went into the sitting-room, where Anastasia had laid tea. Franz was there and scrambled to his feet on her entrance, an eager smile on his young face. The radio was on, and the evening news commentary was coming in from England.

" Isn't that our friend Dunning? " asked Sylvia, sitting down by the tea-table. She picked up the tin of tea, always with a little thrill. It seemed so extraordinary to be sitting here in a besieged villa in the Cretan mountains, dipping a spoon into a tin of Earl Grey's Mixture from Piccadilly.

It brought Grandma Day and *Glenarvon* vividly back to mind.

Sylvia put two teaspoonfuls into the pot and mashed the tea. Franz turned off the radio as Randell Dunning completed his report.

" I begin to be sorry for Mr. Dunning ! " said Franz.

" Why ? "

" Poor man ! We are sweeping over Russia, as we've swept over every other place. We're at the gates of Leningrad now—and it must be difficult never to be able to have some good news for his fans ! "

" Of whom I'm one, thank you ! " remarked Sylvia. " And I believe you are, though of course you won't admit it ! "

" Oh, yes, I will. I've come to like the old boy—though I don't believe a word he says."

" You don't ? "

" Well, not all of it."

" Oh, thank you ! " said Sylvia gaily, passing him a cup of tea.

" Roosevelt has given another good example of America's neutrality ! According to Mr. Dunning, he's called our submarines ' the rattlesnakes of the Atlantic.' "

" I think it is a very good description of them ! "

" But it's not a neutral statement ! "

" President Roosevelt has never liked being a neutral."

" You still hope they'll come in ? "

" Yes, they will."

" I don't think so. America—the whole world—knows England's beaten," said Franz.

" But England doesn't ! Franz, you are still a horrid little Nazi, and I won't have my tea spoiled with these futile discussions. We'll change the subject."

" Very well. But, Sylvia, you don't really mind, do you ? You are always so sporting ! "

" Thanks—but I'm very tired," said Sylvia.

" I am so sorry. Please, I did not wish to annoy you."

He paused for a moment, taking a piece of Anastasia's cake, and then, looking at Sylvia, smiling :

" Isn't it odd ! It's like being at Market Harborough again and having tea—and—and——"

" And ? " queried Sylvia as he hesitated.

" If it could only last like this," he said quietly, his young face very serious, his voice husky. " I miss you terribly when you are away."

Sylvia smiled. In some things he was curiously sensitive. She made no reply, but looked at him.

" I'm going soon, Sylvia ? " he asked in a low voice.

" Yes—it's got to be, Franz."

He said nothing for a few moments, and then as they saw Harry, the marine, pass the door he began to narrate a story. Harry had told him about sleeping all night in Covent Garden Market when he was out of work, and " swiping " fruit when he was hungry.

" He says he's enjoyed every minute of this war. I wish I felt like that ! " commented Franz. " And life's been so much kinder to me than to him."

" That probably explains it. Wars give boys like Harry a change of scene, and excitement, and a sense of self-respect. They feel they matter, at last. It's wrong we should have to have wars to give such boys their chance. It mustn't happen again ; we all feel that," said Sylvia. " How's the guitar ? Have you learned anything new ? "

" No, but I've remembered one little piece I'd forgotten. It's a song from Shakespeare."

" Shakespeare—' The Wind and the Rain ' ? "

" No, something lovelier, something that belongs to you ! "

" To me ! Play it," said Sylvia.

He gave her a quick smile, picked up his sticks, and went across to the table where the guitar lay. He brought it and tuned it, and then, serious as he played the opening bars, began to sing in his boy's voice. Sylvia recognised the song at once. He sang with great feeling, his voice light and sweet.

> " *Who is Sylvia ? What is Sylvia ?*
> *That all our swains commend her ?*
> *Holy, fair, and wise is she ;*
> *The heaven such grace did lend her,*
> *That she might admirèd be.*

> " *Is she kind as she is fair ?*
> *For beauty lives with kindness :*
> *Love doth to her eyes repair,*
> *To help him of his blindness ;*
> *And, being help'd, inhabits there. . . .*"

When he had finished there was a moment's pause, during which his head was bent over the guitar. Then he put the instrument down on the table and stood up, looking at her with shining eyes.

" Thank you—that was lovely," said Sylvia, glancing up from her chair. He stood there oddly, his mouth trembling. Quickly, in one movement, he was on his knees beside her and seized her hand, covering it with impassioned kisses.

" Franz ! " she cried sharply, drawing back her hand.

He looked up at her dumbly, his face quivering, his eyes shining with adoration.

" I must tell you ! Sylvia, I must tell you ! I love you ! I can't go on and not tell you I love you ! "

" Franz—you are crazy ! Please get up ! " cried Sylvia.

But he ignored her command and knelt there, his hands gripping the arm of her chair, his glowing eyes on her face.

" I've been in agony every minute you've been gone. Whenever you go I am in agony—something might happen to you ! I can't bear it ; I——"

Sylvia stood up. He rose and stood before her. Pity now took the place of her anger, seeing him so tense and shaken before her.

" Franz, I thought you were a sensible boy. I am not in love with you, not the least bit. You must not mistake kindness for love——"

" I haven't, Sylvia ; I——" he began, but she ignored his interruption and continued :

" Even you should know how absurd it is. We are enemies. And you cannot be very observant. Haven't you seen my ring ? "

She held up her hand for him to observe it.

" Yes ? " he said in almost a whisper.

" This is an engagement ring. It was given me by my fiancé, Lieutenant Whatley of the Royal Navy."

Franz made no answer for a few moments, looking at the ring and at Sylvia. Then in a tense voice he said :

" I am very sorry. I have been foolish. Please forgive me."

His young face was so white and strained that Sylvia felt she had been almost brutal.

" If you will excuse me, I—I——" he said in a choking voice, and, incapable of further speech, looked at her, his eyes welling with tears. Then swiftly he turned, picked up his sticks, and went out of the room.

Sylvia heard his feet go down the corridor and waited, confused, the vivid image of his despairing face before her. Once or twice she had wondered, but had dismissed the thought. It was now more urgent than ever that he should go.

She went across to her writing-desk, when the door suddenly opened. Janet stood there, the rain dripping from her mackintosh.

" Janet ! " exclaimed Sylvia, then seeing her friend's face : " Is anything the matter ? " she asked.

Janet grinned, pulled off her hat, and shook her mop of short hair.

" Depends how you look at it. What's the matter with our little Nazi ? "

" What do you mean ? "

" Franz—I ran up against him in the passage. He looked like a school kid that's been walloped. He couldn't see for crying ! "

" Oh—that ! We've had a little scene. I had to be rather brutal with him. He's just told me he's in love with me, poor boy ! "

" Are you surprised ? " asked Janet ironically. " I've seen it coming for weeks. What cheek ! "

" I don't feel like that about it—he's a sensitive boy. I don't like hurting him."

" Bosh, my dear ! Nazis are Nazis ; you can't hurt 'em enough ! It's time he went. I noticed him the other day hopping around pretty lively. He'll bolt one day," said Janet, wiping the rain off her face.

" He's going by the next boat. I don't think he'll bolt. He knows what happens to stray Germans," answered Sylvia.

" I've some news for you. I've come to fetch you to a
wedding."

" What ! "

" To a lot of weddings. We're doing the job wholesale.
We've got a tame bishop and a priest—grand beavers, both
of 'em. We're all getting spliced at midnight in a little
church near Gortyn. You're my bridesmaid—if you'll turn
out this poisonous night. It's all very sudden. We've got
the chance and we're taking it. I've got the mules outside.
Will you come ? "

" But, Janet—you are getting married ! " exclaimed Sylvia,
staring at her friend.

" Yes, Frank's making an honest woman of me. That
ought to please Richard. He thinks I'm a slut. Well ? "

" Oh, Janet, of course I'll come ! " cried Sylvia. She
flung her arms around Janet and kissed her.

" It's all very sudden, but some of those Greek girls are
getting married. ' Expecting,' as we say in Yorkshire. Oh,
don't look at me ! I'm not that soft. But Frank likes the
idea, and it makes things more regular. I'd have been here
earlier, but there's been a bit of trouble on the way."

" Trouble ? "

" The Heinies had a motor patrol on the road outside
Gortyn. We had a scrap, and they scooted, but not before
they'd hit two of our fellows. We got one of theirs. We
had to take the upper path. Things are getting hotter."

" It's getting more difficult at Tymbaki. Is Richard at
the fort ? " asked Sylvia.

" No. He's gone off with three hundred men to the
White Mountains. Mandakas is planning a big raid on
Maleme. I hear they shot sixty people in Canea last
Tuesday, including the mayor and two priests."

" Do you want anything to eat ? "

" No, thanks. We must get going. It's pitch-black to-
night. It's a Greek service. I shan't know whether I'm
being married or buried. I don't seem able to pick up
this lingo very quickly. Frank jabbers it like a monkey,
and those Greek girls have taught the boys. Lord knows
what those boys have taught the girls ! One day there's
going to be little bits of England, Australia, and New
Zealand running all over these mountains."

Ten minutes later the mule party set off. The rain poured down. The night was impenetrably dark. A wind buffeted them. Of all strange journeys Sylvia had undertaken, this was the strangest.

Toward midnight they came to the small mountain village they sought above Gortyn. Guards had been posted at all the approaches and challenged them. The thick voices out of the darkness added to the strangeness of this journey. Presently the little church loomed up, dimly white in the darkness. Its octagonal tower was crowned by a cupola carrying the Byzantine cross. They dismounted and stumbled up some cobble steps to doors that opened immediately. They passed in. The scene that met their eyes had a weirdness and beauty beyond description. The little church was packed with Cretan men and women, with soldiers, Greek, English, Australian, New Zealand, in oddments of uniforms. The air was heavy with incense. Candles flickered before the crude, gaudy icons hanging on the walls. The light was dim, except up at the altar where tall candles burned, touching the rich embroideries of the cloths and vestments with reflective splendour. A male choir stood on either side of the altar, men so rugged, some dark and bearded, that they might have been the Apostles themselves. In the centre, before the gleaming altar, waited the bishop and two priests. They were magnificent patriarchs, long-bearded, long-haired, with venerable faces and immense dignity. A heavy gold cross hanging from a neck-chain glinted on the chest of the bishop, whose rich cope proclaimed his eminence.

The service had not begun. A low murmur of voices filled the church. Everybody stood, a parti-coloured assembly of peasants and soldiers, solemn in mien, only dimly visible in this incense-clouded church.

Sylvia was greeted by Lieutenant Walker. Captain Pierce had gone with Richard to join Mandakas. Presently Janet appeared, pulling the bridegroom forward. He was a huge Yorkshire lad with a big wet mouth and shy, smiling eyes. He put a heavy, rough paw into Sylvia's hand, his face reddening with embarrassment as she congratulated them. Then Janet and her escort went off to join the line before the choir. There were eighteen bridal couples. All

the women except Janet were Greeks, robust, black-haired
girls with dark, shining eyes.

The singing began. The two choirs chanted anti-
phonally. They had deep voices of moving beauty. The
music, the incense, the lights, the glimmering icons, the
high mosaic dome, the dim peasant faces, the resplendent
impressive priests, gave to this midnight service the quality
of a dream. Here on a mountainside, in the church of their
ancient faith, men and women, hunted, surrounded by the
threat of death, were gathered together to witness the union
of their daughters with men of another race, from far
corners of the earth. Their future was obscure. Long
endurance, suffering, perhaps death, were in the days to
come. Courage and faith were their sustainers, the love of
liberty their torch through the darkness of oppression.

The priests were intoning. Strophe and antistrophe rose
in the richness of those blended voices. The gusty night
struck the dim windows. Out in the darkness armed men
kept vigil, but here within there was no sense of alarm.
The choral beauty of the service, the exhortations, the
responses, the reverent murmur of the congregation, were
all part of the slow solemnity of this holy rite of matrimony.
Dream-like, dim, and pervasive, the service brought a quiet
exaltation to the hearts of this mountain people. Standing
there, Sylvia closed her eyes. Listening, as those blended
voices raised their Gregorian chant under the glimmering
dome, it seemed as if the echoes of centuries of simple
faith sounded here in witness of man's unconquerable spirit.

After the service, which lasted about three-quarters of an
hour, there was a wedding feast given in the house of a
prosperous villager. No one in the midst of that happy
throng, with its dancing, laughing, and such feasting as the
scanty supplies of these poor people could offer, would
have believed that this was a beleaguered community upon
whom the Nazi might descend, shooting and burning in
savage reprisal.

Somehow the British lads and radiant Greek lasses found
a *lingua franca*. There was much kissing and squeezing and
rustic horseplay. The benign bishop and the two priests
sat with their host along one wall and watched the dancing.
Happily no one foresaw that within a month this village

would be given to the flames and be a charred ruin on the
mountainside, its priest and leaders executed, its women
and children driven out into the wintry forest, all because
it had harboured these British allies.

It was three o'clock when the revellers went out into the
dark night. Most of the men were returning to Fort
Minotaur from which they had come. Sylvia went along
with them in Lieutenant Walker's company. The bridal
couples were being accommodated in houses in the village,
and while they enjoyed the nuptial bed a guard kept watch
over all the approaches.

Sylvia was awakened around ten o'clock by Janet shaking
her. She had slept soundly in the cell-like chamber, shut
off in one of the caverns, which became her bedroom when
she stayed at the fort. Janet chatted to her while she
washed in a wooden bucket and tidied her hair. After a
little while she became aware that her friend seemed nervous
in her manner. It was very unusual for the downright Janet.

" You're quite happy, Janet ? He seems a nice lad,"
said Sylvia.

" Oh—Frank ? Oh, he's all right. I knew what I was
picking," replied Janet. She began to fidget with her
holster.

" There's something the matter—what ? " cried Sylvia,
looking at her.

" I want you to talk to Walker. He's outside."

The two women looked at each other.

" Let's go," said Sylvia quietly.

They found Lieutenant Walker at an improvised desk in
a small cave looking out on to a compound. It was H.Q.
and living quarters combined. He stood up as they came in.

" Good morning. You've something to tell me ? " said
Sylvia directly.

Young Walker glanced at Janet Farr and then spoke.

" I've bad news, Miss Day. Some of our fellows went
over to join Mandakas in a raid on Maleme. It was very
successful. They destroyed a hangar. On the way back
a small party, sixteen, was ambushed. They had to fight
it out. Unfortunately, seven were killed. I'm terribly
sorry—Richard was one of them.''

Sylvia did not speak. She heard him ; she knew what was coming before his name was mentioned.

" Two of the lads with him are back. Would you like to see them ? "

" Yes—let me see them," said Sylvia steadily.

He went out. Janet's hand took Sylvia's.

" Oh, my dear ! " she said quietly, and kissed her.

Sylvia did not answer. She held Janet's hand. In a few moments two soldiers came in, a tough New Zealander of about thirty, and an English lad, a mere boy, with a bandaged head. They told their story of the raid and the ambush as they returned, very simply. Richard had fallen with two others. A hidden machine-gun had swept them as they raced for cover.

" He was quite dead ? "

" Oh, yes, miss. I could see him lying there with two others. He couldn't have felt anything, miss. We was 'iding behind a rock after we'd got across. We was there quite 'alf an hour—and seeing the lieutenant all the time."

" Thank you," said Sylvia to the lad. " You are wounded ? "

" Oh, that's nothing, miss. We're all very sorry about Lieutenant Day. We all liked 'im. He was a brave gentleman."

" He was that ! " added the New Zealander.

" Thank you. What is your name ? " asked Sylvia, of the lad before her.

" Philip Lovegrove, miss, 2nd Leicesters."

Sylvia looked at his rugged companion.

" James Stevenson, 5th New Zealand Brigade. We're very sorry, miss. We all liked him."

" Thank you. He was very proud of you all—as I am."

The men withdrew.

§ 2

Sylvia arrived back at the villa that evening. She was collecting another cavalcade of sick and wounded men to take to the coast on the morrow. Only the sick were willing to leave now. The others wished to stay and fight. Janet insisted on accompanying her. When they arrived the first person to greet them was Franz Kleber. He had been sitting on the terrace. Instantly, as he hailed them, he was aware something had happened. Sylvia told him briefly. He became very silent and watched her with sad eyes ; then he disappeared into his room until supper. Old Anastasia, on hearing of Richard's end, had sat down, wailing in a paroxysm of grief. Helen and Macpherson, always reliable, attended to the meal. Franz scarcely ate anything.

" You'll be hungry before morning," said Sylvia kindly, and saw that she had almost provoked an outburst. The boy turned his quivering face away. He left the room immediately when supper was finished.

" I'll never understand these Nazi boys," said Janet. " They're chock-full of murder and they're chock-full of sentiment at the same time. I thought that kid was going to howl any minute. He was a regular tiger when we brought him here. Remember how he clawed at us over his darling Fuehrer ? Now he's almost a domestic cat."

" Franz has some nice qualities—he's really very sensitive," observed Sylvia, picking up her sewing.

" I've no doubt they all have—till they get their marching boots on," retorted Janet. It was all so very odd. Here was a German sitting at their table, choking with tears, and there was poor Richard, rotting in a mountain gully.

Half an hour later the door opened. Franz Kleber stood their, pale, wide-eyed. He did not come into the room. They looked at him.

" I feel I must tell you. There have been planes over the house all day. Two of them came very low. I am sure they know the villa is inhabited and that people come and go. It has become much more dangerous. They might bomb it."

He stopped speaking. Every word had been an effort. There was a silence. Sylvia looked at him.

" Thank you, Franz. It's quite likely to happen some day. I've faced that," she said. " I appreciate your warning."

" Good night. Good night, Miss Farr," he said.

" Won't you stay with us ? " asked Sylvia.

" No, thank you. I—it is not right for me to see your grief," he said quietly, and turned to go.

" Franz ! " called Sylvia, rising and going towards him. He stood, a little puzzled as she approached.

" Thank you," said Sylvia, and kissed his cheek. " Good night ! "

His eyes rested on her for a few tense moments. Then quickly he withdrew.

Sylvia sat down again. Presently she looked up from her sewing and addressed Janet, who was reading.

" I expect you're a little surprised to see me kiss a German, but Franz, somehow, is often like an English boy to me. I suppose I'm not very good at being an enemy."

" I wouldn't say that of you in action. From what I've seen, you're pretty thorough. I've only one criticism about our Franz. I think you're making him very wretched. Take the arrogance out of a Nazi and what is he ? It's as well he's going. How soon ? "

" On Friday."

" You've not told him, I hope ? " asked Janet.

" The day, no."

" My God, he's lucky to be alive ! I suppose he knows what would happen to him if he stayed ? I marvel Anastasia hasn't poisoned him ! "

" Anastasia's been wonderfully correct," said Sylvia.

Janet left the next morning. " You know, I'm not free any more," she observed with a wry smile. Towards noon Sylvia made her own preparations. It was to be a larger cavalcade this time. She hoped to get twenty men back to the villa by to-morrow afternoon and then, that night, down to the cove they used near Tymbaki, ready for embarkation. She was taking twelve mules this time, with Macpherson, four orderlies, old Jannis, the muleteer, his son, and the boy Nikephoro.

By lunch-time Franz was aware of these preparations. Hitherto he had tactfully asked no questions and had affected not seeing Sylvia's preparations, but now for the first time he mentioned them.

" You must be very careful. They're watching us," he said.

" Us ? " asked Sylvia with a smile.

He looked confused and abashed.

" There's no one to look after you, now Mr. Richard isn't—isn't——"

" Thank you, Franz. That's nice of you. But I am not in the least afraid. At the worst what could happen has happened to so many of my friends. I shall be back to-morrow afternoon."

" And then I go with you to the coast ? " asked Franz.

Sylvia did not answer for a few moments. She looked frankly into his eyes.

" I see you know. Yes," she said. " Franz, I would not advise you to escape. The people have suffered so atrociously, they are in an ugly mood. Every woman I know carries a dagger and uses it."

" I understand," replied Franz.

At three o'clock he waved good-bye as the cavalcade went down the path, across the ravine, and into the wood.

When they had gone he called for Harry, who came out of the kitchen.

" Harry, I'm leaving to-morrow," he said to the cheerful Cockney marine.

" You're leaving, sir ! "

" Yes—and I've not worn my boots for three months. I think I should try them on."

" You can't do that, sir ! "

" No ? "

" No, sir. My instructions are not to let you 'ave any boots, sir. You might find yourself taking a walk ! " said Harry, grinning.

" Oh—I hadn't thought of that."

" Well, we 'ave, sir ! And I wouldn't want to be using this—we've got on very nicely, sir."

Harry tapped the revolver holster over his hip.

" Yes, we've got on very nicely—so nicely I've almost forgotten I'm a prisoner. I'll stick to my slippers and the guitar. And you can stick to my boots and your revolver, eh ? " said Franz cheerfully.

" That's the idea, sir."

" Thank you."

" Thank you, sir."

The marine saluted and left the terrace.

Franz Kleber sat on a stone bench and looked over the valley he now knew so well. Below him was the path coming out of the fir forest by which Sylvia brought back her cavalcade, crossing the ravine before making the ascent to the villa. He sat on for a while, sad and contemplative, until the cold drove him in.

CHAPTER IX

GREATER LOVE HATH . . .

THE following morning, a little after noon, Franz Kleber was writing a letter in the sitting-room. It was a letter to Sylvia which she would find after he had gone. He was so engrossed in this that he did not hear the door open. A voice broke the quiet, bidding him harshly, in German, to stand up.

He swung round in his chair to find himself facing a young German in uniform, levelling a revolver at him. Paralysed with surprise, he stared at the intruder.

" Stand up ! " cried the soldier.

Franz Kleber rose to his feet. Then he found speech.

" Who are you ? What are you doing here ? " he asked in German.

The soldier stared to find himself addressed in his own tongue. The tone and quality of the speech made him aware of superior rank.

" I am Lieutenant Kleber. What are you doing here ? Where is your officer ? " demanded Franz.

" We've captured the house, sir," replied the soldier.

Footsteps sounded in the corridor. Odd, but not a shot had been fired. Then in the doorway a soldier appeared, in a captain's uniform. The private stood aside. The captain walked in and addressed Franz.

" You are our prisoner," he snapped in English, and then stared to find him wearing a German service tunic. " What are you——? "

" I am Lieutenant von Kleber, 17th Air Squadron, General von Löhr's 5th Corps, sir. I am a prisoner here," said Franz in German.

The captain stared. He was a man of about thirty-five, tall, spare, with an alert manner.

" I am Captain Wilhelm Kleinlein, 2nd Division, Para-chute Troops. What are you doing here ? " he asked.

Franz told him briefly. When he had finished the captain began to cross-question him. He seemed aware of everything. He even named Sylvia Day, Janet Farr, and Richard. They were running an underground escape organisation. The women had taken part in the fighting, in violation of their calling. That was a capital offence. He was still questioning Franz Kleber aggressively, when a shot rang out.

" What's that ? " he demanded, turning to the private, his hand flying to his holster. There was a sound of scurrying feet. A sergeant appeared.

" One of our men is shot, sir—on the terrace," he said.

" By whom—how ? " demanded Captain Kleinlein.

Another shot rang out, then another. They all stared at one another.

" *Gott in Himmel!* " exclaimed Kleinlein, and hurried out of the room. The sergeant and private followed, ignoring Franz. He went after them, to find a group of soldiers taking cover at the end of the terrace. The firing was coming from the garden-house overlooking the terrace. Two soldiers had been hit fatally. Their bodies lay crumpled up as they had fallen. The invading party had rushed off the terrace, out of the line of fire.

" Have you got everybody ? " demanded the captain.

" We think so, sir."

" Think so ! Let me see them. Who's escaped ? Who's firing ? "

The captives were brought out of the villa. Franz's eyes ran down the line of defiant captives—Christopoulos, the man of all work ; Aleko, a lame boy who fed the mules, and, openly truculent, old Anastasia. She turned as Franz passed by her and spat in his face. One of the guards was about to strike her, but he stopped him. There was a man missing. Franz knew who had been firing. Harry, the Cockney marine, was not in the line. He had taken refuge in the garden-house. It had one small window commanding the terrace, and could be entered only by a door in it.

A private came up and saluted.

" The firing's from a window at the end of the terrace—a sort of summerhouse, sir. He can't come out of it, but it's difficult to get him."

Captain Kleinlein looked at his sergeant.

" Let me have three men ; we must settle this," he said. He turned to Franz. " You know this place. Who's in there ? Can't we get into it ? "

" It's one of the orderlies, I think. He's not here. There's no entrance to the garden-house except from the door on the terrace."

" Since you know the place, I put you in charge of the party, Lieutenant Kleber. Get that man out, dead or alive ! " commanded Kleinlein.

" I'm not much good, sir—I'm still lame," said Franz.

Kleinlein glanced at his sticks.

" You seem to get about all right. You are in charge of the party," he said curtly. " I want to lose no more men. You understand ? "

" Very good, sir," answered Franz.

It was not an easy task. The garden-house could not be approached. The marine had been quick to recognise the fact, but he had taken a desperate stand. No one could go in, and no one could come out. Franz had only one hope. The boy, realising his futile state, must be made to surrender.

It was possible to shout from the sitting-room window. Franz went there, while the men covered the garden-house with their rifles, from behind a ledge at the opposite end of the terrace.

" Harry—the house is taken. There is nothing you can do now but surrender. It's quite useless, Harry. Put down your rifle," called Franz.

" Useless, is it ? I've killed two Nazis. Send me some more ! " came back the defiant voice.

Rifle fire broke out from behind the terrace and was answered from the window. It was ineffective on either side.

" Stop that fire," said Franz to the sergeant. The firing stopped.

" This is a last appeal, Harry. If you don't surrender we must take the place by assault. It is quite useless. There are fifteen of us. Take my advice, please," called Franz.

" Your advice ! You dirty little Nazi ! After all Miss

Sylvia's done for you—surrender to a little swine like you ! Just step out a minute and see ! " cried the voice inside.

There was a pause. Something desperate must be done.

" I've got an idea, sir—a grenade. I can crawl in under that wall and pitch it in."

Franz hesitated. The sergeant looked at him.

" Very well," he said finally, " but don't throw until I give the signal."

The sergeant went off. Presently he came round the corner of the garden-house on his hands and knees. The man inside could not see him or bring him into the line of fire.

" Harry—I am making a last appeal to you. Unless you surrender immediately, we shall bomb you. It is quite useless bravery. It achieves nothing. Harry, I beg of you—please surrender at once," pleaded Franz.

" Shut your clap and throw your bomb ! "

A rifle shot rang out. One of the men had incautiously looked over the wall. Harry must have been a deadly shot. The man rolled over, drilled through the head.

" Three Nazis ! Send up some more ! " called the triumphant voice behind the window.

" This is my last appeal. Will you surrender ? " cried Franz.

" No, Mr. Hitler ! To hell with you ! "

The sergeant under the window had the grenade in his hand. He looked across at Franz. Then with a swift upward movement he threw the grenade in through the open window.

There was a terrific explosion. Glass and brickwork strewed the terrace ; a cloud of thick brown dust obscured everything. When finally it cleared away, a gaping hole where the window had been was revealed. The sergeant and two men, revolvers in hand, advanced cautiously. The sergeant clambered in over the broken window sill and disappeared. Presently he came back to the shattered window.

" That got him all right—it blew his head off ! " he said grimly.

§ 2

In the next hour, during which Franz Kleber was closely questioned by Captain Kleinlein, it became clear to the younger man how the villa had been taken so rapidly. The place had been under aerial reconnaissance for several weeks, increasingly so in the last few days, as Franz had suspected. It was known that Villa Vouni was a clearing-house for wounded soldiers who were then taken down to the coast where, hidden along the rocky coast, they awaited the supply boats that put in by night. The traffic had been maintained with a daring that had exasperated the German Command. Peremptory orders for it to be stopped had been given the regional command, but the difficulty of the terrain, the cunning of the enemy, assisted by the elusive Cretans, had defeated all their efforts. Secret access to the villa by mule paths was quite impossible in such treacherous country. It had been decided to take it by a parachute landing on the mountain above, and to descend upon it. This had been done. The secret route through the stables and down through the caves towards Fort Minotaur had not been suspected.

"Well, we'll sit here now until they walk into the trap," said Kleinlein to Franz Kleber in the sitting-room. "You seem to be very comfortable here. You must have seen and heard quite a lot."

"I was not allowed on the other end of the terrace," replied Franz.

"What kind of a pair are those women, Sylvia Day and Janet Farr? We have a pretty reckoning for them. It's a court-martial with only one possible verdict. I grant you, they're plucky. What a pity! We don't like shooting women, Kleber. They tell me the tough one, Janet Farr, is an ugly little bitch, but Sylvia Day's a heart-stopper. I expect you had no success?"

"Our relations were very correct. She is a lady, and German officers are gentlemen," retorted Franz, scarcely hiding his disgust.

"Well—it's a good theory—but perhaps you were too young."

He laughed at his own comment, and then his eyes caught the radio.

" Oh—so they weren't cut off from the world ! " exclaimed Kleinlein.   He rotated the dial and waited.   It began to crackle.

" . . . The Germans are still held up around Leningrad.   Their seige is not succeeding.   For almost two months now they have been kept out of the city.   Moscow also is still beyond their clutches.   Their sweep over Russia has been at a price, too great a price, according to official observers.   There are signs of exhaustion showing in the German ranks.   Moscow sounded the death knell of Napoleon.   It may sound the death knell of Hitler. The Russian bear is wounded, but it is not down.   It is angry and aggressive.   The Germans may bitterly repent their rash adventure. . . ."

Kleinlein shut off the radio.

" What fools the English are !   They believe stuff like that ! " he said contemptuously.

" That's one of their best announcers," observed Franz.

" Their best !   Who ? "

" Randell Dunning."

" They're all fools !   The British Empire's dead, but the corpse is so sprawling, mortification hasn't reached the heart yet.   So you listened to the radio ?   Did you live with them ? "

" I had some meals with them when I became convalescent.   They were kind to me," answered Franz.

" Did you ever try escaping ? " asked Kleinlein, with a note of suspicion.

" What, like this ? " said Franz, pointing to his sticks. " And with no boots ? "

Kleinlein looked at his slippered feet before speaking.

" It was just as well, anyhow—the country crawls with assassins.   The women are terrible.   Every one of them uses a dagger.   Every day we lose men.   I wish they wouldn't fight.   I don't enjoy shooting women—if you can call them women."

The sergeant came into the room.   The villa had been

well posted. All the men were hidden. A machine-gun
had been erected on the corner of the terrace, commanding
the ravine and the mule-track out of the wood. The cavalcade would come that way to the villa.

" Keep a sharp look-out. They'll come before sunset.
What have you done with the prisoners ? " asked Kleinlein.

" Locked them up in the stables, sir, and put a guard
over them."

" Good. Now I want the whole place mined. We ought,
with any luck, to get away before dark. We don't want
to be trapped here. Lieutenant Kleber will show you
where to put the mines. He knows the place."

Kleinlein looked at Franz Kleber, who rose to fulfil the
order.

In half an hour the mines were all placed. It was now
almost three o'clock. It began to grow dark after four.
Sylvia always returned before dusk. She would not be
long now.

Franz went out on to the terrace. Two men crouched
by the machine-gun. It commanded the path out of the
wood by which Sylvia and her cavalcade always came.
There was no possible chance of escape. They would be
riddled with bullets. It was cold-blooded massacre. Sylvia
carried no Red Cross flag. She was a combatant.

Along the terrace, by a stone bench, and hidden behind
a pillar of the pergola, Kleinlein waited, his field-glasses
dangling on his chest. He had given strict orders that no
one was to be in view. Six men with rifles crouched behind
the parapet made by the terrace wall. They had been
spread alongside the machine-gun, mounted so that it could
mow the mule-track and the crossing below. Franz Kleber,
his sticks beside him, sat waiting on the inner side of the
terrace, opposite the two machine-gunners. A damp sweat
stood on his brow. The minutes were creeping on. Captain
Kleinlein coolly lit a cigarette. The pale sun had sunk,
amid rain clouds, beneath a shoulder of the western range.

It was a quarter to four when the expectant silence was
broken by a man at the end of the terrace.

" They're coming, sir ! " he shouted.

The gunners stiffened to the alert.

" Hold your fire till I give the command ! " called

Captain Kleinlein, standing up and sweeping the view with his glasses.

Franz Kleber stood up. Over the edge of the wall he could see the cavalcade in the valley below. Three mules had emerged from the wood. He recognised old Jannis leading, then two ambulance mules with Macpherson, and, just coming out into the clearing, Sylvia walking beside a mule ridden by a soldier.

Discarding his sticks, Franz Kleber stepped forward towards the machine-gunner.

" Stand aside, I'll take it ! " he said peremptorily. Before the astonished gunner could make any reply he had knelt and pushed him aside, seizing the gun. The next moment a staccato hammering shattered the silence of the valley as the machine-gun rat-tat-tatted fiercely. But as it barked it swept wildly upwards in the air as the frenzied youth fired and swung the gun in a skyward arc of fire.

Captain Kleinlein dropped his glasses with an oath. The next moment he was firing savagely with his revolver at the figure swinging the gun. The machine stopped in its uproar, and Franz Kleber slumped down behind it.

" Fire, you fools, fire ! " yelled Kleinlein to his paralysed men.

The rifles began to bark. Down in the valley the cavalcade had suddenly halted and was now rushing to cover. The soldiers, firing wildly, failed to stop a single member of the party. The valley was clear again, except for a kicking mule that had broken away, riderless, and lay on its side, wounded.

Captain Kleinlein cursed. That traitorous young cub had cheated them of their prey. He turned on the two quivering men by the machine-gun, then he stooped down over Franz Kleber and pulled him over. He was dead. Blood trickled from one of the wounds behind his ear. Captain Kleinlein pushed him away with his boot in angry disgust. Then he began to give orders, curtly, swiftly, controlling his fury.

§ 3

That wild burst of machine-gun fire had warned the mule party. For a moment they were too stunned to act, so fierce and so surprising was the source of the firing. Then frantically they had scrambled back into cover, but not before a mule had been brought down and old Jannis had been hit in the foot. Bullets splashed about them as they entered the forest, and one of these, perhaps ricocheting from a rock, had struck Sylvia, wounding her above the left wrist. She had felt nothing but a rap, and it was only when they were well back into the wood, breathless and in some disorder, wondering what might happen next, that a flow of blood and some pain made her aware she had been hit. Jannis and herself apart, they had escaped miraculously.

" I always said those Heinies were rotten shots. Blimey, did you 'ear that machine-gun mowin' around ? Gawd, wot shootin' ! " exclaimed a soldier in their party of wounded.

Pursuit was not out of question, but the wood was dense, the track tortuous. The darkness was falling fast. Here among the trees it was already dark.

Sylvia had her wound bound up. Jannis, in considerable pain, was put on a stretcher. Swift decisions had to be made. The villa was occupied by the enemy. That lair was gone. There was only one thing to do, to take a detour that came out above Vori, to find some safe refuge there, or in the vicinity, for the night, and in the morning to push on to their secret base on the coast near Tymbaki.

They began the difficult trek to Vori. Black night closed down on them. The going was rough and tortuous, but old Jannis directed them, despite the torture of his foot. Outside Vori, towards moonrise, he sent the boy Nikephoro to scout ahead. He came back to report that Vori was clear. One of the elders came with him.

At midnight the party had been accommodated in some huts on the edge of the village. Sylvia was taken to a peasant's house where her wound was washed and dressed. She lay awake half the night, wondering what was the fate of those up at the villa, Anastasia, Helen, Harry, the young

marine. And Franz Kleber—what of him? Well, fate
had perhaps done him a good turn ; he had escaped being
a prisoner and going to Alexandria. She dismissed firmly
the suspicion that he might have betrayed them. It was
hardly feasible had he wished to, and she would not believe
it of him. But how much would he tell, and how much
had he really seen ? Speculating on this and other things,
and still heavy at heart for Richard's fate, she fell into a
troubled sleep.

At dawn they were on their way again. They reached
their destination late in the afternoon, and took refuge in
the cave from which they awaited the signal of the visiting
destroyer.

Two days passed. Sylvia took counsel upon future plans.
She had fears that someone from Fort Minotaur might use
the secret route through the stables and fall into the hands
of the Germans at the villa. To prevent this, she hastily
sent off a special messenger to the fort, but the length of
the journey was now almost doubled and more hazardous.

Towards evening of the third day she was startled to see
Helen, the young maid at the villa, step out of a boat at the
foot of the precipitous cove. The girl had escaped, reached
Tymbaki, and had been brought by boat to Sylvia's lair.
She had a bandaged head, and her face was badly cut and
bruised. The story she brought was astonishing, and she
told it with great clarity.

When the Germans came and rounded up Anastasia, old
Christopoulos, and the boy Aleko, she had climbed up
through a trap-door into a cistern-room in the tower. From
its slit window she had a full view of the terrace below. She
stayed there and saw the terrible incidents of the next
three hours ; Harry's fight from the garden-house, with
the German boy, Franz, trying to get him to surrender,
until the grenade blew him to pieces.

" It was terrible, Miss Sylvia. It blew out the window
and the door. I couldn't see anything until the next
morning. There his poor body was, all mixed up with the
bricks and——"

She paused and then with an effort continued her story.

" After that—he'd shot three Germans before they got
him—there was a long wait. They'd put a machine-gun

on the corner of the terrace, and I knew then they were waiting for you. They meant to murder you. There was a captain watching through his glasses. When you came I hadn't noticed before that the German boy was standing near the gun. All at once he pushed the gunner away and began firing, pointing it right away from you, and swinging it deliberately up in the sky. The captain drew his revolver and shot him dead. He knew what he'd done—he'd given you warning."

" So that was it ! " exclaimed Sylvia.

Helen paused. She saw how moved was her listener. After a few moments, Sylvia told her to go on with her story. In about half an hour, narrated Helen, the sergeant gathered his men on the terrace, and then with their captain they left the villa. Something seemed to have frightened them ; they left so hurriedly. While she was watching this the light had almost gone ; suddenly there was a terrific explosion. The whole villa seemed to rise in the air.

" That was the dull roar we heard later as we went through the forest," commented Sylvia. " I wondered what it was."

" I can't tell you how I'm alive now," said Helen. " I was buried and stunned under a heap of rubble. I was saved by a joist which kept the masonry off me. In about half an hour I crawled out. It was quite dark then, and I was too exhausted to do anything. I went round to the stables to sleep there, and when I unbarred the door of the end one, there in the dark were Anastasia, Christopoulos, and Aleko. We stayed there until dawn. Then I sent Aleko off to the fort to warn them."

" That was wise of you, Helen. What a terrible experience ! "

The Greek girl was quiet for a while, then she said very slowly, " The worst was burying them—the English boy and the others. Anastasia found some food in the ruins, and while she got a meal we dug the graves—but not for the three Germans Harry had killed."

" What did you do with them ? "

" We burned them," said Helen fiercely.

" Where did you bury Franz and Harry ? "

" It was a hard job. In the little garden—between the

mimosa trees. They used to like sitting there, you remember. The German boy played his guitar there—I used to see him from the kitchen—and Harry played the mouthorgan with him. That was a wonderful lad, though I had to be firm with him at times when he got cheeky. We buried them side by side. It was terrible, with no priest and no service. I said a prayer, and Christopoulos made two crosses and—and——"

Helen began to cry and buried her face in her hands. Sylvia noticed they were badly cut. She put her arm around the girl. They were both crying now. Presently Sylvia recovered herself.

"You can tell me more later, Helen. I'm going to make you rest. You've had a terrible ordeal," said Sylvia.

She left the girl lying down in the little military cot she used and went out. Macpherson came up to speak to her, but she waved him aside. She wanted to be alone. There was a path from the cove up through the scrub. It led to a ledge overlooking the sea. The sun was setting. The great expanse reflected the glow in the upper sky. Southward, unseen, lay Egypt.

Sylvia sat on a rock. So much had happened these last days, and she felt crushed by the successive blows of fate. Was it worth struggling on ? Richard was gone, the villa ; the life they had lived at the villa was only a dream now. So many had gone from the scene. Cesare Morosini, Richard, young Harry with his Cockney quips, poor brave boy, and Franz Kleber. It was of him particularly she thought now. He had sacrificed himself for her—perhaps for more than her. Possibly, deep down, he had seen the meaning of the struggle and known in his secret heart the side to which his shaken loyalties were leading him. There had been a change in him this last month. "I'll admit Randell Dunning believes what he says. I never could really dislike him—he gets you, somehow," he confessed one day, and then, with his alluring smile, added, "Damn him !" Poor Franz ! Strange how they had detested him at first, how they had been compelled to like him—to love him at the last.

And now ? Should she carry the fight on, Richard gone, the villa gone, and Janet married and almost a creature of the wild mountainside? She felt frighteningly alone. Yet these men needed her; she could do something for them. The fight went on, would go on, until the day of deliverance.

It grew dark and cold on the mountainside. She was aware that her arm was becoming increasingly painful. It was greatly inflamed, and she could not use it. The little Greek doctor from Tymbaki though the bullet might still be buried in the flesh. She had had to stop his probing. That, too, must be considered. She was one of the wounded now. When would the boat come? This was the third night they had watched for the signal. Two of her charges were in urgent need of surgical attention.

She got up and walked down through the gloaming to the cove.

§ 4

At one o'clock in the morning a signal was reported. A little later a boat slid in out of the darkness. It was from the destroyer lying off. A young lieutenant leaped from the boat. He was brought to Sylvia, waiting by the stretcher party.

" Nurse Day? " he asked, saluting.

" Yes."

" Lieutenant Francis. How many this trip? "

" Twenty-five serious cases."

" I have a message for you. From Lieutenant Whatley. His ship is refitting at Alexandria. If I saw you I was to persuade you to make a trip across. He was terribly cut up this wasn't his show."

" I wish I could go," said Sylvia, and questioned him. Then she began to direct the embarkations. They were slow and difficult. The boat would have to make several trips. They had brought supplies also.

Derek in Alexandria. Her arm was very bad. Why not go? It was no dereliction of duty. If she went now she would see him and get surgical treatment. If she went now, finding him there, she would deny him no longer; she would marry him, and when he went away again she would return. She was alone now, too alone. Her longing for him, for his comfort and protection, was intense.

With characteristic swiftness she made her decision when
the second boat came in. She would go on the last boat,
the fourth trip, she told the lieutenant.

"Splendid!" he exclaimed cheerily. "You'll have a
great welcome. You're a legend, you know!"

She hurried back to her sleeping quarters. Helen was in
her room, awake. She told her and began to gather her
things. Then she scribbled a note for Janet.

"Miss, I've something to tell you. I meant to this
afternoon," said Helen.

"Yes?"

"When we buried the young German he had a ring on
his finger. Christopoulos didn't want me to, but I did it.
I took it off. It seemed a shame to bury it like that—and
I thought you'd like it in memory of him. Here it is, miss."

She unwrapped the ring from a piece of cloth. Sylvia
recognised it. It was the seal ring with his mother's
portrait in it. She looked at it for a few moments without
speaking.

"Thank you, Helen. Yes—I am glad to have it," she
said.

§ 5

The fourth boat came. The last of the wounded were
on board. Sylvia said her farewells. The boat pulled
away. Slowly they crept out towards the waiting destroyer,
across the silken water. There was no moon, but the stars
glittered in a dark sky. The great cliffs towered up dimly
above them. Not a light showed on that dark mountain
wall.

The distance grew. They were alone now on the water.
Crete was fading in the night. Sylvia's straining eyes
watched it recede. Some day she would see it again. That
company of the brave still fought for it.

She thought of them, the hardy Cretans, the New
Zealand, Australian, and British lads, hidden in those
mountain fastnesses. A long procession passed in her
thoughts : a captain dying in a room in Canea, Cesare and
his guitar on the terrace, a Greek Red Cross nurse, Joanna
Stavridi, tending the wounded in the caves after the retreat

from Maleme, sturdy Janet on the trek over the mountains to Sfakia, dear Richard and Franz and Harry, the Cockney boy. A gallant company dwelt there. Crete was not lost. The day of deliverance would come. Liberty was an immortal flower. It had been well planted.

The dim outline of the destroyer rode into view.

THE END